Praise for #1 *New York Times* bestselling author

LISA JACKSON

"[B]estselling Jackson cranks up the suspense to almost unbearable heights in her latest tautly written thriller."
—*Booklist* on *Malice*

"When it comes to providing gritty and sexy stories, Ms. Jackson certainly knows how to deliver."
—*RT Book Reviews* on *Unspoken*

"Provocative prose, an irresistible plot and finely crafted characters make up Jackson's latest contemporary sizzler."
—*Publishers Weekly* on *Wishes*

"Lisa Jackson takes my breath away."
—#1 *New York Times* bestselling author Linda Lael Miller

LISA JACKSON

ABANDONED

HQN™

Recycling programs
for this product may
not exist in your area.

ISBN-13: 978-0-373-77650-4

ABANDONED

Copyright © 2012 by Harlequin Books S.A.

The publisher acknowledges the copyright holder
of the individual works as follows:

SAIL AWAY
Copyright © 1991 by Lisa Jackson

MILLION DOLLAR BABY
Copyright © 1992 by Lisa Jackson

CONTENTS

SAIL AWAY

PROLOGUE

MARNIE MONTGOMERY tossed her briefcase onto the antique couch near the windows of her office. She marched straight to her desk, removed an earring and grabbed the phone. As she punched out her father's extension, she balanced a hip against the polished rosewood and waited, her fingers drumming impatiently, a headache threatening behind her eyes.

"Victor Montgomery's office," a sweet voice sang over the wires. Kate Delany. Efficient Kate. Victor's mistress and administrative assistant. She'd been with him for years, and hoped to become the next Mrs. Victor Montgomery.

"Is he in?" Marnie asked.

"Not yet. But I expect him any time." Poor Kate. So helplessly in love with Marnie's father. Loving Victor was easy, as Marnie could well attest. But sometimes that love became overpowering, and Marnie felt as if she'd lost a part of herself, hadn't been allowed to grow into the woman she wanted to be.

She heard Kate flip through the pages of what she assumed was Victor's appointment book. "Your dad called from the course about half an hour ago," Kate said thoughtfully. "He should be on his way back here, and it looks as if his schedule isn't too full this afternoon."

Marnie's lungs constricted. She cleared her throat. "Tell him I need to see him the minute he gets in."

"It's important?"

"Very," Marnie replied, replacing the receiver and suddenly feeling cold inside. Slipping her earring back in place, she noticed the expensive furnishings in her office, the thick mauve carpet, the panoramic view of Seattle's skyline from her corner office. Everything a girl could want.

Except Marnie didn't want any of it. She didn't want the forced smiles of the staff, she didn't want the knowing glances in the coffee room, and she especially didn't want the engraved brass nameplate that read: MARNIE MONTGOMERY, PUBLIC RELATIONS. It could just as well have read: VICTOR'S DAUGHTER. The people who worked "for her" in her department could function well without her. Victor had seen to that.

She tossed her pen into her empty In basket. Was it ever full? Were there ever papers and messages overflowing onto the desk? Did she ever have to put in extra hours? Did she even have to come back from lunch? No, no, no and no!

A nest of butterflies erupted into flight in her stomach at the thought of what she had to do. Rounding the desk she found a piece of letterhead, and rather than have her secretary type her letter of resignation she started writing it out in long hand.

How did one quit being a daughter? she wondered, her brow puckering as she chewed on the end of her pen.

How did she tell a loving father, who had tried all his life to do everything for her, that she felt suffocated?

How could she explain that she had to do something on her own, become her own person, live her own life?

Absurdly, she felt an urge to break down and cry tears of frustration, but because that was exactly what the weaker, dependent Marnie would have done, she gritted her teeth, refused to shed one lousy tear and started writing again in quick, sure strokes.

She couldn't quit being Victor's daughter, but she sure as hell could quit being dependent upon him.

CHAPTER ONE

ADAM DRAKE FELT the skeptical gaze of every man who sat around the polished table. They'd listened to him, scanned the thick sheaf of papers that was his proposal and leaned back in their chairs, without questions but exchanging knowing glances.

The three men in the room were potential investors from California, men who, so far, hadn't turned him down. Yet. However, Adam knew they each had doubts about his proposal—and concerns about Adam himself. He didn't blame them. His reputation was more than a little tarnished.

It was surprising that these investors had stuck around this long.

The lawyer, Brodie, reached into his pocket for a fresh pack of cigarettes. It seemed to take forever for the cellophane to drop onto the table. "I think I can speak for my associates," he said, looking to the other two men and receiving quick nods of approval. "We like the idea of expanding to Seattle, but we've got some reservations."

"This wouldn't be an expansion," Adam reminded the smooth man in the expensive suit. This was a point they'd haggled over before. "I'll own the majority of the hotel. Your capital will be returned, with interest in the amount specified in ten years." He flipped to page six of his proposal and slid it across the table.

Brodie lit up, scanned the neatly typed paragraphs, then flipped through the remaining pages of the contract. He shot a stream of smoke out of the corner of his mouth. "Right, right," he said thoughtfully. "But for the next ten years we would be part owners of *your* hotel."

"That's right," Adam replied, managing a tense smile. God, he hated this kind of politics. Depending upon other people, wealthy men, to finance his business operation. The thought of being tied to anyone bothered him. That was his problem. Bucking authority. Refusing to bend to the power of the almighty dollar.

So why was he here?

Because he had no choice. Victor Montgomery had seen to that.

At the thought of Montgomery and especially the low-lifes who worked for him, Adam's blood boiled for revenge. He forced his thoughts back to the present.

Brodie, eyeing him still, thumped on the contract with one manicured finger. "This looks good, Drake. Only a couple of clauses to reword, but what's really bothering me—" he blew more smoke to the ceiling and squinted at Adam, sizing him up for the thousandth time "—is what happened at Montgomery Inns last year..."

There it was. The noose again. The rope that would strangle him.

Adam felt the tension in the room. *Be cool,* he told himself, not showing a flicker of emotion though the sweat was running down his back and his nerves were strung tight as piano wire. "I was never charged with embezzling," he said evenly. His eyes moved from one man to the next.

"But Montgomery never hired you back," a tiny, apprehensive man sitting to Brodie's left, Bill Peterson, interjected. Behind glasses as thick as the bottom of a soda bottle, Peterson's nervous gaze shifted to each of the other men around the table.

"I didn't want to go back," Adam stated. That much

was true. He'd never work for a snake like Montgomery again, though he itched to know who had set him up. The memory was still painful. Once, he'd respected Victor Montgomery and he'd thought the older man had felt the same for him. *Stupid,* he chided himself silently. Victor had shown his true colors and fired Adam swiftly, pressing charges against him, then, when there was no indictment, sending a severance check to him through his lawyer—*through his damned lawyer!* Victor hadn't even had the guts to face Adam himself. Only the lawyer had been witness to Adam's wrath and stared in uncomfortable silence as Adam had ripped up the check and tossed the confetti-like scraps into the air.

Brodie's voice brought him back to the present. "Look, Drake, before we go into direct competition with Victor Montgomery, I think we should clear this matter up. The way I hear it, there wasn't evidence enough to indict you, and yet the money that was skimmed off the Puget West project was never located."

The collar around Adam's neck felt tight, the blood thundered through his veins. The money had just vanished. No amount of going over the books had uncovered the missing cash. And in that respect, he was, as project coordinator, responsible.

"That's what we don't understand," Peterson said, while the third partner, a silent man with flat features, said nothing. "There should have been a trail. How could anyone have walked away with—what was it? Half a million dollars?"

Adam nodded tightly, though he hoped his expression was calm. "Five hundred sixty-three thousand and change."

The silent man whistled.

"That must have taken some doing," Brodie said, stuffing his copy of the proposal into his briefcase.

"I wouldn't know," Adam responded dryly.

Brodie's brows jerked up as he jabbed out his cigarette in the hotel ashtray. Apparently he didn't believe Adam. "You have to understand our position. We can't very well hand over several million dollars until we're absolutely certain that what happened over at Montgomery Inns won't happen to us." He offered Adam a regretful smile. "If you could ever clear up exactly what happened over there, then maybe we could talk business. In the meantime, I don't think we have a deal."

The other men nodded in silent agreement. Adam didn't blame them. If he were in their shoes he wouldn't trust a man who'd nearly been indicted for embezzling, a man still proclaimed a thief by one of the largest hotel chains on the west coast. Trouble was, Adam was sick of being a scapegoat.

Pushing himself upright, Adam pulled together a grim smile and shook each man's outstretched hand. He watched as Brodie shepherded the small group from the room. Only when the door slammed shut behind the Californians did he let out a series of invectives that would have made a sailor blush. He yanked off his tie and threw it over the back of a chair, then loosened the top buttons of his stiff white shirt. What had he expected? This meeting had been no different than the two others he'd put together.

Face it, Drake, he told himself, *you were convicted even though you were never tried.* With leashed fury, he knew that the black stain on his reputation wouldn't disappear with time. No, he had to find out who had set him up and why. Otherwise, he was finished.

He had his suspicions, of course. There were several people with whom he'd worked at Montgomery Inns who had been jealous of his rapid rise in the corporation, a few who were desperate, and still others who were just plain greedy. Any one of those people could have set him up to take the fall. And fall he had. Once one of Victor Montgomery's golden boys, he was now the black sheep. The Judas.

Until he could prove himself completely blameless, he would never be able to set himself up in business. As he saw it, he had no choice. He had to do some digging and find out just who had hated him enough to frame him for embezzling money he'd never seen. For the past year he'd tried to put the damned incident behind him, but it kept rising like a phoenix from the ashes of his career at Montgomery Inns, to torment and thwart him. Fortunately, he'd already started an investigation to prove his innocence once and for all.

"QUITTING?" VICTOR'S EYEBROWS shot up, and he stared at his only child in disbelief. He'd just walked into the office and found Marnie sitting, waiting, in one of the client chairs. Then she'd lowered the bomb. "Have you gone out of your mind?"

Marnie dropped her letter of resignation on his desk. This scene with her father was going to be worse than she'd imagined. Her father was shocked. Pain showed from his blue eyes, pain at the thought of her betrayal.

"Why for God's sake? And just what do you think you're going to do?" he demanded, slamming his golf bag into a corner closet, then ripping off his plaid cap and sailing it across the office in frustration.

Marnie opened her mouth to answer, but her father wasn't finished raving. "You can't quit! You're my daughter, for crying out loud!" He mopped the sweat from his brow and stuffed his handkerchief into the pocket of his golf slacks.

Marnie had been waiting for him for half the day. She wasn't about to back down now. She'd spent too many hours arguing with herself and gathering her courage to give in.

"I'm serious, Dad," she said quietly, her voice firm. "This is just something I need to do."

"Bull!" Her father crossed the thick expanse of putty-colored carpet and glanced at the calendar lying open on his huge mahogany desk. He flipped through the pages while Marnie surveyed his office with jaded eyes.

Opulent, befitting the reigning monarch of a hotel empire, the suite boasted inlaid cherrywood walls. Brass lamps, etchings, sculptures and buttery leather furniture added to the effect. Behind the office, a private bath with a Jacuzzi, a walk-in wardrobe and king-size bedroom, were available whenever Victor was too busy to drive home.

Grabbing the receiver in one hand, Victor punched a series of buttons on the phone. "Kate?" he barked, still flipping through his appointment book. "Cancel my two o'clock with Ferguson—no, on second thought—just stall him. Ask him to meet me at the site tomorrow at—" he ran his finger down a page "—ten-thirty." Scowling across the room at Marnie, he added, "Just tell him that something important came up, something to do with the opening of the Puget West hotel."

Marnie refused to meet the anger in his eyes and stared instead through the bank of windows in his office. Glimpses of the rolling gray waters of Puget Sound were barely visible through the tall spires of Seattle's skyline. Thick pewter-colored clouds blocked the sun and threatened rain. A jet, headed north, was nearly invisible through the low-hanging clouds.

She heard her father slam down the phone. "Okay, let's get out of here," he said, and dropped the letter of resignation she'd worked so hard to write into his wastebasket.

"Can't we talk here?"

Grabbing his keys, Victor shook his head. "Not a good idea."

Then she understood. Shoving her arms through the sleeves of her coat, she asked, "Do you still really think you've got some spies in the company?"

"Don't know."

"I thought all that was taken care of when you fired Adam Drake."

Her father jammed a hat onto his head. "And I thought you were convinced he was innocent."

"He was," she said flatly. "He got off, remember?"

"He just had a damned good attorney," Victor grumbled, snagging his jacket from the back of his chair. "But that's over and done with."

"Then why're you still paranoid?"

"I'm *not* paranoid," he snapped. "Just careful. Come on, I've got to check things out at the marina, see that the repairs on the *Vanessa* are up to snuff. We can talk on the way."

"Okay," she muttered, barely holding on to her temper. "But you can't just toss my resignation into the trash and expect me to forget all about it. I'm serious, Dad."

"You don't know what you want."

"That's where you're wrong," she said quietly.

The firmness in her tone must have caught his attention. His head snapped up and for the first time since he'd entered the office, he seemed to see her as she really was. His lips pursed tightly and beneath his tan his skin took on a paler hue. "Let's go," he said, his voice much lower.

He didn't even bother changing from his casual pants and sports coat.

In tense silence they strode abreast through the corridors to the elevator. Marnie barely kept herself from quaking at his anger. He was a handsome man, a man who accepted authority easily. His features were oversized, his hair thick and white with only a few remaining dark strands, his eyes intense blue, his nose aristocratic. For a man pushing sixty he was in good shape, with only the trace of a paunch near his waistline. And right now he was beginning to seethe.

"I don't know what's gotten into you," he said when the elevator doors had whispered shut and with a lurch the car sped down sixteen floors only to jerk to a stop at the subterranean parking lot.

"I just think it's time I stood on my own."

"All of a sudden?"

She slid a glance in his direction. "It's been coming on a long time."

"Ever since that business with Drake," he surmised with disgust.

"Before that," she insisted, though it was true that nothing had been the same since Adam Drake had been fired. There had been a change in attitude in the offices of Montgomery Inns. Nothing tangible. Just a loss of company spirit and confidence. Everyone felt it—including Victor, though, of course, he was loathe to admit it.

"And then you decided to break up with Kent," her father went on, shaking his head as he searched the pocket of his jacket for his pipe. "And now you want to leave the corporation, just walk away from a fortune. When I was your age, I was—"

"—working ten-hour days and still going to night school, I know," Marnie cut in. Her heels clicked loudly against the concrete. Low-hanging pipes overhead dripped condensation, and she had to duck to escape the steady drops as she hurried to keep up with her father's swift strides.

She stopped at the fender of Victor's Jaguar. He unlocked the doors and they both slid into the cushy interior.

"You should be grateful…"

Marnie closed her eyes. How could she explain the feeling that she was trapped? That she needed a life of her own? That she had to prove herself by standing on her own two feet? "I *am* grateful, Dad. Really." Turning to face him, she forced a wan smile. "This is just something I have to do—"

"Right now? Can't it wait?" he asked, as if sensing her beginning to weaken.

"No."

"But the new hotel is opening next week. I need you there. You're in charge of public relations, for God's sake."

"And I have a capable assistant. You remember Todd Byers—blond, wears glasses—"

Victor waved off her explanation.

"Well, if he's not good enough I have a whole department to cover for me." That was what bothered her most. She didn't feel needed. If she walked away from Montgomery Inns, no one, save Victor, would notice. Even Kent would get by without her.

Her father fired up the engine and shoved the Jag into reverse. "I don't understand you anymore." With a flip of the steering wheel, he headed for the exit. "What is it you really want?"

"A life of my own."

"You have one. A life most women would envy."

"I know," she admitted, her spine stiffening a bit. How could she reach a man who had worked all his life creating an empire? A man who had raised her alone, a man who loved her as much as he possibly could? "This is just something I have to do."

He waved to the lot's attendant, then nosed the Jag into the busy streets of downtown Seattle. "A few weeks ago you were planning to marry Kent," he pointed out as he joined the traffic easing toward the waterfront. Marnie felt a familiar stab of pain. "But now, all of a sudden, Kent's not good enough. It doesn't matter that he's practically my right-hand man—"

"No, it doesn't," she said swiftly. Surprisingly, her voice was still steady.

"Why don't you tell me what happened between you two?" he suggested. "It's all tied up with this whole new independence kick, isn't it?"

Marnie didn't answer. She didn't want to think about Kent, nor the fact that she'd found him with Dolores Tate, his secretary. Rather than dwell on Kent's betrayal, Marnie stared at the car ahead of them. Two fluffy Persian cats slept on the back window ledge and a bright red bumper sticker near the back plates asked, Have You Hugged Your Cat Today?

Funny, she thought sarcastically, she hadn't hugged anyone in a long, long while. And no one had hugged her. At that thought a lump settled in her throat, and she wrapped her arms around herself, determined not to cry. Not today. Not on this, the very first step toward her new life.

Victor switched lanes, jockeying for position as traffic clogged. "While we're on the subject of Kent—"

"We're not."

"He loves you."

Marnie knew better. "Let's just leave Kent out of this, okay?"

For once, her father didn't argue. Rubbing the back of his neck he shook his head, as if he could release some of the tension tightening his shoulder blades. He slid her a sidelong glance as they turned into the marina. Fishing boats, sloops, yachts and cabin cruisers were tied to the piers. Whitecaps dotted the surface of the restless sound, and only a few sailing vessels braved the overcast day. Lumbering tankers moved slowly inland, while ferries churned frothy wakes, cutting through the dark water as they crossed the water.

Her father parked the Jag near the pier and cut the engine. "I can see I'm not going to change your mind," he said, slanting her a glance that took in the thrust of her jaw and the determination in her gaze. As if finally accepting the fact that she was serious, he snorted, "God knows I don't understand it, but if you think you've got to leave the company for a while, I'll try to muddle through without you."

"For a while?" she countered. "I resigned, remember?"

He held up his hands, as if in surrender. "One step at a time, okay? Let's just call this…sabbatical…of yours, a leave of absence."

She wanted to argue, but didn't. Maybe he needed time to adjust. Her leaving, after all, was as hard on him as it was on her.

Her expression softened, and she touched his arm. "You and Montgomery Inns will survive."

"Lord, I hope so," he murmured. "But I'm not accepting anything official like a resignation. And I want you to wait just a couple of weeks, until Puget West opens. That's not too much to ask, is it?" he queried, pocketing his keys as they both climbed out of the car.

Together, hands shoved in the pockets of their coats, they walked quickly along the time-weathered planks of the waterfront. Marnie breathed in the scents of the marina. She'd grown up around boats, and the odors of salt and seaweed, brine and diesel brought back happy childhood memories of when her father had taken as much interest in her as he had in his company. Things had changed, of course. She'd gone to college, hadn't needed him so much, and Montgomery Inns had developed into a large corporation with hotels stretched as far away as L.A. and Houston.

A stiff breeze snapped the flags on the moored vessels. High overhead sea gulls wheeled, their desolate cries barely audible over the sounds of throbbing engines. *Free,* she thought, smiling at the birds, *they're free. And lonely.*

Her father grumbled, "Next thing I know you'll be trading in your Beemer for a '69 Volkswagen."

She smothered a sad smile. He didn't know that she'd sold the BMW just last week, though she wasn't in the market for a VW bug—well, at least not yet.

"So it's settled, right?" he said, as if grateful to have finished a drawn-out negotiation. "When you get back, we'll talk."

"And if I still want to quit?"

"Then we'll talk some more." He fiddled in his pocket for his tobacco, stuffed a wad into the bowl of his pipe, and clamping the pipe between his teeth, searched in his pockets for a match. Trying to light the pipe, he walked quickly down the pier where his yacht, the *Vanessa,* was docked. "Maybe by the time you think things over, you'll come to your senses about Kent."

"I already have," she said, controlling the fury that still burned deep inside her. Kent had played her for a fool; he wouldn't get a second chance.

"Okay, okay, just promise me you'll stick around until the new hotel is open."

"It's a promise," she said, catching up to him. "But you're not talking me out of this. As soon as Puget West opens its doors, I'm history."

"For a while." He puffed on the pipe, sending up tiny clouds of smoke.

"Maybe," she said, unwilling to concede too much. Her father wasn't a bad man, just determined, especially when it came to her and his hotel chain. But she could be just as stubborn as he. She climbed aboard his favorite plaything as the wind off the sound whipped her hair in front of her

face. Someday, whether he wanted to or not, Victor Montgomery would be proud of her for her independence; he
just didn't know it yet. She'd prove to him, and everyone
else who thought she was just another pampered rich girl,
that she could make it on her own.

ACCORDING TO THE *Seattle Observer,* the grand opening of
Puget West Montgomery Inn was to be the social event of
the year. Invitations had been sent to the rich and the beautiful, from New York to L.A., though most of the guests
were from the Pacific Northwest.

The mayor of Seattle as well as Senator Mann, the State
of Washington's reigning Republican, were to attend.
Local celebrities, the press and a few Hollywood types
were rumored to be on hand to sip champagne and congratulate Victor Montgomery on the latest and most glittery link in the ever-expanding chain of Montgomery Inns.

Adam Drake wasn't invited.

In fact, he was probably the last person good old Victor
wanted to see walk through the glass doors of the main
lobby. But Victor was in for the surprise of his life, Adam
thought with a grim smile. Because Adam wouldn't have
missed the grand opening of Puget West for the world!

As the prow of his small boat sliced through the night-
blackened waters of Puget Sound, he guided the craft
toward his destination, the hotel itself. Lit like the proverbial Christmas tree, twenty-seven stories of Puget West
rose against a stygian sky.

Wind ripped over the water, blasting his bare face and
hands, but Adam barely felt the cold. He was too im-
mersed in his own dark thoughts. Anger tightened a knot
in his gut. He'd helped design this building; hell, he'd even
outbid a Japanese investor for the land, all for the sake of
Montgomery Inns and Victor Montgomery!

And he'd been kicked in the face for his efforts—

framed for a crime he'd never committed. Well, he'd just spent the past three weeks of his life dredging up all the evidence again, talking with even the most obscure employees who had once worked for the company, and he'd started to unravel the web of lies, one string at a time. He didn't have all the answers, just vague suspicions, but he was hell-bent to prove them true. Only then would he be able to get on with his own life.

And never again would he depend upon a man like Victor Montgomery for his livelihood. From this point on, Adam intended to be his own boss.

Close to the docks, Adam cut the boat's engine and slung ropes around the moorings. Before he could second-guess himself, he hopped onto the new deck and walked briskly beneath the Japanese lanterns glowing red, green and orange. Tiny crystal lights, twinkling as if it were the holiday season instead of the end of May, winked in the shrubbery.

His jaw tightened, and a cruel smile tugged at the corners of his mouth as he considered his reasons for showing up uninvited. Adrenaline surged through his veins. What was the phrase—revenge was always best when it was served up cold?

He'd soon find out.

Nearly a year had passed since he'd been hung by his heels in public, humiliated and stripped bare, and tonight he'd seek his own form of justice.

Thunder cracked over the angry waters, and Adam cast one final look at the inky sound. He found poetic justice in the fact that a spring storm was brewing on the night Victor Montgomery was opening his latest resort.

He didn't waste any time. The pant legs of his tuxedo brushed against the wet leaves of blossoming rhododendrons and azaleas as he walked briskly, moving instinc-

tively toward the side entrance and the French doors he
knew would be unlocked and, with any luck, unguarded.

Music and laughter floated through the night as he
stepped onto the terrace. Through the open doors, he saw
that the party was in full swing, bejeweled guests talking, dancing, laughing and drinking from monogrammed
fluted glasses.

Adam tugged on his tight black tie, plowed his fingers
through his wind-tossed hair, then slipped into the opulent foyer. No one seemed to notice. As a liveried waiter
passed, Adam snagged a glass of champagne from a silver
tray and scoped out the milling guests.

A piano player sat at a shiny baby grand, and the nostalgic notes of "As Time Goes By" drifted through the
crowd. Silver and red balloons, tied together with long
white ribbons, floated dreamily to the windowed ceiling
four stories above the foyer. Near the back wall a glass
elevator carried guests to the balconies surrounding the
lobby, and on the opposite wall an elegant staircase curved
upward to the second story. In the center of the room, the
trademark Montgomery fountain, complete with marble
base, spouted water eight feet high.

Oh, yes, this hotel was just as grand as Victor Montgomery had envisioned it, the opening party already a
success. Adam tamped down any trace of bitterness as he
wandered through the crowd. It took a cool mind to get
even.

In one corner of the lobby near a restaurant, a ten-foot
ice sculpture of King Neptune, trident aloft, sea monsters
curling in the waves near his feet, stood guard.

Just like good old Victor, Adam thought to himself as
he spied Kate Delany, Victor's administrative assistant
and, as rumor had it, lover. Dressed in shimmering white,
her dark hair piled high on her head, Kate acted as host-
ess. Her smile was practiced but friendly, and her eyes

sparkled enough to invite conversation as she drifted from one knot of guests to the next.

Scanning the crowd, Adam decided Victor hadn't made his grand entrance yet. Nor had his daughter. He looked again, hoping for a glimpse of Marnie. Spoiled, rich, beautiful Marnie Montgomery was the one possession Victor valued more than his damned hotels. An only child, she'd been pampered, sent to the best schools and given the post of "public-relations administrator" upon graduation from some Ivy League school back east.

Despite his bitterness toward anything loosely associated with Montgomery Inns, Adam had found Marnie appealing. Regardless of her lap-of-leisure upbringing, there had been something—a spark of laughter in her eyes, a trace of wistfulness in her smile, an intelligence in her wit and a mystique to her silences—which had half convinced him that she was more than just another rich brat coddled by an overindulgent father and raised by nannies. Tall and slender, with pale blond hair and eyes a clear crystal blue, Marnie was as hauntingly beautiful as she was wealthy. And as he understood it, she'd become engaged to Kent Simms, one of Victor's "yes" men.

Bad choice, Marnie, Adam thought as he took a long swallow of champagne. Maybe he'd been kidding himself all along. Marnie Montgomery was probably cut from the same expensive weave of cloth as was her father.

Kent Simms fit into the picture neatly. Too ambitious for his own good, Kent was more interested in the fast lane and big bucks than in loving a wife. Even if she happened to be the boss's daughter. The marriage wouldn't last.

But Kent Simms was Marnie's problem. Adam had his own.

He heard a gasp behind him. From the corner of his eye he caught the quickly averted look of a wasp-thin woman with dark eyes and a black velvet dress.

So she recognizes me, he thought in satisfaction, and lifted his champagne glass in silent salute to her. Her name was Rose Trullinger, and she was an interior decorator for the corporation.

Rose's cheeks flooded with color, and she turned quickly away before casting a sharp glance over her shoulder and heading toward a group of eight or nine people lingering around the bar.

Adam watched as she whispered something to a woman draped in blue silk and dripping with diamonds. The woman in blue turned, lifted a finely arched brow and sent Adam a curious look. There was more than mild amusement in her eyes. Adam noticed an invitation. Some women were attracted to men who were considered forbidden or dangerous. The woman in blue was obviously one of those.

She whispered something to Rose.

Perfect, Adam thought with a grim twist of his lips. It wouldn't be long before Victor knew he was here.

CHAPTER TWO

MARNIE JABBED A GLITTERY comb into her hair, then glowered at her reflection as the comb slid slowly down. Shaking her head, she yanked out the comb and tossed it onto the vanity. *So much for glamour.* She brushed her shoulder-length curls with a vengeance and eyed the string of diamonds and sapphires surrounding her throat. The necklace and matching earrings had been her mother's; Victor had pleaded with her to wear them and she had, on this, the last night of her employment at Montgomery Inns. Just being in the new hotel made her feel like a hypocrite, but she only had a few more hours and, then, freedom!

"Marnie?" Her father tapped softly on the door connecting her smaller bedroom to the rest of his suite. "It's about time."

"I'll be right out," she replied, dreading the party. On the bed, a single suitcase lay open. She tossed her comb, brush and makeup bag into the soft-sided case and snapped it shut.

Sliding into a pair of silver heels, she opened the door to find her father, a drink in one hand, pacing near the door. He glanced up as she entered the room, and the smile that creased his face was filled with genuine admiration. He swallowed and blinked. "I really hadn't realized how much you look like Vanessa," he said quietly.

Marnie felt an inner glow. He was complimenting her. Her father had never gotten over his wife and he'd vowed on her grave that he'd never remarry. And he hadn't. Even though Kate Delany had been in love with him for years, he wouldn't marry her. Marnie knew it as well as she knew she herself would never marry Kent Simms.

He reached for the door but paused. "Kent's already here."

"I know."

"He's been asking to see you."

She knew that, too. But she was through talking to Kent about anything other than business. "I don't have anything to say to him."

Victor tugged on his lower lip as if weighing his next words. Marnie braced herself. She knew what was coming. "Kent loves you, and he's been with the company for ten years. That man is loyal."

"To Montgomery Inns."

"Well, that's something. The years he's worked for me—"

"If longevity with Montgomery Inns has anything to do with my future husband, then I should marry Fred Ainger."

"Don't be ridiculous," her father scoffed, leaving his glass on a table near the door, but Marnie could tell her comment had hit its mark. Fred Ainger, a tiny bespectacled accountant in bookkeeping, was about to retire at age sixty-five. He'd been with Montgomery Inns since Victor had purchased his first hotel.

"Okay, okay. We both know that Kent's time with the company doesn't really matter when you're choosing a husband," her father reluctantly agreed, smoothing his hair with the flat of his hand. He looked out the window to the city of Port Stanton flanking the banks of the sound. Smaller than Seattle, Tacoma or Olympia, Port Stanton, as gateway to the sound, was growing by leaps and bounds, and Montgomery Inns was ready and waiting with the

Puget West as the city required more hotels for business-men and travelers. "But Kent is loyal to the company."

Bully for Kent, she thought, but held her tongue on that point. "I'd rather have a husband who's committed to me."

"For what it's worth, I believe Kent is committed to you, honey."

Marnie knew differently. She also realized that she was going to have to tell her father why she was so adamant about rejecting Kent, or her father would badger her for-ever. In Victor's eyes, Kent was the perfect son-in-law. "I didn't love him, Dad." That much wasn't a lie, though she'd convinced herself during the duration of their en-gagement that she had. "Kent wasn't the man for me. He was your choice, not mine."

For a few seconds Victor didn't speak, and Marnie could almost hear the gears whirling in his mind. Her father didn't back down quickly.

He made a big show of glancing at his watch and purs-ing his lips. "Come on," he said, his keen eyes glinting. "Let's go downstairs. We can talk about Kent later."

Marnie shook her head. "*You* can talk about him later. I'm done."

Victor held up a hand to forestall any further argu-ments. "Whatever you say. It's your life."

Marnie wasn't fooled, and cast him a glance that told him so.

Victor held open the door for her, and Marnie stepped onto the balcony. The sounds of the party drifted up the four flights from the lobby. Even from this distance she recognized a few employees of the hotel chain, dancing or laughing with guests who had been sent special invita-tions, the chosen few who mattered in the Northwest—the mayor of Seattle and Senator Mann, several city coun-cil members as well as reporters for local television and newspapers. There were only a few faces Marnie didn't recognize.

All of Seattle's social elite had come to Puget West, drinking and laughing and showing off their most expensive gowns and jewelry, hoping that their names and pictures might find a way into the society columns of the *Seattle Observer* and the *Port Stanton Herald*.

Forcing a smile she didn't feel, Marnie stepped into the glass elevator, her father at her side. As the car descended, she stared through the windows, noticing the lights in the trees in the lobby, the ice sculpture of King Neptune and the three-tiered fountain of champagne wedged between tables laden with hors d'oeuvres. A pianist was playing from a polished ebony piano where a man listened, a handsome man, she guessed from the back of him. She noticed the wide breadth of his shoulders, the narrowing of his hips, the way his wavy black hair gleamed under a thousand winking lights.

There was something familiar about him, something about his stance, that brought back hazy memories. He turned to reach for a glass of champagne from a passing waiter, and as the elevator doors opened, Marnie found herself staring across the room. A pair of mocking, gold-brown eyes met hers, and she nearly missed a step.

Adam Drake!

What in God's name was he doing here? Didn't the man have a sense of decency, or at the very least, an ounce of self-preservation? Her father would love to have a chance to throw him out of the hotel! Even though he'd been proved innocent of the charges Victor had leveled against him, Adam Drake was definitely on her father's ten-least-wanted list.

Adam didn't seem concerned. A slow, self-mocking smile stretched across his jaw as his gaze collided with hers. He winked lazily at her, then took a long swallow from his champagne.

Marnie almost grinned. She'd forgotten about his irreverence, his lack of concern for playing by society's unwritten laws. Well, he'd really done himself in this time. Though she'd never really believed that he was a thief, there was a side to him that suggested danger, and she wondered just how much he knew about the half million dollars skimmed from the funds to build this very hotel. The guy had nerve, she'd grant him that!

Amused, she turned to see if her father had noticed their uninvited guest, but a crowd of well-wishers suddenly engulfed them. Victor tugged on Marnie's arm, pulling her along as he wended his way to the circular fountain and stepped onto the marble base, hauling her up with him. Newspaper reporters followed, elbowing and jostling to thrust microphones into Victor's face. Cameras flashed before her eyes as photographers clicked off dozens of pictures.

Victor laughed and answered each question crisply. Her father was always at his best in front of a crowd, but Marnie was uncomfortable in the spotlight. She tried to slip away unnoticed. However, Senator Mann, always hungry for press, fought his way through the throng to stand at her father's side, blocking Marnie's exit. Even Kent appeared. Predictably, he wended quickly through the tightening group to take his place next to her. She was trapped!

Gazing up at Kent's even, practiced smile, Marnie decided this wasn't the time to bring up the fact that Adam Drake had somehow turned up uninvited.

"Hi," Kent whispered, flashing a thousand-watt grin at her, though Marnie suspected the smile was for the press. He tried to slide his arm around her waist.

Marnie sidestepped him and somehow managed to keep her balance. "Don't," she warned.

"Come on, Marnie," he cajoled. "Just try to be reasonable—at least for appearances' sake."

"I can't—"

"Kent! Congratulations!" Mayor Winthrop's voice boomed as he approached and stretched out his hand. He was short and round, his straight gray hair painstakingly combed to cover a bald spot. "Beautiful hotel, Marnie, just beautiful!" he gushed, before turning all his attention on Victor and Kent.

Marnie managed a thin smile for the man, then, before Kent realized what she was doing, excused herself quickly and stepped into the sea of guests.

Enough with the spectacle, she thought, moving quickly away from the fountain. She had promised her father she'd show up at his party, but she wasn't going to pretend to care about Kent. How could she have ever made the mistake of thinking she loved him? Or that he had loved her? She must've been desperate.

Unconsciously, she glanced back to the piano, but Adam had disappeared and the pianist, taking his cue from Victor, had stopped playing so that the mayor and other city dignitaries could publicly congratulate Victor Montgomery on another glamorous project well done.

Marnie felt little of the pride she'd experienced at the completion of other hotels. Puget West had been different from the beginning. There had been problems and delays with acquisition, zoning, planning, architecture and then, of course, the scandal. At first Adam Drake, Victor's personal choice to supervise the project, had smoothed out the bumps, but later, when Kate Delany had discovered the errors in the books, all hell had broken loose and her father had blamed Adam for the mismanaged money.

The money had never been located. Over five hundred thousand dollars had seemed to vanish into thin air. Marnie had never believed Adam to be a thief, but no one had been able to explain what had happened to the missing funds.

Adam had never been indicted, but the public humiliation had been tremendous, the scandal reported daily in the business section of the *Seattle Observer*. And now he was here? Why?

Scanning the waves of people, she found Adam again. With one shoulder propped against a marble pillar, the jacket of his tux open, his tie loosened, his black hair wind-tossed, he looked rakish and self-satisfied. A small smile played on his thin, sensual lips. His eyes, dark above chiseled cheekbones, were trained on the fountain where Victor stood.

It was strange that he'd decided to come, but fitting, in a way. Adam Drake, before his downfall, had been invaluable to the company, one of the few in Victor's small circle of advisers. Adam had been the man who had found this very piece of land on the western shore of the sound and had negotiated a very good deal for Montgomery Inns. Without Adam Drake, Puget West never would have been built.

Marnie wondered why he had risked having his reputation blackened again. The man must be certifiable.

With difficulty, she forced her gaze away from him. Unfortunately she discovered Dolores Tate, Kent's secretary, lingering near the open bar, her wide brown eyes focused lovingly on Kent.

Marnie thought she might be sick.

Dolores didn't notice her; she was too involved with the scene at the fountain and her own appearance. Unconsciously, she lifted a hand to the springy brown curls that framed her Kewpie-doll face. Draped in a dress of gold sequins and chiffon, Dolores moved gracefully among the people near the fountain, smiling and stopping to talk with this group and that, seeming more a part of this party than Marnie felt herself.

Dolores probably was more at home here, Marnie thought as she tore her gaze away from the woman Kent had chosen as his mistress. Surprisingly, she didn't feel any surge of jealousy, just an annoying embarrassment that she could have been duped by Kent.

Rather than dwell on Kent, Marnie half listened to her father's prepared speech. Victor, public smile in place, was heartily thanking the community leaders for the privilege of building this "...dream-come-true on the banks of the sound for our fair community..."

On and on he went, interrupted occasionally by bursts of clapping or laughter as he related some funny anecdotes about the construction of the hotel. Marnie had heard similar speeches dozens of times before. For her father's sake, she hoped she appeared interested, though she couldn't keep her gaze from wandering across the expansive foyer to the pillar against which Adam leaned.

Marnie could almost feel Adam's hostility sizzling across the room. But Victor went blithely on, unaware that the man he was sure had tried to cheat him was present.

Kate Delany, too, didn't seem to notice Adam as she found Marnie and joined her. "Your father's pleased," Kate whispered into Marnie's ear.

"He should be," Marnie answered automatically.

"Mmm." Kate nodded. Her auburn hair was piled in loose curls atop her head, her silk dress shimmered as it draped over one shoulder. Emerald earrings, shaped like teardrops, matched the bracelet encircling one slim wrist—gifts from Marnie's father. The small white lines of disappointment near her lips were barely visible.

Marnie felt a pang of pity for Kate. She obviously still

clung to the hope that she would someday become Mrs. Victor Montgomery.

As Victor finished, Kate slipped through the crowd toward the fountain. The guests erupted with enthusiastic applause and good wishes while photographers shot rolls of film of her father with the mayor, or senator, or with a dour-faced city councilwoman wearing a simple linen suit and an outrageous magenta hat.

Marnie slid another glance in Adam's direction and decided it was time she found out what he was doing here. They were compatriots, in a perverse way, she thought. Neither one of them belonged here. Only Adam had shown up despite the fact that he wasn't wanted; she, on the other hand, was wanted and would do anything to leave.

She accepted a glass of champagne from a waiter and then slipped through the guests toward the one man who had the guts to defy her father.

Adam saw her coming. He'd watched as she had disentangled herself from Kent and mingled among the clusters of people. She had been smiling at her father's jokes but not really listening. It was almost as if she were playing a part, putting in her time, and she'd cast more than one curious glance in his direction. Good.

She was beautiful, he had to admit that. Her wavy hair was pale blond, almost silver, her eyes were an intense shade of blue and even though she was often serious, Adam remembered that she laughed easily.

But she wasn't laughing tonight. No, Miss Montgomery appeared uncomfortable with all the hoopla, though she was dressed for the occasion in a silky dress that must have cost a fortune and in diamonds that sparkled around her wrist and neck. No one would doubt that she was Victor Montgomery's spoiled daughter.

He found it interesting that when she'd first spotted him she hadn't run to Daddy to tell him that a traitor was in their midst. Instead, she'd appeared mildly curious and now she was walking toward him.

The ghost of a smile crossed her full lips and her eyes twinkled for just a second. "Mr. Drake," she said, stopping just short of him.

"It's Adam, remember?"

"Impossible to forget," she replied, showing off a dimple. "Your name will probably be whispered in the corridors of Montgomery Inns for years. You're a legend, you know."

"As part of the poor and infamous?"

She plucked a shrimp canapé from a tray. "What're you doing here? Don't you know you'll be drawn and quartered before the night is out? That's what they do to party crashers." She plopped the canape into her mouth and washed it down with a sip of champagne.

He couldn't believe that she was actually baiting him. Adam's mouth slashed at a sardonic angle. "And here I thought my invitation had just gotten lost in the mail."

"Right," Marnie replied dryly, her ice blue dress glimmering seductively under the lights. "If I were you, this is the last place I would've shown up."

"Never was one to miss a party."

"You must be a glutton for punishment. My father will flip when he finds out you're here—and he will, you know. It won't take long."

"I'm counting on it."

"Why?" For the first time, the teasing glint disappeared from her eyes. She lifted her glass to her lips and appraised him solemnly over the rim.

"He and I need to talk, and he's been dodging my calls." Adam glanced back to the fountain-cum-podium where Victor was introducing Kent Simms and congratulating him on his promotion to executive vice president. Adam finished his drink in one gulp, as Simms accepted Victor's hearty congratulations, shook hands with the mayor and rained a brilliant pretty-boy smile on the crowd.

"You've *called* Dad?" Marnie asked, apparently stunned.

Adam swung his gaze back to her. "Several times. Never got past Kate. Victor didn't bother to call me back."

"But—"

"I even stopped in at the offices. Kate ran interference. Wouldn't let me in to see him."

Marnie couldn't believe it. Her father hadn't said a word about Adam trying to contact him, and she would have thought, given Victor's feelings about Adam Drake, he would have ranted and raved for days at the younger man's impertinence. "What did you want to talk to him about?"

"Believe me, I have a lot to discuss with your father— or if I can't talk to him, Simms'll do." He cocked his head toward the fountain. "By the way, your fiancé seems to be enjoying himself. Shouldn't you be up there, basking in some of the glory?"

"It got a little crowded," she said, her lips tightening.

"I noticed."

"Adam Drake?" Kate's voice was low and cold. When he turned, her large eyes were suspicious, the color in her cheeks high. "What do you think you're doing here?" she whispered, then before he could answer, asked, "How did you get past security?"

"I helped design this building, remember—including the security system."

"You bastard," she shot back, ignoring Marnie. "You want to ruin it for him, don't you? This is Victor's night, and you're going to make sure that it blows up in his face!"

"I just want to talk to him."

"Well, you can't. Not tonight," she said, her features hardening. "If the press gets wind that you're here, it'll ruin everything! You've got to leave! Now!" Her voice had taken on a frantic tone that seemed to surprise Marnie as she watched the exchange in stunned silence.

"I'm not taking off just yet."

"But why would you want to stay? It'll just cause problems." Kate glanced nervously toward Victor.

Marnie laid a hand on her arm. "Relax, Kate," Marnie said, as if she, too, were trying to avoid a scene, but Kate raged on.

"Please, Adam, just go quietly, before you do something that can't be undone and everything's dredged up again. This is Victor's night. Please don't spoil it!"

"I need to talk to him."

"But not here—"

"I tried the office," he replied, fighting to control his anger. "You wouldn't let me see him."

"My mistake. Come back next week, I'll get you an appointment," she promised, pinning a winning smile on her face and slipping her arm through his, obviously intending to escort him to the door.

"I'll wait, just the same."

Frustrated, Kate stormed away in a cloud of exasperation.

"I don't think that's the way to win friends and influence people," Marnie said dryly.

"I'm not very popular around here, am I?"

She grinned. "I'm afraid you're persona non grata at Montgomery Inns. But my father still keeps your picture in his office—taped over his dart board."

He laughed, surprised that she would joke with him. The pianist began playing again, filling the lobby with a vaguely familiar big-band hit of the forties.

"Do you want me to tell my father you're here?" she asked, and he shook his head.

"I think it would be better if you stay out of it."

"Why?"

"It could get bloody."

"Then I'd better be there," she decided. "Someone—maybe you—might need a bandage."

"And soon," he said, spying Kent Simms, face flushed, plunging through the crowd and heading straight for Marnie. The glare in Kent's eyes was unmistakable—the territorial pride of the spurned male.

"What the hell are you doing here?" Kent demanded in a voice so low it was hard to hear over the crowd.

Adam finished his drink. "I was hoping to talk to Victor, but I guess you'll have to do."

"Forget it. Come on, Marnie, let's go," Kent ordered, grabbing her arm and propelling her toward a banquet room near the back of the lobby.

"Let go of me," she whispered furiously, half running to keep up with his longer strides. She considered making a scene, but thought better of it. No reason to call undue attention to Adam—he'd do enough of that for himself.

In the banquet room, she whirled around and yanked her arm free of Kent's possessive grasp. "What is it you want?"

His expression changed from anger to sadness. "You already know what I want," he said quietly. "I just want you, Marnie."

She couldn't believe her ears. What did it take to make the man understand? "I already told you it's over! I don't need to be manhandled or made a spectacle of! Where do you get off, hauling me in here like some caveman claiming his woman?"

"Caveman?" he repeated. "Weren't you just talking to Drake? Now there's someone who's primitive." He shook his head, as if sorry that she was so dense. "You know, Marnie, sometimes you can be impossible."

"Good!"

"You enjoy being perverse?"

"I just want you to leave me alone. I thought you understood that. If you don't, let me make myself clear," she said, drawing up to her full height and sending him an icy glare. "I'm sorry I ever got involved with you and I never want to see you again."

He glanced to one of the chandeliers high overhead. "I made a mistake with Dolores."

She didn't respond. She'd learned that his affair with Dolores had been going on for over six months. All the time that she and Kent had been picking out china, planning a wedding, looking for a house, sailing in the boat Victor had bought them as an engagement present, Kent had been sleeping with his secretary.

"You know I still love you," he said, and his expression was so sincere, she almost believed him. But she wasn't a fool. Not any more. "Give me another chance," he pleaded. "It'll never happen again. I swear it."

Marnie shook her head. "You can do what you damn well please, Kent. It doesn't matter anymore."

"I really did a number on you, didn't I?"

"I prefer to think that you did me a favor."

A light of challenge sparked in his hazel eyes. He leaned down as if to kiss her, and she ducked away. "Stop it!" she commanded, her tone frigid.

He ignored her and grabbed her quickly, yanking her hard against him. "Don't tell me 'no,'" he whispered, his face so close that his breath, smelling of liquor, fanned her face.

"Don't pull this macho stuff on me!"

"You love it." His grip tightened, and his eyes glittered in a way that frightened and sickened her. He *enjoyed* this fight.

Squirming, unable to wrench away, she stomped on his foot in frustration. The heel of her shoe snapped with the force. "Let go!"

Kent let out a yowl and backed up a step. "What the hell's gotten into you?" he cried, reaching down to rub the top of his shoe, as if he could massage his wounded foot. Wincing, he turned furious eyes on her. "I thought we could work things out, you know? I thought tonight would be the perfect time. Did you see me with your father and Senator Mann? The man knew my name! God, what a rush! And I come back to share it with you—the woman I love—and what do I get?"

"Maybe you're getting what you deserve," Adam drawled, coming up behind Kent.

A wave of heat washed up Marnie's neck. Oh, Lord! How much of their argument had he overheard?

Kent straightened, resting his foot gingerly on the floor as he eyed Adam. Adam was slightly taller, with harsher features, his hair a little longer, his whole demeanor laid-back and secure. Kent, on the other hand, looked military spit-and-polished, his tuxedo crisp, his hair clipped, his spine ramrod-stiff.

"I thought you were leaving," Kent said, glowering at Adam.

"Not yet."

Kent straightened his tie and smoothed his hair. "Does Victor know you're here?"

Adam lifted a shoulder nonchalantly, but his features were set in stone. "I hope so."

Instinctively, Marnie stepped closer to Adam, and Kent shot her an irritated glance, his eyes slitting. "Just what is it you want, Drake?" he demanded, stuffing his hands into the back pockets of his pants and angling his face upward to meet Adam's hard glare. "Why don't you just leave?"

"Not until I ask Victor if he knows who Gerald Henderson is?"

"Henderson?" Kent repeated, his expression so bland it had to be false. "Didn't he work for us?"

"In accounting," Adam clarified.

"I remember him," Marnie interjected, refusing to be left out of the conversation. "He left because he had health problems—asthma, I think. He had to leave the damp Northwest. And he got a better job with a hotel in San Diego."

"Still lives in Seattle," Adam replied. "Spends a lot of time fishing. If I'm not wrong, I think he's drawing some sort of disability or retirement."

Marnie glanced from one stern face to the other. "Didn't the job in California work out?"

"Who cares?" Kent replied. "Henderson's history."

"Maybe," Adam said, and the undercurrents in his voice jarred her. She was missing something in this conversation, something important.

Kent swallowed. "I don't think Victor would be interested," he said, but his voice lacked conviction.

"Not even if Gerald had an idea about the missing funds?"

"What?" Marnie demanded, shocked.

"It's nothing," Kent snapped. "Henderson couldn't possibly know—"

"Adam Drake?" Judith Marx, a reporter for the *Seattle Observer* who had obviously seen some of the hubbub, walked briskly into the banquet room. "I'm surprised to see you here," she said, her eyes taking in the scene in one quick glance.

The understatement of the year, Marnie thought.

"I wouldn't have missed this for the world," Adam drawled.

"Can I quote you?" she asked.

"No!" Kent cut in, his face flushed, a vein throbbing near his temple. "Mr. Drake is an uninvited guest, and if you print that I'll march over to the *Observer* and talk to John Forrester myself!"

"Mr. Forrester would never suppress news," the woman replied smartly.

Kent whirled on Adam, his voice low. "Whatever it is you want, Drake, it can wait until later."

By now, more than a few guests had drifted into the room. Kent was beginning to squirm. Whispers began to float around them, like tiny wisps of fog that lingered for a second, then drifted by.

"Mr. Drake?" Judith Marx obviously smelled a story. She wasn't about to give up. "I thought you vowed vengeance against this company."

"What I said was that I'd prove my innocence."

From the corner of his eye, Adam saw Kent motioning with a finger to a beefy security guard in the doorway.

"Wasn't that all taken care of?" Judith asked Adam, and he turned his attention back to the reporter. "You weren't even indicted." She reached into her bag for her pocket recorder. Kent glanced across the room, nodding to the two guards making their way inside.

Adam was ready for the two sets of hands that collared him and firmly guided him through a back door connecting the banquet room to the kitchen. He didn't struggle. There was no point. Obviously Victor hadn't seen him, or had decided to leave his dirty work to Kent. Either way, Adam wasn't finished. Not by a long shot. But his next move would be more subtle.

Hauling him through the service entrance, the security guards deposited him roughly on the wet asphalt near a delivery truck.

One of the two guards, a big bear of a man with sandy hair and a flat face, muttered under his breath. "Still gettin' yourself into trouble, ain't'cha?" Sam Dillinger had worked with Adam for years before the scandal.

"Looks that way, Sam." Adam brushed himself off as he stood. He managed a grim smile.

"I'm sorry, Mr. Drake. You know, I never believed you were involved in any of that thievin'."

"Thanks, Sam."

The other guard, a thickset man with short salt-and-pepper hair, snorted. He fingered the pistol strapped to his belt. "Don't show up here again," he warned. "Just haul your butt out of here and don't come back!"

"Be sure to tell Mr. Simms he hasn't seen the last of me," Adam said to Jim before sketching a wave to Sam. "See ya around, Sam."

"You bet, Mr. Drake. Good luck to you."

But Adam wasn't counting on luck as he left the two guards arguing about his guilt. He ducked his head against the rain that slanted from the pitch-black sky.

The dock was slick, the wind raw and cold as he strode purposefully back to his boat. Now that he'd come face-to-face with Kent Simms again, he realized that nothing had changed. And since he didn't have any proof other than Gerald Henderson's side of the story, he couldn't very well make accusations that could end up as slander. But from his reaction tonight, Adam was sure Simms knew more than he was telling. Adam had suspected Kent might be involved in the embezzling, of course, but he'd suspected a lot of people within the company.

Now, he decided, he'd start with Simms. He didn't like the way the guy was manhandling Marnie, and the thought of giving Kent a little of his own back caused Adam to smile.

So, his next step would be to have a little chat with Kent before he tackled Victor. The more information he could lay at Montgomery's feet, the better. And somehow, he sensed, Kent could tell him a lot.

Fortunately meeting Kent Simms face-to-face would be a simple matter. The *Marnie Lee,* a gleaming white cabin cruiser, and Simms's personal vessel, was moored on the second dock.

Adam wasted no time. He looked over his shoulder

to make sure the two guards were still watching as he stepped into his small boat. Unleashing the moorings, he settled behind the wheel and gunned the engine. The boat took off, churning a white wake as the engine roared loudly and he headed toward Seattle.

Twenty minutes later, when he was sure the guards were satisfied that he'd left the shores of Port Stanton and had returned to their posts in the hotel lobby, Adam circled back toward the Puget West and the docks where gleaming vessels rolled with the tide.

He wasn't finished. Not by a long shot. Adam intended to board the *Marnie Lee* and wait in the cabin to have it out with Simms once and for all. As he spotted the showy white vessel he thought of her namesake, the lady herself, Marnie Lee Montgomery. How could a woman as bright as Marnie obviously was link up with a loser like Simms?

It was a mystery, he thought, then he remembered the tail end of their fight and decided that all was not bliss in the relationship between Victor Montgomery's strong-willed daughter and the man she'd chosen for a husband.

Adam felt a twinge of conscience as he lashed his boat to the dock, then climbed stealthily aboard Simms's expensive cabin cruiser. He didn't want to hurt Marnie; she'd always played fair with him. Though she'd been raised in the lap of luxury and been given anything she'd ever wanted, she seemed sincere.

Don't forget she's engaged to Simms. Even if they did have a lovers' quarrel, they were, as far as he knew, still planning to marry. That thought left a sour taste in the back of his throat, but he ignored it. Marnie's fate was just too damned bad. Any woman who gave her heart to a jerk like Simms deserved what she got.

MARNIE COULDN'T BELIEVE her ears! The minute Adam was escorted out of the hotel, Kent turned the interview with the reporter around and now, with his arm wrapped securely around Marnie's waist, he was confiding in the woman that Marnie and he were making plans to marry in mid-September.

"Congratulations!" Judith said, snapping her small tape recorder on. "What day is that, the sixteenth—seventeenth?"

"No!" Marnie cried, aghast. What had gotten into Kent? In all the years she'd known him he'd never been so bullheaded or downright stupid.

Kent's fingers tightened around her. "What she means is that we're not completely certain on the date. We've still got to accommodate everyone in the family—"

"What I mean is that there isn't going to be a wedding!" Marnie declared firmly, plucking Kent's fingers off her and stepping away from him. "Kent and I aren't getting married, not in September. Not ever."

"But—" Judith looked from one to the other.

Kent lifted his hands and shrugged, as if Marnie's announcement came as a complete surprise to him. He acted as if she were just some fickle female who couldn't decide what she wanted, for God's sake!

"You explain this!" Marnie commanded, her voice as cold as a winter day. Shaking with rage, she turned on the reporter. "I'd better not read about any wedding in your paper. Not one word!" Spine stiff, she marched straight through the banquet-room doors and to the elevator in the lobby.

Pounding on the button for the fourth floor, she bit her tongue so that the invectives forming in her throat would be kept inside. The elevator doors shut softly, cutting off the sounds of the party, and the car ascended. Furious, her insides shaking with anger, Marnie leaned her forehead against the cool glass. "Calm down," she ordered to herself. "Don't let that bastard get to you!"

The elevator stopped and she stepped through the opening doors, storming into her father's suite. What was Kent trying to do? He'd been acting strangely all night! How had she ever been foolish enough to think she wanted to marry him?

She stalked into the smaller bedroom. Her suitcase, packed and waiting, was where she'd left it near the foot of the bed. Good. She peeled off her gown, threw her jewelry into a case and stuffed the velvet box back into her father's safe.

By the time Victor knocked softly on the door to her room, she had changed into faded jeans, a sweatshirt and a down-lined jacket. "Marnie? You in here?"

"For the moment."

He opened the door and shook his head at the sight of her. "And where do you think you're going?"

She sent him a chilling glance. "I'm leaving. Remember?"

"Of course I remember," he said, holding out his palms as if to forestall an argument, "but I thought you might change your mind and wait a bit. Kent just told me he had Adam Drake thrown out of the party while I was wrapped up with Senator Mann. God only knows what's going to be in the papers tomorrow! I need you to talk to the press—"

"I just did." Marnie wasn't about to be sidetracked by her father's ploy. "*That* was a dirty trick, Dad," she said, yanking her suitcase onto the bed and snapping it open to double-check the contents.

"What?"

Satisfied that she'd packed everything she needed, she clicked the case shut. "You told Kent to give the press a wedding date, didn't you?"

"Of course not—"

"He never would have done it without getting the okay from you," she insisted. "He wouldn't do anything that might threaten his precious career with Montgomery Inns."

"I didn't—"

"Don't lie to me, Dad! It's belittling to both of us."

Her father seemed about to protest, then let out a long, weary sigh. "Okay, I suggested that Kent—"

"Oh, Dad, how *could* you!"

"We needed a distraction. I saw Adam Drake and knew he was here to stir up trouble and then that reporter woman, Judith Marx…" He shuddered. "She can be a barracuda."

"Then why didn't you confront Drake?" she asked, astounded.

Her father shook his head. "Only cause a worse scene. Anyway, I saw Drake and started to follow him into the banquet room when Senator Mann came up to me. Then the reporter started snooping around and I put two and two together. Instead of a big spread about opening this hotel, tomorrow's edition of the *Observer* would probably just bring up Adam Drake and all the problems we had getting this damned hotel built! Believe me, Marnie, we don't need any more bad press."

"Great. So *I* became the distraction," she whispered, exasperated beyond words.

"When Kent talked to me earlier I wasn't for it, but then I saw Drake and the reporter and I gave him the high-sign to go ahead and announce your wedding plans."

"You're incredible," she whispered in exasperation. "Absolutely incredible!" Hooking a thumb to her chest, she added, "We're talking about *my* life, Dad. Mine!"

"Marnie, you have to understand—"

"Oh, I do, Dad," she said, feeling sad as she realized that the company meant more to him than her happiness. "You can give Kent a message for me. Tell him that I'm taking the *Marnie Lee*. If he throws a fit, remind him that half of it is mine. So I'm taking my half—too bad his half is attached."

"Wait a minute—at least tell me where you're going."

"I don't know," she admitted.

"You don't know?" he repeated. "You can't just leave without a plan."

"That's exactly what I'm going to do. The next few days I'm going to figure out just what I want to do with my life. Take some time to think about it, then, when I get back, I'll let you know. Goodbye, Dad." More determined than ever, she headed out of the suite and down a short hall to a private elevator, which took her to the underground parking lot. From there it was only a few steps to the back of the building.

Outside, the wind ripped through the trees and the black water of the sound moved in restless waves. Marnie followed the path beneath the line of dancing Japanese lanterns.

Reaching the dock, she spotted the *Marnie Lee* and smiled faintly. Wouldn't Kent be tied in knots when he learned she'd taken the boat he'd come to think of as his? Kent had used the boat for the past six months. He'd be shocked to his toes when he found out she had taken command of the sleek vessel Victor had given them as an engagement present. Let him stew in his own juices—September wedding indeed!

Tossing her suitcase on board, she felt better than she had all night. She unleashed the moorings holding the *Marnie Lee* fast then climbed to the helm. The engine started on the first try, the dark waters of the sound churning white. Biting her lip, Marnie maneuvered the craft around the other vessels and toward the open waters of Puget Sound.

She decided to head to Orcas Island.

There was an old resort on the island, a resort her

father planned to refurbish, and the old hotel would be the perfect place to camp out the first night. From there she would decide what she was going to do with the rest of her life. She couldn't be Victor Montgomery's baby forever. Nor did she want to be Kent Simms's wife. That left Marnie Montgomery, a single woman who had dutifully done everything her father had requested, from college to her career at Montgomery Inns.

Marnie let out the throttle and the boat sped forward, the prow knifing through the choppy dark water, the wind tearing at her hair. She let out a whoop of pure joy!

For the first time in her twenty-four years, she felt completely free. She closed her eyes and felt the soft caress of the wind on her face.

The next few weeks were going to change the course of her life forever!

CHAPTER THREE

ADAM TRIED TO MOVE his cramped muscles. He'd been hiding in a storage closet in the hold for forty-five minutes, according to the luminous face of his watch, and for the last fifteen the boat had been moving, cutting through the water at a pretty good clip. The *Marnie Lee* pitched and rolled as they traveled, and Adam guessed that the storm was stronger than the weather service had predicted. The force of the gale didn't seem to deter Simms though; he never turned about.

Good. The farther they were from Port Stanton, the better. Adam couldn't wait to see the look on Simms's face when he appeared on deck.

Adam gave Kent another fifteen minutes, then eased himself from the tight quarters. He'd stashed an overnight bag in the galley because he'd learned over the past year to be prepared for anything. He didn't know how long he'd be stuck with Kent—he hadn't worked that out yet. A lot depended upon Simms's attitude and what kind of deal they could cut, because, Adam was sure that Kent Simms was up to his eyeballs in the embezzling mess. There was a chance that Simms hadn't been involved, but the probability was slim. From his overreaction at the sight of Adam, to his insistence that security be called, Simms looked guilty as hell. Yep, Simms was hiding something. Adam just had to find out what it was and how it was tied to the embezzling.

He glanced up the stairs, felt the lash of rain and wind

and decided to give Kent a couple more minutes while he
changed. Tossing his bag into an empty cabin, he stripped
out of his tux and slid into jeans, flannel shirt, sweater and
high-tops. Finally he flung a black poncho over his head.

Using sea legs he'd acquired in the navy, he climbed
up two flights to the bridge and twisted his lips into a
grim smile at the thought of scaring the living hell out of
Simms. If nothing else, Simms's reaction would be worth
the rocky ride.

Flinging open the door of the bridge, he stopped stock-
still. A blast of wind caught the door, ripping the door
latch from his hands. Papers rustled and caught in the icy
breeze. Marnie Montgomery, planted at the helm, nearly
jumped out of her skin. With a scream that died in her
throat, she whipped around and fumbled in the pocket of
her jacket, presumably for a weapon. The helm spun crazily and the boat shuddered.

"Drake? What the hell are you doing here?" she cried,
her face ashen, her hair blowing in the wind as she scrabbled to regain control of the spinning wheel. "You nearly
gave me a heart attack!"

He was as stunned as she. Marnie? Here? At the wheel
in the middle of a gale-force storm? The wind was fierce,
the waters of the sound rolling and unpredictable.

"I asked you a question," she said, her blue eyes dark
as the angry ocean. "And close the door, for crying out
loud!"

Damn his rotten luck! Adam caught hold of the latch
and pulled the door shut behind him. The door slammed
tight, shutting out the wind and rain.

Papers stopped blowing, and Marnie's blond hair fell
back to her shoulders. "Well?"

His entire plan—spontaneous as it had been—depended upon getting Simms alone. Now he had to deal

with Simms's angry lover. Terrific! Just damned terrific. "I'm looking for Kent Simms."

"Here?" she said, laughing bitterly. The disgusted look she sent him accused him of being out of his mind. "You expected him on board?"

"Isn't he?"

"Not if he has a brain," she muttered. Scowling, she added, "I think Kent's back at the hotel, living the good life, kissing up to my father." She turned her concentration back to the sea.

So she was still furious. Good. Her anger might work to his advantage, Adam thought. Now that he was on this pitching boat in the middle of a storm, he had to improvise his hasty plan, and though he wasn't quite sure how, he knew instinctively that any rift between Simms and Victor Montgomery's daughter was a good sign.

"What do you want with him?" she asked, never taking her eyes off the boat's prow.

"We need to talk."

"About what?" Her voice was casual, but he noticed a glint of suspicion in her gaze as she hazarded a quick glance in his direction. "No, don't tell me. Let me guess. This has something to do with the reason you crashed the party, doesn't it?"

When he didn't immediately respond, she plunged ahead. "And since I don't think you're interested in filling out a job application for Montgomery Inns, you must want to talk about the money that's missing from the Puget West project. Right?"

It galled him the way she talked about the embezzlement so flippantly. He'd gone through hell in the past twelve months, and she acted as though it didn't really matter, just a little inconvenience.

She wasn't finished. "If you want my advice—"

"I didn't come here for—"

"You should just get on with your life."

"I'm not here for advice."

"Then you shouldn't have stowed away on my boat."

Her boat? "The *Marnie Lee* belongs to Simms."

She smiled at that, and her face softened a little. Even under the harsh lights of the bridge, with her hair still wet and her face without a trace of makeup, she was a beautiful woman. "*Half* of the *Marnie Lee* belongs to Kent. Unfortunately for him, his half is nailed to my half and I decided to leave the party early."

"Why?"

She sent him another hard look, a line forming between her brows. "It was time," she replied, without giving him a clue to her motives.

"Does it have anything to do with your fight with Simms?"

Marnie started to answer, then held her tongue. *She* should be the person asking questions, not the other way around! What the devil was Drake doing on her boat? She felt nervous and hot, though the bridge was barely 50° F. Adam had always put her on edge; his angled features, thick hair and intense eyes fairly screamed "sexy," but she'd ignored his rakish good looks when she'd worked with him. She knew a lot of attractive men, but Adam was different. He was more than just simply handsome. There was a restlessness about him, an earthiness coupled with repressed anger that caused her to react to him on a primal level. Kent had called Adam primitive and for once he'd been right: there was a certain primal sexuality to the man.

So here he was, in the tiny bridge, a storm thundering outside, the boat lurching and tilting, and all she could think about was keeping distance between herself and him.

"You made a mistake," she said flatly.

"Just one?" One side of his mouth lifted.

Marnie gripped the helm and felt her palms dampen with sweat. All she wanted was to escape her past and sort out her identity. But now she had to deal with Adam Drake. Even though he had come to her rescue at the party, she didn't want him fouling up her first real bid for freedom. "Look, you've got to get off the boat."

"Why?"

"You're not part of my plan."

He snorted and tossed back the hood of his poncho. "We've got more in common than I thought. You weren't part of mine."

"Let's get one thing straight—we've got nothing in common."

He glanced at her sharply. "So you're a believer in the great lie, too. You really think I skimmed off money from the Puget West project."

"There's been no other explanation," she said, hedging.

"I was cleared, damn it!" In two swift strides he was so close to her that she noticed the gold flecks in his brown eyes. His nostrils flared in outrage.

"You weren't cleared," she said evenly, "there just wasn't enough evidence to indict you."

He drew in his breath sharply; the air whistled through his teeth. "Well, Miss Montgomery, I guess I was wrong about you. I thought you might be the one person in the entire Montgomery Inns empire that realized I'd been set up. But you're just like the rest, aren't you?"

"No, I'm different. I ended up with you as a stowaway. I didn't ask you to come on board, did I? As far as I'm concerned you should get off my boat." She considered telling him that she'd stood up to her father and the board, declaring him innocent, but decided the truth, right now, was pointless.

Adam's gaze raked down her. "What do you want me to do? Walk the plank?"

"If only I had one." He could joke at a time like this? The man was incorrigible! There was a slight chance that he was a thief, and now he'd stowed away on the boat, proving that he obviously had no scruples whatsoever. And yet there had been a time when Marnie had relied upon his judgment, had trusted his interpretation of the facts. She had sat through many meetings with Adam in attendance. He always spoke his mind, arguing with her father when necessary. Unlike Kent, who worked diligently to have no mind of his own and think exactly like her father. The proverbial yes-man. She shivered at the thought that she'd once believed she loved him. She'd been a blind fool, a rich girl caught up in the fantasy of love.

The *Marnie Lee* groaned against the weight of a wave, and a tremor passed through the hull. The wheel slid through Marnie's fingers, and Adam grabbed hold of the helm, his arms imprisoning her as he strained against the wheel. "Only an idiot would sail in a storm like this," he muttered.

An idiot or someone hell-bent to have a life of her own, she thought angrily, surrounded by the smell of him. The scent of after-shave was nearly obscured by the fresh odor of water and ocean that clung to his skin. His hair gleamed under the fluorescent bulbs in the ceiling and his features were set into a hard mask as unforgiving as the sea.

"Do I have to remind you that you've shown up uninvited twice in one night? That must be some kind of record, don't you think?"

"I don't know what to think right now," he admitted, his eyebrows thrust together and deep lines of concentration etching his forehead, "but I sure as hell can come up with a hundred places I'd rather be."

"That makes two of us," she snapped, as his arms relaxed and he stepped back, giving her control of the vessel again. "We'll put into port at Chinook Harbor."

"That's where you're going?"

"It's a little out of the way." *But worth it, to get rid of you,* she thought unkindly. She didn't need any complications on this trip, and any way she looked at it, Adam Drake was a complication. He stepped away from her, and she commanded the boat again, glad for the feel of the polished wheel in her hands. A hundred questions plagued her. What did he want with Kent? Why had he stowed away? How involved in the embezzling was he? And why, oh Lord, why, did she find him the least bit attractive? The man was trouble—pure and simple.

The storm didn't slow down for a minute. Harsh winds screamed across the deck and waves curled high to batter the hull repeatedly. Marnie's stomach spent most of the trip in her throat, and she didn't have time to consider Adam again. He made himself useful, helping read the charts and maps as they headed into the cluster of San Juan Islands.

Her plan was to drop him off in Chinook Harbor, spend the night on the boat, then, as soon as the storm passed, sail around the tip of the island to Deception Lodge, an antiquated resort her father wanted to restore. Making camp in a potential Montgomery Inn bothered her a little; the lodge still belonged to her father and as long as she was seeking shelter on Montgomery soil, she wasn't truly free.

"But soon," she muttered as she spied a few lights winking in the distance, lights that had to be on Orcas Island.

"But soon—what?"

She shot him a look that told him it was none of his business, and was about to turn inland when she spotted the buoy bobbing crazily ahead.

"Watch out," Adam commanded, but the sea swelled

under the boat like a creature climbing from the depths. "Marnie, you're too close!"

Panicked, she checked the gauges. "Too close to what!"

CRACK! The *Marnie Lee* trembled violently, and for a second Marnie thought the boat was about to split apart.

"Damn it, woman, get out of the way." Adam shoved her aside and threw open the door.

"You can't go out…" Her voice was carried away by the cry of the wind.

"Just steer the boat, for God's sake!"

Horrified, still trying to set the *Marnie Lee* back on course, she watched as Adam tied a rope around his waist, then worked his way around the bow, rain beating on his head, his hands moving one over the other on the rail. He paused at the starboard side, leaned over, then braced himself as another swell rolled over the deck, engulfing him. Marnie's heart leaped to her throat. She saw the lifeline stretch taut. Her stomach lurched as the wave retreated and Adam, drenched, still braced against the force of the wave, appeared again.

"Thank God," she whispered, her throat raw, "Now, Drake, damn your stubborn hide, get below deck and dry out."

Another torrent of water washed over the deck and once again Adam vanished for a few terror-filled seconds. This time, when the water receded, he moved along the rail again before disappearing on the stairs.

She guided the ship by instinct; she'd learned sailing from her father years before. But all the while her nerves were strung tight, her ears cocked to the door.

Nearly ten minutes later, Adam returned to the bridge, dripping and coughing saltwater and glaring at her as if she were responsible for the storm. "There's a crack in the hull—a small one on the starboard side, on line with the galley," he said. "Not a big gash, but it's not going away. You're taking on water—slowly. I used some sealer I found downstairs, but it won't hold, at least not forever." His eyes were dark and serious. "You've got to turn inland."

"But there's no port for miles."

"You don't have a choice. The island's close enough. Just head for land. We'll worry about a harbor when we get closer." He picked up the microphone for the radio and started to call the Coast Guard, but Marnie flipped the switch, turning off his cry for help.

"We'll make it ourselves," she said, refusing, in her first few hours of freedom, to give up any small bit of her independence. "Besides, I think the storm's about over, the rain's stopping."

"Did you hear me, Marnie?" he demanded, ignoring her assessment of the situation. "Rain or no rain, sooner or later, this boat is going to sink like a stone. And we're going to sink with her."

"But not for a while. Right?"

"Unless we hit something else."

"How long do we have?"

"How the hell should I know?"

"Ten minutes? Twenty? Two hours?"

"Hell, I don't know, but you can't take a chance like this!"

"Why not?" she demanded, cranking hard on the wheel and checking the maps of the area again. They weren't far from her destination, the point where Deception Lodge was sprawled on high cliffs over the ocean. If she could beach the *Marnie Lee* soon, she wouldn't have to call for help and suffer the indignities of having Victor running to save her only to remind her that she wasn't yet ready to fly on her own wings. Well, damn it, he was wrong. And so was Adam Drake. "Don't tell me you're worried about your neck, Mr. Drake."

"No more than I am about yours." Sarcasm tainted his voice.

"Then help me get this boat to shore."

He eyed her for a minute. "And for that, I get what?"

"A bargain? Now, you want to bargain with me?" she asked incredulously. She couldn't believe her ears. "Isn't staying alive enough?"

His lips curved crookedly. "Give me a little more incentive. My life this past year hasn't been that great."

Unbelievable! While the boat rocked beneath them, he wanted to barter. Marnie didn't have time. "Okay, okay already. So I'll owe you one," she said, furious until she saw the glint of satisfaction in his dark eyes.

"All right, Marnie. You steer. I'll keep the gash from getting any worse." He started for the door but stopped, glancing back over his shoulder, his hair falling over his eyes. "What is this, anyway—some sort of quest? What're you trying to prove?"

When she didn't answer, he strode out the door. Marnie wasn't about to confide in him; he could bloody well think what he wanted. After all, he hadn't been invited along. She owed him nothing. Not even an explanation. Besides, if anyone had an explanation coming, it was she. What the devil was he doing looking for Kent on this boat?

She struggled with the helm until her muscles began to ache. Then, as she turned east, the storm abated. Waves still washed over the deck, but the wrath of the storm was spent, the wind no longer keening over the black water. The clouds, which had so jealously covered the moon, thinned to become a gauzy filter for weak moonlight.

Squinting, Marnie saw the island, a huge black shape rising from the frothy swell of the ocean like a sea monster. They couldn't be far from Deception Point, she thought wildly, but in the darkness she couldn't see well enough to make out the rocky cliffs. No lights glowed in the dark, guiding her to a port, but she wasn't about to complain.

She slowed the engines, creeping in with the waves. In too close and she'd scrape bottom; too far out and they'd have a helluva fight in the life raft to get to shore.

Below decks, Adam heard, rather than felt, the change in speed. So they were going to dock. Finally. Victor's daughter had more guts than he would've given her credit for—maybe more guts than brains, considering the situation. He sealed the cut in the hull again with the sealer he'd found in a storage closet, and decided the craft wouldn't sink as long as she was stable. The gash was above the waterline and had only leaked when the boat had listed badly. Unless the sea rolled the *Marnie Lee* onto her starboard side again, the boat wouldn't settle to the bottom of the ocean. Or at least he hoped not.

So why hadn't she let him radio for help? What kind of game was she playing? Was she the kind of rich woman who needed thrills?

She'd always seemed so down-to-earth. Beautiful but never too flashy. Elegant but not extreme. So why the sudden boat trip in the middle of a storm? And why not call the Coast Guard?

Could Marnie Montgomery be a woman running from her past?

That particular thought intrigued him. He climbed the slippery steps to the bridge. Marnie barely glanced his way. "You'd better drop anchor," he said, checking the charts again. "Any closer and you're asking for trouble." His gaze slid to hers, and for an insane moment he thought he read more than anger in her stare. But that was crazy. As far as he knew, she hated him, thought he was a traitor to Daddy's precious company. She looked away, but not before he recognized female interest for what it was.

"Okay, let's do it." She released the anchor, and the boat settled, rolling with the tide but no longer listing.

Adam, still wondering about her reaction, worked on the inflatable life raft and loaded it with supplies.

"Get your things," he ordered when the raft was pumped up.

While she climbed to the lower cabin, he hurried back to the bridge and made a quick call to the Coast Guard. She'd be furious with him, but so be it, he thought, as he loaded his pockets with matches, flares and a first-aid kit he found in a cupboard beneath the radio.

Within minutes they were both in the life raft. Leaning his back into the oars, Adam rowed for shore. Marnie reached for the second set of oars, but he shook his head. The air was still cold, the wind still gusting, and he felt an unlikely sense of chivalry. "I can handle this. Relax."

"No reason," she said, her back stiffening as she threw her weight into the task.

Adam didn't argue with her. If she thought she was helping, fine. He wasn't up to another argument. Rowing backward, he watched her arms strain, the muscles of her back move fluidly. She wasn't a wimp by any stretch of the imagination, and he grudgingly admired her gameness. The *Marnie Lee,* lights blazing, was stark against the dark sky. They rowed without speaking; only the sound of the waves and the occasional burst of wind disturbed the silence as they approached the beach.

Adam dropped his oars, climbed over the side and slid into the chest-deep icy water. Towing the raft inland, he said, "I radioed the Coast Guard."

She snapped her head around. "You did *what?*"

"I didn't think you'd want your father to worry, and the Guard needs to know about the *Marnie Lee.*"

"You had no right!" she cried, outraged.

"Probably not. And it's not that I care a lick about your

dad. I just thought, from the looks of things, you wouldn't want him sending the cavalry after you. Hey—stop—you don't have to—"

But Marnie slid into the frigid sea and together they pulled the raft onto the beach.

"Anyone ever call you stubborn?"

She laughed a little, even though she was shivering.

Adam sized her up and realized he'd never really known her in the few years they'd worked together. "What is it with you, anyway, Montgomery? You've got a helluva chip on your shoulder."

"Isn't that a little like the pot calling the kettle black?" she threw back, her teeth chattering, as the two of them dragged the raft high onto the sand, away from the tide.

"Yeah, but I didn't grow up in the lap of luxury."

"Well, I did!" she replied, tossing her wet hair out of her eyes and reaching for her bags. "And that's the problem. Look, I'm not going to argue with you anymore. There's a lodge where I'm going to camp out for the night, and if you want to come along, fine. If not, I don't really care. It's about a two- or three-hour hike into town. That way—" She pointed the beam of her flashlight south. "Your choice." With that she grabbed the bags and started, with the aid of a flashlight, north along the beach.

Adam didn't ask any more questions. He didn't really give a damn. He was only interested in Marnie to further his cause. Period. Whether Miss Montgomery knew it or not, she was going to help him find out what happened to the missing half million dollars.

CHAPTER FOUR

SWEARING UNDER HIS breath, Victor Montgomery slammed down the phone in his suite. Damn Marnie and her stupid independence! His hands were shaking so badly, he stuffed them into his pockets. What was wrong with that girl? Downstairs in the lobby, two hundred of the most important people in the Northwest were milling through the hotel, sipping his champagne, toasting Montgomery Inns while Marnie could have lost her fool life! If she were here now, he'd wring her neck! Instead, he had to act as if nothing were wrong. As if his wayward daughter hadn't walked out of his life. As if he weren't worried sick about her.

"Problems?" Kate asked, smoothing his lapel with her long fingers and offering him an encouraging smile. Kate was a good woman, he thought, trying to get a handle on his emotions. At least *she* had enough sense to do what she was told!

"Marnie."

Kate raised an interested eyebrow and sighed. "She's almost twenty-five."

"And therefore can do anything she damned well pleases, is that it?"

"She's not a baby, Vic. You can't tie her down forever."

"I can try, damn it!" He shoved a hand through his hair and wondered when he'd lost Marnie. And why? Hadn't he given her everything money could buy? Hadn't he put her through the best schools, hired the best nannies, spent as much time with her as he possibly could have? If only Vanessa were still alive. Maybe then...

"Senator Mann's waiting for you," Kate reminded him gently. She refilled his glass and handed him the fresh drink.

"I know, I know, probably hoping for a campaign contribution," Victor grumbled.

Kate chuckled deep in her throat. "Probably."

Still worried about Marnie, Victor took a swallow of the whiskey and waited for the fiery warmth to settle in his stomach. Maybe then he'd calm down. He thought about confiding in Kate but didn't. He'd never confided in a woman except his wife. Even Marnie hadn't heard his worries or dreams, not really. God, he missed Vanessa. She'd been gone so long...

Pulling himself back to the present, he touched Kate affectionately on the shoulder. "Tell the senator I'll be down in a minute and send in Kent, will you?"

"Of course." With another smile, she swept out of the room in a billow of familiar perfume and white silk. A beautiful woman, he thought. A gracious woman. A woman he could live with. If it weren't for the memory of Vanessa.

Adjusting his cuffs, he glanced in the mirror and frowned at his reflection. He was getting old. Not that fifty-seven was near the end of the line, but more than a few crow's-feet were carved near his eyes and his hair was thinner and whiter than it once had been. His weight was starting to become a problem, and sometimes, damn it, he just felt tired.

As he grew older, he wanted more from life than a string of hotels, not that the business wasn't important. It was. But he wanted, *needed,* a daughter who worked with him, a daughter who was happily married, a daughter who would become the mother of the grandchildren he intended to spoil rotten.

A quick rap on the door and Kent, not one hair out of place, strode into the suite. Shutting the door behind him, he turned back to Victor. "Kate said you wanted to see me." He flashed his easygoing smile.

Victor liked Kent. The boy was so eager. He reminded Victor of himself twenty-five years before. Waving the younger man into a chair, he said, "It's about Marnie."

The all-American smile faded as Kent sat down. "I thought she left."

"She did. And apparently she took the *Marnie Lee* with her."

"What!" Kent blanched and leaped back to his feet. Then he sank back into his chair. "But she couldn't have," he said, one hand rubbing the opposite forearm.

"I just got a call from the Coast Guard—"

"Oh, my God, there's been an accident!"

"Marnie's fine," Victor assured the younger man, though Kent didn't seem relieved. In fact he appeared more agitated than ever. Well, he'd just had a helluva shock. Hadn't they all? Victor poured Kent a stiff shot and handed him the glass. The drink shook in the boy's hands.

"What happened?" Kent asked, tossing back most of the bourbon.

"As I said, Marnie took off in the *Marnie Lee*. She thinks she owns half of it, you know. And really she does. I did give it to the both of you as an engagement present."

"So that gives her the right to take off and leave me stranded?" Kent asked, dumbfounded. "God, what's gotten into her?"

"She wants to be independent."

"But it's like a damned hurricane out there." Kent strode to the windows and stared out at the gloomy night.

"Well, it's not quite that bad," Victor said, though he halfheartedly agreed with the man he'd hoped would become his son-in-law. "But Marnie has this…thing—ambition, if you will…to be her own woman. She tried to resign, but I talked her into taking a leave of absence instead, and she's off to, quote, 'find herself.' Whatever the devil that means."

"In the *Marnie Lee*." Kent yanked hard on his tie, and his face became a mask.

"The boat's in a little trouble," Victor admitted. "At least that's what the man said."

"Trouble?" Kent said, alarm flashing in his eyes.

Victor was touched. Despite anything Marnie said to the contrary, Kent Simms loved her. "Nothing serious, but it could have been."

"Wait a minute," Kent said, his eyes narrowing. "What man are you talking about—someone from the Coast Guard?"

Victor sighed. "Well, no. I heard it from the Guard, of course, a Captain Spencer, but he was radioed by some man, a passenger Marnie had on board."

"*Passenger?* This just gets better and better, doesn't it? So now she's with some man! Good God, Victor, what's going on?" Kent finished his drink and wiped the back of his hand over his lips.

"I don't know." Victor tugged thoughtfully on his lower lip. Kent's worries infected him again. He'd half calmed himself down, but now he felt a rush of concern as Kent poured himself another drink and paced from the windows to the door.

"I don't like this, Victor. I don't like it at all." He tossed back his second bourbon in two swallows.

"Neither do I."

"She's been acting crazy lately." Kent jammed his hand

through his hair in frustration. "I wonder who the devil is with her."

"I wish I knew." Swirling his own drink, Victor asked, "Maybe this new independent streak has something to do with why you two broke up."

Kent shook his head. "It's been coming for a long time," he said, effectively closing the subject. "Do you have any idea where she put into port?"

"That's a problem. The boat is anchored off Orcas Island, the westerly side. My guess is that she plans to spend the night camping on the beach or…"

"Or what?" Then Kent appeared to understand. "You think she may be holed up in Deception Lodge."

"Quite possibly."

"Then let's go get her." Kent strode to the door, eager to charge off and retrieve his lost maiden.

Victor admired the boy's spunk, but he motioned him back into the room. "It's just not that easy. I promised Marnie I wouldn't interfere."

Kent's mouth went slack with disbelief. "So you're letting her—and this *man*—hang out alone in the lodge?"

"Yes." Victor drained his glass as he remembered the determination in his daughter's fine chin. And the *man,* whoever he was, had had the decency to call the Coast Guard. His curiosity was burning as to the man's identity. Victor nevertheless decided that this time he had to trust Marnie. Though she hadn't spoken of a male passenger on the boat, she was entitled to live her own life.

"You can't just let Marnie and some guy shack up in Deception Lodge!"

"I don't think I've got any other choice."

"But you're her father," Kent protested, his face flushed, his lips thin and hard.

"That's the problem."

THE LODGE OCCUPIED a long stretch of the headlands, three rambling stories of sloping roofs and shingled gables. Most of the windows were still intact, Marnie noted, as she swung the beam of her flashlight over the weathered siding and covered porch. Only a few glass panes had been boarded over. The old structure had once been grand, a unique out-of-the-way retreat for those who spent their summers in the San Juan Islands.

Now the lodge's grandeur was little more than a memory. One creaky shutter banged against the wall, and the porch sagged a bit at the northerly end. Dry leaves rustled as they blew against the door.

"Needs a little work," Adam remarked, eyeing the rustic old building as he set his bags on the creaky floorboards of the porch.

"Nothing the Montgomery touch can't fix." She fit a key from her ring into the heavy lock chained across the double doors and twisted. The lock held firm for a second before springing open. Marnie let the chain fall to the porch and shoved open the doors.

Inside, she swung the beam of her flashlight over the lobby. Yellowed pine paneling dominated the room. There was a massive rock fireplace and all around the room, scattered like leaves in the wind, were tables with upside-down chairs stacked atop them. Furniture, draped in sheets, had been shoved into one corner of the cavernous lobby.

"You planned on staying here?" Adam asked, scanning the dusty interior with a grimace.

"Just for a few days." The beam of light dancing ahead of her, she walked to the wall behind the desk and found a bank of light switches. She flipped each switch in turn, but nothing happened. The room was still dark except for the pale lights from their flashlights.

"You're staying until..."

"Until I figure out my next destination."

"Another Montgomery Inn?"

She threw him a dubious smile over her shoulder. "No."

Adam rubbed the crick from his neck, and Marnie could feel his eyes following her. She couldn't quite figure him out. Sometimes she felt as if there were a hidden side to him, as if he were, as her father claimed, evil. Victor had told her often enough in the past year that Adam Drake was a predator, always on the move, ready to stalk his next prey.

She wasn't anxious to believe her father's opinion that Adam was such a lowlife. From her own dealings with him, she'd found Adam Drake to be honest and hardworking. He'd been tough, but Adam's toughness, mixed with pure cunning, had worked many deals in her father's favor. In those days Victor had praised Adam Drake for his ruthlessness, for his sense of knowing "when to make the kill."

So was he really a wolf in sheep's clothing? Or a man who'd been turned into a scapegoat? Marnie wondered if she'd ever know the answer. Not that it mattered. Adam was an inconvenience for one night. Nothing more.

"So this is Victor's next project," he mused, running the beam of his flashlight over the staircase and upper balcony. Cobwebs caught in the light, and dust swirled in the illumination.

"One of many." Spying a short hallway that separated the bar from the kitchen, Marnie headed toward the back of the lodge. She remembered seeing blueprints of this place in her father's office and had listened with interest as Victor had expounded on the "renovation and rejuvenation" of the old lodge where he'd spent many happy summers as a boy.

Following the bobbing trail of the flashlight, she walked briskly down the hallway and found the door she was looking for, a door, according to the aged drawings of Deception Lodge, where a narrow flight of steps led to the wine cellar. She pulled on the knob, but the door wouldn't budge. "Great," she muttered, setting her flashlight down and grabbing the old knob in both hands. The door wasn't locked, she thought, just swollen in its frame. She tugged hard, throwing her weight backward. Finally the old wood gave and she nearly fell as the door popped open. The dank smell of water seeping through cement permeated the air, but she found what she was looking for: an electrical panel.

Crossing her fingers, she threw the switch and immediately the old lodge was awash with light. "Bingo," she whispered, before trying to find a thermostat for the furnace. Certainly there was one somewhere. She walked through the back halls until she discovered not one thermostat, but three, one for each floor of the old building. She flipped the switch, and heard a clang and rumble as the furnace for the first floor kicked on. "Two for two," she told herself, smiling with satisfaction as she dusted her hands on her jeans. Now, if only her father didn't rush out here in a panic when he received a call from the Coast Guard. Facing Victor again tonight wasn't in her plan.

Nor was Adam Drake, for that matter. What in the world was she going to do with him? He didn't seem inclined to leave her, and she experienced ambivalent feelings about his being here. Sure, she could use the company and he'd helped her save the *Marnie Lee,* she thought guiltily, but he cramped her style as far as her independence was concerned. She could hardly claim to be a self-reliant woman when a man had linked up with her.

"But only for one night," she reminded herself again. "Tomorrow he's history." *If* the *Marnie Lee* could limp into harbor, she'd take Mr. Drake back to civilization, put the boat up for repairs, then wait until the *Marnie Lee* and the weather cooperated.

And where will you go? she asked herself for what seemed to be the ten thousandth time. Alaska? Hawaii? L.A.? Mexico? "Wherever I want to," she muttered as she made her way back to the lobby.

Adam hadn't been idle. He'd stacked yellowed newspapers in the grate, and with the help of a few dry leaves and a chunk of fir, attempted to light a fire. He struck a match and held it to the tinder-dry fuel. The leaves and paper caught instantly, and flames crackled over the dry logs.

Marnie caught him leaning back on his heels, surveying his work and warming his palms against the small heat. His poncho had been discarded, hung on a peg by the front door, and his wet shirt clung to him like a second skin. His hair was beginning to dry, but still shined beneath the light shed from the wagon-wheel chandeliers suspended overhead.

He glanced her way when she entered, and rose to his feet. "Success," he said, motioning toward the sconces mounted against the walls.

"Some. At least we'll have light and heat, though I don't know about the furnace. There might not be much oil in the tank. But so far," she said, crossing her fingers, "it's humming along."

"All the comforts of home." His eyes met hers, and his expression turned jaded. "Well, at least all the comforts of *my* home. I can't speak for yours."

"Are you going to badger me for the night? If so, you may as well start walking. There's a town a few miles down the road."

"Believe me, *you* weren't part of my plan."

"Then we've got something in common."

"I doubt it."

Boy, did he know how to get under her skin. "For your

information, not that it matters, until today I lived with my father."

"And now?"

She lifted a shoulder. "I guess I don't have a home."

"Unless you count the waterfront condominium in Seattle?"

"My father signed the lease."

"But you lived there."

"It wasn't mine."

"What about the Tudor on Lake Washington?"

"My father's."

"So you *are* on some kind of independence kick, aren't you?" His eyes narrowed dangerously before he turned and using a long stick, prodded the fire. "The poor little rich girl. Had to leave all Daddy's money, but had no other means of transportation than her yacht. Sorry, Marnie, it just doesn't wash."

"Then what do you think I'm doing?"

"Having a temper tantrum—an adult temper tantrum, but a tantrum nonetheless."

"And you," she said, shoving her hands in her pockets and crossing the room to show him that she wasn't the least bit frightened of him, though in truth, he did scare her. "What're you doing?"

"Just lookin' for the truth."

"From me?"

"You'll have to do," he said, beginning to unbutton his shirt. "I'd really hoped that I could deal with Simms tonight." She watched his fingers as the buttons slid through their holes, and the back of her throat turned desert-dry. What was he doing? Stripping? Right in front of her?

He didn't seem the least self-conscious as he said, "I have to admit, getting the truth from Simms isn't likely to happen. But you...I don't know." His shirt was halfway unbuttoned, revealing a hard chest with curling black hair and tanned skin stretched taut over corded muscles.

"What do you want to know?" she asked, forcing her eyes back to his face and flushing when she caught just the trace of amusement in his eyes.

"Everything."

Oh, God, he was pulling his shirttails from his jeans and slipping his arms from the sleeves! His torso was rock-hard and solid, the muscles moving fluidly as he tossed the shirt over the fireplace screen and positioned the screen in front of the grate.

Marnie let out the breath she hadn't even realized she'd been holding. He was only drying out his clothes. Of course. And in the back of her mind she'd half expected him to try to seduce her. What an idiot she was! He wasn't interested in her sexually.

And she wasn't interested in him. Yet her gaze kept wandering to his chest and the sinewy strength of his arms.

"What do you think Kent could tell you?"

"How he embezzled the money."

"Kent?" She turned her gaze back to his face to see if he was joking, but his features were stone-sober. "Embezzle?"

"Why not?"

"And jeopardize his future with the company? No way." Marnie shook her head. She'd seen Kent Simms in a new light these past few weeks, and she knew that nothing was more important to Kent than his position at Montgomery Inns. Tonight had proved it.

Snakes! They were both snakes! Victor and Kent. "Five hundred thousand dollars isn't enough for Kent to risk everything." She rubbed her chin thoughtfully, inadvertently smudging her jaw with dirt. "In fact, I wouldn't think he'd do it for a million."

"A half million is a lot of money."

"Not to Kent's way of thinking," she said bitterly.

Adam sat on the hearth and took off his shoes. Water dripped onto the floor. "You're not very kind to your fiancé."

"Ex-fiancé," she said swiftly.

"Lovers' spat?"

"Something like that." She didn't see any reason to confide in Adam. She hadn't even told her father about Kent's infidelity and might never. Kent's betrayal was too humiliating. To keep looking busy, she found a mossy log propped against the hearth and tossed it onto the fire. The moss ignited in a spit of flames. She barely glanced at Adam again, afraid she'd already said too much, afraid her eyes would wander over his broad expanse of naked skin. "So are you going to get dressed?" she asked, unable to keep the irritation from her voice.

"Do I bother you?"

"Yes!" She spun on her heel and felt her cheeks go warm as she saw the firelight play against his skin.

His gaze touched hers for a heartbeat, then he walked, barefoot, leaving wet footprints in the dust, to the door, where his bag was lying open, and withdrew a shirt—the same white shirt he'd worn to the party. Rumpled silk and muddy denim—a new fashion statement.

"So why do I bother you, Marnie? You think I'm a thief?"

"I don't know what to think," she admitted. "All I want to do is get through this night."

"If I took the money, why would I show up at Victor's party, hmm?" He finished tucking his shirt into his Levi's and looked up at her, his dark eyes intense and probing.

"Maybe you want to clear your name so that you can dupe someone else into hiring you."

"No way. I'm through working for someone else." He

smiled coldly. "I guess I'm on an independence kick, too. You know, Marnie, we're more alike than I'd ever guessed." Laughing bitterly at his own joke, he reached for her bag and tossed it to her. "You should change, too. Wouldn't want Victor's daughter to catch her death."

"I didn't say I was on an independence kick."

"Aren't you?" He regarded her so intensely that she was uncomfortable.

"I'm just taking a vacation."

"Sure. In the middle of a tempest."

Rather than get caught in this argument, she grudgingly took his advice and decided to change. Her shoes squished and her jeans and sweatshirt were soaked in seawater. Shooting him an angry glare, she carried her bag to the rest room behind the lobby desk.

The sinks were dirty and stained. She twisted on a knob, but no water flowed from the spigot. "Give me strength," she prayed, stripping out of her wet clothes and tossing on a dry pair of jeans and a sweater.

When she finally returned to the lobby, she found Adam had moved a couple of old couches close to the fire. "I figured we needed something to sleep on," he explained.

Sleep. She doubted she'd even close her eyes tonight. She ran her fingers over the back of an old, dusty couch. Sleep would be impossible while lying this close to a man who had nearly been indicted for embezzling from her father, a man who had the nerve to stow away on her boat, a man who was too damned virile for his own good.

THIS WAS GETTING him nowhere, Adam thought darkly. He hazarded a glance at Marnie asleep on the other couch, her hair falling in a lustrous blond wave against her cheek, her breathing deep and even. She'd told him nothing. Nothing!

Disgusted, he rolled over, biting back an epithet at the

broken spring that was poking into his back. Somehow he had to convince Marnie that he wasn't the enemy, that she could trust him, that she should open up to him. But how? She was angry with Simms and her father right now; maybe he could play upon that. If he could just keep her with him, there was even a chance that he could pretend interest in her. Most women couldn't resist male attention, but Marnie Montgomery wasn't most women.

And she, though she claimed otherwise, could still be involved with Simms. A slow smile spread across his chin at the thought of making love to her, at claiming Simms's woman for his own. But as soon as the thought came, he shoved it aside. Though making love to Marnie held a certain appeal, he wasn't into primal male urges. Seducing her to get back at Simms was beneath even him.

He'd done his share of womanizing years before, and nothing good had come of it. He'd grown up on the wrong side of the tracks in Chicago, been raised by an elderly aunt whom he'd easily duped and had gotten into more trouble with the law than he should have. Along the way there had been girls and women, and not one face he could remember.

The minor scrapes with the law had convinced his aunt that Adam needed more direction, and he'd been forced to sign a hitch in the navy, where he'd spent four years finding out how tough life could really be.

From the navy he'd gone on to college, where he'd met more women—coeds. By this time, he'd figured out that most women were more trouble than they were worth, always after something.

After graduation, he'd landed a job with a hotel in Cleveland and been transferred to San Francisco, where he'd caught the eye of Victor Montgomery.

The rest was history. From the time he'd been hired on with Montgomery Inns, Adam had thought his life was right on course. Victor had taken to him, and Adam's quick rise up the corporate ladder had surpassed all of his contemporaries, including Kent Simms.

Kent, who had been with the company longer than Adam and had graduated at the top of his class at Stanford, had never liked Adam Drake. Simms had let Adam know more than once that he didn't approve of Adam's less-than-conventional methods of business.

Adam had never cared much for Simms, either, though he hadn't given the man much thought. And he'd never considered Simms capable of anything more devious than greed. Raised in an upper-middle-class family, Kent had always been seduced by money—he'd had a taste of it growing up in California, but he'd always hungered for real wealth.

However, Adam doubted Kent had the guts to sabotage Adam's career just to gain more favor with Victor. The plan could too easily have backfired.

No, subterfuge wasn't Kent's style. However, wooing Victor's daughter was right in character. Adam didn't think Kent was capable of love—and in that respect they were twin spirits. Adam thought love was overrated and probably nonexistent. However, he imagined Kent's supposed love of Marnie was tied up in the golden ribbon of Montgomery wealth.

Snorting in disgust, he rolled over again. This time he faced her, saw the firelight play upon the slope of her cheek. He noticed the sweep of her lashes and the regular rise and fall of her chest, as if she hadn't a care in the world.

Poor little rich girl, he thought again, the unhappy princess. With a soft sigh, she flung one arm out, and the old bedding they'd scrounged from an upper hall was tossed aside. Though fully dressed, her sweater was untucked, exposing a slice of abdominal flesh that, even in repose, appeared taut and nubile.

Stop it! He squeezed his eyes shut. *Enough!* He had to quit thinking of her as a woman—she was Victor Montgomery's daughter. Nothing more.

All he had to do was get through tonight and use her tomorrow. Find out what she knew about the embezzling scam and get the hell out!

CHAPTER FIVE

OPENING ONE EYE, Marnie noticed an old coffeepot nestled in the warm coals of the fire. On the hearth, a half-full jar of instant coffee, two spoons and a few ceramic cups had been set out.

A gift from Adam? she wondered, stretching and rubbing the sleep from her eyes. She glanced at his couch, found it empty, and blinked herself awake. Her mouth tasted rotten, and she felt dirty and grimy. A cup of coffee would help.

As she twisted off the cap of the jar, she thought about Adam. He must've found the utensils in the kitchen, though the coffee and the water to make it with had obviously come from the galley of the *Marnie Lee.*

So why the uncharacteristic act of kindness? He needn't have troubled himself. Stretching her cramped shoulders and neck, she looked around the room, half expecting to see him, though she could tell by the atmosphere in the lodge—the silence and the cold, stagnant air—that he wasn't around. But he'd be back. His bags were still by the front door, and his clothes, stiff and dirty, were strung across a fireplace screen. Only his poncho and beat-up running shoes were missing. He might just be outside searching for more firewood, or walking to the nearest town to phone for help.

Or maybe not. He hadn't exactly made a beeline to get off the boat when he'd found her at the wheel. Sure, there'd been a storm, and he couldn't have done anything but stay on board, and yet once he'd gotten over the shock of discovering her on board, he hadn't been in a hurry to abandon her.

Not that she cared, she told herself as she poked at the smoldering logs. Right now, Adam Drake was just extra baggage.

She grabbed the handle of the metal pot and sucked in her breath as she burned her fingers. Dropping the kettle, she stuck her fingers in her mouth. Some of the water spilled onto the coals, hissing loudly. "Son of a…gun!" she muttered, shaking her hand to cool her reddened skin. "Smooth move, Marnie. Real smart. Now you know why you should have been a Boy Scout!"

One step backward for independence, she thought wryly as she glanced over her shoulder, half expecting Adam to appear on the balcony and laugh at her. But there wasn't so much as the scrape of leather on the dusty floorboards, not the flicker of a shadow. He'd obviously taken off early this morning while she'd slept. Lord, she must've been dead to the world. Hard to believe. Marnie Montgomery, the world's greatest insomniac, sleeping as if drugged, while a strange man—perhaps a thief—was stretched out only a few feet away. She hadn't even surfaced when he'd rattled around with the coffeepot.

Slowly the pain in her hand retreated to a dull ache. She wondered about Adam and his cockamamy story. Why unearth all that scandal about the embezzling again? Was he really so innocent that it mattered? The fire popped, and she kicked at a spark that spewed onto the hearth. Adam Drake, the eternal mystery and bane of Montgomery Inns.

What would her father say? She could picture Victor now, his face suffused in red, his lower lip trembling in rage when she told him she'd spent the night with Adam Drake. It would be better if Victor never knew. After all, this whole trip was about her bid for freedom, wasn't it?

Wrapping her hand in an old towel, she picked up the coffeepot more carefully this time and poured a stream of hot water into the chipped cup. Steam rolled from the hot water as she stirred in a spoonful of the dark crystals. The smell of coffee mingled with the scent of burning wood, and surprisingly, she relaxed, sipping from her cup.

Despite a night on a lumpy, dusty couch, no food for hours, the feel of grit against her skin and her disturbing companion, Marnie Montgomery felt better than she had in a long, long time. She was on her way to being her own woman, she could feel it in her bones. Tucking her knees to her chin, she cradled her cup and let the steam caress her face.

For years she had craved adventure. And now, feeling the hot coffee burn down her throat, she'd gotten the adventure of a lifetime. With some twists she hadn't expected. Between last night's storm and Adam Drake, all her plans had been shot to shreds. And the surprising part was, she wasn't even worried.

She, who had fussed that every press release, every meeting, every party be perfect down to the very tiniest detail. She, who had spent hours color-coordinating napkins and linen, balloons and flower arrangements, seeking out opinions from Rose Trullinger, her father's interior decorator. She'd labored over brochures, and if one line wasn't to her liking, she'd insisted it be fixed. At the news conferences she'd been poised, every hair in place, wearing expensive suits, her speeches prepared to the letter.

And why wouldn't she be a perfectionist? After her mother's death she'd been raised by several nannies, all of whom had assured her that to win her father's approval she should be the new "lady" of Montgomery Manor, the little girl who acted like an adult. Miss Ellison, her favorite nanny, the one who had marched into her father's palatial home a week after her mother had died, had taught eleven-year-old Marnie how to fold her napkin on her lap, which utensil to eat with, and how to write proper thank-you notes on her engraved stationery. Never was she to wear anything wrinkled or soiled, and no dress could be worn twice to a Montgomery Inn function.

Her education had been planned since her birth, and though at college she'd rebelled a little and worn her jeans one whole week without washing them, all her lessons were so deeply ingrained that she was still the epitome of social decorum.

If it hadn't been for those summer vacations with her father, when he taught her how to fish and swim and steer a boat, she might have turned into the perfect little angel Miss Ellison had tried to mold.

No wonder a man like Kent had been attracted to her... and repulsed. The Ice Maiden, as she'd heard herself called on more than one occasion.

Spontaneity hadn't been a part of her vocabulary. Until she'd written her letter of resignation to her father. Well, she'd certainly changed. Almost overnight. She swallowed a smile when she thought of feisty, birdlike Miss Ellison. In her own way, Marnie had loved the pert Englishwoman with her smooth, implacable expression and warm eyes that were always partially hidden behind rimless glasses. Miss Ellison had been kind and warm to Marnie, though unbending in her perception of who Victor Montgomery's daughter should be. Miss Ellison's interpretation was that Marnie was to become the princess of Montgomery Inns and heir to the throne—that worn boardroom chair now occupied by Marnie's father. Of course, Miss Ellison had anticipated that Marnie would marry well, and her husband, the new prince of the Montgomery empire, would be handsome and intelligent and kind and ride up on his white charger to swoop Marnie away.

With a short laugh, Marnie glanced down at her hands

and noticed the small wedges of dirt beneath her nails. If only Miss Ellison could see her now. How appalled the tiny Englishwoman would be. Miss Ellison had never approved of Victor teaching Marnie how to tie a half hitch, use a jackknife or site a gun. In fact, Miss Ellison would have been absolutely apoplectic if she could have witnessed Marnie last night as she'd attempted to steer her boat through the driving rain and howling wind.

As for Adam Drake, surely Miss Ellison would cluck her tongue and find him "...entirely unsuitable! Too earthy, darling, too dangerous. Mark my words, he's the type of man who uses women to get what he wants. And we all know that he was involved in that nasty business with your father. Stole from him, he did. No matter what the court decided. You can see it in his eyes. He's no good. No *breeding,* you know. I don't trust him. Not at all..."

Marnie rotated her cup in her hands and pondered her situation. Standing, she stretched her spine and heard the bones in her back pop. The first order of business, she realized with a frown, was to get rid of Adam Drake. She didn't want him and he didn't want her. He had been shocked to his socks to find her behind the helm last night. At the thought of his stricken, rain-washed face, she smiled. He'd been ready to tear Kent limb from limb, and he'd ended up facing Victor Montgomery's daughter.

She finished her coffee, poured another cup and wondered what Adam hoped to learn by talking to Kent. Kent knew nothing of the embezzlement; he'd even admitted feeling foolish having not discovered the discrepancies in the books himself. Fortunately, Kate Delany, Victor's ever-vigilant assistant, had noticed that certain receipts hadn't balanced with actual checks and that the computer entries had been tampered with.

Kent had been flabbergasted. He'd never been fond of

Adam, that much was true. They were both too competitive, and Adam had always outshined Kent.

Marnie thought back to those days when she'd been in business meetings with Adam. He'd been the apple of her father's eye. Always on the lookout for a new hotel site, first with the figures on the competition. He had a way of explaining a future project so that everyone in the room understood him.

Adam had been popular with the employees, especially the women, who found his hard edge and competitive spirit a challenge. Even Marnie had considered him attractive, though she hadn't let him know it. No, until Kent had started wooing her so relentlessly, she'd made it a personal policy not to date anyone remotely connected with the company. If only she had stuck with her own unwritten law and never gone out with Kent.

Refusing to dwell on the humiliation that being engaged to Kent Simms had caused, she walked onto the front porch, half expecting to find Adam, but he was nowhere to be seen. She strolled across the wet beach grass of the headland and stared down sheer cliffs to the restless sea churning wildly over fifty feet below. Angry blue gray waves pounded the rocky shoreline, sending up a salty spray that smelled of brine and kelp. Sea gulls floated on the gusts high overhead, and far in the horizon, blending eerily into the fog, fishing boats trolled the waters.

Knowing the fishermen were out there comforted her a little. She and Adam weren't entirely alone in this deserted stretch of the islands. But she was free. Looking south, she spotted the *Marnie Lee,* not listing, thank God, but rocking gently on the swells. The boat's white hull gleamed in the morning's gray light. She thought she spied the inflatable raft riding the waves near the yacht and realized Adam had gone back to the boat, probably to check the damage to the craft. For a heart-stopping second, she wondered if he intended to take off and leave her stranded. Panic seized her, but she forced herself to calm down. If Adam's intention had been to abandon her and steal the boat, he could have left at any time last night. And he probably wouldn't have taken the time to leave hot water and coffee for her. Relaxing, she realized that whether she liked it or not, she had no choice but to trust him.

Her brows drew together. Trust a man her father considered a traitor of the worst order? "This could get messy," she thought aloud.

She considered Adam again. There was certainly something dangerous about him, a hidden side to him that was as dark as it was ruthless. A fascinating side.

So THIS WAS WHERE Simms spent his hours away from the office, Adam thought harshly as he eyed the largest cabin on the *Marnie Lee*. He scowled at the brass fittings, oiled teak furniture, all bolted down, of course, and the silk bedspread and sheets. Yep, Simms really knew how to live in style.

With Marnie.

How many hours had Marnie spent lying in this very bed, making love to Simms? Adam's stomach clenched, and a sour taste inched up his throat. She claimed she was through with Simms, and Adam was inclined to believe her. And yet, she'd once been Kent Simms's lover, had once intended to become his wife. "No accounting for bad taste," he muttered, leaving the room and ignoring the pounding in his head at the thought of Marnie and Simms making love. It wasn't any of his business. Period. She was Victor's daughter and Simms's ex-fiancée. Nothing more.

She might have information that would help him get to the bottom of the embezzling scam, but then again, she might know nothing of the vanished half million. He'd have to find out one way or another because he was running out of time. Brodie, Peterson and the rest of that particular investment group had slipped through his fingers. And the next group would, too, unless he proved himself innocent.

He made his way to the galley. Checking his handiwork on the hull, he noted the *Marnie Lee* seemed watertight. She wasn't in any immediate danger of sinking, which was good, because the plan that was forming in his mind wouldn't work unless the boat remained afloat.

He grabbed some more provisions, clean towels and a couple of sleeping bags. Up in the bridge he radioed the Coast Guard again, this time identifying himself at the captain's insistence and explaining that he and Marnie would be taking the boat in for repairs as soon as possible. He asked for the weather report and was told that there wasn't another storm front coming in for at least three days.

"It's supposed to be overcast, a little rain, but nothing serious for a while," Captain Spencer assured him. "You sure you don't need any assistance?"

"I'll call if there's trouble. We'll put up at Chinook Harbor within a couple of days," Adam replied, his mind spinning the lies that were part of his scheme.

"Anything else?"

Adam thought for a second and smiled slowly, gripping the microphone until his hands ached. "Just one more thing," he said slowly. "Pass the word along to Victor Montgomery at the Puget West in Port Stanton. If you can't reach him there, he's probably at corporate headquarters in Seattle. Tell him that I'm with Marnie and we're both fine. We'll spend a couple of days up at Deception Lodge while the boat is being repaired. I wouldn't want him to worry about his daughter."

"Will do, Mr. Drake. I'll let him know you radioed."

"Thanks," Adam said, wondering if Victor would show

up in the company helicopter to personally throw Adam out of the lodge and make sure that Marnie's virtue remained intact. After all, in Victor's opinion, Marnie was keeping company with a thief and traitor—the very devil himself. That thought warmed the cockles of Adam's vengeful heart. There was a chance that Victor would confide in Simms, and Simms, outraged that his lady fair was in the hands of a criminal, would come charging up to the island as well. That would be even better.

Adam would be waiting. But he had to convince Marnie to spend another couple of days in the lodge. That shouldn't be too hard; he'd just have to lie a little, and lying was becoming easier all the time. As he saw the situation, he was battling for his reputation, for his ability to make a living. He thought of the California investors who'd dismissed him so summarily. Brodie had said it all. "We can't very well hand over several million dollars until we're absolutely certain that what happened over at Montgomery Inns won't happen to us."

So Adam had to clear his name, and the only man who had been able to help him at all had been Gerald Henderson. But even Henderson's information had been sketchy. Gerald had been a CPA and worked in accounting with Fred Ainger. He was convinced that Adam was innocent, but Adam hadn't been able to pry any more information out of him. Either Gerald didn't know who the guilty parties were or he was afraid of retribution.

Adam's back was to the wall. And if he had to lie to Marnie to get what he wanted, so be it. It only followed that if he had to use Marnie as bait to get to her father, that's what he would do. After all, it wasn't as if he were putting her in any danger. But once she discovered that he'd deceived her, all hell was sure to break loose.

He only hoped it happened after he got his audience with Simms or Victor Montgomery.

MARNIE COMBED HER wet hair. Shampooing had been difficult without hot water. She'd had to heat water on the fire, then she'd sponged all the dirt from her skin. She was drying her hair near the flames when she heard Adam's tread on the porch. The door burst open and he strode in, as grungy as she was clean, and deposited a huge bag on the floor.

"You brought more supplies?" she asked, eyeing the bag.

"Everything I could carry."

"But why? We're leaving…" Her voice faded as she understood. "Something's not wrong with the *Marnie Lee,* is it?"

"She'll be fine," Adam said easily. "But there's another storm brewing—might be worse than the last. The Coast Guard advised us to stay put."

She dropped her comb, her hair forgotten as she glanced at the window and the overcast day beyond. "Another storm?" she said, her heart sinking at the thought of being cooped up with Adam any longer. His restless energy made her nervous, and the way he stared at her, as if trying to read her mind, bothered her. "You called the Guard again?"

"Mmm." He was unpacking the bags, laying out more food and supplies on the hearth. "I thought I should explain our position. And I wanted an updated weather report."

"It would be better if you hadn't," she said, walking to the window where she balanced a knee against the sill and rubbed her arms. The horizon was bleak. The waters seemed lonely. Where once she'd spied three fishing boats, now only one trolled the steely depths.

As a young girl she'd spent a lot of time on the ocean. Her father had taught her to read the weather's slightest signals. A fragile breeze stirred the branches of fir trees near the lodge, but the sky was far from dark.

"When's this storm supposed to hit?" she asked, trying to keep the suspicion from her voice.

"Early afternoon. Maybe sooner. No way to tell." He tossed a piece of mossy oak onto the fire and kicked it into place. The flames crackled and hissed. Adam rubbed his hands on his jeans. "The weather can turn quickly up here."

"I know, but I think we could limp into port," she said, testing him, though she really doubted that he would lie to her. What would be the point? No doubt he was as anxious to be rid of her as she was to lose him.

Adam shrugged. "It's your call, Marnie, but it wouldn't hurt to wait it out. The boat's holding water now, but one more shot against that hull and it might split wide open."

"It wouldn't take long to make it to Chinook Harbor or even Deer Harbor." She bit on her lower lip thoughtfully, resting her hands on the windowpane. She wasn't used to making these kinds of decisions alone, and Adam wasn't much help. Not that she wanted his help, she told herself. This was, after all, her bid for independence.

"You're right," he said suddenly, before she could change her mind. "We can probably make it. Okay, let's go." He grabbed his bag and the two sleeping bags and shouldered open the door. "Kill the fire."

"It couldn't be any worse than last night," she pointed out as he walked outside. She ignored the fire and followed him onto the porch. The wind blew harder than she'd expected, and she watched as the first thin drops of rain began to drizzle from the leaden sky.

"Last night was bad enough," he said, squinting as he stared at the horizon. "But this storm, bad as it's supposed to be, should blow over soon and why take a chance?" He was across the porch now, starting for the path. "However, if you're sure you want to try it, just pack what you need. We can leave the supplies here." Head bent against the rain, he started along the sandy path that led through the rocky forest, to the beach.

Indecision tore through Marnie. What if he were right? What if she, in her foolish anxiety to leave this place, put the *Marnie Lee* in jeopardy? Then all her quick words about standing on her own would come back to haunt her. Her father and Kent would never let her forget her aborted attempt at freedom. "Adam! Wait!" She ran the length of the porch and watched as he turned on his heel, his back rigid, his face, as he spun to glare at her, a mask of impatience.

His jaw was dark with the start of a beard, his lips thin and compressed, his brown eyes reflecting anger. "Make up your mind, Marnie. What's it gonna be?"

She checked the sky again. It suddenly seemed more ominous. The clouds were burgeoning. The timeworn phrase, better safe than sorry, flitted through her mind. "We can wait. A few more hours won't hurt, I suppose."

Tossing her a look that silently called her a wishy-washy female, he hauled the bag onto his shoulder, brushed past her and headed back inside.

"Women," he muttered, making the word an insult.

Marnie bit back a hot retort and waited a few seconds before she followed him back into the lodge. The man really got under her skin. Who was he to sneer at her? It wasn't as if he'd been invited on her ill-fated cruise. He'd stowed away, like the thief he probably was. She stormed inside where Adam was once again opening up his packs. To look busy, she stoked the fire and prodded the logs, causing flames to shoot to the back of the blackened fireplace. Adam's eyes never left her backside. She could feel his gaze boring into her. Well, he could look all he wanted. She'd put up with him for a little longer, but if the storm didn't break by mid-afternoon, or if she didn't see any evidence of a serious squall on the horizon, she'd pack everything up herself, if she had to, and sail to Chinook Harbor. Adam Drake could do whatever he damn well pleased.

"DRAKE? SHE'S WITH Adam Drake?" Kent sputtered, his eyes rounding incredulously as he stood in the middle of Victor's Seattle office. "What the hell's she doing with him?"

"I wish I knew." Victor reached into the inner pocket of his jacket, withdrew his pipe and opened the humidor on his desk. "I would've known earlier, but the captain of the Coast Guard ship that took the message called Port Stanton before he reached me here."

"We've got to go get her! That man's crazy. You saw how he barged in on your party, and I don't have to remind you what he did to our publicity!" Kent snapped the local section of the paper onto Victor's desk. The headlines, bold and black, announced:

Disgruntled Employee Returns
To Opening Of Puget West

Adam Drake, whose employment with Montgomery Inns was terminated last year when half a million dollars disappeared...

"I know what it says," Victor grumbled, clicking his lighter to the bowl of his pipe and inhaling. He let out thick puffs of smoke. "I just don't know what to do about it."

"Well, the first thing I'd do is impound that damned boat of his—the one he left at Port Stanton. The security guards saw him take off in a boat, so he must have doubled back and left it at the hotel."

"Maybe—"

"Then, I'd go up to Deception Lodge and haul Marnie

back here! For God's sake, Victor, no one can even guess what Drake's got up his sleeve!"

"You think he'll hurt Marnie?" Victor asked, eyeing Simms as he paced nervously in front of the desk.

"He's desperate. After that fiasco last night, I did some checking through a P.I. who owes me a favor. I'd already had him looking into Drake because of the problems last year. Anyway, according to the P.I., Drake's planning to get back into the business. But there's a catch. Anyone he approaches for financing turns him away. He's talked to groups from L.A., Houston and Tokyo. No one will touch him."

Victor drummed his fingers on his desk as he considered his nemesis. Once he had trusted Drake with his fortune, and had anyone asked him about the most ambitious vice president he'd ever promoted, Victor would've replied that he would trust Drake with his very life—or the life of his daughter. He'd had that much faith in the bastard. But, of course, his opinion had plummeted when he'd realized that Drake had slowly but surely embezzled him out of a sizable chunk of his wealth.

The money hadn't really been an issue, but the lack of loyalty had. Victor required absolute loyalty from his employees. In return, he treated them well. But not, apparently, well enough for a scoundrel like Drake. He glanced up at Kent, edgy as he paced from the windows to the bar and back. It took all of Victor's willpower to remain calm. "Look, I don't like this any more than you do, but there's nothing I can do."

"*Nothing you can do?* Marnie's your daughter, for crying out loud!"

"Precisely." Victor's fist connected with the top of his desk, jarring his arm. "And if I interfere in her life, she'll never forgive me!"

"She might not get the chance," Kent said, his face

flushed. "Drake's backed into a corner. And we all know how a cornered wolf reacts. You could press charges against him for kidnapping—or trying to steal the *Marnie Lee!*"

"We don't know what the hell happened to put Drake on the *Marnie Lee,* so I can't start making wild accusations. Besides, I don't give a damn about that boat."

"Well, I do!" Kent said, his face reddening. "Remember, half of it's mine. *I* should press charges."

Victor waved off that argument. "Forget it. At least for now. According to the Coast Guard, Drake plans to put up for repairs in Chinook Harbor."

"*He* plans. What about Marnie?"

Victor clamped his teeth onto the stem of his pipe. As far as he was concerned, Marnie had gotten herself into this mess, she could damn well get herself out.

"Well, what're we going to do?" Kent demanded, coming over to stand in front of Victor's desk and leaning over the cluttered surface.

At that moment Kate tapped lightly on the office door and poked her head in. "Ty Van Buren on line two."

"Thanks, I'll take it," Victor said, then noticed the nervous twitch of Kent's mouth. The poor kid was worried sick about Marnie. "There's nothing we can do right now." He reached for the phone. "Except wait. It's Drake's move."

CHAPTER SIX

THE AFTERNOON WORE ON, the weather growing slightly worse, but the storm that had been predicted never developed into anything more serious than a slight squall. As the hours dragged by, Marnie was on edge, overly aware of Adam in the lodge, his maleness seeming to fill the cavernous rooms. She felt the weight of his gaze, smelled his musky scent, heard his tread as he moved from room to room, pacing the lodge like a lion. Some of the time he'd spent chopping wood, as if he expected to be here longer than a few hours, or to focus some of his energy, she didn't know which. He'd also scouted and explored the lodge stem to stern and top to bottom. Marnie hadn't accompanied him. The less she was forced into contact with him, she figured, the better for both of them.

They hadn't said more than a dozen words to each other. Marnie had done some exploring herself, kept the fire burning, and sorted out the supplies Adam had brought from the boat, all the while keeping one eye on the weather. If only they had a radio, she thought in frustration as the night loomed ahead, then she'd hear the weather updates and know what to expect.

As it was, she was facing another night alone with Adam, and the hours marched steadily onward. The shadows in the rooms lengthened, and Marnie silently kicked herself for not following her instincts and taking the boat to port. She should never have trusted Adam. He'd probably invented the whole story. But why? No, his lying to her didn't make any sense. She wasn't about to kid herself into believing that he *wanted* to stay here with her.

Her stomach grumbled, and she eyed the sorry prospects for a meal. She heard Adam walk into the room, and without looking over her shoulder, she snagged two pieces of bread and a jar of peanut butter. "So what happened to your storm?" she asked, spreading a thin layer of peanut butter on one slice of bread. Not exactly hearty fare, but the sandwich would have to do.

She took a bite and twisted on the hearth so that she faced him. Adam, who had been in the basement, brushed the cobwebs from his hair but didn't answer immediately.

"The storm," she repeated. "Remember? The one that kept us trapped here all day? The one with the gale-force winds that the Coast Guard was so worried about?"

He shoved up his sleeves. "Maybe it'll hit tonight."

"Maybe," she replied, studying him as she took another bite. Would he lie to her? But why? It just didn't make sense.

She watched as he moved to the window and scanned the sky, as if he were looking for something, expecting something to appear in the gloomy heavens. Perhaps he had been telling the truth. Maybe he did expect a storm of hurricane proportions. Still, she wasn't convinced. She decided to call his bluff. "Maybe you didn't even call the Guard."

Tossing a glance over his shoulder, he rained a sarcastic smile in her direction. "Why would I lie?"

"You tell me."

He snorted and faced her again, his hands resting lightly on his hips. She tried to keep her gaze on his face, but couldn't help noticing the way his fingers spread over the pockets of his jeans where the faded denim stretched taut across his lower abdomen. She quickly averted her eyes, focusing on the window instead.

"You disappoint me, Marnie."

"*I* disappoint you?" she repeated, startled. Why, all of a sudden, was she so aware of him? Was it the storm gathering outside, the charge of the forces of nature, or the warm atmosphere in the lodge that made her realize just how intimate the situation had become? Her stomach clenched, and she pushed the remains of her sandwich aside. A few seconds before she'd been ravenous, now she couldn't swallow another bite.

"I thought you were different." He turned back to the window and propped his foot on the sill as he stared toward the sea.

Knowing she shouldn't ask, but unable to stop herself, she said, "Different from what?"

"The rest."

When he didn't elaborate, she waited, her senses all keyed on her reluctant companion. The back of his neck was tanned bronze, and his hair curled behind his ears. His buttocks, beneath his jeans, shifted as he threw one hip out to balance himself.

Marnie's throat was suddenly as dry as a desert wind, and she realized that she'd been holding her breath, waiting. But for what?

Adam was the sexiest man she'd met in a long, long while and, damn it, she was responding like a boy-crazy teenager. Perhaps it was just the surroundings and the fact that she was imprisoned here with him, but she was more attuned to his lazy sensuality than she'd thought possible.

His voice caused her to jump. "Everyone at the company thought I ripped off your old man. But you—" he pressed his palms against the damp panes "—well, I guess I expected too much."

She felt an immediate need to explain herself, as if she should be ashamed for her actions, though she hadn't done anything wrong. What did she care what Adam Drake thought of her? He could be the sexiest man alive and there was still a chance that he was a thief. Maybe that was the cause of her fascination with him, she thought darkly. The fact that he was truly forbidden fruit.

"You said you knew Gerald Henderson?" he asked, before her thoughts took her too far from the conversation.

"Mmm." She slammed back to reality and hoped the heat in her cheeks was from the fire and not from her ridiculous fantasies.

"What kind of a man would you say he is?"

She lifted a shoulder. "I only knew him as an employee," she admitted. "He worked in the accounting department with Fred Ainger and Linda Kirk. I met him at meetings and company parties and occasionally in the halls or cafeteria, but I never got to know him personally." She was glad for a turn in the conversation, though she sensed that Adam was leading her into dangerous waters. Nonetheless, talking about Montgomery Inns was better than the emotion-charged silence and her own imagination.

"Would you say Gerald was dishonest?" Adam asked, rubbing his index finger over his thumb.

"Absolutely not." Henderson had worked for Victor Montgomery for twelve years before his sudden retirement last spring. There had never been a word of impropriety linked to him.

"He wasn't even close to sixty-five. Why do you think he retired?" Adam lifted his head, his hard gaze locked with Marnie's, and Marnie's breath caught in her throat. For a heart-stopping second she thought she saw more than just a single question in Adam's eyes, as if he were just as aware of her as a woman as she was of him as a man. She swallowed with difficulty, and his gaze, golden brown and unwavering, held hers.

"I told you earlier that I thought Gerald was having

health problems," she finally responded when she captured control of her tongue again. Oh, God, if only he'd quit staring at her! "Stress-related, or allergies, I think. Anyway, he didn't come back to work for the hotel and was supposed to go on to another job."

"You ever see the medical bills?"

"No, but I wouldn't. It's not my department..."

His razor-thin lips curled into a smile that was a blatant sneer at her naïveté, and her temper started to rise.

"He reported to Fred," she said quickly, wondering why, all of a sudden, his opinion of her mattered in the least.

"And Fred reported to...?"

"Personnel on matters like this, otherwise to...Kent."

"Who, in turn, reported to your father," he said, filling in the obvious blanks.

"Yes." Suddenly defensive, she felt as if she owed it to her father to straighten Adam out. "I don't know what you're trying to say, Drake, but my father didn't steal money from himself. That's ridiculous."

One side of his mouth lifted in a crooked likeness of a smile. But his eyes were cold and serious. "Henderson seems to think that someone close to Victor is cheating him. And despite the general low opinion of my reputation at the company, Henderson believes I was framed."

"By whom?"

"That's the half-million-dollar question, isn't it?" he drawled, his eyes still trained on her face as if he expected some sort of reaction from her.

"How were you 'framed'?" she asked, unable to keep a hint of sarcasm from her words.

"I don't know," Adam admitted, and for the first time since she'd discovered him aboard the *Marnie Lee,* she was convinced of his sincerity. He let out his breath in frustration and shoved both hands through his hair.

"Henderson couldn't tell you?"

"Couldn't or wouldn't. He's afraid, I think. I couldn't get any more information from him." Adam eyed a scuff mark on the floor and rubbed it with the toe of his worn running shoe. The room was beginning to grow dark, only pale light filtered through the glass to illuminate the rough angles of his face. For a second Marnie wondered about him, about his private life. As far as she knew, he'd never married, but she wished she knew why. He was handsome, his features sensual, his body firm and hard. He was intelligent; he'd displayed his sharp business acumen on more than one occasion. Until last year, when all hell had broken loose, he'd been a successful corporate executive. At that point he'd had good looks, money and a future that could only be described as stellar.

Until he'd been accused of theft, Adam Drake had been considered a real catch—one of the most eligible bachelors in Seattle.

If one were looking.

Marnie wasn't. Or at least she told herself she wasn't.

Even so, her gaze was drawn to the vee of his shirt front and the dark hairs that curled against his tanned skin. Afraid he might catch her staring, she focused on the wall behind him and ignored the irregular beat of her heart. It was natural to be uncomfortable around him. She was a woman, after all, and she obviously wasn't immune to his rugged maleness. A pity. If only she could look past that raw sexuality that seemed to emanate from his deep-set eyes.

"So you think Kent set you up?" she finally asked, though her throat was uncomfortably tight.

Adam looked pained. "I never would have guessed he'd have the brains or the guts to do it."

"Henderson could be wrong."

"He could be. But he isn't."

"Well, even if he's right—and I'm not saying I go along with this—he could be talking about someone else in the company, someone other than Kent."

"Still trying to defend that bastard, are you, Marnie?" Adam shook his head and muttered something indistinguishable under his breath before adding, "Some women never learn."

The words cut like the bite of a whip. She, alone, had stood up for him to her father, pointing out that a man was innocent until proven guilty. Though she wasn't completely convinced of his innocence, she couldn't believe he was actually a thief. Oh, she'd been back and forth on the subject, never really knowing, but she'd argued Adam's case bitterly to her father. Not that it had made any difference. In Victor's book, Adam had done the unthinkable: he'd betrayed a trust.

Of course, Adam had no way of knowing about her feelings or the fact that she and her father had been at odds over his dismissal. Though she wanted to rub it in Adam's face right now, she didn't. He wouldn't believe her anyway. His last cutting remark had been testimony to that.

"Believe me, Drake, I *do* learn from my mistakes. And the mistake I made was in believing you and letting you stay here with me. If you ask me, *you're* the bastard," she said coolly, though her blood was beginning to boil. "Ever since we got on this island, you've insulted me and made innuendos about my father." Involuntarily, her fingers curled into tight fists. "If you don't like the present company, I suggest you hike to the nearest town. There's a map in the *Marnie Lee*."

A ghost of a smile played on his lips. He reached into his back pocket and whipped out a folded piece of paper. "Got it," he said. "But if I leave, what will you do?"

"Muddle through somehow," she replied. "I really can take care of myself."

He cocked an insolent eyebrow. "That remains to be seen."

"Watch me!"

"Oh, I will," he said, and his voice was suddenly silky smooth. To Marnie's consternation, he sauntered across the room to the archway leading to the old dining room.

She couldn't help herself. Knowing that she was flirting with danger, she shoved herself from the hearth and walked quickly across the dusty plank floors, through the arched entrance to the dining area and down two creaking steps to the bar where Adam, behind the counter, was wiping a glass with the tail of his shirt. On the bar, thick with dust and cobwebs, was a bottle of whiskey. The label was yellowed and blurred with grime.

"You're not really going to drink that, are you?" she asked, appalled.

Mocking her, he poured a stiff shot into the glass and threw her own words her way. "Watch me." He tossed back the drink and didn't so much as flinch as the liquor hit his throat. He held up a glass to her.

"I'll probably have to get you to a hospital to pump your stomach," she said. "Who knows what was in that…" She walked closer and motioned to the bottle.

"Who cares?"

"I do," she said crisply. "I didn't want you on this trip in the first place and I certainly don't want to clean up after you…or play nursemaid."

"No?" His gaze strayed from her eyes to her neck and lower still. "Playing nursemaid could be fun."

Goose bumps appeared on her flesh. "What it would be is a disaster," she countered, and wished her voice didn't sound quite so breathless.

As if he caught the subtle change in her attitude, he motioned to the bottle. "Join me?"

"I don't think liquor's the answer. Especially not that—" she wrinkled her nose "—bottle."

His eyes gleamed. "Liquor's not the answer to what question?" he asked, and his voice sounded fuller from the whiskey.

"I think we should keep our wits about us."

"Speak for yourself." He poured himself another drink, then propped one arm on the bar and vaulted over the counter to land lithely beside her.

She felt smaller then, with him so close. His scent, earthy maleness blended with the faint muskiness of old Scotch, wafted across her face.

"Anyone ever told you you're too uptight?"

"Thousands," she retorted.

"Well, they're right." One side of his mouth lifted, exposing teeth so white they gleamed in the shadowy room. He touched her arm and she drew away, stepped back from fingers that felt warm and inviting.

He didn't back down. "Afraid, Marnie?"

"Of what? You?" She shook her head, lying a little. She was petrified of him, but not for her life. Physical violence wasn't his style; however, he could be devastating in other ways.

She quivered as he touched her again and saw his gaze flicker to her mouth. Without conscious thought, she licked her lips and heard him respond with a low groan.

Marnie knew she was in trouble.

"Why the hell do you have to be so damned beautiful?" he growled as he lowered his head and molded his mouth to hers. She knew she should stop him, that kissing him was madness, but the feel of his lips, warm and supple, caused a response so deep she actually shook.

Don't let me fall for a man like this, she thought, and

willed herself to remain impassive. Though the blood in her veins heated and pulsed, she didn't move, but trembled slightly when he drew her close. His lips moved urgently against her mouth; his tongue, prodding, sought entrance.

Every instinct told her to let go, fall against him, give in once. What would it hurt? But in the back of her mind, she heard a warning, and with all the willpower she could muster she pressed her palms against his chest and shoved. "Let me go," she said, her voice a breathless whisper. "What do you think you're doing?"

He yanked his head back, but still his strong arms held her firm. "So all those stories about you are true?" he asked, cocking an insolent brow over his laughing brown eyes.

"What stories?"

"The stories of the ice maiden," he said, and she wanted to die. Her face washed with color, but she set her jaw and forced a cool smile.

"You thought you'd be different?"

A muscle bunched in his jaw, but was quickly tamed. "No, but I thought a woman whose standards were so low that she'd bed a snake like Simms, might have hotter blood than rumor had it."

She slapped him. Without thinking, she raised her hand and smacked the palm against his cheek and he, damn his black heart, had the nerve to laugh.

"So the lady does have some passion after all."

"Get out, Drake," she insisted, quivering with rage. "Remember when you said you were disappointed in me, well the same goes for me! I had faith in you. I even told my father that you couldn't possibly have stolen anything from him. I argued with the board of directors. And I was wrong, wasn't I? You're just as bad as everyone said."

His dark eyes sparked, and before she could react, he grabbed her. Whirling her off her feet, he maneuvered her against the bar, cutting off her escape. This time his mouth crashed down on hers with a punishing force that ripped through her body. His hands clamped her close, and she could barely breathe as his tongue pressed hard against her teeth.

She tried to fight him. This was no way to start any kind of relationship, but she couldn't help but yield to emotions that were tearing through her. Love or hate, she couldn't tell, but her breathing was labored, her heart hammering in her chest, the rational side of her mind losing a battle with her war-torn emotions.

His kiss was as impatient and demanding as the man himself. His arms surrounded her waist, pressing against her spine and forcing her breasts and abdomen to flatten against the solid length of his body. Through her clothes, she felt male muscles straining, a hard, lean frame moving against hers. Her back was pressed against the bar, and he leaned over, forcing her backward, his heaving chest nearly crushing her as she half lay on the dusty counter.

"Dear, God," she whispered, her voice rough when he pulled his mouth from hers and stared down into her eyes. "What—what are you doing?"

"Making a point." His hand moved slowly upward, past her ribs to her breast, which was rising and falling with each of her shallow breaths.

"Don't—"

His fingers caressed the sweet mound as his lips found hers again, and this time the kiss was more gentle, his mouth wet and hot, his tongue quietly prodding.

She sighed, and in that split second he shifted, his legs moving between hers, his tongue gaining entrance to her mouth. A warm whirlpool of desire swept her in its loving current, and all her skin tingled in anticipation. The smell of him invaded her nostrils and she tasted the tangy salt of his skin.

This is sheer madness, she thought, but couldn't stop the current of passion that carried her without protest as he lifted her sweater over her head and she felt the chill of the old lodge brush against her skin.

"Marnie, sweet Marnie," he moaned, gathering her close, his face pressed into the hollow of her breasts, the air from his lungs torrid. His tongue was rough and erotic as he licked her skin, skimming the sculpted lace of her bra. Her breast grew heavy and anxious, her nipple tightening into a hard bud of anticipation.

He didn't disappoint her. His lips surrounded her nipple, and his teeth and tongue parried and teased, causing her body to silently beg for more of this sublime torture.

He was all too willing to comply. She felt the heat of his body, the hard thrust of his hips against hers, the exquisite torment of his mouth as he moved lower, unsnapping her jeans, his tongue licking a path of liquid fire around her navel to delve even lower.

Marnie sucked in her breath as he eased the rough fabric of her jeans over her hips, past her thighs, to her knees. Only when his fingers slid upward past the elastic of her panties to caress her buttocks, did reason invade the dreamlike fog of her mind.

Self-respect grappled with passion, and she dug her fingernails into his shoulder. "Please," she whispered, "I can't...I just can't do this..."

Still he perused her, his hands shifting to the warmth between her legs.

"Adam, please, no!" she cried.

His body stiffened for a second before he drew away, his face contorted as he struggled to rein in his galloping desire. "Sweet heaven," he whispered, his hands shaking as he tried to steady himself. "So you're not an ice maiden after all," he muttered, his eyes still smoldering. "You're a tease."

"No, I—"

"You wanted me, damn it!" he thundered, before jamming his hands deep into the pockets of his jeans.

"No—I…" His expression accused her of the lie as she struggled back into her clothes. Ridiculously she felt close to tears, but she wouldn't let him see that her emotions were frayed, her nerves strung tight. Her fingers trembled as she zipped her jeans. She could feel his gaze on her, and from the corner of her eye she saw him move to the wall, and crossing his arms over his chest, continue to stare at her. At least he was several feet from her, she thought, finally lifting her head.

"I just want the truth."

"I don't understand—"

"You wanted me," he repeated, eyes blazing.

For several heartbeats she didn't answer, couldn't. The truth was more than she could bear. How could she want this man—the very man who had probably cheated her father? And even if he hadn't stolen the money, he'd hidden in her boat and practically forced himself on her. And the lies. She knew that the storm that had been predicted had been fabricated, but why? So he could seduce her?

A tingle of delight skittered along her arms, and she ignored it. She was *not* the kind who enjoyed the thought of men lusting after her…

"Yes," she finally allowed, her fingers trembling as she snapped her jeans and straightened her sweater. "I wanted you."

"But you stopped. Why?"

"Things are too complicated between us," she said, her voice wavering. "You're the last man in the world I should…" She motioned with her hand frantically.

"The last man in the world you should bed?"

She sucked in her breath. "Yes. The *last* man."

"That's probably why you want me."

"I don't think—"

"Well, it's certainly not love, is it?"

"No, but..."

He advanced slowly on her, and it took all her willpower to stand her ground. "You know what I think?" he asked, his eyes deepening to the color of dark chocolate.

"I'm not sure I want to."

"I think you'd like to let loose, I mean really let loose. That's what your journey into the storm was, wasn't it? So why not take it all the way?" He touched her hair, his fingers groping beneath the pale strands to capture her neck and draw her face next to his.

She swallowed and stared into his eyes, her heart racing, her pulse throbbing all over again.

"Come on, Marnie," he whispered, "take a chance." He kissed her then, and this time she wound her arms around his neck. Nothing that felt this wonderful could be wrong, she told herself, kissing him back and drinking in the smell and feel of him.

His weight pushed them both to the floor, and this time there was no holding back. As he stripped off her clothes, she worked on the buttons of his shirt and shoved it off his shoulders. Her fingers explored the sinewy strength of his arms and chest, flexing in the springy hair that covered his sleek muscles. Groaning, he kicked off his jeans and rolled over her, his tense male body gleaming and naked in the growing shadows.

"That's better," he whispered as she twined her hands in the thick strands of his hair, kissing him with all the passion that ripped away her pretenses. He moved, slowly at first, letting her feel the length of him against her sensitive skin.

Instinctively, she dragged him closer, and he kissed first her lips, then her closed eyes and then her breasts. Her nipples ached until he suckled, and a molten heat swirled deep in her core, causing an ache to burn between her legs.

A final protest deep in a dark corner of her mind told her that she was dancing with the devil, that only heartache would come of this, but she was past the point of caring, teetering on the brink of sensual fulfillment. His knees wedged her legs apart. She moaned low in her throat, waiting, wanting and feeling every inch of him as, with one swift thrust, he entered her and a blinding light flashed behind her eyes.

"Adam," she cried, her voice as raw as the sea.

"I'm right here," he whispered against her ear.

She moved with him, feeling each glorious stroke as he claimed her for his own with ever-increasing tempo. Her body fused with his, his skin sliding against hers, as the explosion rocked them both, sending her over the edge of desire and into the sweet oblivion of afterglow.

"Marnie," he whispered over and over again, as his breath slowed and the beating of his heart echoed her own. "Oh, Marnie." Strong arms surrounded her, and again she felt tears prick her eyelids, but she fought them back. She'd have no regrets, she told herself, not ever. This one moment of passion, be it forever or fleeting, she would treasure. Nothing could destroy it.

CHAPTER SEVEN

ADAM SPENT A GOOD PART of the night making love to Marnie. In the hours between their passionate bouts of lovemaking, he lay on his back, listening to her breathing, and wondered if he was losing his mind. Though physically he wanted her as he'd never wanted another woman, he knew that loving her so intensely was a mistake. But he couldn't stop himself. Her luscious body called out to his baser instincts, and her soft blue eyes touched his intellect.

He'd known more than his share of women in the past. Hell, he was no saint. But no woman had confused him so.

Marnie was different. Sometimes utterly naive, other times fiercely self-sufficient, she was a sensual enigma that, had he more time, he might be inclined to unravel.

But she's Montgomery's daughter, he kept reminding himself as he stared down at her. Sunlight was streaming through the windows of the lodge, and Marnie, curled next to him, looked almost angelic.

A very sexy angel. After her initial reluctance, Marnie had turned out to be a willing and responsive lover, as insatiable as he was.

He rubbed his chin impatiently. What the hell was he going to do with Victor's willful daughter? Make love to her until he was satisfied and had his fill of her? Or lie to her and use her in his quest for absolving himself of all blame in the embezzlement? Or let himself get involved with her and see just how far it would go?

Seeing her sleeping peacefully, her pale hair falling over her cheek, her dark blond lashes lying against her creamy white skin, his gut reaction was to stretch out beside her and start kissing every inch of that perfect, delicious body. Let the future bring what it would. Right now, all that mattered was Marnie.

"God help me," he muttered, knowing that she was bound to get hurt, as he overcame the urge to slowly drag the sheet from her shoulders and see the morning light against the perfect skin of her breasts. Just thinking about her rosy nipples, hidden coyly by the sheet, caused a hardening in his loins all over again.

You're the bastard, she'd accused him yesterday, and damn it, she'd been right. He couldn't get enough of her, and yet that's exactly what he would have to do, get his fill of her before he dropped the bomb: he was only using her to get back at Victor. Inside he winced at his own cruel calculations, but he overcame his squeamishness where Marnie was concerned. After all, using her had been part of his plan—hadn't it? And maybe some small part of him had thought that by bedding Montgomery's daughter, he would gain some sort of convoluted revenge against Victor, a man who had scorned his loyalty.

Adam had been the fool, of course. The military had instilled in him a sense of loyalty, and he, upon joining Montgomery Inns, had transferred that loyalty to Victor Montgomery. Talk about misplaced faith!

So he'd planned to use Marnie, and maybe even had started his sexual advances with thoughts of revenge. His strategy had backfired, of course. Now he didn't want to hurt Marnie, and yet he saw no other alternative. She was in the way. Again he glanced at her, and it was all he could do not to touch her hair and smooth her cheek with his palm.

When she'd challenged him yesterday, he'd planned to

prove to her that she was no better than other women, that she, too, had emotions and feelings and passion, that just because she was Victor Montgomery's daughter didn't make her any different.

And he'd proved his point—very well. Too well.

He felt like the proverbial heel, but there was nothing he could do to rectify things. What would the next step be? Offer to marry her out of some misguided sense of duty? No, that was too Victorian. Besides, Victor would only claim that he was a fortune hunter, bent on ruining everything he cared about. And truth to tell, Victor would be right. Because he didn't love Marnie. He couldn't. And she didn't love him. Oh, sure, they cared about each other…at least a little. But what had transpired between them was pure animal lust.

They were trapped, forced into intimacy, and they found each other darkly alluring. All that sexual tension had exploded into unbridled passion, and there was nothing more to it—no complicated emotions, no need to make promises for a future that didn't exist.

He buttoned up his shirt and stared down at Marnie— the princess. What he was planning to do to her was brutal, but he had no choice.

Swearing under his breath, he finished dressing and walked outside. Victor hadn't taken the bait yesterday, so Adam would have to make sure that this time Marnie's old man had no options.

VICTOR MONTGOMERY didn't like being manipulated. Not by anyone and especially not by Adam Drake. Nonetheless, that's exactly what had happened, he thought angrily. So here he was, feeling totally helpless, about to jeopardize his daughter's trust by playing into Adam Drake's hands. He strapped himself into his seat in the company's helicopter and noticed his companion, Kent Simms, doing the same. The pilot was already checking gauges and flicking switches, and the chopper's huge rotating blades picked up speed.

"I told you we shouldn't have just sat on our butts," Kent complained over the noise of whirring blades as the chopper lifted off.

The pilot steered the craft upward before heading north, flying over tall skyscrapers and the vast waters of the sound. "The minute I heard Drake was involved, I knew there would be trouble," Kent continued, fiddling with his seat strap and trying to get comfortable."

"I only did what Marnie wanted." Even to his own ears, the excuse sounded lame.

"The only way to deal with a man like Drake is to take the offensive. Once he's got the upper hand, it's all over."

"Marnie doesn't want my interference."

"You don't know that. We haven't heard from her, have we?" When Victor shook his head, Kent rubbed his chin nervously. "Yeah, right. For all we know, she's being held hostage by Drake—"

"He wouldn't go that far," Victor intervened. "There are laws—"

"He got off scot-free once before, didn't he? A viper like Drake always slithers out of the trap. As for Marnie, she's a woman. And I don't have to tell you that sometimes she doesn't make the right decision."

"Amen," Victor said under his breath. He didn't want Kent to know how upset he was, so he held his tongue. But when he'd spoken to Drake, he could barely talk. Claiming that the phones on the *Marnie Lee* were inoperable, Drake had mustered the gall to have the Coast Guard patch a call through to Victor. The conversation had been short but to the point. The *Marnie Lee* was still anchored near the beach at Deception Lodge, but Drake didn't know when they'd put up for repairs. It had been all Victor could do to respond civilly to Drake, but he'd had no choice. Marnie was with the bastard.

That situation had to change. Especially given Marnie's emotional state right now. The breakup with Kent, this ludicrous bid for independence, and her own ambivalent feelings for Drake all added up to trouble—deep trouble.

Victor sighed. When Kate had told him of the embezzlement, Victor had informed the board members. It had been Marnie, alone, who had tried to convince Victor and the rest of the board that Adam Drake had been innocent. At the time Victor had assumed that she was just being her normal, trusting-the-underdog self. Now he wasn't so sure. Was it possible that his straitlaced daughter could fall for the sensual much-touted charms of Adam Drake?

Disaster! That's what it was. Pure, unadulterated disaster! Victor should never have let her leave the other night! He should have put his foot down.

From the corner of his eye, he saw Kent squirm. Kent's tanned face was unnaturally pale, his usual smile missing. He was agitated and tense and had tried to talk Victor out of flying north with him. "I'll take care of this," he'd said, when Victor had explained about Drake's phone call. "Marnie's my responsibility."

"She doesn't think so," Victor had pointed out, as he'd grabbed his jacket and punched the intercom button to have Kate request a pilot for the chopper. Kate, too, had voiced her concerns, but that was because she'd felt a little like Marnie's mother. Well, she wasn't. And Victor was still president of the corporation, and no one, including Kent Simms, Kate Delany or Adam Drake, for that matter, was going to tell him how to handle his corporation or his daughter. He watched Kent nervously scratch his arm. The boy was sweating bullets over Marnie.

"I just hope she's okay," Kent said, wiping an unsteady hand across his lips.

"She will be." Victor's gaze moved to the bubblelike windshield and beyond to the restless green-gray water. "It won't be long."

"I can't get there fast enough," Kent said, nervously biting his lip.

Victor silently agreed, but they would just have to hang on for a couple of hours. A quick copter ride to Deer Harbor and a rental car to Deception Lodge. He and Kent would see Marnie by nightfall. And then, by God, she was going to listen to reason!

As for Adam Drake, if he'd so much as laid one finger on Marnie, Victor would personally skin him alive!

MARNIE WAS GETTING used to Adam's long absences. In the few days they'd been on the island, he'd been out as much as he'd been in the lodge. Both mornings, she'd awoken to find him gone. But their relationship had altered since yesterday, and she didn't know if the changes were for the better or the worse.

For all of her twenty-four years she'd lived her life on a single track, a track carefully laid by her father. And now, in the span of forty-eight hours, she'd jumped rail and headed off in new directions that were both frightening and exhilarating.

She changed clothes and folded the sleeping bags, still smelling of sex, and her mind was filled with blistering memories of passion she'd never known existed, passion hidden deep within her. Blushing at the vivid thoughts, she poured herself a cup of coffee and headed outside, where she balanced one hip on the porch rail, sipped from her cracked cup and waited for Adam to return. The morning was brilliant and warm. A vibrant sun climbed steadily in a clear blue sky, and a breath of sea wind stirred the fir branches and fluttered the new leaves in the oak trees. Birds skimmed the surface of the calm sea. Either Adam had lied about the storm or the weather service had been badly mistaken. All trace of clouds had disappeared, and the sunshine was warm against her face.

She tucked her chin on her hand. Adam Drake was a complication she hadn't anticipated, a wrinkle in her life she wasn't prepared to deal with. They'd become lovers, but she could hardly call them friends. Their lovemaking had been so explosive, so fierce and savage, that she felt drained afterward, as if she'd been in an emotional battle in which both sides were victorious.

"Silly girl," she chided herself, and brushed a pebble off the rail and onto the damp earth surrounding the porch. She'd never been a romantic and she wasn't about to start having idle fantasies now. She couldn't stay up here with Adam forever, and yet, as anxious as she'd been to leave Montgomery Inns behind, she now felt ready to settle in for a while, let this love affair run its natural course... But that was impossible. They hadn't talked much, though he had asked her questions about the company, questions she wouldn't answer. He'd brought up the embezzlement, but she wouldn't speculate about what had happened, not with the man her father presumed to be the thief.

She heard the sound of footsteps and trained her eyes on the stone-strewn path, which cut through the thick stands of trees and lush ferns. Within seconds Adam appeared and her stupid heart did a quick little flip at the sight of him. This wasn't supposed to happen, this lust, but she couldn't seem to control her emotions.

"Did you go back to the *Marnie Lee?*" she asked, dusting off the seat of her jeans as he stepped onto the porch and shifted the bag he'd slung over his back from one shoulder to the other.

He sent a quasi-smile her direction. "Yep."

"And?"

"And she's still above water," he answered. For a millisecond a hint of reluctance glimmered in his eyes.

"But everything was okay?" Marnie pursued, sensing he was holding back on her, that he was hiding something from her, protecting her from bad news.

"Everything's fine," was his gruff reply. Shoving open the door, he hauled his bag of supplies into the lobby and dropped the heavy bundle on the floor. Without another word, he walked into the dining room, and Marnie had the odd sensation that something was terribly wrong. Suddenly Adam had grown sullen and distant.

Because of last night? she wondered. Did he think she'd expect some sort of commitment from him now? Nothing could be further from the truth. She was her own woman, able to make decisions regarding her body on her own.

But still his glum mood bothered her. And he was now in the dining room, where their first explosive encounter had occurred. Marnie struggled to keep her breathing even.

Knowing that he was avoiding her, but unable to leave well enough alone, she followed him and found him seated on an old bar stool near the window, the opened bottle of liquor in one hand, a half-full glass in the other.

"Something happened," she stated, boldly pulling up a stool next to his and straddling it.

He flicked a glance her way, then drained his glass. "What?"

"Nothing," he muttered, and she noticed that his expression was as hard-edged as ever, any sign of tenderness wiped away.

"For God's sake, Adam, *something's* going on."

He stared at her a long while, his eyes going over every contour of her face, as if he were memorizing each tiny detail. "I just think it's time to celebrate," he said, his jaw sliding to the side.

"Celebrate?" she repeated, a kernel of fear settling in her heart. "Celebrate what?"

"The cavalry."

He was making no sense whatsoever, and yet there was something in the way he considered his words that indicated he wasn't telling her everything—that indeed he did have a secret he hadn't shared with her. "What cavalry?"

His lips quirked. "Oh, you know. Those mighty fighting men from Montgomery Inns."

Marnie's stomach contracted as he poured a second glass. She shivered from the sudden coolness in the room, as if they'd never shared a second of passion, a drop of love, as if they were, again, mortal enemies. "Someone's coming here? Someone from the company?" she whispered.

"Good old Victor, unless I miss my guess."

She was suddenly stone-cold. He had to be kidding. "My father's in Seattle."

"Correction. He *was* in Seattle."

"He wouldn't come up here."

"I invited him."

"You *what?*" she cried, her voice as rough as the whiskey he'd poured into his glass. "But how?"

"Through the Coast Guard."

"But why?" She thought about their passionate lovemaking. It had all been an act, a way to bend her will to his so that she would trust him, and the minute she let down her guard he had the nerve to contact her father! "You used me!"

For a flickering moment she thought she caught a glimpse of regret in his face, but it was gone so quickly she wondered if she'd imagined a shred of remorse in his hard features. "What have you done, Drake? What did you say to him?"

"Only enough to get him here."

"You told him about *us?*" she nearly screamed, denying the overpowering urge to lunge at him. "You had no right—"

"I just said I didn't think we'd be back for a while. That's all."

"But you intimated that there was something going on between us!" she guessed, livid. Who was this…this beast she'd slept with? Warm and loving one minute, treacherous and deceitful the next! "How could you?"

"I didn't say anything about last night," he shot back.

"But you said enough to get him up here!"

"I might be wrong," he replied, his gaze cutting. "Maybe Kent will come to the rescue on his white steed. That would be better yet." He studied his liquor for a second, then took a long swallow. "Nah," he said finally, "Simms doesn't have the nerve. Not unless he shows up *with* Victor."

Marnie's entire world tilted. "Oh, God," she groaned, her future suddenly bleak. Her father would be furious. He'd label her a traitor, brand her as disloyal for openly consorting with the enemy. "You're out of your mind," she whispered, trying to think straight.

"I think you could use a drink," he said, and his voice was kinder. He touched her hand, but she drew quickly away.

"Don't!" she snapped. "Don't touch me!"

He started to hand her his drink, but she swatted the glass to the floor, and liquor spattered his jeans and splashed against the window to drizzle down rough pine walls. She wanted to cry but wouldn't let herself, wouldn't give him the satisfaction of seeing her fall apart. Slowly inching up her chin to meet his gaze, she demanded, "Why do you hate me? What have I done to you?"

"I don't hate you, Marnie," he said quietly, and a fleeting sliver of conscience showed in his expression. "But you're Victor's daughter."

"And for that you're trying to ruin my life?" Agony mingled with remorse in his expression, before his face turned hard again. He started to pour yet another drink, then, cursing, screwed the cap back onto the bottle. "You *slept* with me, damn it," she charged, outraged and wounded.

"And you slept with me!"

She opened her mouth, then let it snap closed. She'd been a fool to let him get close enough to hurt her. "Yes, I did. As if that makes what you did all right. Don't turn this argument around!"

In frustration, he pinched the bridge of his nose between his index finger and thumb. His eyes squeezed closed. "I didn't mean to hurt you," he said. "I had no intention of—"

"Seducing me?" she cut in, remembering the first time he'd kissed her. "Or forcing me?"

His eyes flew open, and purple color suffused his neck. "I didn't *force* you to do anything you didn't want to!"

That was true enough, she supposed, but she was aching inside from the wounds he'd inflicted. "You didn't hurt me," she lied, managing to keep her voice steady.

"I hope not, Marnie." The way he said her name was like a balm. He stared into his glass. "I've done a lot of things I'm not very proud of, some of them happened in the last couple of days, but I've never stolen from your father and I've never forced any woman to sleep with me."

"So why don't you leave?" she said, hoping to pull together a little of her shredded dignity.

"I thought you could help me find some answers, and if you couldn't, then I knew Victor or Kent could supply them."

"So you did use me," she said, her voice tight and weak.

"Yes, damn it!" he exploded, leaping from his bar stool and striding back to the bar where he slammed the bottle on the counter next to the mirror. "I only want my life back, my self-respect!"

"So do I," she threw back at him. "And I'd like to think that what we shared last night was more than a cheap trick to lure me into a compromising position with my father. What is it you want from me, Drake?" she finally asked, her voice shaking as she climbed off her stool and marched up to him. She stopped when she was mere inches away, the toes of her shoes close to his battered sneakers.

"I don't want anything from you," he said slowly. "I'm after Simms or whoever the hell set me up. I just thought you could give me some information."

"About what?" she demanded.

"About who in the corporation would be a suspect."

"I thought you'd decided Kent was your scapegoat."

He sent her a look that was absolutely chilling. "I suppose I deserved that," he admitted with a cold smile. "And I'd put money on Simms being the culprit, but I don't understand his motive. Unless he had debts I don't know about, I don't know why he'd jeopardize having it all—by marrying you—for half a million."

"*I'm* not marrying anyone."

"That's encouraging," he said, and his mouth shifted into his first honest smile of the day.

"I can't tell you anything about Kent that you don't already know. I thought I loved him and that he loved me, but I was mistaken and I thank my lucky stars that I wasn't foolish enough to marry him. But I don't think he stole from my father. He's not that stupid…and it would take a lot more money for him to betray Dad."

"But he would do it?"

"Loyalty isn't Kent's strongest quality," she said grimly, thinking of Kent's affair with Dolores.

"So what about Fred Ainger? He's about to retire and he lives the good life. I don't think Social Security and his pension at Montgomery Inns will cover his wife's extravagances."

"Fred's too honest."

"Is he?" Obviously Adam wasn't convinced. His eyes narrowed thoughtfully, as if he were squinting to read extremely small print. "How well do you know Rose Trullinger?"

"Well enough. You can't possibly imagine *she* would embezzle. She's in interior design. How could she possibly juggle the books?"

"Doesn't she have access to a computer terminal?"

"Yes, but—"

"And isn't it linked to the entire Montgomery Inns chain?"

"By secret access codes." This was too farfetched. Adam was really reaching.

"Rose has an ailing husband who can't hold a job, and three daughters in college."

"Just because people need money, doesn't mean they'd steal!" she said in exasperation. This conversation was getting them nowhere, and they were avoiding the issue that was on both their minds. Marnie could think of nothing but their lovemaking, and though Adam had changed the topic, she wasn't finished having it out with him.

"I have a question for you," she finally admitted.

"Shoot."

His golden brown gaze held hers. "What about sleeping with me?" she demanded, bracing herself for the pain of his rejection. "Didn't it mean anything?"

He hesitated just a second before answering coldly. "Last night was sex."

"And that's all?"

His eyes bored into hers, and the air between them fairly sizzled with electricity. He swirled his drink, tossed it back and slammed the empty glass on the bar. "That's all it could ever be."

She wanted to hit him. To slap him so hard he would take back the ugly words, but she couldn't. Because he was speaking the truth. They had no future together, no love, just sex.

"They're right about you," she finally said, her jaw wobbling ever so slightly and hot tears building behind her eyes. "You're just as bad as Dad and Kent think."

"Probably," he agreed as she spun and stumbled blindly up the steps and through the lobby. She had to get away from him, had to pull herself together. She shoved open the door with her shoulder as tears started to stream down her face. She couldn't break down in front of him, wouldn't let him see her cry.

"Marnie!"

Oh, God, he was following her!

She ran, around the corner to the back of the lodge. His footsteps crunched in the gravel behind her, and he caught up with her at the weed-strewn parking lot, near a spreading maple tree with branches that provided a green canopy. "Marnie—wait. Just listen to me." He grabbed hold of her arm, and though she tried to pull away from him, he was much stronger than she, and she was wrenched back against the solid wall of his chest.

His arms surrounded her. "Marnie, Marnie, Marnie," he whispered against her hair. "Don't hate me."

"I do!" she lied, wishing she could pull away. "All you are is trouble. My father was right!"

"Your father's wrong about a lot of things, and so are you." He stared down into her shimmering eyes, and she wanted to collapse against him, to beg him to take back the cruel words, but of course he wouldn't.

"Just leave me alone!"

But he didn't. Instead his lips crashed down on hers, possessive and hard, demanding and comforting, and she struggled hard to pull away. But his arms were powerful, his mouth hot and wet, his will as strong as her own.

Her body reacted, sagging against his hard male contours, her arms slackening until she fought no longer and was aware of only Adam. The smell of the sea wafted over the musky scent of him, and deep in the distance she heard birds startled at the sound of a car's engine. Closing out all sounds, she clung to him and molded her body tight against his.

Groaning, he moved so that her back was pressed hard against the rough bark of the maple, but she didn't care, and when his hands moved upward along her arms, she shuddered with want. Her mouth opened easily to his practiced tongue.

Vaguely she was aware that something was wrong, that the sounds of the day had changed, but she didn't know or care why. She was lost in a savage storm of emotion, and as his hand surrounded her breast, gently massaging her flesh through her sweater while his tongue tickled the inside of her mouth, she gave in to all the wanton pulses firing her blood.

Until he stopped. As quickly as he'd pulled her to him, he released her. "Someone's coming," he said as the whine of a car's engine split the air and the nose of a white sedan rounded the final curve in the gravel lane.

Quickly Marnie straightened the hem of her sweater and swiped at the tears still standing in her eyes, but not before she met the furious gaze of the driver of the sedan. Her heart plummeted. Right now, she wasn't ready to face her father.

Victor's polished leather shoes landed on the gravel as the car rolled to a stop. "What the hell's going on here?" he said in a voice so low and menacing Marnie could barely hear it over the dull pounding of the surf. His gaze landed in contemptuous force on Adam. "Well, Drake, you got what you wanted. I'm here. Now what?"

"I just want to talk to you."

Marnie hadn't even noticed Kent in the passenger seat of the car, but there he was, climbing out of the sedan, his shoulders stiff, his mouth a white, uncompromising line. His whole attitude reeked of disdain, as if he could barely stomach the scene unfolding before him. However, Marnie knew him better than most and she saw something more than he'd like to show, something he was trying to hide, something akin to fear that touched his features.

The wind picked up, shoving Marnie's hair in front of her eyes, as her father reached her side. "Are you all right?" Victor asked, grabbing her in a huge bear hug. His face was filled with fatherly concern, and Marnie realized she'd wounded him bitterly by leaving with Adam.

"I'm okay."

"You're sure?" He held her at arm's length, as if he could see the scars on her soul, scars inflicted by Adam Drake.

"Dad, believe me. I never felt better." From the corner of her eye she saw Adam stiffen.

"And what about him?" He motioned to Adam, and Marnie recognized a spark of rebellion in Adam's eyes. "He treat you right?"

"No one 'treated' anyone," she said evenly. "And you're here now. Why not talk to him yourself?"

A muscle flexed in Victor's cheek, and the wind blew his tie over his shoulder. He hesitated just a second, but finally said, "All right, Drake. Let's get this over with. What's on your mind?"

Adam told him. Right there in the old parking lot with the first few storm clouds rolling in from the west. Rain began to fall from the dark sky as Adam explained his theory of being set up and he didn't stop, not even when Kent scoffed at him.

Victor listened, though Marnie guessed he wasn't buying any of Adam's theories.

"All I want is another chance to prove that I'm innocent," Adam finally said, "and a public apology from you, absolving me of all guilt when that proof is uncovered."

"You're out of your mind," Kent said. "You've got no proof of a conspiracy against you or whatever you think happened. You're grasping at straws, man."

"Maybe your straw," Adam said with a slow, cold smile, challenging Kent without so much as lifting a finger. Kent rose to the bait, his jaw set and his handsome face flushed dark. He was ready to fling himself at Adam, but he must have thought better of his actions, for he straightened his tie instead and backed down. For the moment.

Victor remained unswayed. "All right, Drake, you've had your say. And I've listened. And I only have one thing to say to you—keep the hell away from my daughter. As for your cockamamy theories, keep them to yourself. You screwed me over, Drake, and I have a long memory. So don't try to drag innocent people's names through the mud, because it won't work with me." He'd slowly built himself into a rage. "Come on, Marnie—" He reached for her arm.

"I'm not leaving."

"What?" Her father stared at her as if she'd lost her mind. "Of course you're coming with me, now get your things and—"

"Listen, Dad. Nothing's changed," she said, wincing at the lie. "I'm not coming back to the company. The paper I gave you was a resignation, not a request for a leave of absence. And I haven't forgotten what you did on the night of the party." From the corner of her eye, she saw Kent go white.

"But you're coming back to Seattle," Kent said.

"Not yet."

"For God's sake, what's gotten into you?" he sputtered. "Has Drake brainwashed you?" Flinging one hand in the air, he turned to Victor and as if Marnie hadn't a mind of her own said, "You talk some sense into her and take her back with the car. I'll sail the *Marnie Lee* into port and have her repaired."

"Over my dead body," Marnie cried. "*I'm* responsible for the boat, and I'll take care of her."

"And what about him?" Kent hooked an insolent thumb in Adam's direction.

"He's his own person. He got what he wanted from me, didn't he?" she said, coloring a little. "He got you both up here. He can do whatever he pleases."

"For God's sake, Marnie, listen to reason," her father begged, but she turned swiftly on her heel and headed back to the lodge. She was tired of men—all men—manipulating her, using her, thinking about her from their own selfish perspectives. Well, the whole lot of them could rot in hell. Victor for smothering her, Kent for betraying her and lying to the press about marrying her, and Adam for seducing her and playing with her heart.

If only she could run to a nunnery, she thought sarcastically, but stopped dead in her tracks. She wasn't running *away* from her problems, she was running *to* a new self-sufficient life. She'd start her own publicity firm, just as soon as the *Marnie Lee* was repaired.

She threw things in her bag and listened, hoping for the sound of a car's engine as it left, but instead she heard the door of the lodge open and slam shut. "You're leaving." Adam's voice startled her. She'd expected her father.

"That's right."

"Where're you going?"

"Don't know."

"Marnie, I—"

She shouldered her bag and brushed past him. "Don't bother apologizing, Adam. It's not your style." With one last glance that she hoped appeared scathing, she pressed forever into her memory how he looked just then, with three days' worth of stubble on his chin, his hair uncombed, his clothes unclean. Her father was right. She was better off without him. So why, then, did her heart ache so?

She left Adam in the lobby. Her father would see that Adam was duly thrown out and that Deception Lodge was secured. Oh, she'd bungled this first attempt at independence, she thought miserably as she hiked down the trail leading to the beach where the rubber raft awaited, but her mangled attempt was because of Adam. She should never have let him get so close to her.

Rain peppered the ground, puddling in the sandy path and giving the forest a fresh, earthy cleanliness that reminded her of Adam.

"You'll get over him," she predicted, but wondered just how long it would take.

CHAPTER EIGHT

HE'D BLOWN IT. With Marnie. With Victor. With Montgomery Inns.

Adam threw his few new belongings into a nylon bag and slung it over his shoulder before heading to the office of the fleabag of a motel he'd called home for the past week. He'd stayed in Chinook Harbor, knowing Marnie had checked into a hotel on the other side of town. Several times he'd tried to contact her. So far, she hadn't responded.

He didn't really blame her.

Ever since the confrontation with Victor in the parking lot of the lodge, Adam had relived the scene over and over again in his mind. He should have anticipated the outcome. Marnie, furious with all of them, had left without so much as a glance over her stiff shoulder, and Adam had felt the unlikely urge to run after her. And what? Apologize? Ridiculous! He couldn't start letting a woman foul up his plans—especially when that woman was Victor Montgomery's only child, his princess.

As for Victor, the old man had looked as if he wanted to kill Adam right on the front porch of Deception Lodge. Somehow, Victor had managed to control his thirst for blood and had, instead, made a big show of kicking Adam off Montgomery property. Victor had been white with rage, shaking as he'd chained the front door and slammed the padlock shut, swearing and threatening to call the police.

"This is it, Drake," he'd growled, his voice so hushed Adam had barely heard it over the sound of the surf. "You've pushed me too far this time. The inns were one thing. Money, I can always make. But my daughter..." By this time Victor's lips were bloodless, his blue eyes colder than ice. "I'll never forget how you used and humiliated her to get to me. If you breathe one word of this to anyone, I swear I'll call the authorities and then I'll personally wring your worthless neck!" With that, he'd stalked to his car, and Adam, every muscle aching with restraint, hadn't lunged at the man, nor begged forgiveness. He'd just stood there and when Victor had opened the door of the Mercedes and stared at him, Adam had met Victor's unwavering hate-filled gaze with his own steady scrutiny.

Victor's reaction had been predictable. As had Marnie's. The odd man out had been Simms. Everyone else had acted right in character. Victor had been the indignant, furious father; Marnie a proud woman who'd discovered that her lover hadn't cared for her. But Simms had been strangely quiet and subdued for a jilted fiancé.

Thinking of Marnie, Adam winced. She had been an innocent in all this. Sure, she'd been in love with Simms, but she'd never done anything directly against Adam. In fact, if she were telling him the truth, she'd protested his innocence to the board of directors of Montgomery Inns and she'd trusted him not to hurt her.

He closed his eyes, willing the image of Marnie's beautiful face from his mind and concentrating instead on Simms—the man she was supposed to marry. Simms's reaction to the scene at the lodge had been odd, to say the least. Instead of being pleased with Adam's dressing down by Victor, instead of reveling in Adam's verbal lashing, Simms had seemed more interested in Marnie and their damned boat. It had been all Victor could do to restrain Simms from chasing down the path after Marnie. No smug smile cast in Adam's direction, no supercilious look down Simms's nose. No, in fact, once over the initial shock of seeing Adam, Simms had only been interested in Marnie, the yacht and the well-being of both.

Maybe the bastard really did care for her, Adam thought with a grimace, as he checked out of the motel. He handed the cashier his credit card, hastily scribbled his name and stuffed the receipt in the pocket of his stiff new jeans.

Outside, the weather was warm, sunlight spangling the waters of the marina several blocks downhill. Boats of all sizes and shapes were tethered to the docks. The shipmasts looked like telephone poles spaced too closely together. Hulls gleamed in the sunlight, and sails flapped noisily before catching the breeze that blew steadily across the harbor. The air was thick with the smells of fish and seaweed, the cloudless sky littered with gulls and terns.

He spotted the *Marnie Lee* as he walked toward the waterfront. Chinook Harbor was a sleepy little village where people knew everything about each other and loved to gossip. Adam, from nights spent at a local watering hole and from days lingering over coffee at a popular diner, had learned from a few discreet inquiries that Marnie had placed her yacht in the care of Ryan Barns, a sailor with a reputation of caring more for boats than for his wife and small daughter.

He'd also learned that the repairs would take several weeks.

Marnie would either have to stay on the island and wait, or return to Seattle, or continue on her flight for freedom by some other means of transportation. Though she'd never fully confessed that she'd left Montgomery Inns to start a life of her own, Adam had guessed as much. Her argument with Victor at the lodge had confirmed his suspicions. Her bid for independence won his grudging approval. Few women, or men for that matter, would give up the good life just to prove themselves.

Yep. Marnie was one helluva woman.

Marnie, Marnie, Marnie. It would be best if he stayed away from her. But right now, he couldn't. Not yet. Despite all the pain he'd already caused her, he had to convince her to help him again.

Fat chance, he thought, irritated with how he'd bungled their relationship. *What relationship?* he thought irritably, and sighed in self-disgust. He'd destroyed any chance of her trusting him again.

A few tourists and townspeople wandered along the streets of Chinook Harbor. The air was clean and clear, the only evidence of the storm of the past week the streaks of mud lining the sidewalks and clogging the gutters.

Adam trekked the two blocks to the pier, hoping to spy Marnie, but was disappointed. The woman behind the desk of Barns's Charters and Repairs, Renada, if the smudged nameplate on her desk could be believed, cast him the same patient smile she always gave him, but she wouldn't let him near the *Marnie Lee.*

"Sorry, Mr. Drake, no can do," Renada said, as she had each time he'd visited. "You know the rules. Now, if you'd like to talk to Mr. Barns, I'll just call him…" She reached for the phone on the corner of her desk, but Adam shook his head. He'd already talked to Barns and gotten nowhere.

He turned to leave just as Ryan Barns himself swung through a back door. The man was short, wiry, with several tattoos decorating his beefy forearms. Sweat stains darkened the faded blue material of a T-shirt that matched the color of his eyes.

"Mr. Drake, back again, I see," Barns drawled, snapping a grimy cloth from the hip pocket of sagging jeans and wiping black oil from his hands on the rag. He smelled of diesel and tobacco. "Don't tell me. Ya come wantin' to get on board the *Marnie Lee* again."

"I'm looking for Miss Montgomery."

Barns sniffed and stuffed the oily rag back into his pocket. "She ain't here, but I told her you came snooping around here the other day and she was fit to be tied. Told me in no uncertain terms that you weren't allowed on her boat, that you and some guy named Simms were strictly off-limits."

"Is that so?"

Barns nodded and let out a whistle between slightly gapped front teeth. "I don't know what you did to that little lady, but she's madder'n hell at you."

"Just tell her I'd like to talk to her."

"Already did," Barns replied amiably. "And she told me to tell you to—" he glanced at his secretary who was just lighting a cigarette "—how'd she put it, Rennie? Something about buying a one-way ticket to hell—no, no, that wasn't it."

Renada let the smoke roll out her nostrils. "I think it was more like, 'Tell Mr. Drake he can stow away on the next steamer bound for hell, but he's not to set foot on the *Marnie Lee*.'"

"That was it!" Barns grinned and snapped his fingers. "I thought she was jokin', but she never once cracked a smile."

"Just tell her I was here again," Adam said as he left Renada and Barns chuckling at his expense.

In the motel's parking lot, Adam tossed his bag into the trunk of his rental car, then climbed behind the wheel. He knew where Marnie was staying, he'd just wanted to give her time to cool down before he showed up on her doorstep. But she'd refused to return his phone calls, and the one time he'd stopped by her hotel, she'd refused to meet him for a drink.

Adam couldn't wait any longer. He had to talk to her. Whether she wanted to see him or not.

So what're you going to do? Shanghai her? That particular thought brought a lift to the corners of his mouth and a warm feeling deep in his gut. Though he'd tried, he couldn't forget making love to her—hot and wild, savage and yet laced with tenderness, their lovemaking had burned bright in his mind. Especially at night.

He'd thought about finding himself another woman; there were lots of bored women in this town who had cast interested glances in his direction, but he'd never so much as tried to catch their eyes. No, right now, all of his sexual fantasies were tied up with Victor Montgomery's daughter.

Forbidden fruit.

Nonetheless, no other woman would do. Not until this mess with Montgomery Inns was resolved and Marnie was out of his blood forever. He flicked on the Ford's engine and edged into the slow flow of traffic.

One way or another, he had to convince Marnie to see things his way.

THE NOON SUN BEAT down with the intensity of July rather than late May, though no one had jumped into the pool, which sparkled invitingly near Marnie's table. Beneath a striped umbrella, Marnie sipped her tea and finished the crumbs of her croissant. She scanned the headlines of a Seattle paper she'd purchased in the lobby, unable to keep from looking for any information on Montgomery Inns.

The last time she'd seen her father, he'd been as angry as she'd ever seen him.

And Adam. She couldn't think of him without hurting inside.

"Moron," she muttered at herself as she sipped her tea. For the first time in days she'd felt like eating. So she'd ordered lunch on the veranda and settled in at this table flanked by planters overflowing with pink-and-white tulips and pale yellow daffodils. Only a few feet away, the aquamarine water in the pool shimmered invitingly.

Maybe she was finally getting over Adam, she thought, still scanning the paper.

Right. And maybe horses have learned to fly. Idly, she stirred her tea.

Somehow, she had to get on with her life. Without Adam Drake messing it up. She thought about how he'd planned her seduction, how he'd played with her emotions and how gullible she'd been. Believing him. Trusting him. She'd even fantasized that she'd been falling in love with him.

Silly, spoiled little girl. Used to getting your way. Well, when it comes to men and love, you just don't seem to learn. First Kent. Now Adam. What a pathetic list of men to fall in love with!

"I'm not, never have been and never will be in love with Adam Drake." She shoved her plate aside, licked her fingers and flipped through the classified section of the paper. Maybe having the *Marnie Lee* put up for repairs was a turn of good luck. She couldn't just climb on the boat and sail away from her problems. She had to face her future. A future without Kent, without Montgomery Inns and definitely without Adam.

She could move anywhere she chose. She had enough money to start her own public-relations firm, and if she were frugal, she could manage for nearly a year before she'd have to get a job to supplement her income.

She couldn't just take off on the boat and put off her decision about where she was going to live forever. She ran her fingers down the classified section of "business opportunities." Maybe there was a firm she could buy—on a contract, of course—and in time…

"Marnie?"

The sound of Adam's voice was like a jolt of electricity. She visibly jumped and snapped her head around to find him standing just outside the shade of the umbrella. *Oh, please, God, no!* Her heart thumped crazily at the sight of him, but she set her jaw and eyed him coolly. "I thought I made it clear—I don't want to speak to you."

"I got the message." He grabbed a chair from a nearby table, twisted it around and straddled it, his eyes squinting against the sun as he looked at her.

"I don't think you did. I never want to see you again."

"Never's a long time."

"Not long enough." She scooted her chair back, intending to leave, but he reacted too quickly, reaching out with the speed of a striking snake, his fingers closing tightly over her wrist. "Just hear me out, okay?"

"Why?"

"Because it's important."

"Believe me, Mr. Drake, we don't have anything to discuss."

"I don't blame you for being angry."

"I'm *way* past angry, Adam. In fact, I'm beyond furious and enraged. Even livid doesn't quite describe—"

"Just listen to me."

"No—"

"Please," he said softly, and her heart turned to mush. She had to remind herself what a black-souled bastard he really was. "There's no point, Adam," she said, pulling hard on her hand, but he didn't budge. "Let me go."

"No."

"I'll call security."

"And cause a scene?"

"Yes! You don't have an exclusive on creating a scandal, you know," she gambled. She'd been brought up believing in decorum and doing the right thing, but Adam blew all her beliefs right out of the water.

"Don't I?" His mouth stretched into a crooked, dangerous smile, and his golden brown eyes seemed to catch the rays of the sun. "We'll see about that," he drawled, standing, the pads of his fingers moving slightly against the inside of her arm. Marnie's pulse trembled and he felt it; she knew he did, by the spark of recognition in his gaze.

"What're you doing?" she whispered, conscious of more than a few pairs of eyes turned in their direction.

"Convincing you to listen to me."

"How?" she asked, her heart fluttering tremulously though she was still trying to draw away as she realized he intended to kiss her! "Oh, no—"

"See that man in the corner—about forty, round glasses?"

She couldn't help casting a glance to the edge of the veranda where the man, wearing a plaid sport jacket and brown slacks, was watching them intently. She froze.

"He's a photographer for the local paper."

"Sure," she said, hoping to sound sarcastic.

"He is."

"I don't have to listen to this," she said quickly, though she spied a camera on the table next to the man in question. She tried to yank away again and Adam, standing, drew her from her chair, wrenching her close so that her body slammed into his. His arms surrounded her, and he lowered his head as if he were going to kiss her. "Adam, don't—"

"Struggle if you want to. Make a scene. But think about it," he whispered against her ear. "Because if that man takes your picture and it somehow finds its way to the front page of the *Seattle Observer,* your father will probably see it."

"You're bluffing," she accused, but her heart nearly stopped when the man in the corner, as if looking for a cue from Adam, picked up his camera. Adam nodded imperceptibly and Marnie gulped. "You hired him, didn't you?" she whispered, horrified at the realization. "You hired him to do this so that—"

"Now listen, Marnie," Adam cut in, all humor leaving his face. "He's not going to do anything unless I give him the high sign."

"You wouldn't!" she whispered. How devious was Adam? To what lengths would he go?

"Watch me." His lips brushed over hers and even though a part of her was mortified, her body, at least, was thrilled. Her skin tingled where he touched her.

"Let go of me," she commanded. But if anything his grip tightened, and when he kissed her again, her breath was lost somewhere between her lungs and her throat, her mind caught between now and forever.

"Just listen to me," he said softly, when he raised his head from hers and she was conscious only of the rush of blood in her ears, the dizzy sensation in her mind.

"You're crazy! If you think I'm going to—"

"Come on, Marnie, what've you got to lose?" he asked, and when his gaze found hers, her throat squeezed at the tenderness in his eyes. *It's all an act! He's using you again! Don't let him! Marnie, use your head!*

"Just hear me out. I promise I'll be good."

"I don't think that's possible," she said, her voice sounding odd when she finally found it again. "Just remember I don't *owe* you this, you know."

"Of course not. You're doing it out of the goodness of your heart," he quipped, but when she looked for a spark of levity in his expression, she found none.

She tried to remember why she should be furious with him, and though the reasons flitted through her mind, she refused to listen to them. And her temper, usually quick to flare, wouldn't ignite. Not with everyone on the verandah staring at them. "Let's get out of here."

"Now you're talking." He slid his fingers to the crook of her elbow and propelled her forward on a straight path between the tables to the foyer of the hotel. She scrabbled for her purse, but didn't put up any further argument. In her peripheral vision she noticed the blur of red-and-white flowers, early petunias, she guessed, and heard the clink of glasses as diners turned their attention back to their lunches, but everything else, save Adam's strong presence, faded into the background.

This is nuts, Marnie kept telling herself as he guided her past the front desk and into the elevator.

"What floor are you on?"

"Four."

He slapped the button, and the elevator doors closed before he finally trusted her not to bolt and released her. Her head started to clear. She realized they were headed for her hotel room and trouble. Big trouble. She couldn't be confined in a small room with a bed with Adam Drake! She couldn't trust him and she certainly couldn't trust herself!

The elevator stopped with a thump. The doors parted, and Adam stepped onto the floral carpet of the corridor. Marnie didn't move. Before the doors closed again, Adam reached inside, grabbed her and hauled her out of the elevator car.

"Don't!"

"Come on, we don't have all day."

"For what?" she replied, her old fire returning as she jerked her arm back.

"For me to convince you to help me."

"W-what?" she sputtered, then laughed. "You're not serious, are you? You think *I*, after the way you treated me, would help *you*. Oh, come on, Drake! Never."

"Don't you want to know the truth?"

"I think I do. You were involved. Period. I don't know how deeply. I'm not sure if you were the brains behind the operation or just plain duped by someone else. Whatever the explanation is, I don't care."

"I don't believe you."

She turned a corner and stopped at 431, her room. But she didn't unlock the door. "Thanks for the escort. Not that I needed one. And as for that dirty trick—the one with the photographer—it was your last!"

He grinned at that. "Don't count on it."

His smile touched a corner of her heart, but she refused to be drawn into his web of lies again. "As far as I'm concerned, you're out of my life."

"Remember, you owe me one."

"I—what? As I said I don't owe you anything—"

He leaned closer, and his thumb touched the slope of her jaw. "I remember distinctly you telling me that you owed me. Remember the deal we made? In the storm? You wanted me to help you get the boat to shore…"

His breath swept across her ear, and she licked her lips as she remembered that first fateful night of the storm and the pitching deck of the *Marnie Lee* when Adam had told her of the crack in the hull. "All deals are off," she said firmly.

"I never thought you'd be the kind to welsh, Ms. Montgomery."

"And I never thought you'd sleep with me just to get back at my father!"

He sucked in his breath. "Marnie, I—"

"I think you should leave."

He didn't move so much as an inch. "Then you don't want a partner?"

She was reaching into her bag, searching for the room key. "Partner? What kind of partner. Never mind—" she held out her palm and shook her head "—I don't want to know."

"A business partner."

Her heart dropped to the floor in disappointment. "Now I *know* you're joking," she said, finding her key and trying to sound cool and sophisticated. She couldn't let him know that she cared for him—even a little.

"I'm dead serious. I need you and you need me."

"I don't *need* anyone," she said, "especially not you." She shoved her key into the lock. Glancing over her shoulder, she said simply, "You're too much trouble, Mr. Drake, and right now I don't want or *need* any more trouble than I already have."

She took one step across the threshold before his hands grabbed her hard on the shoulders and spun her around, pushing her against the door frame. She barely caught her breath before his mouth crashed down on hers with a kiss as strong and demanding as the waves pounding the shore. His lips moved expertly along the contours of her mouth, gliding easily, molding to her skin until slowly her stiff resistance yielded and she kissed him back. Her mouth opened slightly, and his tongue darted between her parted lips, flicking and teasing as he pressed her body hard against the doorjamb, the wood cutting into her back as his hips pushed forward to pin her abdomen tight against him. "You're a liar," he breathed into her hair, and a familiar warm ache began to throb deep inside her. "You do need me."

"No." Oh, God, why did she sound so weak?

"And I get the feeling you like trouble. You need some spark in your life—a little shot of danger to spice up that dreary existence of the spoiled little rich girl."

"You bastard," she hissed, struggling again. "You don't know anything about me! How dare you—ooh!" Cupping her nape, he drew her head to his and kissed her so hungrily her knees threatened to buckle. She tried to resist, to fight him, but her arms and legs wouldn't respond and all her defiance slipped away.

She sagged against him, suddenly anxious to feel the sinewy muscles of his body straining through his clothes. When he at last dragged his mouth from hers, her breathing came in short gulps and her mind was reeling out of control, stumbling into risky territory, a region where she might just let herself trust Adam again. Her hands trembled as she pushed him away. "I…hate you."

"I know." He kissed her again, and she couldn't breathe.

"You…I…we can't do this."

"Sure we can," he drawled.

"*I* can't. This madness has got to stop."

"Not yet, Marnie. Not until I convince you that it's not madness. I need your help."

"We tried this once before. It didn't work! It'll never work!"

A lock clicked two doors down the hall.

What now?

An elderly man, wearing a fedora and carrying a wooden cane and newspaper tucked under his arm, stepped into the hallway from his room. Locking his door, he sent a cursory glance in Adam and Marnie's direction. A soft smile bowed beneath his snowy moustache as he passed, and Marnie blushed to the roots of her hair as she guessed his thoughts. He probably concluded that she and Adam were involved in a lovers' spat.

Ridiculous! But close enough to the truth to bother her. "I don't have anything else to say to you," she insisted, as, over the top of Adam's shoulder, she observed the elderly gentleman pushing the elevator call button before leaning on his cane.

"Just hear me out."

The elevator doors opened and a family of four exited,

two boys clamoring down the hall while their parents struggled with shopping bags.

This was outlandish! She hated the scene they were making, inwardly wincing at the knowing glance the twelve-year-old boy sent her as he raced past.

"Okay—but you've got five minutes," she said, already deciding that listening to him was a mistake. She shoved open her door and they stepped inside. Adam locked the door behind him, and Marnie felt an overwhelming sense of desperation. She crossed to the bureau and rested her hips against the polished edge, refusing to even acknowledge the queen-size bed dominating the small suite.

"What I've got is a simple business proposition for you," Adam said.

"I'm all ears." She couldn't help the sarcasm.

"Oh, no, Marnie, there's more to your body than that," he drawled, sitting on a corner of the bed and staring at her with those golden brown eyes.

"Just get to the point." She walked to the window and fiddled nervously with the blinds. She felt his gaze on her backside, and her skin prickled.

"Okay," he said, smiling at her obvious discomfort. "I know you want to start your own business and that you haven't quite figured out where to land yet."

"How do you—oh, never mind. Go on."

"So—why not settle in Seattle?"

She snorted. "Are you crazy? I'm trying to get away from Montgomery Inns."

"I know, but maybe that's a mistake." He stretched out on the bed, and Marnie was aware of how good he looked. Freshly shaven, with clean clothes, his body long and lean against the slate blue spread, he smiled up at her, and her heart melted.

"A—a mistake?"

"You're killing the golden goose. I bet your father

would hire you as a freelance publicist. You could have the Montgomery Inn account, as well as drumming up your own business. You could cultivate other accounts, start your own little empire."

"My father demands absolute loyalty."

"You wouldn't be disloyal."

She hurled him a glance that called him a liar. "He doesn't like sharing."

"You're freelancing. It's not a matter of sharing. Besides, what better way to build client confidence than by snagging one of the best accounts in the business?"

"Because I'm Victor's daughter. Back to square one." She yanked hard on the blinds, drawing them open before sitting on the window ledge and staring out at the warm afternoon. From her vantage point, she saw the glittery waters of the bay and the fishing boats and sailing vessels moving along the horizon. "So where do you come in? What was all this talk of a partnership?" She glanced over her shoulder.

His eyes locked with hers, and an indecent flame flickered in those sienna orbs. "I can think of a few ways," he said, smoothing a wrinkle from the quilt.

"Name them."

"I'd hire you."

"As what?" she asked suspiciously, while dragging her eyes away from the seductive movement of his hand against the bedspread.

"As a publicist for the first Hotel Drake."

"Which doesn't yet exist," she pointed out.

"It will, once I've settled a few things."

"And this fictitious hotel—will it be located in Seattle?"

"It would be easiest for me. After all, I already live there."

She knew that he resided in Seattle in a condominium on the shore of Lake Washington, complete with a mooring for his own boat—the boat he'd probably left in Port Stanton when he'd stowed away on the *Marnie Lee*. "And if you never get this hotel off the ground—"

"I will," he said emphatically, then sighed. "Look, I know a lot of people—more than you," he added, when she was about to point out that she'd been around people in the hotel business for years. "Contacts that could get you off your feet and away from the golden handcuffs of Montgomery Inns."

"I'm already there," she said.

"But you've got to start somewhere."

That much was true.

"And if things don't work out in Seattle, you're no worse off than you are now."

Except you'll be near Dad again. That part she could handle, as long as she was her own boss. *And Kent?* She'd avoid him. And wouldn't it be pleasant showing him that she could make it on her own? Without a man.

Adam Drake's a man.

Dealing with Adam would be the hardest part in all of this. She'd just have to find a way to keep him at arm's length. "This would be strictly business?" she asked.

"Whatever you want."

Her voice wouldn't work for a second. "Our relationship would have to be only professional."

"What else?"

She blushed, damn it, but managed a cool, sophisticated loft of her brow. "There isn't anything, is there?"

"Just the fact that you still owe me one."

"Don't remind me."

Slowly he rolled off the bed, crossed the small expanse of carpet and placed one hand on either side of the windowsill, holding her prisoner. "Then we have a deal?"

Nodding, she tried to shrink away, but was drawn by the magnetism in his eyes. "We have a deal." She thrust out her hand, expecting him to take it, but a crooked smile slowly curved his mouth.

"I think we should seal this bargain with a kiss." Before she could answer, his mouth found hers again and she didn't even try to stop him. She felt her body molding to his of its own accord, and she lost herself in the feel and taste of him.

A partnership with Adam Drake would be no better than dealing with the devil, but right now, wrapped in his arms, Marnie didn't care.

CHAPTER NINE

TRYING TO FORGET the memory of making love to Adam, Marnie hammered another nail into the freshly painted wall of her new office and carefully hung a painting she'd picked up at a local gallery.

Why couldn't she forget him? she wondered, surveying her work with a critical eye. It had been two weeks since she'd awoken in the hotel room alone in Port Chinook. Though she hadn't slept with him, his image had lingered in her mind and had been imprinted on her heart. She'd forced herself to leave him, but she hadn't gone far. In fact she'd taken his advice and located her new business in Seattle, less than a mile from the corporate headquarters of Montgomery Inns. And she couldn't stop thinking about him.

Shoving the hammer into an empty desk drawer, she muttered, "You're hopeless, Montgomery." Sighing, she flopped onto the edge of the credenza, clasped her hands between her knees and remembered their goodbyes.

"I'll call you," Adam had said, gathering her into his arms, smelling so earthy and male.

"Give me time to settle in—think things through," she'd replied. "Remember I'm not really convinced that moving in next to my father is the smartest thing I've ever done."

"No," he'd agreed, his eyes twinkling as he looked down at her. "Linking up with me is the smartest thing you've done."

She'd laughed. "I'm afraid linking up with you will be the end of me."

"Never." He'd lifted her up, twirled her off her feet, and when she'd slid back to the floor, kissed her with such breathless passion that, even now, seated in the office, she tingled.

"Remember, we're partners," he'd reminded her.

"But I need time to be my own person before I can be partners with anyone," she'd replied, and she'd left without him, wondering if he would return to Seattle.

Now, two weeks later she knew he, too, was living somewhere near the city. He'd tried to contact her, but she hadn't been ready to talk to him or deal with the conflicting emotions that he always seemed to ignite. Their meetings had been brief. Sometimes she was sure she loved him. In other, more rational hours, she thought she hated him, or should hate him.

She brushed her hands on her skirt and stood in the middle of her office. It was small, even cramped, but was located in a decent part of town. It also came with a part-time secretary and wasn't too expensive.

Marnie had found it herself after a week of reading the paper, talking to realtors and touring available sites. She'd repainted the walls, bought a desk, chairs and a credenza, and set out a few plants near the window. A skylight offered a view of the clouds shifting in the sky. "Home, sweet home," she told herself.

So now all she had to do was drum up business. Her first appointment this afternoon was with her father.

"Fitting," she muttered, checking her watch as her stomach clenched. She'd already approached two other hotel chains, the marina and a local restaurant without much success, but today she was scheduled to walk back through the hallowed halls of Montgomery Inns.

Adam's idea. Right now, she wasn't convinced working for the company again was such a great plan. As for Adam, she'd seen him briefly a couple of times when he'd stopped by the office, but she'd declined any chance to spend much time with him. Her feelings about him were still confused. She didn't know whether she hated him or loved him, but she told herself that she couldn't trust him.

So why did you take his advice and come back here? Because you "owed him one"? Because you want to start a business relationship with him, become "partners"? Get real, Marnie.

"Oh, shut up!" she grumbled at the nagging note of conscience that had been hounding her since she returned to Seattle.

"You talkin' to me?" Donna's voice carried through the partially opened door. Donna came with the building and was secretary-receptionist for Marnie, an accountant and an interior designer, all of whom occupied this floor of the Maynard Building.

"Just to myself," Marnie sang back.

Grabbing her briefcase and purse, Marnie walked briskly through the door to her office. Donna, offbeat compared to the secretaries who pledged allegiance to Montgomery Inns, was bent over the keyboard of her computer terminal and fiddling with the keys. Somewhere close to twenty, with spiky red hair and outlandish jewelry, she managed to juggle her workload and keep all three offices running smoothly, though she spent a lot of time drinking coffee and smoking cigarettes. So far, though, Marnie had no complaints. Donna was refreshing, outspoken and incredibly efficient.

"Damned thing," Donna muttered, her pretty face a knot of frustration as she poked a long, bloodred finger between the keys of the keyboard.

The computer bleeped angrily.

"Problems?" Marnie asked.

"Always. Can't get the printer to work. I've called the company a million times and they can't seem to find the bug in the system." She leaned back in her chair and lit a cigarette, blowing smoke to the ceiling and scowling at the machine as if she could will it to turn on and hum companionably.

"Wish I could help, but I'm definitely on the 'user unfriendly' list," Marnie joked. "I'll be at Montgomery Inns for a couple of hours. If it takes longer, I'll give you a call."

"I'll be here," Donna replied, wrinkling her nose at the terminal. "Probably all night if I can't get this thing to work."

Marnie waved and walked outside, bracing herself for the battle that she was sure would erupt when she came face-to-face with her father again.

"MARNIE!" KATE DELANY clasped her hands together and grinned broadly as Marnie walked toward her desk. Piped-in music played softly from hidden speakers and recessed lighting offered soothing tones in the administrative offices of Montgomery Inns. "It's good to see you again!" Kate enthused. "You know, it hasn't been the same here without you—and him—" she motioned to the closed door of Victor's private suite "—he's been an absolute bear!"

"I can imagine," Marnie drawled.

"Please, for the rest of us, reconsider and come back," Kate begged, though her dark eyes sparkled with a teasing light. "If you were around, things would go *sooo* much smoother."

Marnie laughed. She was surprised, but it felt good to be in familiar surroundings again. She relaxed a little as Kate rapped softly before shoving open one of the twin mahogany doors. "She's here," Kate said, closing the door behind Marnie and leaving father and daughter alone.

Victor was seated on the couch, pretending interest in a sailing magazine. "You're late."

"I don't think so—"

He looked up then, his face a little paler than she remembered. "God, it's good to see you."

"You, too, Dad." And she meant it. They stood staring at each other for a few seconds, and all the horrible words and accusations that had kept them apart seemed to fade away. She knew she should still be angry with him; he had, after all, encouraged Kent to lie to the press about their engagement, but despite all Victor's faults, Marnie knew he loved her. Everything he did was simply because he was trying to make her life easier. "Oh, Dad," she whispered, her throat suddenly tight.

Tossing his magazine aside, he rose to his feet and hugged her so fiercely she nearly cried. "Sorry about all that business with Kent," he said, his voice unusually gruff. "Kate advised me to 'butt out of your love life.'"

"A wise woman, Ms. Delany. Maybe you should marry her," Marnie said, lifting her head and swallowing back her tears. She held her father at arm's length and cocked her head to one side. "What d'ya think?"

Victor chuckled as he released her and smoothed his jacket. "Far as I'm concerned, I am married."

"Dad, Mom's been gone a long time."

"I know. And when I die, I'm going to be put into the ground right next to her." He shoved his hands into his pockets and jangled his keys. "Well, have you come to your senses, yet?"

She felt a knot of anxiety tighten her nerves. "About what?"

"About coming back, that's what! I thought you were here to talk business!"

"Yes and no," she hedged. "Come on, Dad, let's sit down." She motioned toward his desk, and Victor, casting her a suspicious glance, settled into his wide leather chair.

"What's this all about?"

"I do want to work for you," she said, "but not as an

employee. This is what I think we should do..." She launched into her speech, explained about her new business, how she wanted to freelance, and how she hoped to develop her own set of clients. *And become publicist for the Hotel Drake?* she thought guiltily.

As she spoke, rapidly at first, her father said nothing, just tented his hands under his chin and, while his expression turned dark, stared at her over his fingertips.

When she finally finished, his lips were pursed tightly, and his nostrils had flared. With worried blue eyes, he continued staring at her, and the clock mounted on one wall struck three.

Marnie's insides twisted. She couldn't stand the suspense. "Well?"

He hesitated, but only slightly, and Marnie's heart sank. "The answer is no."

"No?" All her soaring hopes nose-dived back to earth and crashed on the stones of cold reality. What had she expected? She was, after all, still dealing with Victor Montgomery.

"You either work for me or you don't. Period."

"But, Dad—"

He shook his head. "I'll not be used, and I won't allow this corporation to be a springboard for you. This company has been good to you, and so have I. I'm willing to pay you top dollar to work for me as an executive, but I'm not going to subsidize your talent so that you can go out and work for the competition."

"I'm only working for myself. Like you."

"Bull." His fist crashed onto the desk, jarring his humidor and photographs. "Unless I miss my guess, this has something to do with Drake, doesn't it?"

"Adam's not involved—"

"Like hell!" Victor's face suffused with color. "That

miserable bastard. First the company, then you. What's the man got against me?"

"Maybe he doesn't like the way you convicted him without a trial," she said sharply, surprised at her quick defense of a man she, herself, didn't completely trust.

"So now you're on his side. When he practically kidnapped you and God only knows what else?"

"He didn't kidnap me, Dad. If anything, I took him where he didn't want to go. And as for sides, I'm not on his or your—"

Her father made a dismissive sound just as Kate knocked and poked her head into the office. "Mr. Simms would like to see you. He asked that I interrupt."

"Not now," Victor snapped, but Kent had already brushed past Kate and strode into the office.

"You're back?" Kent asked, his handsome face breaking into a smile of relief.

Marnie had to grit her teeth to be civil to him. "It doesn't look that way."

Kent stared from Marnie to Victor and back again. "But you're here and..." He gestured toward her briefcase and she noticed him staring at her clothes—the neat black suit and royal blue silk blouse.

"I'm here on business, yes," Marnie replied, lifting her chin, "but your boss isn't interested."

"Victor?" Kent asked.

Victor grumbled as he reached for his pipe and humidor. "She's here because of Drake."

"No, Dad. This is *my* business."

"Humph." He unscrewed the lid of the humidor and filled his pipe with his favorite blend of tobacco.

"Drake?" Kent repeated. "What's he got to do with this?"

"Nothing!" Marnie insisted.

"Everything. He's behind this, you know." Victor struck a match and puffed furiously as he tried to light his pipe.

The flame burned his fingers, and he cursed around the stem of his pipe, waving the match out before lighting another. "He's concocted some harebrained scheme about Marnie going out on her own, starting her own publicity business, for crying out loud, and then holding this company up for ransom while working for my competitors! Well, I won't have it!" He shook out his match.

Marnie climbed to her feet and leaned over her father's desk. Her temper was slowly getting the better of her. "You haven't even heard me out," she said, ignoring Kent. "You have no idea what I'd charge. Hiring me freelance would be cheaper than paying me all those employee benefits and taxes you keep complaining about."

"Hey—slow down. You want to work here?" Kent inquired, his gaze as skeptical as her father's.

"On my terms."

"Out of the question." Victor tried to hand her back her proposal, but she reached for her briefcase, snapped it closed and turned her back on the neatly typed pages in her father's fingers.

"Read it, Dad. You might find it interesting." She crossed to the door, and Kent, with a high-sign to Victor, followed her past Kate's desk and down the hall.

"Let me talk to him for you," he suggested, once they were out of Kate's earshot.

"No, thanks. I can speak for myself." Kent was a good reason to be glad she didn't have to work with Montgomery Inns. She wasn't sure she could stand being around him.

"I know, but I think we could work something out." When she didn't reply and kept marching toward the elevators, Kent grabbed her arm and tried to twirl her around. "Marnie, if you'll just listen—"

"Let go of me!" She yanked her arm back as the doors of the elevator opened. Why had she come here? She'd known how her father would react. Now she had to deal with Kent! Shooting him a withering glare, she climbed into the waiting elevator and pressed the button for the lobby. Kent slid between the closing doors.

She was trapped alone with Kent. Damn Adam Drake and his stupid ideas! She should've known this would blow up in her face. She stood in one corner of the car, watching as the lights to the floors flickered on and off. Fourteen...thirteen...twelve...

"Marnie," Kent said softly.

Eleven...ten...

"I want you back."

She uttered a sound of disbelief. "No." Nine...

"I want to see you again."

"It's over, Kent." Eight...seven... Come on, come on, elevator, she thought, wishing it would land in the lobby or some other soul would stop its downward descent and climb on board.

"It doesn't have to be."

She held her silence and heard him swear softly before he slammed his palm on the "stop" button. The elevator jerked to a halt somewhere between the fourth and third floors. Her feet nearly slipped out from under her, and her briefcase banged against the walls of the car. "What are you doing?" she nearly screamed.

"I'm going to talk, damn it, and you're going to listen!"

"No way!" She reached behind him, trying to press the control panel, but he caught her wrist and shoved her back against the wooden panels of the elevator car. "Are you out of your mind?" she whispered, shocked at his nerve. Who did he think he was? "Let go of me!"

"You're the one who should come to your senses."

"About what?"

"Us, Marnie. We could be good together."

"Oh, *pleeease*." She couldn't believe he still thought

she cared. What an incredible ego! She pulled hard on her arm, but he didn't release her. "Let go of me, Kent," she warned, wondering if she should scream or kick. Screaming would attract attention—probably the wrong kind—and kicking him might make him all the more violent.

"I mean it," he persisted, his face close to hers. "We've got so much going for us already. Your dad approves of me, he bought us the boat—"

"A big mistake. We've got nothing, Kent. Release me immediately and I won't cause a scene."

He didn't hear her, but rambled on. "I'm sorry for Dolores and for talking out of turn to the press. I made some mistakes, and don't you think I've paid for them?" For a second a glimmer of intense pain surfaced in his hazel eyes.

She didn't buy it.

"Come on, Marnie. Why don't you and I take the boat for a cruise, try to patch things up?"

"I don't want to hear this, Kent," she said, her voice edged in steel as she glared at him. Motioning toward the control panel with her briefcase, she said, "You've had your little drama, now take your hands off me and let's get going. I have another appointment."

"With whom?"

"It doesn't matter."

"Drake?" Kent demanded, and his fingers tightened around her wrist, pinching her skin. Her stomach roiled.

"Stop it—"

"He doesn't care for you, you know. You saw that up on the island." Kent's face was so close to hers she could see the beads of sweat on his upper lip. "He's using you, Marnie. To get back at your father, or me, or whoever else he thinks hurt him. He doesn't care for you and he never will."

He voiced all her own insecurities, but she managed to

lift her chin a fraction and stare into his eyes. "Let me go, you bastard. Or I'll call security."

Kent sneered, and his breath was hot against her face. For the first time since entering the car with him she felt real fear. "You think he loves you, don't you? Oh, God, Marnie, you're such a fool." He laughed coldly before his lips crashed down on hers with a possessive force that repelled her. Her stomach roiled again, and she struggled, pushing against his shoulders and trying to kick him in the shins. But he sidestepped her blow and kissed her all the harder, groaning low in his throat and pinning her hard against the elevator wall. His mouth ground down on hers with a savagery that scared her to death. She stopped struggling, went absolutely rigid in his arms.

He tried to turn her on. His hands moved against her back, his lips played across hers, but she remained stiff and unresponsive as a statue, knowing instinctively that if she fought him, he'd misconstrue her struggle for passion. When he lifted his head for a second, she moved quickly, biting his lip, then lunging past him and hitting the control panel with both hands.

He yipped. The car jolted, nearly toppling them both before resuming its downward flight.

"Don't you *ever* touch me again," she warned furiously, brandishing her briefcase as if she'd hit him with it. "If you ever, *ever* lay so much as one finger on me, I'll have you up on charges so fast your head will spin."

Blood surfaced at the corner of his mouth, but she didn't feel a shred of remorse. He reached into his pocket for his handkerchief and dabbed at the corner of his mouth. "You're making a big mistake," he said, his eyes narrowing as he attended his wound.

"Not as big as the one I made when I got engaged to you."

His face twisted as if he really were in pain. He blinked

hard, and his voice cracked when he whispered, "I love you, Marnie," but he didn't try to reach for her again.

"No, Kent," she replied as the elevator hit ground level. "You love yourself. And my father's money. And the boat. Nothing else really matters to you." She turned and left him, pretending she didn't hear when he called after her.

"That boat is half mine! I've still got my things, *my* things on board," he yelled.

Marnie didn't bother turning around. She crossed the tiled foyer of the hotel, walked through a revolving door and took big gulps of rain-washed air. She was shaking all over and she thought she might throw up at the thought of Kent's hands on her. She went to the nearest phone booth and dialed Adam's number. If only she could see him, touch him…but that was crazy. She was lucky to be rid of Kent; she couldn't rush things with Adam. She wasn't even sure that she wanted Adam as part of her life.

But he already was.

With that disturbing thought, she hung up the unanswered phone, walked back into the building and ran down the stairs to the parking lot.

IT TOOK ANOTHER WEEK for Victor to call. In that time Marnie hadn't seen much of Adam, but that was her choice. No men. No complications. "And no fun," Donna informed her when she heard about Marnie's philosophy. "You know what they say about all work and no play."

"'They,' whoever they are, could be wrong," Marnie replied.

She and Donna had just finished lunch—take-out Chinese food—and Donna was getting ready for an afternoon of typing late tax returns for the accountant by touching up her fingernails with a coat of raspberry-ice polish. Why Donna polished her nails before typing was a mystery to

Marnie, but she didn't complain because Donna's work was flawless and they were fast becoming friends.

"Who are these guys anyway?" Donna said, motioning with her head toward a stack of phone messages in Marnie's mail slot. "Victor, Kent, Adam and some guy named Ryan Barns. They never leave you alone."

Marnie grinned impishly, and she threw back her head. "They're all my lovers," she teased, glancing at Donna from the corners of her slitted eyes.

"Sure. The career woman who wants no complications." Donna's plucked brows raised expectantly. "Tell me another one."

"I thought you knew that Victor's my father."

"I'd guessed that much," Donna admitted.

"And Kent—he works for Dad." She purposely left out the fact that they had once been engaged. It was over. No reason to bring up the sorry past.

"He sounds desperate." Her gray eyes appraised Marnie. "And he keeps talking about some boat. Your boat?"

"Believe me, it's a long and boring story," Marnie said, stuffing her empty chow mein carton into a white sack.

"What about Adam Drake?" Donna asked, blowing on her nails.

Good question. What about Adam? She couldn't spend a waking hour without thinking about him. "Adam used to work for my father. Maybe you read about him. It was in all the papers a year ago."

"A year ago I was in Santa Barbara."

"Another long and boring story," Marnie assured her as she tossed the sack into the trash. "Let's just say he and my dad are mortal enemies."

"Sounds interesting. Besides, I don't think anything about *that* man could be boring. He stopped by yesterday."

"He did?" Marnie was flabbergasted.

Donna read the expression on her face and frowned. "You know, I should've told you, but you were gone at the time and he said it wasn't important, that he'd come back in a few days and then I got busy with tax reports for Miles and—"

"It's all right," Marnie assured her, though she wasn't up to another meeting with Adam. Not yet. She needed more time for her emotions to settle. If that were possible.

"If he shows up again, what should I tell him?"

"That I'm busy...well, no," she retracted. She couldn't avoid him forever, and she really didn't want to. Sooner or later she'd have to confront him as well as her own feelings. "Tell him I'd be glad to see him," Marnie said against her better judgment. There was a part of her that couldn't resist Adam Drake, no matter how many times she told herself that being with him was only inviting disaster.

Two hours later, her father called. "I've reconsidered," he said, and Marnie, sitting precariously on the corner of her desk, nearly fell over. Victor Montgomery wasn't known for changing his mind once he'd taken a stand.

"And?" she said.

"I spoke to several people on the board who want to give you a chance, and it goes without saying that Kent is in your corner. He tells me I'm a fool to let pride stand in my way."

"I don't know what to say." Instantly, Marnie's defenses were up.

"You don't have to say anything. Just show up at the meeting next Monday morning, 9:00 a.m. sharp and lay out your proposal. I want Simms, Byers, Anderson and Finelli to see what you've come up with. Then I'll let you know."

"Fair enough, Dad," she said, trying to keep the smile from her voice. Maybe doing business with Montgomery Inns would work out after all. This might just be the first step to reconciling with her father. She and Victor were the only members of the Montgomery family. And she never doubted that her father loved her; he was just misguided in his attempt to control her life. Finally it looked as if he was about to treat her as an independent woman.

"But I think we should be clear on one point," Victor said, his voice taking on that old familiar ring of authority.

Here it comes—the bomb. "What's that?"

"Adam Drake."

Her heart nearly stopped. "What about him?"

"I never want to hear his name mentioned again."

"Don't you think you're being a little theatrical?" Marnie asked. "He was your employee once. His name is bound to come up."

"Not from you."

"I can't promise that, Dad. But I'll try," she conceded.

"Fair enough. I miss you, Marnie. We all do."

"And I miss you, Dad." She hung up feeling better than she had in weeks. Most of her anger had cooled, and she was ready to deal with him as businesswoman to businessman. She wasn't sure just how she would handle the father/daughter relationship yet, but she was buoyed that Victor had taken the first step toward mending fences.

"One step at a time," she told herself firmly.

THE AFTERNOON SUN was pale behind a hazy layer of clouds. The smells of diesel and dead fish floated on the air and in the water. Adam shoved his sunglasses onto his head and lifted his binoculars, focusing on *Elmer's Folly,* a charter fishing boat churning toward the docks of Ilwaco with Gerald Henderson on board.

It had taken him nearly a week to track down Henderson, who had fled Seattle the day after Adam crashed the party at the Puget West. The way Adam figured it, Gerald had read about Adam being thrown out of the hotel in the *Seattle Observer,* realized there was going to be trouble and decided to disappear for a while.

Unfortunately for Henderson, Adam knew about his sister's beach cabin in Longview and also knew that Henderson enjoyed deep-sea fishing and usually reserved space on the same charter boat which moored in Ilwaco, a small fishing village located on the Washington shore of the mouth of the Columbia River. *Elmer's Folly* chugged into the small marina, located not far from the fish-processing plant, where you could buy anything from clams to salmon or have your trophy gutted, skinned and canned or smoked, depending upon your preference.

Adam spied Henderson on board with eight other men. Good.

Lowering his binoculars, content to wait until all the fishermen disembarked, he leaned against the sun-bleached rail and shoved his sunglasses onto the bridge of his nose.

Gerald Henderson took his time about getting off the boat, but finally he appeared on the dock, wearing worn jeans, flannel shirt, jacket and a hat decorated with fishing lures and hooks. He hauled a couple of fishing poles and a tackle box with him.

"Any luck?" Adam asked, once he'd closed the distance between himself and Henderson. He'd waited around most of the afternoon and now he wanted answers.

"Nah, not even a nibble," Henderson replied before looking up and realizing Adam wasn't just another interested fisherman asking about the salmon run. Henderson's face fell. "What're you doing here?"

"Waiting for you."

"Why? I've already told you everything I know."

"Have you?" Adam surveyed the smaller man. Henderson was nervous, glancing over his shoulder and gnawing at his lip.

"I just want to know how deeply Simms was involved in the embezzling mess."

"Kent?" Henderson shrugged. "We went over this, Drake. I'm not sure who was involved. It could've been you."

"But it wasn't."

"Probably not," Henderson admitted, reaching into the inside pocket of his jacket for a crumpled pack of cigarettes. "Kate and I found the discrepancies on the books and brought them to Kent's attention. He took it from there. But he seemed as surprised as I was that there was something wrong." He tried to shake out a single cigarette, but three or four dropped onto the dock. Swearing, Henderson bent over and picked them up.

"Maybe Kent was just surprised that you figured it out," Adam offered.

Henderson stuck one cigarette between his lips and shoved the others back in the pack. "Maybe." He began walking again, toward the sandy parking lot.

"And you were paid to keep your mouth shut."

"I wasn't paid a dime." He cupped his cigarette against the wind and clicked his lighter to the tip.

"Then how're you surviving?"

"Disability."

"What?"

"And my pension. You should've stayed on with the company a few more years. Great benefits."

"If you say so."

"I do." Henderson took a deep drag on his cigarette. "Look, Drake, I don't know why you think I'll say something more than you don't already know, but I won't. You know everything I do, so why don't you just bug off?" With that he stalked across the lot to a dusty red pickup and threw his fishing gear behind the seat back.

Adam was right on his heels. "There's more that you're not telling me."

Henderson tossed his cigarette into the gravel where the butt burned slowly, a curling thread of smoke spiraling into the clear air. "I don't *know* anything. I just have hunches."

"What are they?"

"Nothing that I can prove." He started to climb into the cab of the pickup, but Adam grabbed his arm and spun him around, slamming him up against the back fender.

"I'll do the proving," he said, shoving his face next to Henderson's and seeing a drip of perspiration as it slid from beneath the smaller man's hatband. "Who agreed to pay your disability?"

Henderson gulped. "The old man himself."

"Montgomery?"

"Yeah."

Adam didn't let go of Henderson's lapels. "And who told you that you'd be paid?"

"My boss. Fred."

"Fred Ainger?"

"Right."

Adam's hard gaze pinned Henderson to the fender. Henderson was shaking by this time, sweat running down his neck in tiny streams. "You think he was involved?"

"I told you, man, I *don't* know." Henderson's gaze slid away, and he smoothed the front of his jacket. "Fred has money problems—I don't know how serious."

"What kind of money problems?"

Chewing on a corner of his lip, Henderson said, "Fred's still paying off Hannah for their divorce—she took half of everything they owned and even got part of his pension, I think. Good old community property." Gerald lifted his hat and wiped the sweat from his brow. "And now he's got Bernice for a wife. She's the daughter of some bigwig doctor back east. Used to expensive things. Fred tries to get them for her. And she's hell-on-wheels with a credit card. Seems to think credit means free money."

Bernice Ainger was thirty years younger than Fred. He'd met her at a convention, become obsessed with her and divorced Hannah to marry the younger woman. He'd been in his early fifties at the time and he'd been paying for that mistake ever since. So how did Fred connect with Simms?

"Funny," Adam drawled, though he wasn't the least in the mood for humor, "but every time I'm around Simms, he seems nervous—like he knows more than he's telling. The thing is, I don't believe that he'd intentionally get caught up in anything that might ruin his career."

"Sometimes people do things on impulse."

"No, this was planned for a long time. Otherwise the money would've been recovered."

Gerald's gaze shifted again, and Adam got the feeling he was wrestling with his conscience. For that, Adam respected him. Ratting on his friends didn't come easy to Henderson. Or else he was just trying to save his own neck.

"I heard something once," Henderson admitted, as the scent of dead fish wafted across the parking lot.

"What?"

"It was Simms, I'm sure it was, though he didn't know that I was on the other side of the partition in the accounting room. I'd been in the vault, and when I came out I didn't say anything. Simms was on the other side of that partition that separated Fred's office from mine...you know the one I mean."

Adam nodded, his heartbeat accelerating slightly. Now, finally, he was getting somewhere.

"Well, anyway, Simms was angry, really angry, telling someone off, but I didn't see who it was. They were walking out the door."

Adam could hardly believe his good luck. For the first time he was learning something new, that Simms *was* directly involved, but that he had an accomplice. Adam had to force himself not to shake every detail out of Henderson.

"Who was in Fred's office when you went into the vault?"

"No one."

"Not Fred?"

"Nope, he'd gone home for the day. Saw him leave myself."

"And Kent?"

Henderson shook his head slowly. "He wasn't there either, but I was in the vault for a good five or ten minutes. And when I came out, Simms and whoever he was talking to were on their way out."

"And you don't think Fred came back? Couldn't he have returned to the office for something he'd forgotten, his keys or wallet or something?"

Henderson took off his hat and slapped it against his thigh. A ring of sweat curled his thin sandy hair. "I don't think so. But I don't know."

"So you think Kent, with or without Fred's help, took some of the Puget West funds?"

"I can't say. I don't know much about Simms. He's kind of a pretty boy, and I doubt he'd do anything to jeopardize his job. After all, he's engaged to the boss man's daughter."

"*Was* engaged," Adam said quickly, irritated that anyone, even Gerald Henderson, who probably had been out of touch with the gossip at Montgomery Inns for a while, would think that Marnie and Kent were still an item. "Past tense."

Henderson stuck out his lower lip and shrugged. "Well, then, who knows. He might have got himself into a heap of debt somehow. That's what happened to Fred. He's hurtin' for cash." He hesitated a second, but then, like so many men when they can finally get something off their chest, Henderson added, "This might sound strange, but...well, I got the feeling that Simms was talking to a woman—not by what he said, but by the scent in the room. You know, like some kind of expensive perfume."

Adam's heart nearly stopped. "Would you recognize it again?"

"I..." Henderson shrugged, then shook his head. "Probably not."

"But who do you *think* it was?" Henderson's intuition might naturally come up with the right suspect.

"I said I don't know. There's got to be seventy-five women working in that building. Simms was probably on a first name basis with half of 'em. I couldn't begin to guess."

"Linda Kirk works in accounting," Adam ventured, turning his thoughts away from a dark possibility.

"But she was home sick that day. In fact she was gone for over a week with the flu."

Marnie. She'd been going out with Simms at the time... But she had no reason to embezzle funds. Just because Marnie was involved with Simms wasn't any reason to think that she would steal from her own father...no, that line of thinking was preposterous.

Henderson was obviously thinking he'd said too much. His face was flushed; his eyes showed a hint of panic. "Look, Drake, that's all I know. Really."

This time Adam believed him and stepped away from the truck.

Climbing quickly into the cab, Henderson flicked on the ignition. The engine sparked, died, then caught with a roar and a plume of foul-smelling exhaust. Above the rumble of the engine Henderson said, "Fred's not such a bad guy, you know. Just got himself into a little trouble. And Simms—hell, what can you say about that guy?"

"And the woman?"

"*If* there was one. I'm not sure…" He rammed the truck into first, pulled the door closed and took off, spraying gravel and dust behind him.

Adam didn't know if Henderson's information had helped him or not. All along he'd thought Kent Simms was responsible for framing him and that he'd done it alone. Had he been wrong? Was Ainger or a mystery woman involved? Or was Henderson just blowing smoke? Trying to save his own tail?

Adam didn't think so. The man was terrified that he'd slipped up by spilling his guts. So now, he had to try to locate a woman…a woman involved with Kent. But *not* Marnie!

Angrily Adam stomped out Henderson's still-smoldering cigarette and watched as Gerald's pickup wound down the dusty road. Without any answers, he walked across the gritty parking lot and slid into the interior of his rig. Spinning the steering wheel, he headed north to Seattle.

Next stop: Marnie's place. She'd been avoiding him for too long. She'd had enough time to think things through. Besides, he needed her to help him get to the bottom of this.

And you want her. Scowling, he twisted on the radio, hoping to drown out the voice in his head. A jazzy rendition of an old Temptations song came on the air. Yes, he wanted Marnie. Damn it to hell, he'd wanted her from the second he'd seen her trying to helm that boat in the middle of the storm. And wanting her was all right. Making love to her was okay. But falling in love with her could never happen.

Falling in love? Now, why the hell did he think of that?

CHAPTER TEN

AS SHE WALKED OUT of the boardroom, Marnie couldn't believe her good luck! After all his blustering and blowing about company loyalty, Victor had actually signed a contract with her. Of course he'd tried to talk her into coming back to the company and she'd declined. And of course Kent had tried to maneuver her into a quiet corner to convince her that they should get back together.

Now Kent tagged after her. As if their last encounter hadn't been violent and revolting. "Let's just take a boat ride Saturday," Kent suggested with that same all-American smile Marnie had once been dazzled by. "We can try and work things out while we're sailing the *Marnie Lee* together. Come on, Marnie, what d'ya say?"

The man didn't understand the word "no." She didn't bother answering, just continued down the hallway from the boardroom toward her father's office.

"You're still mad at me, aren't you?" Kent insisted, touching her lightly on the arm.

"Mad doesn't begin to describe how I feel," she said furiously, jerking away from him, her shoulder banging against the wall.

"You know, the boat's half mine."

"I'll send you a check."

"But the *Marnie Lee* was a gift. You can't just buy me out. I won't sell."

"I don't think you'll have much of a choice, unless you want to buy my half."

"I don't have that kind of money!"

"Then you'll have to borrow it, or we're at an impasse." She started down the hall again.

Kent swore under his breath as he raced to catch up with her.

"This has gone far enough, Marnie. You've had your chance at being independent. Hell, you've even had your little fling with Drake. But now I'm tired of playing your little games and—"

"How many times do I have to say it?" she declared vehemently. "It's over!"

"Why? You seeing someone else?"

"None of your business."

"Drake?"

"Leave me alone." But he grabbed her arm, spinning her around. She braced herself for the same kind of assault as in the elevator. "Touch me and I'll scream or worse," she warned, and he must've believed her for he dropped his hand to his side and didn't blow up as she'd expected. Instead he became deadly calm, his mouth tightening into a thin line of fury, his hazel eyes frigid as he stared at her. A chill slid down her spine.

"There you are!" Victor, who had been delayed by one of the architects, flagged her down. Ignoring Kent, he strode to Marnie and patted her on the back. "Nice presentation," he said, finally noticing his executive vice president. "Went well, didn't you think, Kent? Now, Marnie, if this doesn't work out, you can always have your old job back."

"If this doesn't work out, we're both in real trouble," she joked back.

Kent didn't crack a smile.

"Come on, drinks are on me," her father insisted. "We'll celebrate our new partnership."

Marnie's stomach did a peculiar flip at the mention

of partnership, but she indulged her father. They sipped champagne and nibbled on hors d'oeuvres at a French restaurant with a view of Elliott Bay, and Victor wasn't satisfied until the three of them had toasted their new alliance.

The fact that Kent had come along as well made Marnie uncomfortable, but she suffered through it because of Victor. She loved her father, and finally he'd really tried to give her the freedom she so desperately needed.

Two hours later, Victor drove her back to the parking lot where she'd left her car.

"It was like old home week with you here today," he said, a hint of nostalgia in his voice.

"Dad, I've only been gone a little while."

"Seems like forever. Oh, well, we'll just look to the future, right?"

"Right."

He opened the door of her Ford and chuckled. "This isn't your BMW, but I guess it's better than the twenty-year-old Volkswagen I thought you'd purchase."

"It'll have to do. Looks like I'll have to buy out Kent's half of the *Marnie Lee*."

"Don't be too hasty, Marnie."

"Or else he has to buy me out," she said, lacing her fingers through her father's. "I think Kent finally understands that I don't love him, probably never did, and that I'll never marry him. Now, if I could just convince you..."

"Ahh, Marnie," her father said, smiling sadly. "I was only thinking of you, you know." As she slid into the driver's seat, he leaned over and kissed her cheek. "It's good to have you as part of the team."

"Thanks, Dad."

She started the ignition, but Victor hesitated before closing the door. "I don't suppose you've heard anything from Drake, have you?"

"I thought you didn't want his name mentioned."

"I don't."

"Well, since you brought up the subject, you may as well know. I will be seeing him," Marnie said, deciding that she had to be honest with her father from the beginning. Not that it was any of his business, but she wanted to start off on the right foot.

Her father's face drooped. "I was afraid of that."

"Trust me, Dad. I'm a big girl now."

Glancing over the hood of the car, Victor sighed. "Whatever you do, Marnie, just don't let that bastard hurt you." He slammed the door shut, and as Marnie backed out of her parking space, she caught a glimpse of him in the rearview mirror. He looked older and paler than he had earlier, as if all his vigor had been drained by the mere mention of Adam's name.

She steered the car out of the lot and joined the thread of late-afternoon traffic clogging the city streets. Mist seemed to rise like ghosts from the streets as fog settled over the bay and crept steadily up the steep hills of Seattle.

Pleased that she finally had a paying client, she nevertheless felt a little niggle of guilt. Just how far away from Victor's influence had she really gotten? And was she making her own decisions or allowing Adam to manipulate her? Seeking Montgomery Inns for a client had been Adam's idea. Maybe, like the fog settling against the hillside, she was clinging to the past.

Refusing to be glum, she flipped on the radio and hummed along to soft rock as she followed the line of taillights leading out of the heart of the city. Pulling into the reserved carport of her apartment unit, she switched off the engine, her thoughts turning once more to Adam and her father. Oil and water. Suspect and victim. Her lover and her next of kin.

Raincoat tucked under her arm, she hurried up the exterior stairs to her second-story unit.

Adam was waiting for her.

She saw him seated against the wall, arms folded over his chest, and she nearly dropped through the floor. He glanced up at her. A warm grin stretched slowly across his face, and his eyes seemed a shade darker with the coming night. His black hair gleamed an inky blue in the glow from the security lights, and Marnie's heart leaped at the sight of him.

"'Bout time you showed up," he drawled, rising to stand next to her as she unlocked the door.

"I wasn't expecting company." She slid a glance his way, and her pulse skyrocketed at the sight of his angular jaw and sensual lower lip. "But that's how you operate, isn't it? Always showing up where you're not expected."

"Keeps people off guard."

"Keeps you in trouble." She shoved the door open. "Come on inside. You'll talk your way in anyway. And this way maybe we can keep from being the gossip of Pine Terrace Apartments." Inviting him inside wasn't the greatest idea she'd ever come up with, but she felt like celebrating and the fact that he was here, sitting in the dark, waiting for her, touched a very feminine and romantic side of her nature.

He followed her inside. She heard his footsteps, and her heart thrilled at the familiar sound. "I thought I'd take you out to dinner."

"A bona fide date?" she mocked, glimpsing him over her shoulder.

His grin slashed white against his dark jaw. "That surprises you?"

"More like knocks me off my feet."

"Well, true, our relationship has hardly been flowers, wine, poetry—"

"Oh, *pleeease*..." She tossed her raincoat over the back of the couch and turned to face him. Her tongue was loosened by the champagne, and she was in a mood for honesty. "We don't even have a 'relationship,' remember? Just 'sex.' Isn't that what you said?"

He had the decency to frown. "I was oversimplifying."

"Oh." She lifted her brows, silently inviting him to explain himself.

"We're partners."

"Unwilling," Marnie reminded him, but he touched her then, his fingers surrounding her nape as he drew her to him.

"Why do you keep fighting me?" he whispered.

Staring into his intense gold-brown eyes, she hesitated only a second. "It might be because you have a history of lies," she managed, her voice trembling a little. "I have a long memory, Adam, and it seems that you hang around me whenever it's convenient for you. Most of the time I think you're interested in me because I'm Victor Montgomery's daughter."

His eyes searched her face. "It would be easier if I hated you."

"Don't you?"

"What do you think?" he said, his gaze delving deep into hers.

"I wish I knew, Adam."

"Unfortunately, I find you the most fascinating woman I've ever met."

"Unfortunately?"

"I never wanted to care about you, Marnie. Not even a little." His eyes swept her lips, and her stomach knotted at the thought that he might kiss her. "Believe that I never intended to hurt you."

"You couldn't," she lied easily, though her pulse was fluttering wildly. "I don't care enough."

"Good," he replied with a knowing smile that accused her of the lie. "Then you'll go out with me."

Of course she would. Was there any doubt that, if she saw him again, she'd go along with any of his wild schemes? When Adam Drake was around, it seemed as if all of her hard-fought independence disappeared, that she willingly cast away any vestiges of being her own self-reliant woman. "Why not?" she said, "just give me time to change."

"You don't have to. You've dressed perfectly for what I have in mind."

"I hate to ask," she said, but decided that her white dress with a wide leather belt looked professional and tailored, dressy enough for a nice restaurant but a little too sophisticated for corn dogs on the beach.

Adam took her arm and whirled her around, propelling her back down the stairs to his car, some sort of four-wheel-drive rig that looked as if it should be tearing up some winding mountain road rather than racing from red light to red light only to idle in the city.

He threw the truck into gear and drove south, through the hilly streets toward the waterfront. Curling fingers of fog climbed over the water and into the alleys, creating a gauzy mist that seemed opalescent as it shimmered beneath the street lamps. Neon signs winked through the thin veil of fog, and the city seemed to shrink in upon itself.

Adam drove to the waterfront and they dined in a funky old restaurant located on one of the piers. Adam had requested a specific table with a window that offered a panoramic view of the dark waters of the bay. The bowed glass was angled enough that through the rising mist some of the city was visible. The tower of Montgomery Inns, Seattle, with its glass-domed ceiling, rose like a thirty-story cathedral on the shores of the sound.

"You must've hunted all over the city for this view,"

she remarked as the waiter poured white wine into their
glasses.

"Nope. I used to come here often when I worked there."
He hooked a finger toward the corporate headquarters of
Victor's empire. "Remember?"

She didn't bother answering, just sipped her wine as the
waiter concentrated on other diners. They ordered salmon,
clams and crab, drank Riesling wine, and avoided any ref-
erence to Montgomery Inns. Some of Adam's hard edges
seemed to retreat in the flickering light from the sconces
on the wall. Or was it the wine that caused her perception
of him to change? Or maybe the cozy restaurant with its
rough cedar walls and eccentric antiques caused her to be
a little less critical, slightly nostalgic, more forgiving.

"I saw Henderson today," he finally said, after the
waiter had cleared their plates and they were left with
two mugs of Irish coffee.

"And? Did he help you, 'unravel the mystery'?" she
quipped, unable to keep a trace of scorn from her voice.

Adam scoffed, swigged from his cup and swallowed
slowly, his Adam's apple moving sensually in his neck.
Marnie tore her gaze away from his throat, but not before
her stomach tightened a fraction and the shadows of the
darkened restaurant seemed to close around them. She
heard the clink of silver, the rattle of dishes, the soft laughter of other patrons. There was also the sound of soft-rock
music drifting from the bar and the hint of smoke lingering in the air, but she was so aware of Adam that everything else seemed distant and faded.

Adam's gaze touched hers for a heart-stopping second,
and without thinking, she took a swallow of her drink,
then licked a lingering dab of whipped cream from her
lips.

A fire sparked in his eyes, and she cleared her throat.
"You were talking about Henderson?" she prodded, hating

the breathless quality of her voice. If only she could feel cool and sophisticated and completely immune to his earthy sensuality.

"Right. Henderson." He swallowed again, his eyes shifting to the window and the dark night beyond. "Well, Henderson's not as much help as I'd hoped he'd be." He told her about his meeting with the man at Ilwaco, purposely omitting Henderson's hunch about a woman, wanting to wait a few minutes before he dropped that particular bomb.

"He thinks Fred Ainger took the money?" Marnie shook her head. "No way. The man's too loyal."

"But to whom? Victor or Bernice?"

"I don't believe it." She drained her mug.

"You don't believe anyone at Montgomery Inns would steal," he said, then amended, "except maybe for me."

"No," she said slowly, running a finger over the still-warm rim of her empty cup, "I don't think you took the cash."

"Well, someone did."

"I know." She sighed, hating to think about it, wishing the money could just be found—discovered to be only misplaced—and they could all get on with their lives.

She glanced up at him sharply and caught him examining her with such absorbed concentration that her skin prickled. She looked quickly away.

Adam paid the bill and they walked outside, along the wet docks into the deep purple night. The wind teased her hair, and along with the odor of the sea, it carried the very real and masculine scent of Adam Drake.

When he stopped before they reached the car and his fingers laced with hers, her heart began to pump more wildly than she ever thought possible. Beneath the hazy glow of a street lamp, with the vapor swirling around them, he caught her around the waist, lowered his head and kissed her, hard and fast, his lips seeking hers with such hunger that she felt dizzy.

Lord, why was it always this way with him? What was it about him that literally took her breath away? She felt the fog clinging to her hair and skin, tasted the coffee and whiskey still clinging to his lips, heard the thunder of blood rushing through her ears.

"Come home with me, Marnie," he whispered against her ear.

She trembled, trying to find the strength to say no. "I don't think I can."

"Sure you can."

"This is dangerous, Adam."

"Why?"

She gathered all her courage and tried to break free of his restraining embrace. "I—I can't be involved with a man just for sex. There has to be more."

"Moonlight and roses? Champagne and promises?" he asked, his eyes darkening with the night. "Diamonds and gold bands?"

"Trust and love," she said, her voice quavering. "That's hard to have when your entire relationship—excuse me, *non*-relationship—is centered around one person using another," she said, disentangling herself so that she could breathe, so that she could think.

His jaw grew hard and she could see from his expression that he was fighting an inner battle. "You know I care about you. Damn it, it wasn't what I wanted, what I'd planned, but I *do* care." He jammed both hands into his pockets. "I can't tell you what you want to hear. I can't make you promises, Marnie. And I can't pretend to be something I'm not. You just have to accept me for what I am."

"And what's that?" she asked.

His lips twitched. "A man who can't seem to keep his hands off you."

Her heart melted and she wanted to fling herself back into his arms, but she resisted, knowing that loving him would only cause more heartache. All of a sudden loving him seemed so easy. Or was it a lie—was she confusing love with sexual desire? She'd thought she had once loved Kent, but that had been a fantasy and her feelings for Kent hadn't scratched the surface of her emotions for this man. As for Adam, at least he wasn't pretending to feel undying passion and love for her. But was his brutal honesty about his very reserved feelings any better?

She sucked in her breath and gathered her courage before she poured out her heart. "I'm too old-fashioned for quick affairs or one-night stands or any of the above," she said, smiling faintly at this ridiculous maidenly retreat after their nights of passion. But she couldn't lie.

"You want me to marry you?"

The question echoed off the bay and through her heart. "No!"

His dark brow arched insolently, silently accusing her of lying through her teeth.

"I—I just need more of a commitment than that I'll wake up with you in the morning and then, maybe, never see you again. Call me old-fashioned, but that's the way I feel."

He sighed, frustrated. "I don't think it's possible to consider you a one-night stand or a quick affair, Marnie. But I'm in no position to promise you a future that just doesn't exist—and that's because of your father. I don't even know what my future will be. I can't promise you anything. Come on." Without waiting for a response, he grabbed her hand and pulled her across the street to his rig.

They drove in tense silence back to her apartment. He flicked the radio on, and tunes from the "fabulous

fifties, sensational sixties and spectacular seventies" filtered through the interior between blasts of some inane
radio announcer trying to be a comedian. Marnie was in
no mood for jokes.

She was in no mood for arguing with Adam.

She rested her head against the passenger window and
caught a glimpse of Adam, his features drawn, his mouth
tight as he drove. To avoid an issue that had no answers,
she changed the course of the conversation. "Tell me more
about Henderson."

Adam's expression changed as he switched mental
gears. "Henderson. Boy there's one nervous guy. He really
couldn't confirm that Fred Ainger was part of the setup."

She turned to face him. "I thought you were convinced
that he was the man."

"Just one suspect. But there may be others." He down-
shifted, rounded a corner and glanced at her from the
corner of his eye. "Henderson overheard an argument,
well, from the sounds of it, more like a dressing down,
right after the embezzling. Simms was really telling someone off, but Henderson, who had just come out of the
accounting-room vault and was on the other side of the
partition, couldn't see who it was."

"He doesn't have an idea?"

"He thinks it might be a woman."

"A woman? Why?" Marnie asked, her mind spinning
with the names of a dozen women who worked at the hotel
and had access to the accounting records. "Linda Kirk?"
she said, thinking of the petite middle-aged woman with
a quick smile and sharp mind. "I don't believe it!"

"Neither does Henderson. Linda was out sick that week."
Adam told her about Henderson's hunch and the perfume.

"That's not much to go on," she said when Adam finished. "Just because Kent was arguing with someone in

the accounting department isn't any big news. At least I don't think it's enough to indict anyone."

Adam flinched at her sarcasm.

"Sorry. Sore subject," she said.

"You have any idea who would be involved with Simms?"

"Besides me?" she said smartly, then sighed and ran her fingers through her hair. She thought about Dolores Tate. And Stephanie Bond. And Lila Montague, all women whom Kent had dated. "I'm afraid the list is miles long."

"Good thing I'm so patient," he replied, smothering a cynical smile, and Marnie almost laughed.

"Right."

"Just think about it."

"I will," she promised as he stopped at a red light.

When the light changed, he stepped hard on the throttle, sped through the intersection and turned into the small drive leading to her apartment building.

He pulled into a vacant space, threw the rig into park, clicked off the headlights and turned off the ignition before turning all his attention in her direction. The cab of the truck seemed suddenly intimate. Mist drizzled down the windshield and the warmth of their bodies was beginning to cloud the glass. Adam's presence seemed to fill the interior, and she knew that she had to escape before she made the same mistake with him that she had in the past.

Her voice was scarcely a whisper. "Thanks for dinner. I—"

"I want to come up."

Her throat went dry. "You never give up, do you? You just keep pushing and pushing and never stop."

"When something's important, I go for it."

She knew he wasn't speaking of her, couldn't be. He'd made that perfectly clear. "And when something's dangerous, I leave it alone," she said. "You know the old saying 'once burned, twice shy'?"

"You don't have to be shy with me." He touched her hand, and she felt a shiver of delight. "As for that business about the danger, I don't believe it."

"Well, you're wrong!" she argued, as his fingers wrapped over hers and she felt the pads of his fingertips, warm and enticing against the underside of her arm. *Think, Marnie, think!* But she didn't pull her arm away. "Look, Adam, I don't mountain climb, or play with rattlesnakes, or run into burning buildings."

"But you do sail a boat in the middle of a storm, you do stand up to one of the most intimidating men in the state—"

"Meaning you?"

"Meaning your father. And you are willing to take a few risks, if you feel strongly about something."

She blushed in the deep interior and reached for the door handle, pulling up on the lever and getting nowhere. Adam had electronically locked the door by means of some sort of child-protection device and she was trapped inside the rig with him.

"You barely knew me and you stood up to your father, as well as the board, in my defense." With his left hand, he withdrew the keys from the ignition, and the only sound inside the four-wheel-drive vehicle was the soft jangle of metal. "You were willing to take a risk then."

"That was before I knew that you'd use me or anyone else to get what you want."

"All I want is the truth."

The keys clinked softly—like wind chimes disturbed by a stealthy breeze. "I don't see how I can help you," she said, suddenly aware of a knot in her throat and the restless energy that seemed to radiate from him.

"It's simple really. You've been hired by your father's company, right? As a freelance publicist."

"Yes, but how did you find out?"

"I still have a few friends at Montgomery Inns."

"Spies, you mean," she said, flabbergasted. Hadn't her father always been suspicious of disloyal people within the tight fabric of Montgomery Inns? Marnie had always thought that Victor was jumping at shadows, that his paranoia over the embezzlement was playing tricks in his mind. Apparently she had been wrong.

"No one 'spies' for me." But the look he sent her caused her to shiver.

"Yet." Cold certainly settled in the pit of her stomach.

"Yet."

Oh, God! "But now you're hoping that I'll do your dirty work for you," she guessed, sickened.

"Of course not."

"I won't betray my own father!"

He tugged at her arm, so swiftly she didn't see him move. Dragging her close so that his nose was touching hers, he growled, "Let's get a couple of things straight, Marnie. I'm not asking you to betray anyone or spy on anyone. And I'm not going to put either your personal career or your physical well-being in jeopardy. That's not the way I work. Whether you believe me or not, I don't expect you to plunder the company files, or sabotage the computer system, or be involved in any other corporate espionage b.s."

She gulped, but managed to meet his gaze with her own. "Then what is it you want from me?"

"Nothing," he ground out, then swore loudly and violently. "Or everything. I can't decide which." His gaze burned like molten gold as he glared down at her. "Damn it, Marnie, you've got me so messed up, sometimes I don't know up from sideways. But I do know this much. I have never, *never* wanted a woman the way I want you!"

"And it frightens you," she surmised with sudden clarity.

"It scares the living hell out of me!"

His fingers tangled in the pale strands of her hair, and his lips descended upon hers skillfully. He groaned as he felt her yield and give herself to him. She wound her arms around his neck and, lifting her face from his, managed a tremulous smile. She wanted him as much as he wanted her. If not more. "What're we gonna do about this?" she wondered aloud, breathless.

"Give me twenty minutes, and I'll show you," he vowed, reaching behind him and unlocking the doors.

"That quick?"

His grin turned wicked. "Or two hours. Your choice, Miss Montgomery. Your every wish is my command."

Once inside, he carried her into the bedroom and laid her gently on the bed. Marnie quivered as he kissed her, removing clothing and brushing his lips intimately against her skin.

She was on fire. All the emotions of the last few weeks running rampant through her willing body. Her skin aflame, her breasts aching for his touch, her lips anxious as they melded to his.

He took his time with her, touching her and running his hands and mouth against her skin, teasing her and waiting until she was ready, until she took his hand and pressed it to her breast, until she felt as if the hot, aching vortex within her would be forever empty.

Stripping him of his clothes, she closed her mind to all doubts, opened her eyes and watched as slowly his hard body found hers. She gasped at his entrance, and words of love sprouted to her lips, only to be lost as he began to move and she could no longer control her tongue or voice.

"Oh, Marnie," he whispered against her ear, his skin slick with sweat. "Sweet, sweet Marnie."

CHAPTER ELEVEN

"IT'S GOOD TO HAVE you back, even if it's only temporary."
Kate Delany set a cup of coffee on the corner of Marnie's
desk, the desk she'd occupied while she still worked full-
time for the firm, in the office that she'd come to look
upon as a prison.

"Thanks. I need this." She picked up the mug, let the
steam drift toward her nostrils and sighed. "You know, I
never thought I'd admit it, but it's good to be back." Despite her bid for independence, Marnie surprised herself
by missing some of the people she'd worked with. She'd
also had trouble adjusting to the slower pace of her own
office. Now, working at Montgomery Inns, she discovered she enjoyed the bustle and energy of a hotel swarm-
ing with hundreds of guests and employees.

Cradling her own cup of coffee, Kate dropped into
one of the chairs near the desk. "So how's it going for
Montgomery Public Relations? Any new accounts?" She
crossed one slim leg over the other.

"A couple. But this one—" she tapped the eraser end
of her pencil on a press release she was working on for
Montgomery Inns "—takes up most of my time."

"Your father will be pleased." Kate's dark eyes twinkled. "He's never gotten over the fact that you walked out
on him."

Marnie shifted uncomfortably in her chair. She didn't
expect a reprimand, not even a gentle one, from Kate. "I
only needed a little breathing space."

"I think he understands that now."

"You talked to him about it?" Marnie guessed, sipping the strong, hot coffee.

Kate laughed. "For hours. It takes a long while to convince your father of anything." At that her laughter died, and a cloud appeared in her eyes. Marnie guessed she was thinking of Victor's reluctance to remarry.

Marnie said, "Well, since you championed my cause, maybe I can champion yours."

"I wish *someone* could," Kate admitted, "but I don't think it's possible. Oh, well, no one can say I didn't try." She took a long swallow of coffee and seemed lost in her thoughts—nostalgic thoughts from the expression on her face. "I'd convinced myself after Ben and I divorced that I'd never find anyone else. Not that I was still in love with him or anything like that. Ben was far from perfect, a little boy who never grew up. Didn't like the responsibility of marriage, wasn't ready to support a wife, and wouldn't hear of starting a family." She smiled sadly. "But he was fun. The kind of boy you'd love to date but hate to marry. Anyway, it didn't work out and I came to work here and I met your father and he was everything Ben wasn't. Strong, dependable, steady as a rock. I couldn't believe it when he noticed me, plucked me out of the secretarial pool…" Kate's voice trailed off, and she cleared her throat. Tiny lines of disappointment surrounded her lips. "Well, that was a long time ago."

Marnie hated to see Kate so defeated. "Don't give up on him just yet," she said.

"Never say never, right?" Kate asked, finishing her coffee.

"Right!"

"Okay. So enough of me crying in my beer—or coffee. What about you, Marnie?" Kate asked as she stood. "Why don't you give Kent a second chance?"

Another little push from Kate. Marnie was surprised. "I'm not a glutton for punishment."

"Was it that bad?"

"Worse, but it doesn't matter," Marnie said, uncomfortable at the turn in the conversation.

"Is there someone else?"

Marnie thought of Adam and his reluctance to commit to her. Yes, she was falling in love with him. They were treading water, waiting for the tidal wave that would eventually drive them apart. "No one serious," she said when she caught Kate's probing gaze.

Kate lifted a skeptical brow. "Victor told me you were seeing Adam Drake."

Marnie didn't comment, but Kate sighed and drummed her fingers on her empty cup. "Take my word for it, Marnie. That man's trouble with a capital *T*. And if you ever want to hurt your father to the point that he'll never forgive you, then I suppose you can just keep on seeing Adam. When Victor finds out, he'll be devastated."

"My father can't choose whom I date."

"Or marry?" Kate asked, and Marnie's head snapped up. For a second a fleeting look of understanding passed between them and Marnie realized that she was much like Kate, caught in a love affair that could only end badly, emotionally tied to a man, who, for reasons of his own, couldn't or wouldn't allow himself to be tied down forever. Depression weighted her heart.

Kate stood, rounded the desk and touched her lightly on the shoulder. "Kent's a good man, Marnie, though I know he has his faults. But he knows he hurt you, and I believe he'd never hurt you again. As for Dolores—"

Marnie's eyes widened. *Kate knew?* Her cheeks flushed hot with embarrassment. How many other employees knew or guessed that Kent had two-timed the boss's daughter? What about her father?

Her anxiety must have registered, because Kate said, "Victor doesn't know. And not that many people in the firm had any idea that he was…seeing anyone while you were engaged. In fact, the only reason I knew was that I came upon Dolores crying in the ladies' room one day and I took her back to my office to calm her down. She let everything out. She was nearly hysterical, sobbing and carrying on. Kent had told her he didn't want to see her again and she didn't believe him. She wanted to quit Montgomery Inns, but I convinced her to stay, at least for a while. But, from the looks of it, Kent broke up with her for good."

"Doesn't matter," Marnie heard herself saying. She didn't love Kent. Never had. And in the past few weeks she'd seen a side to him that was frightening.

"Probably not. I doubt if I'd ever forgive him, if I were in your shoes. But I thought you should know the full story. Done with that?" she asked, flicking her finger toward Marnie's nearly empty cup.

"Yes. And thanks."

"Don't mention it. I'm just glad you're back and back on your own terms. See ya later." She swept out of the room, leaving Marnie restless and concerned.

She spent the better part of the first week working with the Montgomery Inns account and spending more time at the hotel than she did at her own office. Donna, ever efficient, swore that she had the situation under control, but the most difficult part of Marnie's job was being so removed from Adam. After Kate's rebuff, when he'd tried and failed to contact Victor, he'd decided not to call Montgomery Inns. Marnie had to content herself with seeing him in the evenings at her place. At the thought of their nights together, she smiled.

At the hotel, she worked with Todd Byers, who had assumed her position for the few weeks she'd been gone.

Todd was about twenty-seven, with unruly blond hair and round, owlish-looking glasses.

"That about does it," he said, flopping back in a chair near her desk and resting his heels on another chair. "We should have all the publicity for Puget Sound West done for the next six months."

Marnie rubbed her chin. She couldn't afford to blow this account. "You're right, but I'll follow up just in case."

Todd shrugged, obviously thinking she was overly careful. "The next project's in California. San Francisco. Renovations are half finished," Todd said. "Victor wants us to go there next month."

"I know," Marnie admitted, remembering her conversation with her father about her schedule and wondering how she was going to juggle her time as it was. She thought about leaving Adam, and her heart tugged a little, but she ignored that tiny pain.

"Well, I've got a few loose ends to tie up, then I'm outta here," Todd said, dropping his feet to the floor and slapping his hands on his legs. "It's almost seven."

The time had gone by so quickly, Marnie had barely noticed. "I'll see you tomorrow," she said as Todd smiled, saluted her, and exited.

Twenty minutes later, as she was leaving, she bumped into Rose Trullinger in the hallway. "Just the person I wanted to see," Rose said, though she was wearing a full-length coat and was tugging on a pair of gloves as if she were heading outside to her car. "I don't have time to go into it right now, but I want the Puget West brochure changed. The pictures of the suites don't do justice to the design."

Marnie couldn't believe it. "But you approved those shots." A courtesy, since Rose really had no authority over publicity. But Marnie had tried to please everyone.

"I know, I know. I made a mistake." She finished with

the glove and met Marnie's gaze levelly, as if she were daring Marnie to challenge her.

"The brochures are already being printed."

Rose smiled thinly. "Then get them back," she said. "I'll talk to you tomorrow."

"You bet you will," Marnie said under her breath. She headed toward her father's office, but discovered that he and Kate were already gone for the day. In fact, the executive offices were practically deserted. She should go home, work on the Jorgenson Real Estate account, her latest client, but she was in no hurry, as Adam was out of town, meeting with some investors from Los Angeles.

Rose's strange attitude had reminded her of her conversation with Adam. Hadn't he said one of the accomplices could be a woman? She hesitated as an idea occurred to her—maybe she could help find the culprit. She was alone in the building, with access to all the computer files... This might be her only chance to prove, once and for all, that Adam was innocent.

She walked down a corridor, turned right and entered the accounting area for the entire hotel chain. There were twenty desks, none currently occupied, in the bookkeeping area and three offices, partitioned off from the rest of the workers: a cubicle for Fred Ainger, one for Linda Kirk and one for Desmond Cipriano, the man who had replaced Gerald Henderson.

Feeling a little like a thief, she walked straight to Fred's desk, and using her own code, accessed the computer files for the Puget West hotel. She printed out scores of records, accounting as well as construction and research, hoping for some clue as to who took the money. She believed Adam was innocent. There were times when she didn't trust him, but she really believed that he hadn't taken a dime from her father. If he had, why would he want to dig up all the evidence again? No, Adam was a man hell-bent to clear his name, and to that end, Marnie decided, she could help him.

For the next three nights, she pored over the documents, making notes to herself, reading all the information until the figures swam before her eyes, but she found nothing, not one shred of evidence concerning the missing funds. True, she wasn't trained in accounting, and a dozen lawyers and accountants and auditors had gone over the books when the discrepancy was discovered, but she'd hoped... fantasized...that she would be able to unearth the crucial evidence that would prove Adam's innocence, absolve him of the crime, and give him back his sterling reputation.

"You are a fool," she told herself on Saturday morning as she dressed. Adam was due back in town later in the afternoon, and she planned on using the morning to visit the *Marnie Lee*. There was still the matter of Kent's belongings on the boat, a point he'd made several times since she'd started work at the hotel, and she wanted all trace of him out of her private life. Of course, she'd have to find a way to buy out his half of the vessel, but that would have to wait until she had a little more cash or could talk to her banker. A loan would probably be impossible, though. She'd just started her own business, didn't own her own home and her car was worth only a few thousand dollars. Her savings had to be used to keep her afloat until the receipts for the business exceeded the expenses.

The only person who would loan her enough money to buy out Kent was Victor, and she'd sell the boat rather than crawl back to her father and beg for money just when she was trying to prove she could make it on her own. It looked as if the *Marnie Lee* would soon be on the auction block. Kent had already indicated that he couldn't afford to buy Marnie out—so there was no other option.

She drove to the marina and walked along the waterfront. The sun was bright, the air brisk and clear, the sky a vivid blue. Only a few wispy clouds dared to float across the heavens.

Marnie zipped up her jacket and watched as sails and flags snapped in the brisk breeze. She was almost to the *Marnie Lee*'s berth when she heard her name. "Miss Montgomery!"

Turning, she spied Ed, the caretaker for the marina, scurrying toward her. He was small and wiry, not any taller than she. "Miss Montgomery. I need to talk to you!" he said, a trifle breathless.

"Hi, Ed."

"Hey, you told me to tell you if anyone asked about your boat, you want to know about it."

Marnie grinned. So someone wanted the *Marnie Lee*! Just when she needed the cash! "Did he leave his name and number?"

"Nope. But I know the guy," Ed said uncomfortably. "Name's Kent Simms."

"Oh." All her hopes were crumpled, and anger coursed through her blood. "And what did he want?"

"On board. But I said, 'No dice. Not unless you're with Miss Montgomery.' He left, but he was none-too-pleased about the situation."

"I'll bet not. When was he here?"

"Just yesterday around noon, and once before." Ed explained that Kent had been trying to get aboard the *Marnie Lee* for nearly three weeks, off and on. Marnie was annoyed before she realized that maybe he wanted more than the few belongings stashed aboard the yacht. Maybe he wanted more. Perhaps he thought he owed her one by stealing the boat, just to get back at her for taking the *Marnie Lee* the night of the party.

She didn't really blame him because she knew that Kent, right or wrong, considered the boat his. He'd had a strange attachment to the *Marnie Lee* from the first time he'd seen the boat, as Victor had proudly presented his gift to the two of them for "sailing along life's choppy waters and calm seas." Victor had walked them grandly through the cabins and decks, showing off a boat that was equal to his pride and joy, the *Vanessa*. Nonetheless, half the boat was hers, and the sooner Kent accepted that fact, the better for them both.

What if Kent balked when she put the sleek yacht up for sale? What if he refused to sign the papers?

After thanking Ed for his eagle eye and fierce loyalty, she walked down the sun-bleached planks of the pier and boarded the gently rocking boat. The *Marnie Lee* was a source of pride to her, as well. She rubbed a hand over the rail and eyed the teak decking and polished chrome fittings. Yes, it was beautiful and, now, after discovering Adam aboard this very boat, she had a special attachment to the craft as well. Unfortunately she couldn't afford the upkeep.

Running her hands down the polished rail, she entered the main salon and started rifling through drawers and cupboards, pulling out Kent's personal chessboard, his brass compass, his deck of cards, a few sailing magazines and a couple of paperback murder mysteries. She checked the galley and packed up his gourmet coffee, popcorn and exotic teas. She didn't want him to have any reason to return. She boxed everything she recognized as Kent's and realized how little, she, herself, had added to the belongings on the boat.

In the main cabin, she tossed Kent's clothes, shoes, swimsuit, slippers, cuff links, shaving kit and date book into a box. She started packing his laptop computer, but hesitated, then turned on the machine. Waiting until the tiny monitor warmed up, she wondered what she hoped to find. Her stomach knotted. What if this computer was the key, the proof of Kent's duplicity? As the access screen glowed in front of her, she worked with the various menus, and spent two hours scanning the files. Nothing. Not one shred of incriminating evidence against him. She didn't know whether to be disappointed or relieved.

She unplugged the laptop and packed it in a box with Kent's clothes. After double-checking the bureau a second time, she opened the closet and noticed the wall safe. She'd almost forgotten about it. The combination was easy; the numbers were a sequence of dates, the day, month and year of Kent's birth. Grimly she turned the dial, listening for the tumblers to click.

Nothing. The lock didn't budge.

She tried again, convinced she'd fouled up the number sequence in her haste.

Again the lock held.

"What the devil? Come on, you!" she muttered to the lock.

With renewed concentration, she redialed the combination three more times, giving up when she realized that Kent had changed the code. Probably after she'd broken up with him.

"Well, that's great," she muttered, hands on her hips, perspiration dotting her brow. "Just super!" Now she'd have to get the damned combination from Kent and return to the boat before she could be sure that nothing on board belonged to him. Frustrated, she threw the last of his belongings—a picture of the two of them, their arms wound around each other as if they were really in love—into a box.

It took most of the morning to clean out the boat and, with Ed's help, carry all Kent's belongings to her car, but when she was finished and was driving home she felt a sense of accomplishment, as if she'd managed to break the last remaining link of the chain that bound her to Kent. "Except you still have to dispose of the boat," she reminded herself as she parked in her assigned parking space at her apartment. And there was the small but irritating matter of the wall safe.

As for Kent's belongings, she'd leave them in her locked car and take them to the office on Monday, where in the basement parking lot of Montgomery Inns, they would separate once and for all.

THROUGH THE WINDOW, Adam noticed the sprawling suburbs of Seattle as the plane descended at SeaTac airport. He'd had two drinks on the way back from L.A., where his talk with Brodie hadn't gone any better than the last time. Yes, Brodie and his investment group were interested, but, as before, if Adam couldn't completely clear his name, the investors just weren't able to do business with him.

He'd spoken to another man as well, Norman Howick, an oil man, a millionaire with a reputation for taking risks on new ventures. Howick had been interested, but hadn't been able to commit. He'd been too much of a gentleman to mention Adam's unsavory past, but the inference had hung in the air between them like a bad smell.

"Back to square one," he muttered to himself as the 747 touched down with a chirp of tires and a bump. The big plane screamed as it slowed before taxiing toward the terminal.

Closing his eyes, pleasant thoughts of Marnie rippled through his mind. He realized his feelings for her had changed and deepened. He no longer viewed her as Victor's daughter, and that was probably a mistake, but he couldn't help himself.

Being with her brought a certain brilliance to his otherwise austere world. She was the light and he was night, she was a smile and he was a frown. Not that she didn't have her own dark side and her temper—he'd been on the wrong end of that a time or two. He chuckled softly as he remembered her fury—the scarlet tinge on her cheeks, the fiery spark in her blue eyes, the rapier cut of her words and the haughty toss of her flaxen hair when she was truly angry.

"You've got it bad, Drake," he chastised as he walked along the jetway and through the terminal. It took half an hour to locate his baggage and his car, and then he was speeding along the freeway and back to Marnie.

At her apartment, he took the steps two at a time, rang the bell and scooped her into his arms when she opened the door. She let out a startled squeal as he twirled her back across the threshold and into her living room.

"Miss me?" she asked, her blue eyes laughing.

"Just a little." He kissed her eyes, her throat, her neck… and she giggled like a delighted child. The scent of her was everywhere, and he buried his face in her hair and breathed deeply.

"I missed you, too," she said, caressing his cheeks before she kissed him on the lips.

He couldn't stop. So sensual yet innocent, Marnie unwittingly created a fever in him that raged through his blood, licking like fire to heat his loins and drive all thoughts—save the primal need to make love—from his mind. He kicked the door shut with one foot and carried her straight into the bedroom, then fell with her onto the bed.

"But I have dinner ready—"

"It'll wait." Her skin was warm to his touch, her smell intoxicating.

"So can we."

"Speak for yourself," he said, working on the buttons of her blouse as his lips and tongue touched the soft shell of her ear. She responded by moaning his name.

"Adam, oh, Adam…" Her eyes glazed over, but she smiled and said, "You're incorrigible, you know."

LISA JACKSON   199

"Probably." Her blouse parted.

"And totally without scruples. Oh!"

"Mmm." He pressed hot, wet lips against the hollow between her breasts and felt the fluttering beat of her heart. "Not even one lousy scruple?"

"None," she said, her voice breathy, a thin sheen of perspiration beginning to glow against her skin as he shoved the silky fabric of her blouse over her shoulder.

"Ah, what a lonely, unscrupulous life I lead," he said, his breath whispering across her bare skin as he unclasped her bra and her breasts spilled forward, dusty pink nipples stiffening in the shadowy light.

He sucked in his breath, willing himself to take it slow, while the fire in his loins demanded release. All he wanted to do was thrust deep into her and get lost in the warmth of her body. She moved against him, rocking slightly, reaching up and linking her fingers behind his head, only to draw him downward so that his open mouth surrounded her waiting nipple.

He took that precious bud in his mouth and suckled, hard and long, drawing on her breast as she writhed against him. His fire had spread to her and she held him tight, breathing in shallow gasps, her skin slick with sweat.

She wanted him as much as he wanted her, and he wasted no time ripping off his clothes and ridding her of her jeans and panties. When at last he was over her, poised for entry, he hesitated only slightly, staring at her fair hair, feathered around her face like an angel's halo, her innocent blue eyes staring up at him with infinite trust and hunger, her lips parted in desire.

At that precarious moment he hated himself. For what he'd done to her, for what he'd done to himself, for that frightening and overpowering need to claim her in a way as primitive as the very earth itself.

Yet he couldn't stop himself. In that heartbeat when he

should have told her that they would never have a future together, that their lives would soon part forever, he squeezed his eyes shut against her beauty, swore silently at himself, then plunged deep into the moist warmth and comfort that she so willingly offered.

SOMETHING HAD CHANGED. Marnie felt it. Ever since Adam had returned, he'd seemed different—desperate, but she didn't understand why. They'd made love, and there'd been a savagery to their lovemaking that bordered on despair. As if Adam felt they would never make love again.

"I cleaned out the boat," she said, once they were seated at the small table in her kitchen.

He looked at her, his brows raised.

"All Kent's things. I'm taking them with me to work on Monday." She took a bite of chicken-and-pasta salad. "He must really want them. He's been hanging around the docks trying to get on board the *Marnie Lee*."

"What was on board?" Adam asked. He'd eaten half his salad and was drinking from a long-necked bottle of beer.

"Nothing special. Just the usual male paraphernalia. You must've seen most of it when you were rooting around the boat looking for supplies." Memories of the storm and rain running down the windowpanes as they'd made love in Deception Lodge floated through her mind. She swished her wine in her glass and studied the clear liquid. "But I don't think he wanted his things. There wasn't anything that valuable on board, though I couldn't get into the safe—he changed the combination." At that, Adam's head jerked up. "I don't think there's anything really important in there, it's too risky. Remember I had keys to the boat. Oh, and he left his laptop computer—or one of them. I think he has a couple. But I checked it out. Nothing."

Adam scowled in frustration, and Marnie rambled on.

"I think Kent really wanted back on the boat to steal it from me. You know, tit-for-tat, since I took the boat from him. Fortunately Ed, the caretaker, caught him and threw him out."

"Why would Kent steal the boat?" Adam asked, his gaze keen as he took a long swallow of his beer.

"To get back at me." She explained about Kent's feeling of ownership for the *Marnie Lee.*

Eyeing her pensively, he finally asked, "What happened between you two?"

Marnie swallowed hard, then set her fork carefully on her plate. This, she felt, was a moment of truth. Could she trust her secret with Adam, the man who had so callously used her once before, a man with whom she knew she was falling in love? She cleared her throat, wondering if she had the courage to tell him the entire embarrassing story and deciding that he deserved the truth. Whether he admitted it or not, they *were* involved in a relationship. "Kent cheated on me," she finally admitted, struggling with the damning words. Though Kent meant nothing to her anymore, her pride was still damaged. "Not just once, not just a fling, but he had an affair with his secretary for the entire duration of our engagement."

"His secretary?"

"Dolores Tate," she said, then felt foolish, like a common gossip. "It doesn't matter, and I guess he did me a favor."

Adam rotated his near empty bottle in his hands. "You loved him?"

Shrugging, she avoided his eyes and stared out the window near the table. Outside, a robin flew into the lacy branches of a willow tree. "I thought I did at the time." She played with her fork. "But I think I was just caught up in the excitement of it all. Dad was so thrilled and the whole office congratulated us."

"Except Dolores?"

"She and I were never close." Clearing her throat, she looked up at him. "What about you? Any near brushes with the altar?"

"Nope."

"That's hard to believe."

It was his turn to glance away. "Any time a woman got too pushy and started talking about settling down, I always found an excuse to end it."

"Why?"

"I just never saw any reason for it."

"No family pressure to get married and father grand-children?"

"No family."

She bit her lip as she had a sudden insight into the man. She'd never heard him talk about his life, and thought he'd just been a private person, never thinking that his child-hood might have been painful.

"Can't remember my folks. My mother never told anyone who my father was, and she left when I was three. Never heard from her again. I was raised by Aunt Freda—really my mother's aunt. She died a couple of years back." He drained his beer, concluding the conversation.

Marnie swallowed hard. For the first time she under-stood some of the anger and pain she'd felt in Adam. "I'm sorry."

"Don't be. It's all ancient history."

"Didn't you ever want to find your parents?" she asked.

"Never!" His face grew hard, and his eyes narrowed in barely repressed fury. "I never want to see the face of a woman who could walk away from her child."

"Maybe she couldn't afford—"

"What she couldn't afford was an illegal abortion."

She swallowed hard. "You don't know…" Her voice trailed off.

"I do know. And I guess you couldn't blame her. She had nothing but a mistake in her gut. But that's not why I don't want to find her."

Tears burned the backs of Marnie's eyes, and her throat clogged, but Adam, staring intently at his hands, didn't seem to notice. "When I was three, she left with a sailor. A man she'd known two and a half days. Took off for L.A., and neither Freda nor I ever heard from her again. That's why she's as good as dead to me."

Oh, God. She wanted to reach forward, to place her hand on his, instead she asked softly, "But what about your grandparents?"

"Never met 'em. They were older—my grandfather fifty-five, my grandmother forty at the time my mother was born. According to Freda, they never really understood my mother and disowned her when she turned up pregnant and unmarried at seventeen. Believe it or not, my grandfather was a minister. He couldn't accept that his daughter ended up a sinner." His voice was bitter and distant, as if it took all his willpower to speak at all. "And I was a part of that sin. Proof that his daughter had fallen. They never even saw me. Freda was the only decent relative in the whole family tree. And she's gone now, so, no, I have no family."

"Does it bother you?" she whispered.

"I don't let it." Scraping his chair back, he carried his plate to the sink. "I don't even know why I told you all this," he said, frowning darkly and hooking his thumbs in the front pockets of his jeans.

Marnie crossed the kitchen, wrapped her arms around his neck and smiled up at him through her tears. "I wish I could say something, anything, that would change things."

"No reason to," he said harshly, but didn't push her away. In fact, his hands moved from his pockets to surround her and hold her close. Marnie held back the sobs that burned deep inside for the little abandoned boy who'd never known a mother's love.

If only he would let her close to him, let her take away some of the pain. She listened to the steady beat of his heart and she knew that she loved him, would always love him, no matter what.

"Marnie," he whispered hoarsely into her hair as the first tears trickled from the corners of her eyes. "Oh, Marnie…Marnie…Marnie." His voice sounded desperate, and Marnie clung to him as he swept her off her feet and carried her to the bedroom.

CHAPTER TWELVE

"YOU HAD THE NERVE to remove my things from the boat?" Kent accused, his voice cracking and his face turning white beneath his tan. He grabbed her arm and propelled her down a corridor.

"Let go of me." Marnie jerked back her arm and glared at him. "I'm sick of you manhandling me. Don't ever touch me again! Got it?" When he didn't respond, she added, "I just thought you'd want to know about your things."

"But you had no right—"

"It's all in my car," she cut in, disregarding his protests of injustice. "I'd be glad to transfer them to yours, if you give me the keys."

"You want the keys to the Mercedes? Are you out of your mind? Do you know what it's worth? You think I'd trust you with it after that stunt with the boat?" He was nearly apoplectic.

Marnie didn't care. "Do you want your stuff or not?"

"Of course!"

"Then let's transfer it now."

Kent checked his Rolex. "I have a meeting in seventeen minutes."

"It won't take long." He hesitated while Marnie walked to the elevator and pushed the button. "No problem. I'll leave it on your hood."

"What the hell's gotten into you?" he growled, but followed her to the bank of elevators, straightening the cuffs of his jacket and tie. "You used to be sane."

"When I was engaged to you?" She almost laughed. Most of the pain had faded with time. And the fact that now she knew what a real relationship between a man and a woman could be, she hardly believed that she had once considered herself in love with Kent. "Let's not talk about it. All right? In fact, let's not talk about anything." She considered the last time she'd been trapped in an elevator alone with Kent, but she wasn't worried. She could handle herself.

The doors to the elevator opened, and she stepped inside, joining Todd Byers, the hotel-services manager and two men from the sales team. She smiled at the other occupants, and Kent made a failed attempt to hide the fact that he was vastly perturbed with her and the entire situation.

Marnie, on the other hand, talked and chatted with Todd, laughed with the men from sales, and was still chuckling when she and Kent landed in the first subbasement, where the executives parked their cars.

The luster of Kent's black sports car gleamed under the overhead lights, in sharp contrast to her used Ford. She didn't care. Unlocking the trunk, she motioned to the three stacked boxes. "Didn't you miss any of this stuff?"

She thought he blanched and swallowed hard, but she only caught a glimpse of his profile as he unlocked his car. "Some of it," he said, lifting one of the flaps and peering inside the largest carton. "You found my computer?"

"Right where you left it—humming and clicking and spinning out information left and right," she said, unable to stop from baiting him.

"What?" he asked, horrified. "But it has an automatic shutoff…" He stopped short, finally realizing that she was joking with him.

"Relax, Kent. Your computer and all you other precious belongings are safe."

"You brought them straight from the boat?"

"After a short layover at my apartment."

"Oh." He yanked at his tie as he carried the first box to his car. It was too large to stuff in his trunk, so he had to place it behind the front seat. "Did, uh, did anyone else see any of this?"

"What do you mean?"

Kent looked at her over the shiny roof of the Mercedes, and she noticed tiny beads of sweat at his hairline. He licked his lips. "I mean Drake. Did he see it?"

She shrugged and thought about lying to him, but couldn't. Instead, she said simply, "He didn't rifle through anything. Why?"

Kent seemed relieved. "It's private, Marnie. That's all. Just between you and me. It's got nothing to do with him."

Suspicious, she dropped a small box into his open trunk. "Well, I hope you didn't have anything specific that you didn't want him to see, because he spent a lot of time alone on the boat."

"On *our* boat? Damn it, Marnie, you won't even let me near the *Marnie Lee* and I own half of it! But that loser, he's allowed to snoop around anywhere he wants! I can't believe you, Marnie." He slammed the passenger door of the car shut. "After what that jerk did to your father, how can you even think of allowing him anywhere near you or the yacht!"

"You knew he was on it," she pointed out, then waved her hands to forestall any further protests. She wasn't going to get into an argument with Kent. "Have you got everything?"

"You tell me. Since I'm not allowed on *my* boat, I can't tell if everything's here."

"If I find anything else, I'll send it to you," she replied, turning toward the elevators but catching a glimpse of the hard set of Kent's mouth.

A WOMAN. Henderson had said he'd thought Simms was in cahoots with a woman. But which woman? Seated at a bar stool in Marnie's apartment, Adam stared at the printouts Marnie had brought from the accounting department. In the corporate headquarters of Montgomery Inns there were over seventy employees, fifty-two of whom were women.

Crossing off those who didn't have access to computer terminals and accounting records, the number dwindled to thirteen; though with Kent's authority, the woman involved could merely have been an accomplice. She could have been the one pulling the strings behind Kent, even though she didn't have the power or wherewithal to actually move the funds. Leaving Kent in charge. No, that didn't work. Unless Kent really was the brains behind the operation.

Adam tapped his pencil against his teeth in frustration. Four women had easy access to the computer terminals as well as authority to access delicate information: Linda Kirk in accounting, Rose Trullinger in interior design, Kate Delany, Victor's assistant, and Marnie.

There were other women who worked in bookkeeping and records, and a few secretaries who were high enough on the corporate ladder to dig into the files. But to create an intricate embezzling scheme? Not likely.

However, he couldn't discount the men. Henderson thought Fred Ainger was involved. And what about Desmond Cipriano? The man who had taken over Henderson's office was young, brash and hungry. He'd had a lesser job during the time of the embezzlement and had been promoted after Henderson left the company. Only with the corporation a few years, Desmond didn't have all that much loyalty or time invested in Montgomery Inns.

A headache began to pound at Adam's temples and he rubbed his eyes. He threw his pencil down in disgust. Who? Who? Who?

MARNIE FELT LIKE a traitor as she walked toward Kate's desk. Of course, no one knew she had taken company records home, but nonetheless she was uncomfortable and she felt like talking with her father, maybe gaining some insight from him or maybe even convincing him to speak with Adam.

No doubt Victor would hit the roof when he found out she'd misused her authority, but better he learn it from her than find out on his own.

"Is he in?" she asked as Kate set the receiver of the phone back in its cradle.

Kate shook her head, and her auburn curls swept the shoulders of her linen suit. "Had to meet with the lawyers. I thought he said something about seeing you later..." She thought for a minute. "Something about dinner?"

"That's news to me."

Kate seemed puzzled. She ran her fingers down her appointment book and sighed loudly. "Nothing here, but I could've sworn..."

"Then you're not going out with him?" Marnie asked, knowing that her father and Kate often had dinner together.

"Not tonight." Kate closed the appointment book. Her lower lip trembled a little.

"Trouble?" asked Marnie.

"Not really."

"But..."

Kate sniffed and cleared her throat. "Your father is... preoccupied right now. Lots going on. The Puget West just opened, the architects are working on the blueprints for Deception Lodge, and the California projects...well, I don't have to tell you about them. San Francisco's due to reopen in October and—"

Marnie held up her hands, palms out, as if in surrender. She understood only too well how easily Victor Montgomery could bury himself in his work. "Enough said. It sounds as if my father has put his personal life on hold for a while and something should be done about it."

"Oh, no!" Kate shook her head vehemently. "He's just busy and he needs that—being busy, I mean. He can't slow down. It would kill him. And besides, this isn't the first time I've been shoved to the back burner. We'll get through it," Kate predicted, but tears shimmered in her eyes, and she suddenly reached forward and grabbed Marnie's hand. "If I can give you one piece of advice, Marnie, it's don't get involved with a man who isn't ready to commit. You could spend the rest of your life waiting." The phone rang, and Kate, obviously embarrassed by her outburst, let go of Marnie's hand and waved her off. "I'll be all right," she mouthed before turning her attention to the phone and saying, "Mr. Montgomery's office."

Feeling totally depressed, Marnie moved quickly down the corridor. Did Kate know about her dead-end relationship with Adam? But how? Just a lucky guess? Or from bits and pieces, snatches of conversation?

Inside her office she shivered and rubbed her arms while surveying this room that she had once claimed; the plush carpet, the expensive furniture, the panoramic view. Did she want it back?

No. Beautiful as the office was, it was made up of carpet and ceiling tile and antiques and brass lamps and piped-in music. Things. Just material goods. And material goods had never seemed less appealing. Especially now that she was forced to consider a life without Adam, or worse yet, to be strung along like Kate, always waiting, while knowing in her heart that the man she loved could never let go of the past or offer her a future. "Oh, Lord." With a sigh, she took off her earrings and dropped them into her purse.

She considered her father's fervent loyalty to a wife who had been gone over a decade. To what purpose? Why wouldn't he marry again?

And Adam. Would he never marry? Would he never find a woman on whom he was willing to take a chance? Well, if he did, his future wife certainly wouldn't be the daughter of a man who had tried to put him behind bars.

But she loved him, Marnie thought painfully. And that was the pure, naked truth. Of all the men in the world, she was senseless enough to fall in love with the one she couldn't have. So, could she live with him and forget about marriage, about children, about a mate for life?

Perhaps her romantic notions were nothing more than dusty fantasies left over from a childhood without a mother, a child who was read stories about beautiful princesses and castles and dragons and knights on white steeds who wanted to do nothing more than live happily ever after with the girl of their dreams.

"Idiot," she chided, as she punched out the number of her own publicity firm.

Donna answered on the second ring. "Montgomery Publicity."

"Hi. How's it going?" Marnie asked, balancing a hip against the desk in her old office at the hotel.

"Mmm. Busy," Donna said, and Marnie could almost imagine her polishing her nails, swigging coffee and smoking a cigarette while manning the phones and typing out complicated corporate tax returns for Miles Burns, the accountant in 301. "You got a couple of call backs from Andrew Lorenzini at Sailcraft. He liked your proposal and wants to meet again next week."

"Good." With a few accounts like Sailcraft, Marnie wouldn't be so dependent upon Montgomery Inns.

"Andrew Lorenzini," Donna repeated. "He sounds interesting."

"He sounds married," Marnie replied.

"Oh, well, too bad," Donna replied with a loud sigh. "Anything else?"

"Nope. As I said it's a real killer today."

"Well, don't work too hard."

"Wouldn't dream of it," Donna replied, before saying, "Oh, yes, there was one more message. Adam called. Couldn't get through to you at Montgomery Inns, and said he'll meet you tonight at the usual spot. Now *he* sounds interesting *and* romantic. I've seen him, you know. Total hunk."

"What you've seen is too many movies."

"Not enough. And definitely not with the right men."

Marnie laughed as she rang off. Her mood improved as she thought of an evening alone with Adam. So they weren't planning to walk down the aisle together, so they didn't have a future all mapped out for them, so her father thought he was as crooked as a pig's tail. So what? The new Marnie Montgomery could take a relationship and her life one spontaneous step at a time! The old Miss Ellison-trained Marnie was long buried. The new Marnie was taking over!

She hummed to herself as she grabbed her briefcase and started for the elevator. Then the thought struck. Hadn't Kate said that her father wanted to take her to dinner? And Adam had left a message saying he and she were to meet at the usual spot, meaning her apartment. So there was a chance that Victor, if he planned on picking up his daughter for dinner at her place would come face-to-face with the man he hated.

Marnie sucked in her breath. The thought of the two

men she loved confronting each other at her place chilled her to the bone. She dashed back into her room and dialed the number of her father's mobile phone. A monotone voice told her that the phone wasn't in service. Quickly she punched out her father's extension and Kate answered. Without explaining why, she asked Kate to try and reach Victor and make sure that tonight's dinner plans were rescheduled. "Anytime later this week," she instructed, and felt a little better when Kate told her she was expecting Victor to call in to the office at any moment.

Marnie's relief was short-lived. How long could she sustain this juggling act? she wondered, her good mood chased away by the horrid memory of Adam and her father, fists clenched, squaring off at Deception Lodge.

"It won't happen. It can't," she told herself as she took the elevator to the employee cafeteria, grabbed a doughnut and poured herself a cup of coffee. She talked with a few of the women from the marketing department, people she'd worked with at Montgomery Inns. Within minutes she caught up with several women—their lives, their children's trials and tribulations and their grandchildren's accomplishments.

"So, now that we've bored you to death. What about you, Marnie?" Helen Meyers asked. "How was your grand adventure in the San Juans?"

"So it's hit the local gossip mill?" she countered.

"And a three-county area," Roberta Kendrick agreed.

Marnie laughed, enjoying the company. She told them bits about her trip in the storm but didn't mention Adam's name and was blindsided by Helen's next remark.

"I heard Adam Drake kidnapped you." Helen's graying brows arched over her rimless glasses.

"Stowed away," Roberta interjected. Picking up her teacup, she shook her head at Helen. "Don't change things around."

"I'm just repeating what I heard."

"He was on the boat," Marnie conceded. "And I hate to admit it, but it was a good thing. The storm was worse than anyone would have guessed. And Adam's a pretty good sailor."

Helen swiped at a stain on the table. "Well, I know it's not popular to say, but I, for one, and I think I speak for everyone in the marketing department, miss Mr. Drake."

"Do you?" Marnie was surprised to hear such anarchy from one of Victor's loyal employees.

"If you ask me, he got the shaft!"

"Helen!" Roberta cried, then made quick, apologetic motions with her hands. "Please, don't listen to her, she's just angry with Mr. Simms today."

"That know-nothing! You were right to break off with him, Marnie. He's useless!"

One side of Marnie's mouth lifted, and Roberta tried to pour oil on rough waters. "We all miss Mr. Drake," she admitted, throwing a speaking glance in Helen's direction meant to still the little woman's tongue. "He was fair and had a sense of humor, and no one worked harder for the company than he did. It looks bad for him, but… well, most of us don't believe that he took any money from your father. It just doesn't make sense." Helen looked as if she were about to add her two cents, and Roberta put in quickly, "However, we all are doing our best to work with Mr. Simms. If your father trusts him, then we—"

"Bull!" Helen cut in, and Roberta rolled expressive green eyes. "The man's a dimwit, and you know it, Roberta Kendrick!"

Somehow Marnie managed to channel the conversation and turn it to a less disastrous course. She listened for a few minutes while Roberta caught her up on the details of her trip to Hawaii the previous February. Finally Marnie escaped.

She spent the next couple of hours with Todd, who assured her that Rose Trullinger's request to change the brochure was out of the question. "You could double-check with your dad on that one," he said, polishing his glasses with a handkerchief as he stood over her desk, eyeballing the pictures in question, "but I've never seen your father change something like this unless there was a good reason."

"I agree. Besides, I think I'm supposed to make that kind of final decision," Marnie replied.

Todd pushed his glasses onto the bridge of his nose. "Right you are. Besides, you can't believe everything Rose tells you these days."

"No?"

Todd shook his head. "She's going through some pretty heavy stuff right now. Her husband isn't getting any better. One of Rose's daughters dropped out of school to help her take care of him, but it looks like he might have to go in for open-heart surgery, and there's some hassle about insurance benefits. So Rose is real tense these days, and everyone around here is trying to cut her a little slack while being as supportive as possible."

"I wish I'd known this earlier," Marnie said, trying to remember her conversation with the slender woman.

"Don't worry about it. She's probably already forgotten the entire issue. My guess is that within a week or two she won't know this shot—" he thumped a finger on the picture "—from the one she says she wanted." He glanced at his watch and scowled. "Are we done for the day? I gotta run."

"Sure. I'll see you Monday."

Todd left, shutting the door behind him. Marnie leaned back in her chair, swiveling to stare through the bank of windows to the Seattle skyline. Skyscrapers loomed upward, seeming to slash through a summer-blue sky. Only a few clouds hung on a lazy, summer breeze. At the sound, boats chugged across the gray blue waters, leaving foaming wakes and reflecting a few of the sun's afternoon rays.

Everyone working for Montgomery Inns seemed to have more than his or her share of problems. Kate Delany and Rose Trullinger were just a few.

And what about you? What about your relationship with Adam? Talk about going nowhere!

"Oh, stop it," she said, mentally chewing herself out and refusing, absolutely refusing, to be depressed. Deciding to call it a day herself, she stuffed some work into her briefcase, grabbed her jacket and swung open the door. One of the elevators was out of order, and a crowd of employees milled around the remaining operable lifts.

Marnie took the stairs, concluding that a little exercise wouldn't hurt her. Her heels rang on the metal steps as she descended, passing each floor quickly. She didn't see the girl huddled on the landing of the eighth floor until she almost tripped over her.

Marnie froze. The girl was a woman. Dolores Tate— and she was sobbing loudly. Her curly brown hair was wilder than ever, her eyes red. A handkerchief was wadded in her fist, and her skin was flushed from crying. She gasped as she recognized Marnie and looked as if she wanted to disappear as quickly as possible.

A tense silence stretched between them before Marnie managed to ask, "Are you okay?"

Dolores sniffed and cleared her throat. "Do I look okay?" Her voice dripped sarcasm.

Disregarding Dolores's unconcealed contempt, Marnie asked, "What's wrong?"

"You?" Dolores responded, blinking hard. "*You* want to know what's wrong with me? God, that's choice!" Her purse, lying open, was shoved into a corner. Dolores pawed through the oversize leather bag. "I need a ciga-

rette." She found a new pack and worked with the cellophane while her hands trembled. Finally she lit up. "You
want to know what's wrong with me? Why don't you take
a wild guess?"

Marnie knew the woman was baiting her, but she couldn't
resist. "This probably has something to do with Kent."

"Bingo!" Dolores threw back her head and shot a plume
of smoke toward the ceiling many stories above. "But
I don't suppose I have to tell you about Kent. He did a
number on you, too."

"Doesn't matter."

"Not to you, maybe." Tears trickled from the corners
of Dolores's eyes. She swiped at the telltale drops with her
fingers. "But I actually loved the bum." Laughing bitterly,
Dolores found her handkerchief again and wiped her nose.
"How's that for stupid?"

"We all make mistakes," Marnie replied, wishing she
didn't sound so clichéd.

"Yeah, well, I made my share." Suddenly her gaze
was fixed on Marnie's. "And, well, for what it's worth—I
didn't mean to hurt you. I was just in love with the wrong
man. But apparently—" her voice cracked, and she drew
up her knees, bowing her head and holding her cigarette
out in front of her as the smoke curled lazily into the air
"—apparently, Mr. Simms doesn't feel the same about
me." She blinked rapidly. "In fact, that bastard told me he
never even cared about me! I guess I was only good for
one thing. He broke it off with me, you know. A couple of
weeks ago, but I thought I could change his mind. Obviously I was wrong about that, too."

Marnie was aware of footsteps ringing on the steps a
few stories up. "Look, you want to go somewhere and talk
about it?" she said, feeling suddenly sorry for a woman
who had so many hopes wrapped up in a man like Kent.

"With you? Are you out of your mind? That's why he

broke up with me, you know. He blamed *me* for him losing you. Can you believe it? Like it was *my* fault!" She finally seemed to hear the clattering ring of footsteps closing in on them and she struggled to her feet, crushing out her cigarette with the toe of a tiny shoe.

"If it's any consolation," Marnie offered, "I think you did me a big favor."

"Why?" Dolores asked, attempting to compose herself as a few men from the personnel department edged passed them and continued down the stairs. Marnie waited until the noise faded and, from far below, a door slammed, echoing up the staircase before silence surrounded them again. "Oh, I get it," Dolores said, her eyes turning bright. "This is all because of Adam Drake, right?" She smiled a little. "That really burned Kent, you know. That you would be interested in Drake."

"Because he was supposed to have embezzled from my father?" Marnie countered, and Dolores sucked in a sharp breath. Her throat worked, before she tried to pull herself together.

"You know something about it?" Marnie asked, reading Dolores's abrupt change of attitude. No longer the scorned, broken woman, Dolores was now looking guilty as sin. All the subterfuge came together in Marnie's mind.

Dolores must be the very woman they were looking for— the woman Kent was talking to when Gerald Henderson overheard the conversation in the accounting department. "You know that Fred Ainger was involved, and Kent?" she asked as Dolores, one hand on her purse, the other hanging desperately onto the rail, began to back down the stairs.

"I don't know anything about it," Dolores responded, denial and guilt flaring in her eyes.

"Oh, come on, Dolores! It's written all over your face! And Gerald Henderson overheard you and Kent in the accounting office."

"Not me!" Dolores shook her head. "I was never near the accounting department with Kent!"

"Then who was?" Marnie asked, following Kent's lover down the stairs and feeling a little like a predator. Dolores was obviously terrified that she'd said too much.

"I—I don't know," she squeaked.

Marnie clasped Dolores's wrist, stopping the other woman cold. "What are you afraid of?" When Dolores didn't immediately respond, Marnie said, "You must be involved."

"No!"

For a minute she stared at her, and slowly Marnie believed her. Stark terror streaked through Dolores's red-rimmed eyes. Yet there was something she was holding back, something important. Marnie gambled. "I have to go to my father with this."

"Oh, God, no," Dolores pleaded. "Really, I don't know anything."

Marnie's conscience nagged her, but she pressed on. This was, after all, her one chance to absolve Adam of a crime he didn't commit and prove his innocence. "Then you won't mind telling that to my father or the board or the police?"

Dolores nearly fainted. Her entire body was shaking, and for a terrifying instant Marnie was afraid the girl might lose her footing and fall down the stairs.

"Listen, Dolores, why don't you just tell me everything you know about the theft? Then I'll decide if my father has to know about your part in it."

"I wasn't part of it!" she cried.

"Then who're you protecting? Kent?" Marnie scoffed. "After what he did to you? Believe me, Dolores, he's not worth it."

Dolores wavered. Chewing on her lip, she said, "If I help you…?"

"I'll talk to my father, explain that you were basically

an innocent bystander—a victim. But you have to tell me the truth—all of it—and I can't promise that you won't be prosecuted if it turns out that you're involved more than you say you are."

Dolores gulped, but her eyes held Marnie's, and for the first time since they'd met, Marnie felt as if a glimmer of understanding passed between them. "You have to believe me, I didn't do anything and I never got a cent," she whispered, licking her lips nervously.

"But you did know what was going on?"

"I—uh—I found out when I caught Kent fiddling with the books." Dolores sank to the step and dropped her head into her hands. "It's all such a mess and I loved Kent so much that…that I didn't…couldn't blow the whistle on him."

"Was Fred involved?" Marnie asked softly.

"I don't know. I don't think so." Dolores shook her head slowly. "I think there was someone else, but I really don't know who. Kent kept me in the dark as much as possible. That's the way he was." Her pouty lips compressed, and anger caused her pointed chin to quiver. "And he never cared about me. Not at all." Her hands curled into tiny fists of outrage.

"Would you be willing to testify against him?"

Dolores stared at Marnie a long time. "I can do better than that," she said at last, finally throwing in her lot with Marnie. "I can tell you where the records are—the books that show how the money was skimmed off the project funds."

Marnie was floored. "Where?"

Dolores smiled through her tears. "In the boat."

"The boat?"

"The damned boat. Your boat. The *Marnie Lee.* Everything you need to prove that Kent's the thief is in the safe in your boat!"

CHAPTER THIRTEEN

THE PHONE RANG in Marnie's apartment, but Adam let the answering machine take the call. He made it a practice not to answer her phone or do anything that might suggest that they were a couple. He respected Marnie's privacy, true, but there was another reason. He couldn't get too tied into this woman, much as he cared for her. It wouldn't be fair to either of them. Until he could prove his innocence, he had nothing to offer her.

On the fourth ring, the answering machine picked up, playing Marnie's tape recording. A few seconds later, Marnie's voice, breathless, rang from the box. "Adam? Are you there?" Marnie asked, her voice ringing with excitement on the telephone recorder. "If you are, pick up. Please! This is important!"

Just the sound of her voice brought a grin to his face. He picked up and drawled, "Gee, lady, sounds like you're in desperate need of a man. What can I do for you?"

"Thank God you're there!" she whispered, relief and delight mingled in her words.

"You know me, just hanging around your place, a kept man," he returned. Her good mood was infectious, and he imagined how she must look, cheeks flushed pink, her flaxen hair tousled, her blue eyes clear and bright.

"Meet me at the *Marnie Lee!* I'll be there in half an hour!"

"Whoa. Slow down a second. Why?"

"I don't have time to tell you now," she said, nearly

laughing, her voice bubbling with enthusiasm. "Just meet me there!" With a profound click, she hung up, and Adam slowly replaced the phone. Whatever she was up to, it couldn't wait.

He glanced at the table, where pencils, pens, a calculator and two half-empty cups were scattered over the reports from Montgomery Inns. After hours of poring over the personnel and accounting records, Adam had come up with nothing that even remotely hinted at who was behind the embezzlement and consequent frame-up. He was tired, his back and neck ached and his mouth tasted stale from cup after cup of coffee. He was getting nowhere fast.

A boat ride with Marnie sounded like just the ticket to get his mind off this mess.

Scooping up his keys from the table, he stuffed them into the pocket of his jeans and saw Simms's name on a personnel report. "You son of a bitch," Adam muttered. "I'll get you yet." But he wasn't as convinced as he once had been. Though Henderson's hearsay tied Kent to the crime, it was just Henderson's word against Simms's. No, he needed more proof: cold, hard facts. Adam had foolishly underestimated Simms and whoever the hell his accomplice was. They were professionals when it came to sliding dollars out of the company accounts. If Kate Delany hadn't noticed the discrepancies, they could have embezzled millions.

He was reaching for his jacket on the curved arm of the hall tree when he stopped short at a sudden thought. Kate Delany. Of course! He didn't need Victor's help; if he could convince Kate to talk to him, to explain how she'd been tipped off, then he might find the answer to how the money was shuffled, to where, and more importantly, to whom.

Feeling that he was suddenly on the verge of a breakthrough, he shoved his arms through the sleeves of his jacket and projected ahead to an evening of sailing, a dinner with candlelight and wine and a night of lovemaking, with Marnie lying beside him, her pale hair, touched by the moonglow, looking as if it were a silvery fire.

First a night with Marnie, then tomorrow he'd tackle Ms. Delany. If the woman would see him. She'd made it all too clear that she thought he was no better than a weasel.

Well, dammit, she'd just have to deal with him.

The doorbell chimed softly through Marnie's apartment. "Marnie? You ready?" Victor's voice boomed through the panels as Adam pulled open the door.

They stood face-to-face, inches apart, the threshold of Marnie's front door a symbol of the rift between them. Adam on one side, Victor on the other, a year of bitterness, lies and mistrust separating them as surely as the threshold itself.

One side of Adam's mouth lifted into a mocking grin. "Well, Victor," he drawled, as the older man's shock turned to simmering rage. "It's been a long time. I'd invite you in, but I'm just on my way out."

Victor tilted his aristocratic head, and the nostrils of his patrician nose flared slightly. "Where's Marnie?"

"I'm going to meet her."

"She's having dinner with me."

"That's not the way I understand it," Adam replied, then added, "excuse my manners." He glanced pointedly at his watch. "I guess I've got a few minutes. Would you like to come in for a drink?"

Victor snorted. "What the hell do you think you're doing hanging around my daughter? I warned you—"

"I figure Marnie's old enough to make her own decisions."

"Or mistakes," Victor declared, gazing past Adam to the interior of the apartment, as if he expected Marnie to walk out of the kitchen, fling herself into his arms and complain that Adam had been holding her hostage against her will. It amused Adam that Victor really expected him to lie at every turn.

"Well, if you're not interested in coming in and shooting the breeze, then I guess I'd better be off. She's waiting for me at the boat. So if you'll excuse me…"

But Victor stood as if rooted to the porch, his gaze narrowing to some spot beyond Adam, his old eyes fixed on the inside of the apartment. "Oh, my God," he whispered, and his throat worked slightly. His face turned bloodless, as if he'd seen a ghost. "What the devil have you been doing, Drake?" he asked in a voice so low it was nearly lost in the rumble of traffic from the street.

"What do you mean? I told you she's not here…"

Ignoring Adam, Victor pushed past him, strode down the hallway to the table where Adam had been seated, where stacks of computer printouts lay sprawled over the white tabletop. Each heading, in bold inch-high letters, announced that the pages were property of Montgomery Inns.

Adam's stomach tightened. In his fantasies about being alone with Marnie and his exuberance of thinking they were about to solve the mystery with Kate Delany's help, he'd forgotten about the sheaves of paper, damning and incriminating printouts, strewn all over the kitchen.

Victor picked up the first few pages, scanned the print and nearly staggered as he slumped into a chair, dropping his head into his hands, one page of a printout still wadded in his fingers. Hearing Adam approach, he looked up, his eyes suddenly old and tired. "You did it, didn't you? You managed to turn my own daughter against me."

"No, I—"

"Damn it, Drake, I'm sick of lies! Sick!" With a renewed rush of energy, Victor struck one stack of printouts, and it skidded off the table to pour onto the floor, sheet after perforated sheet, rolling and folding onto the tile, condemning Marnie in her father's eyes. "She got them from corporate headquarters, didn't she? Hell, yes, she did. She still has access to the files. And then she brought them back to you, like a dog bringing slippers to his master for a pat on the head. God, you're incredible. My own daughter!" His voice trembled perilously, but he didn't break down.

"Marnie was just trying to help me."

"Or ruin Montgomery Inns!" Victor's face had flushed, and his lips shivered in rage.

"She wouldn't—"

"She already did, Drake, and I'm holding you personally responsible. I know you're trying to put together a deal to open a rival hotel, right here in downtown Seattle, and you've convinced my daughter to become involved in some sort of corporate espionage against her own flesh and blood. Well, I won't hear of it! You can tell Marnie for me that she's fired!" he shouted, slamming his fist on the table and scrambling to his feet. "I'm calling my lawyers immediately to press charges against you for stealing company records. And I'm going to change my will. From this moment forward, Marnie's cut off! Understand? Cut off from any more Montgomery money. As far as I'm concerned, I don't have a daughter anymore."

Adam grabbed hold of the older man's lapels as Victor tried to brush past him. "If you just would have talked to me this never would have happened."

"Talk to you? All you had to do was call for an appointment," Victor raged, his voice becoming louder.

"I tried! But you left word with Kate Delany that you wouldn't see me."

"Enough of your lies! Just give Marnie the message."

"Don't you think you'd better tell her yourself?" Adam suggested, as he dropped the collar of Victor's coat.

"Why? She wouldn't believe me. It's you she trusts now. You've got her under some sort of spell, and when she wakes up, I hope to God she realizes what an incredible mistake she made—that you're just not worth it."

"Marnie can make up her own mind," Adam repeated, his jaw clenched so hard it throbbed.

Victor slammed out of the apartment, and Adam felt a tremendous loss. Not for himself. But for Marnie. Victor was the only family she had in the world, and no matter how angry she became with her father, he was still her own flesh and blood. Adam braced himself for the rift that was to come. He knew she loved the old man and would be devastated when she found out that Victor had branded her a traitor and disowned her. He'd seen how much Victor meant to her when they'd discussed family ties.

Adam had ruined everything for her. He leaned heavily against the wall. How could he tell her that her father considered her no better than dead?

The phone rang again and the answering machine clicked on. Adam hesitated, half expecting Marnie's voice to be on the phone. "Marnie?" a woman asked. The voice was high-pitched and sluggish, as if she were drunk or drugged. "Marnie? Are you there? Oh, God, please be there! Marnie? This is Dolores…"

Dolores Tate? Adam froze, listening to Dolores's message.

"…look, I, uh, well, Kent knows that you know about the books. He, um, oooh, God! He came over and…and I told him. But somehow—somehow he already knew. I could see it in his eyes." She was crying now. Her voice faltered. "He flipped out and…he hit me, Marnie," she whispered, sniffing loudly. "He *hit* me. And I think he's on the way to the boat. I wouldn't mess with him if I were you… He might have a gun. Oh, Lord…"

Adam rushed back to the phone and picked up the receiver.

"Dolores, this is Adam Drake," he said, only to hear the sound of the connection being severed. A second later a dial tone buzzed in his ear.

What was she talking about? What books? What did it have to do with Marnie? A gun? Did she say a *gun!*

He didn't waste any time trying to call Dolores back. He didn't bother locking the apartment. Taking the steps to the parking lot two at a time, he raced down the stairs and only hoped that he wasn't too late.

IN THE MAIN CABIN of the boat, Marnie twisted the combination lock for the fifth time, but nothing happened. Not one single tumbler had seemed to fall into place. She wasn't just coming up with numbers at random, she'd taken the time to rifle through Kent's desk, and came up with dates, figures, or series of numbers that held special significance for him.

She tried again using his birthdate, her birthdate, the day he was promoted. Nothing, nothing and nothing.

Racking her brain, she came up with a long shot. The date of their engagement. The tumblers clicked, and the heavy door swung open. Maybe Kent did care for her more than she believed. She reached into the safe and withdrew a small velvet box. Inside was a diamond ring—the engagement ring she'd given back to him. Beneath the box were several stock certificates, and at the very bottom was a ledger book. Marnie opened the book and a computer disk fell out.

She heard brisk footsteps on the deck above. Adam. "Down here," she called, still reading the entries in the ledgers. They were coded, but she could see that vast amounts of money had been moved around the various accounts of Montgomery Inns—or at least that's what she suspected.

Adam's footsteps sounded on the stairs. "We've got it!" she yelled, her voice bubbling. She was practically beaming when he walked through the cabin door. "Look, it's all here—" she said, before her words died in her throat and she met Kent's all-knowing gaze.

"Ah, Marnie," he said, clicking his tongue and sighing. His face was cold and set. A tiny sliver of fear pricked her heart.

"Where's Adam?" she demanded.

"Don't know." He lifted one shoulder. "You expecting him?"

She knew she had to be careful. If she lied, Kent would see right through her. "I *hoped* you were him."

Kent winced. "So what am I going to do with you?"

"I think the question is, 'What are the police going to do to you, Kent?'" she said bravely, though she was cold inside. The glint in his eye was deadly, the determined set of his jaw rock-hard and his mouth was a thin, cruel line.

"That does pose a problem," he admitted, and for a fleeting second his iciness seemed to thaw and he looked again like the man she'd almost married. "I never wanted to hurt you." He glanced down at the books, still lying open in Marnie's hands. "But I got caught up in all this... well, it's over and done with," he said, his regret giving way to harsh reality. "Now, we've got to figure out where we go from here."

"You have to tell my father the truth. You have to give yourself up."

Kent snorted, as if she were a fool. "And spend the next twenty years in jail? I don't think so."

"If you don't tell him, I will."

"Oh, Marnie," he said, shaking his head again. "I don't think you're in a position to bargain." With that, he reached into his pocket and pulled out a small but deadly pistol. Marnie's heart stopped.

"You couldn't—"

"Maybe not. But I don't have many choices left, do I? If only Drake had butted out, this all would've worked."

"You mean if he'd taken the fall."

He motioned with his gun to the door. "Hand me the books, then climb on deck. I think we should take a little cruise until I figure out what I've got to do."

"You're going to kidnap me?" she cried, fear giving way to stark terror. Alone on the open sea with Kent. But it was better than having Adam show up here and innocently walk into the barrel of Kent's gun.

"No, Marnie," he said as surely as if he could read her mind, "I'm not going to kidnap you. You're going to come with me willingly. Otherwise, I might have to find a way to kill your boyfriend and plant some evidence on him that proves without a doubt that he was the man who embezzled from your father."

"I'd never go along with that story," she said, her throat squeezing together so that it was hard to speak.

"Hopefully you won't have to. Maybe I'll bargain with Drake. If he cares anything for you, he might be willing to confess in order to spare your life and his."

Marnie could barely believe her ears. Did Kent actually think that Adam would claim responsibility for a crime he didn't commit, just to save her? Though Kent's pistol worried her, she couldn't accept the fact that he would actually shoot her. Embezzling was one kind of crime; murder was an entirely different story. Though cold fear crawled up her spine, she didn't really believe that Kent was capable of murder. This was all a bluff; it had to be.

Aware of Kent right behind her, she climbed the stairs to the deck, where the wind had picked up speed and sails were snapping loudly. "This is crazy, Kent. You're no killer. You couldn't hurt anyone."

"Tell that to your friend, Ed."

"Ed?" she repeated, her dread and adrenaline causing her heart to beat triple-time. "You didn't—"

"He never knew what hit him, but, no, he's not dead. Just sleeping for a while."

Only then did she realize just how desperate Kent had become. "What did you do to him?" she demanded, turning to face him, though her hair swept in front of her eyes. She thought she caught a movement of something on the bridge, another person, and her heart plummeted. Kent had brought along his accomplice.

"Don't worry about Ed. He'll survive," Kent assured her again. "Now, come on. You're so good at stealing this boat and sailing off into the sunset, why don't you do the honors and man the helm?"

A smug smile toyed at his lips, and Marnie never wanted to strike a person so much as she did just then. Her hand drew back to slap him.

"Don't even think about it," he warned.

From the corner of her eye, she caught a flash of movement. She turned and discovered Adam hurling himself from the bridge, flying through the air and straight at Kent.

"What—" Kent whirled, aimed his pistol, but Marnie, already poised to strike, hit his hand and the gun, flashing fire, spun out of his hand. Adam landed on Kent and sent them both sprawling along the smooth planks of the deck.

The accounting books were knocked from Kent's grasp. They fluttered upward and caught on the wind before dropping and sliding across the deck to drop into the sea. The computer disk followed, and Marnie raced to the rail, trying vainly to capture the evidence before it settled into the cold, dark waters. But the disk settled quickly beneath the surface. Devastated, she dared one look over her shoulder and grinned inwardly.

Adam was on top of Kent, one fist clenched around the front of Kent's expensive shirt, the other poised over his face, ready to pummel Kent's perfect features to a bloody mass.

Marnie didn't hesitate. Kicking off her shoes, she climbed onto the rail, poised for half a second, then dived neatly between the *Marnie Lee* and the boat tethered next to her.

"Marnie! Wait!" Adam's voice rang across the sound as ice-cold water rushed over her in a frigid wave. She swam downward, through the murky water, trying to see the books and the computer disk, hoping to keep some shred of evidence against Kent.

But the water was dark between the boats, and though she searched, she found nothing, not one paper drifting through the depths. Her lungs burned and she swam upward breaking the surface and gasping for air.

She glanced up at the *Marnie Lee* and watched as Adam dived into the water beside her. He surfaced a minute later, treading water and wiping water from his eyes.

"Anything?" he asked.

"Nothing."

He dived again, and Marnie followed suit, hoping against hope that not all of the evidence was lost. But she saw nothing, *nothing* and she knew in her heart that by this time, the pages that hadn't settled to the floor of the sound would be ruined and indecipherable. As for the computer disk, what were the chances that it, if discovered, was still operable?

Something slithered by her toes and she inwardly cringed at the thought of what kind of fish or eel had passed. She kicked toward the surface again.

With a loud roar, the engines of the *Marnie Lee* caught fire and the propeller started to churn in the dark water creating a whirlpool that sucked everything in its current. Marnie felt herself being pulled with papers, flotsam and kelp toward the craft. She struggled, swimming toward the shore against the drag of the frigid water, but the stern of the boat swung hard, coming closer. She managed to break the surface and gulp for air, but caught a mouthful of water.

"Watch out!" Adam cried, swimming toward her in quick, sure strokes. He wrapped one strong arm around her waist and swam with all his might toward the dark piers and the protection of the docks as she coughed and retched.

He only stopped when they were safely beneath the wharf and he could hold on to the barnacled pilings for support. "You okay?' he asked, and genuine concern etched his face.

"I—I'm fine," she gasped, her throat still squeezing shut against the onslaught of foul-tasting water. "But Kent. He's getting away!" Disappointment weighted her down. They'd lost the evidence they so sorely needed!

"He won't get far," Adam predicted. She turned in the water, so that her body was pressed to his.

"Why not?"

Tenderly Adam brushed aside a lank lock of hair that was plastered to her cheek. "I figured he'd make a run for it. I already called the Coast Guard. He'll be picked up before you and I get dried off."

"You didn't!"

"Oh, yes, I did." His brown eyes appeared darker in the shifting shadows beneath the dock. "Besides," he said, his voice thick, "it doesn't matter."

"Doesn't matter? Are you kidding? Do you know what those papers were?"

Adam's arm tightened around her. "If I were a betting man, I'd say they were the records explaining where all the missing funds went."

"Right, and now they're gone!" Her lips trembled from the cold. "And—and Kent, he won't admit to anything."

"Don't worry about it," Adam advised, his face closing the small distance between them.

"Why not?"

"Because it doesn't matter. When I saw Kent with that gun pointed at you, I realized that nothing mattered but your safety. God, I've been a fool." He kissed her then, his lips pressing possessively to hers, his mouth molding along the yielding contours of hers. She wrapped her arms around his neck, and despite the icy cold water, she felt warm and secure. As long as she was with Adam, *nothing else mattered.*

CHAPTER FOURTEEN

As soon as they climbed out of the water, Adam located a phone in the office of the marina and called an ambulance for Ed. The ambulance arrived within fifteen minutes, and Ed, arguing his health, was whisked off to the nearest hospital. After drying off with a couple of towels, courtesy of the locker room of the marina, Adam drove Marnie to the hospital, where they waited until Ed's doctor assured them that he'd be all right. Ed was suffering from a minor concussion. The doctor, a very distinguished man in his sixties whose authority brooked no argument, insisted, over Ed's very vocal protests, on keeping him in the hospital overnight for observation.

Two hours later, after witnessing Ed's cantankerous ribbing with one of the nurses, Marnie and Adam were satisfied that he would manage one night at Eastside General.

"Let's go to my place and clean up," Adam suggested as they climbed back into his car.

"So my apartment isn't good enough?" Marnie teased.

"Not tonight." Adam considered the printouts still strewn across Marnie's kitchen table and his conversation with Victor. He didn't want any reminders of the afternoon. Besides, until he'd heard that Kent was apprehended and locked up, he wanted to keep Marnie safe. The picture in his mind, of Kent pointing a pistol at Marnie's chest, kept returning in vivid and terrifying clarity.

Though Kent might know where Adam lived, he'd be less likely to try to surprise them there.

Adam's condominium was located on the eastern shore of Lake Washington, planted on a wooded hillside with steps that wound down to a private dock where his boat was anchored—remnants of the good life courtesy of Victor Montgomery.

He'd brought Marnie here a couple of times in the past few weeks, but they'd never stayed long and not once had she spent the night. Tonight would be different.

"First dibs on the shower," she said as they walked into the entry hall and gazed through a double bank of ceiling high windows with a view of the flint-colored waters of the lake. The bedrooms were downstairs, and Marnie walked confidently through Adam's room to the master bath, where she peeled off her clothes and stepped under the shower's steamy spray. The hot water rinsed the grit and briny smell from her skin. She washed her hair as well, trying to clean away the memory of Kent, his gun, and the pages of the accounting records as they floated just out of her reach.

She didn't hear Adam enter the bathroom, but felt the cold rush of air as he shoved aside the glass shower door and joined her in the misty warmth of the shower's spray.

"Couldn't wait?" she teased, glancing back over her shoulder to see his handsome face in the fog.

"That's one way of putting it." But he didn't seem all that interested in the soap. Standing behind her, he reached forward, his hands surrounding her abdomen as he pulled her closer to him, his fingers spreading over her skin as he drew her tight enough that her buttocks pressed against his thighs.

Her skin tingled, and the water acted as a lubricant, allowing his hands to move silkily against her skin, as he turned her toward him. Heat, as liquid as the gentle spray, uncoiled within her.

She felt his hardness and the brush of his lips against

her nape as he kissed her damp skin. She moaned low in her throat, and his fingers moved slowly upward, grazing the underside of her breasts, causing her nipples to stand erect.

He captured both her breasts in his hands, and she arched backward as he entered her, driving deeply into that warm womanly void that only he could fill.

I love you, she thought, but didn't dare utter the words. Instead she gasped as he moved within her, long and sure, causing a spasm of delight to ripple through her body as she braced against the wet tiles, receiving all of him eagerly.

"Marnie, love," he whispered against her ear, as he moved faster and faster until she was caught up in a whirlpool of emotion that wound tighter and tighter until she was spinning out of control, her breathing labored, her mind and soul filled with only Adam.

Crying her name, he plunged into her and collapsed and she, too, fell against the tile, her heart pounding in her ears. She didn't want to move, couldn't get enough air.

Finally, when her breathing had slowed to normal, she coughed and Adam chuckled. "We'd better get out of here before we drown."

"Or before the water turns cold," she agreed with a laugh.

They spent the rest of the evening sipping wine, eating wedges of cheese and bread and making love. As if their narrow escape had heightened Adam's need to be with her, he barely let her out of his sight. Even when she insisted on rinsing out her dress and hoping it would dry, he was right at her side, assuring her she looked stunning in his faded old bathrobe.

They were settled on the couch, staring at the sunset when Marnie stretched and smiled at Adam. "I guess it's time to do my daughterly duty."

"What's that?" he asked warily.

"I think I'd better call Dad and tell him what happened."

"Maybe you should wait on that," he suggested, taking her hand and drawing her into the circle of his arms. She was half lying against him, his legs surrounding hers, her back pressed to his chest, and his face was nestled next to hers.

"Until when? Kent calls up and asks for bail money?"

She glanced sideways to catch his gaze. Adam's golden brown eyes held hers, and for the first time a premonition of fear slid down her spine. "There's something you're not telling me."

"I saw your father today," Adam said slowly, as if the words were hard to find. "He stopped by your apartment—seemed to think that you had dinner plans with him."

Marnie's stomach knotted. "Oh. I didn't have any plans with him, but Kate thought the same thing. She was supposed to get hold of him and cancel."

At the mention of Kate's name, Adam's brows quirked. "She must've forgotten. Anyway, the upshot is that he not only found me in your apartment but he also saw the printouts."

"Oh, God," she whispered, a dull roar starting in her ears.

"He leapt to the wrong conclusions—"

"—that I was betraying him!" The dull roar seemed louder, more deafening; it beat through her brain and created a dark cloud at the corner of her vision.

"I tried to explain that it was all my fault, but he wouldn't listen. You know how he can get."

"Oh, yes," she said silently, waiting for the ax to fall. Victor would've been outraged that his only daughter had turned Judas on him. "He fired me, didn't he?"

"For starters."

"Worse?" Her insides crumbled. She'd never meant to hurt her father, and yet she'd done the one thing Victor could not handle. "Don't tell me. He disowned me."

"Something like that," Adam said, and there was naked pain in his eyes. As if he really did care what happened to her.

The glorious evening turned into a nightmare. Yes, she'd wanted her independence; yes, she'd wanted to follow her own path; but she'd never intended to wound her father, only to show him the truth—that Adam was innocent.

Tears stung the backs of her eyes, and she pulled out of Adam's embrace, as if in so doing she could change the past.

"I'm sorry," he whispered.

She laughed bitterly through the tears. "Don't be. It wasn't your fault," she said, flinging his own words back at him when she'd once tried to solace him.

"Yes. But this time it's a lie. This is all my fault. I knew involving you was a mistake, but it seemed the only logical way." Sighing, he threw back his head and stared at the ceiling. "I should never have put you into this kind of a position."

"But you did and I went into this with my eyes open."

"I pushed you."

"Well, maybe a little on the island. You weren't invited. But not since we've been back. Since we landed in Seattle, I chose to see you. I could just have easily chosen not to." *Except that I was beginning to fall in love with you,* she thought desperately, unable to utter the words. She didn't want to chase him out of her life by bringing up an emotion he didn't believe in, and now, after she'd learned that she'd lost her father, Adam was speaking as if he, too, were going to disappear from her life. Shivering, she rubbed her arms and felt the cozy warmth of terry cloth that smelled like him.

"There's more," he finally said as the shadows lengthened across the room.

"What could it possibly be?"

"I think I know who Kent's accomplice is."

"You do?" She was skeptical, and a headache was building behind her eyes. It wasn't every day a girl lost her family in one fell stroke.

"Kate Delany," he said.

"Kate?" She almost laughed. "You're out of your mind! No one is more loyal to my father than Kate."

He looked at her long and hard. "You like her, don't you?"

"Yes! She's like—well, not a second mother, but a big sister to me. Don't tell me she's a part of this mess, because I won't believe you!" Marnie said, her voice rising an octave as a wave of hysteria hit her. Too much had happened in one day and she couldn't believe that Kate, faithful, steady Kate, had stolen from the man she loved.

She scrambled to her feet and began to pace. "I've got to go, Adam. I've got to straighten all this out—"

"No."

"Yes, I—" God, why couldn't she think clearly? He was on his feet and gathering her into his arms.

"Stay with me."

"I can't, not tonight, but—"

"Not tonight," he whispered against her hair. "Stay with me forever."

His words stopped her protests. "I—I don't understand."

"Sure you do, Marnie. Marry me."

Then she understood. His desperation. His guilt. He felt responsible for her because Victor had disowned her. It was sweet and noble, but not a gesture of love.

"You don't mean this," she said.

"I want you to be my wife, Marnie," he whispered, and if she hadn't known better, she almost would have believed him.

The phone rang, and Adam answered. The conversation was long and one-sided. She only heard snatches of it, but guessed that Kent had been apprehended. Lord, what a mess. Her father would be devastated to find that Kent and Kate had betrayed him as well as his only daughter.

Shoving her hands in her pockets, she walked onto the deck and stared at the stars winking high in the sky. She ached inside, ached from the pain of losing her father and worse yet, ached with the thought that she was losing Adam.

Oh, yes, he'd proposed, but out of a sense of duty. Never once had he said he loved her.

She heard the sliding glass door open. "It's over," he said, coming up behind her and standing so close she could almost feel him. But he didn't touch her. "Kent's confessed to everything and Kate's in custody."

"And Dad?"

"He's at police headquarters."

"He must be destroyed."

"Your father has a way of bouncing back."

Marnie curled her fingers over the rail. "Not this time," she whispered, then turned, feeling the warmth of Adam's arms surround her. He kissed her so gently she thought her heart would break. She drowned herself in the smell and feel and taste of him for this one last night. Tomorrow they would both have to deal with reality and the very genuine probability that they'd never see each other again.

"IT'S NOT EASY for me to say I was wrong," Victor allowed, standing near the windows in his office, his hands clasped behind his back. "But I was, and I guess an apology is in order. Adam, Marnie...I'm sorry."

They were standing in his office together because they'd both been summoned. Adam's countenance was grim, and he stared at Victor long and hard. Marnie was nervous. Though her spine was stiff, her chin lifted defiantly, her heart screamed forgiveness. Victor was her father.

"I misjudged you, Adam. Listened to the wrong people and I...well, I was convinced that you were a traitor to the company." Victor took in a long breath. "To that end, I did you a horrible disservice and I intend to make a public statement to that effect. And, if you want it, I'd be glad to offer you a job, a full vice presidency with stock options. If you'll consider it."

"Never."

Victor clamped his mouth shut and nodded stiffly. "You could name your price."

"My price would be too high, Victor," Adam said with quiet authority. "I'd want it all. Including your daughter."

Marnie had to brace herself against the desk for support. *Don't do this,* she thought, *not now.* "No, Adam, I don't think you understand," she said trying to place a hand on his arm. He shook it off.

"I just don't trust anyone who would throw his only daughter out of his life."

Victor sucked in his breath. Marnie knew this was difficult for her father. The past few days, with the arrest of Kent and Kate, along with a few other people who had known about the embezzlement, had been hard on Victor. His usually firm face was lined, his eyes bagged. He reached across his desk and grabbed his pipe, which he stuffed with tobacco.

As he lit his pipe, he stared through the smoke at his only daughter. Marnie felt her heartstrings tug.

"Adam's right. Again. I've been especially rough on you," Victor admitted, his voice coarse from emotion. "I mistreated you, Marnie, and I wouldn't blame you if you never forgave me."

His hands trembled slightly and once again he hid them behind his back. His teeth clamped down on the stem of his pipe as he continued, "I never really listened to you, didn't believe you could make it on your own, threw a fit when you linked up with Adam and then, when you were only trying to help him, I did the worst thing a father can do. I acted as if you didn't exist. I wouldn't blame you if you never spoke to me again." He lowered himself heavily into his chair, broken and lost.

Marnie could barely get any words past the knot in her throat. "I—I love you, Dad," she whispered, sniffing loudly, and Victor's head snapped up.

"I love you, too, precious. I'm so sorry."

All at once he was standing, and Marnie rushed into his arms, crying uncontrollably as she clung to him. Her poor father. According to the police, Kate Delany had admitted swindling the funds because she felt she was in a dead-end situation with Victor. He'd never marry her, and she wasn't even certain he wouldn't eventually tire of her and pick out a younger, prettier secretary to become his next mistress.

Kent, jealous of Adam's influence with Victor, had found out about Kate's scheme. He had agreed to help her work out the movement of the funds and had made sure everything went through Adam's department, transferring the money from account to account and skimming off enough to eventually add up to half a million dollars. When an auditor had started nosing around, Kate, herself, had made the "discovery" of the embezzlement and with Kent's help, thrown the suspicion on Adam.

Now Kent and Kate were facing prosecution, Dolores

was turning state's evidence and even Gerald Henderson was testifying.

"Things will be all right," she told her father, smiling through her tears. "You'll see."

"God, I hope so." Victor swiped at his eyes, then pulled out a handkerchief and blew his nose loudly.

Marnie turned to Adam, but discovered that he'd left. The room was empty except for her father and herself.

"You'd better go find him," her father advised with a grin. "If I were you, I wouldn't let that one get away."

"I won't. But I don't know when I'll be able to work on the publicity for San Francisco—"

"Don't worry about it," her father said. "Just patch things up with Adam. The rest will work out."

She believed him. She ran through the hotel and impatiently waited for an elevator. "Come on, come on," she whispered as the lift eventually stopped and dropped her into the parking lot.

Running to the *B* level, her heart in her throat, she had the horrible thought that Adam didn't want her any longer. That, upon seeing her embracing her father, he assumed she would always be a spoiled little rich girl, Victor's daughter. But he was wrong—so wrong. She loved Adam with all her heart and nothing, *nothing* was going to keep her from pledging her love for him and making him understand that she didn't care about marriage, the future, or the past. She only wanted Adam. For as long as he would have her.

THE CALL FROM BRODIE came in too late. After speaking to Victor Montgomery directly, Brodie had finally come to understand that Adam had nothing to do with the embezzlement. Victor had called Brodie himself and given Adam a personal recommendation to the California lawyer.

Too late. Much too late. Adam had been pleased to give

Brodie the news that he didn't need him or his financing. Norman Howick, the rogue oilman, had promised him a deal that was perfect. Adam already had his plane ticket on the first flight tomorrow morning. He wondered if he'd hear from Marnie, and his heart wrenched at the thought.

If this deal with Howick worked out—and it looked good—Adam would be packed and leaving Seattle by the end of the week. Alone. Without her.

Well, that's what you wanted, wasn't it? You used her. To get what you wanted. So now that you're off the hook for the embezzling scam and she's back with Daddy, everything's just as you planned.

"Dammit all to hell," he growled, grabbing a bottle of Scotch from his liquor cabinet and walking outside to the deck of his condominium. The day was clear and bright and he'd planned on taking a boat ride. A warm summer sun spangled the water with golden light, and sailboats and skiffs were skimming the surface of Lake Washington. He'd even loaded a few supplies into his boat when the phone had rung and he'd raced back to the condo where he'd been able to tell Brodie where to stuff his offer.

But the satisfaction he should have felt, when he'd told Brodie where to get off, wasn't enough. He was still missing Marnie in his life and he felt hollow inside.

He uncapped the bottle and took a long pull before screwing on the cap and walking down the overgrown path to the deck where his small cabin cruiser lay docked. Unwinding the ropes from the pilings, he scanned the cliff where his condominium stood one last time—as if he expected Marnie, with her bright eyes and tinkling laughter to suddenly appear.

Forget her.

Impossible. He climbed aboard, pushed off and started the engine. It coughed, sputtered, then caught with a roar.

He gunned the throttle, and the boat picked up speed, slicing across the water while the wind tore at his face.

Marnie...Marnie...Marnie... Her face swam before his eyes and he knew it would take forever to forget her.

"Where're we going?"

Even her voice seemed to follow him. Stupidly, he looked over his shoulder and there she was. Just as he'd pictured her. He blinked once to believe what could only be an apparition, and she laughed. Braced against the railing, the wind singing through her hair, her smile beguiling and bright, she tossed back her head. "Well? The San Juans? The Caribbean? Maybe Alaska? Where?"

He was momentarily tongue-tied as Marnie reached over and quickly switched off the ignition. The engine died. The boat slowed to a stop and floated on the gentle roll of the lake.

"How'd you get here?" he demanded, finally comprehending that she'd fooled him somehow.

"I'm a stowaway," she said, laughing. "Just like you were."

She'd been in the small cabin below-decks? "But how did you know I'd go out today?" He was beginning to smile, he felt a familiar tug on his lips.

"I watched you. I pulled up to the front of the house and spied you carrying things on board. So I snuck down the hill and hid."

"But why?"

Her smile faded, and her blue eyes turned the color of the sea. "Because I want you, Adam," she said with obvious difficulty. "I can't bear the thought of you leaving. When I turned around in Dad's office and you'd disappeared, it seemed as if a part of me had left with you." She looked away from him now, as if afraid that he would reject her, and he realized how difficult this was for her.

"When you proposed to me, I knew it was because my

father disowned me, that you felt guilty and responsible." When he tried to interrupt, she held out a quivering hand to stop him. "And you thought I was one of those women in your life pushing for a commitment. But that's not true." When she faced him again, tears stood in her eyes. "I want you for as long as we can be together, and then, when it's over, I'll leave. I won't pressure you."

Adam laughed out loud. This beautiful, incredible woman was willing to give him everything and so much, much more. "Pressure me?" He grabbed her around the waist and kissed the tears from her eyes. "Are you crazy? You're the one who's going to get all the pressure, lady. I *want* you to marry me. I didn't propose out of some sense of duty, Marnie. I proposed because I want you to be my wife. The only reason I didn't drag you to a preacher kicking and screaming is that I thought you should resolve your relationship with your father as well as become your own woman. Isn't that what you've been screaming about for the past month?"

"You're serious?" she said, disbelief clouding her eyes.

"More serious than I've ever been in my miserable life," he assured her, his hands brushing a strand of pale hair from her eyes. "Believe me, Marnie. I want you. Today. Tomorrow. Forever. From the moment I saw you standing at the helm, battling the storm and barking orders at the sight of me, I knew you were the one. I just couldn't admit it. Not to you and not to myself."

He watched her swallow hard.

"I love you, Marnie Montgomery. If you don't believe anything else in this world, believe that I love you."

She blinked back her tears. "Does this mean that I'm still in the running for the publicist of Hotel Drake?"

"And anything else that has to do with me," he replied, kissing her soundly on the lips. "Will you marry me?"

"Absolutely."

"This won't interfere with your independence?" he teased.

"I am my own woman, Mr. Drake. And I know my own mind. And all I want is you."

"But you're a businesswoman now."

She smiled coyly. "Then I'll just have to move my business wherever you want. I'll have your children and tend your house. But, believe me, I will be my own woman."

"And my wife?" he asked skeptically.

"I think I can be both."

"You'd better be," he said, his mouth coming down to claim hers possessively, as if he already were her husband. She nearly dropped the keys to the boat into the water, but he didn't care. He had everything he needed in his arms.

Lifting his head, he asked, "Where do you want to go for a honeymoon?"

She grinned slowly. "Anywhere you take me." One of her eyebrows lifted saucily. "You know, we could start right now."

"Now?"

"Well, you do have a cabin downstairs and…if we want to, we can just sail away together."

"You're sure?"

"More sure than I've ever been in my life."

"Miss Montgomery, you've got yourself the deal of a lifetime." One arm around her waist, he plucked the keys from her palm with his free hand, started the engine, rammed the boat into gear, and set on a course that would hold them steady for the rest of their lives.

* * * * *

MILLION DOLLAR BABY

CHAPTER ONE

THE DOG STUCK his wet nose in Chandra's face. He whined and nuzzled her jaw.

"Go 'way," Chandra grumbled, squeezing her eyes shut. She burrowed deeper into the pillows, hoping Sam would get the message, but Sam didn't give up. The persistent retriever clawed at her covers and barked loudly enough to wake the neighbors ten miles down the road. "Knock it off, Sam!" Irritated, she yanked a pillow over her head and rolled over. But she was awake now and couldn't ignore Sam's whining and pacing along the rail of the loft; the metal licenses hanging from his collar rattled noisily.

When she didn't respond, he snorted loudly and padded quickly down the stairs, whereupon he barked again.

So he had to go out. "You should've thought of this earlier." Reluctantly, Chandra pulled herself into a sitting position and shoved a handful of hair from her eyes. She shivered a little and, yawning, rubbed her arms.

Sam barked excitedly, and she considered letting him out and leaving him on the porch. As Indian summer faded into autumn, the nighttime temperature in the Rocky Mountain foothills had begun to dip toward freezing. "It would serve you right," she said ungraciously as she glanced at the clock on the table near the bed. One forty-three. Still plenty of time to fall asleep again before the alarm clock was set to go off.

Grumbling under her breath, she had leaned over and was reaching under the bed, feeling around for her boots, when she heard it: the sound that had filtered through her dreams and pierced her subconscious over Sam's insistent barking. The noise, a distant wail, reminded Chandra of the hungry cry of a baby or the noise a Siamese cat would make if it were in pain. Chandra's skin crawled.

You're imagining things! she told herself. She was miles from civilization....

The cry, distant and muffled, broke the silence again. Chandra sat bolt upright in bed. Her heart knocked crazily. Clutching the quilt around her shoulders, she swung her feet to the floor and crossed the worn wood planks to the railing, where she could look down and survey the first floor of the cabin.

Moonlight streamed through the windows, and a few embers glowed behind the glass doors of the wood stove. Otherwise the cabin was cloaked in the darkness that night brought to this isolated stretch of woods.

She could barely see Sam. His whiskey-colored coat blended into the shadows as he paced beside the door, alternately whining and growling as he scratched on the threshold.

"So now you're Lassie, is that it?" she asked. "Telling me that there's something out there."

He yelped back.

"This is nuts. Hush, Sam," Chandra commanded, her skin prickling as her eyes adjusted to the shadows. Straining to listen, she reached for the pair of old jeans she'd tossed carelessly across the foot of the bed hours earlier. The familiar noises in this little cabin in the foothills hadn't changed. From the ticking of the grandfather clock to the murmur of the wind rushing through the boughs of the pine and aspen that surrounded the cabin, the sounds of the Colorado night were as comforting as they had always been. The wind chimes on her porch tin-

kled softly, and the leaky faucet in the bathroom dripped
a steady tattoo.

The cry came again. A chill raced up Chandra's spine.
Was it a baby? No way. Not up here in these steep hills.
Her mind was playing tricks on her. Most likely some
small beast had been wounded and was in pain—a cat
who had strayed or a wounded raccoon…maybe even a
bear cub separated from its mother….

Snarling, Sam started back up the stairs toward her.

"Hold on, hold on." Chandra yanked on her jeans and
stuffed the end of her flannel nightshirt into the waistband. She slid her feet into wool socks and, after another
quick search under the bed, crammed her feet into her
boots.

Her father's old .22 was tucked into a corner of the
closet. She hesitated, grabbed her down jacket, then curled
her fingers over the barrel of the Winchester. Better safe
than sorry. Maybe the beast was too far gone and she'd
have to put it out of its misery. Maybe it was rabid.

And maybe it's not a beast at all.

By the time she and the retriever crept back downstairs,
Sam was nearly out of his mind, barking and growling,
ready to take on the world. "Slow down," Chandra ordered, reaching into the pocket of her jacket, feeling the
smooth shells for her .22. She slipped two cartridges into
the rifle's cold chamber.

"Okay, now don't do anything stupid," she said to the
dog. She considered leaving Sam in the house, for fear that
he might be hurt by the wounded, desperate beast, but then
again, she felt better with the old dog by her side. If she
did stumble upon a lost bear cub, the mother might not be
far away or in the best of moods.

As she opened the door, a blast of cool mountain air
rushed into the room, billowing curtains and causing
the fire to glow brightly. The night wind seemed to have

forgotten the warm breath of summer that still lingered during the days.

Clouds drifted across the moon like solitary ghosts, casting shadows on the darkened landscape. The crying hadn't let up. Punctuated by gasps or hiccups, it grew louder as Chandra marched across the gravel and ignored the fear that stiffened her spine. She headed straight for the barn, to the source of the noise.

The wailing sounded human. But that was insane. She hadn't heard a baby cry in years…and there were no children for miles. Her dreams must have confused her…and yet…

She opened the latch, slid the barn door open and followed an anxious Sam inside. A horse whinnied, and the smells of dust and saddle soap and dry hay filled her nostrils. Snapping on the lights with one hand, she clutched the barrel of the gun with the other.

The horses were nervous. They rustled the straw on the floor of their boxes, snorting and pawing, tossing their dark heads and rolling their eyes as if they, too, were spooked. "It's all right," Chandra told them, though she knew that something in the barn was very, very wrong. The crying became louder and fiercer.

Her throat dry, her rifle held ready, Chandra walked carefully to the end stall, the only empty box. "What the devil…?" Chandra whispered as she spied a shock of black fur—no, *hair*—a baby's downy cap of hair! Chandra's heart nearly stopped, but she flew into action, laying down the gun, unlatching the stall and kneeling beside the small, swaddled bundle of newborn infant.

The tiny child was bound in a ratty yellow blanket and covered by a tattered army jacket. "Oh, God," Chandra whispered, picking up the small bundle only to have the piercing screams resume at a higher pitch. Blue-black eyes blinked at the harsh overhead lights, and the infant's little face was contorted and red from crying. One little fist had been freed from the blankets and now waved in agitation near its cheek. "Oh, God, oh, God." The baby, all lungs from the sound of it, squealed loudly.

"Oh, sweetheart, don't cry," Chandra murmured, plucking pieces of straw from the child's hair and holding him close to her breast, trying to be soothing. She scanned the rest of the barn, searching for the mother. "Hey—is anyone here?" Her sweat seemed to freeze on her skin as she listened for a response. "Hey? Anyone? Please, answer me!"

The only noises in the barn were the horses snorting, the baby hiccupping and crying, Sam's intermittent growls and Chandra's own thudding heart. "Shh...shh..." she said, as if the tiny infant could understand her. "We'll fix you up."

A mouse scurried across the floor, slipping into a crack in the barn wall, and Chandra, already nervous, had to bite back her own scream. "Come on," she whispered to the baby, as she realized the child had probably been abandoned. But who would leave this precious baby all alone? The infant howled more loudly as Chandra tucked it close to her. "Oh, baby, baby," Chandra murmured. Maternal emotions spurred her to kiss the downy little head while she secretly cursed the woman who had left this beautiful child alone and forsaken. "Who are you?" she whispered against the baby's dark crown. "And where's your mama?"

Wrapping the infant in her own jacket, she glanced around the dusty corners of the barn again, eyeing the hayloft, kicking open the door to the tack room, scanning the corners behind the feed barrels, searching for any signs of the mother. Sam, yelping and jumping at the baby, was no help in locating the woman's trail. "Hello? Are you here?" she called to anyone listening, but her own voice echoed back from the rafters.

"Look, if you're here, come on into the house. Don't be afraid. Just come in and we'll talk, okay?"

No answer.

"Please, if you can hear me, please come inside!"

Again, nothing. Just the sigh of the wind outside.

Great. Well, she'd tried. Whoever had brought the child here was on his or her own. Right now, the most pressing problem was taking proper care of the baby; anything else would have to wait. "Come on, you," she whispered to the infant again, tightening her hold on the squirming bundle. Ignoring the fretting horses, she slapped off the lights and closed the barn door behind her.

Once she was back in the cabin, Chandra cradled the child against her while she tossed fresh logs into the wood stove. "We'll get you warm," she promised, reaching for the phone and holding the receiver to her ear with her shoulder. She dialed 911, praying that the call would be answered quickly.

"Emergency," a dispatcher answered.

"Yes, this is Chandra Hill, I live on Flaming Moss Road," she said quickly, then rattled off her address over the baby's cries. "I discovered an infant in my barn. Newborn, dehydrated possibly, certainly hungry, with a chance of exposure. I—I don't know who it belongs to...or why it's here."

"We can send an ambulance."

"I live twenty miles from town. It'll be quicker if I meet the ambulance at Alder's Corner, where the highway intersects Flaming Moss."

"Just a minute." The dispatcher mumbled something to someone else and then was back on the line. "That's fine. The ambulance will meet you there."

"Good. Now, please contact the emergency room of the hospital...." Mechanically, she began to move and think in a way she hadn't done in years. Placing the child on the couch next to her, she carefully unwrapped the howling infant. Furious and hungry, the baby cried more loudly, his skinny little legs kicking. "It's a boy...probably two or three days old," she said, noticing the stump of the umbilical cord. How many infants so like this one had she examined during her short career as a physician? Hundreds. Refusing to let her mind wander into that forbidden territory, she concentrated on the wriggling child and carefully ran her fingers over his thin body. "He's Caucasian, very hungry, with no visible marks...." Her hands moved expertly over the smooth skin of the newborn, checking muscles and bones, small fingers and toes, legs, neck, spine, buttocks, head.... "Wait a minute..." She flipped the switch of a brighter light and noticed the yellow pallor of the whites of the baby's eyes. "He appears jaundiced and—" she touched the downy hair again, carefully prodding "—there's some swelling on the back of his head. Maybe caput succedaneum or cephalhematoma...yes, there's a slight bleeding from the scalp, and it appears only on the right side of his head. I don't think it's serious. The swelling isn't too large, but you'd better have a pediatrician look him over the minute he gets there." She continued to examine the infant as if he were her patient, her gaze practiced and sure. "I can't find anything else, at least not here without medical equipment. Did you get everything?"

"Every word," the dispatcher replied. "You're being recorded."

"Good." Chandra shone her flashlight in the baby's eyes, and he blinked and twisted his head away from the light. "Notify the sheriff's office that apparently the child's been abandoned."

"You don't know the mother?" the dispatcher questioned.

Chandra shook her head, though the woman on the

other end of the line couldn't see her. "No. I have no idea whom this guy belongs to. So someone from the sheriff's office should come out here and look through my barn again and check the woods. I called out and looked around for the mother, but I didn't have much time. I was more concerned with the child." She glanced to the windows and the cold night beyond. "My guess is she isn't far off. You've got the address."

Chandra didn't wait for a response, but hung up. She pulled a blanket from her closet and rewrapped the tiny newborn. He was beautiful, she thought, with a shock of downy black hair that stood straight off his scalp and a voice that would wake the dead. But why had he been abandoned? Had the mother, perhaps homeless, left him in the relative comfort of the barn as she searched for food? But why not stop at the cabin? Why leave him in the barn where there was a chance he would go unnoticed, maybe even die? Chandra shuddered at the thought. No, any responsible mother would have knocked on the door and would never, *never* have abandoned her child. "Come on, you," she said to the baby, "we've got work to do. You can't just lie there and scream."

But scream he did until she swaddled him more tightly and held him in her arms again. Only then did his cries become pitiful little mews. Chandra clutched him even tighter; the sooner she got him to the hospital the better.

Sam was sitting at attention near the couch. She looked in his direction, and the big dog swept the floor with his tail. "You," she said, motioning to the retriever, "stick around. In case the mother wanders back or the police show up."

As if the dog could do anything, she thought with a wry smile.

She found more blankets and tucked the child into a wicker laundry basket which, along with several bungee cords and the baby, she carried to her suburban. After securing the basket by the safety belt in the back seat, she crisscrossed the bungee cords over the baby, hoping to hold him as tightly and safely as possible.

"Hang on," she said to the infant as she hauled herself into the driver's seat, slammed the door shut and switched on the ignition. She rammed the monstrous rig into gear. The beams of the headlights washed across the side of the barn, and Chandra half expected a woman to come running from the shadows. But no one appeared, and Chandra tromped on the accelerator, spewing gravel.

"Dr. O'Rourke. Dr. Dallas O'Rourke. Please call E.R."

Dallas O'Rourke was writing out instructions for a third-floor patient named William Aimes when the page sounded. He scowled menacingly, then strode to the nearest house phone and punched out the number for the main desk of Riverbend Hospital. Checking the clock at the nurse's station, he realized he'd been on duty for the past twenty-two hours. His back ached and his shoulders were stiff, and he felt gritty from lack of sleep. He probably looked worse than he felt, he thought grimly as the receiver of the phone rubbed against the stubble of beard on his chin.

A voice answered, and he cut in. "This is Dr. O'Rourke. I was just paged."

"That's right. I'll connect you to E.R."

The telephone clicked and a familiar voice answered quickly. "Emergency. Nurse Pratt."

"O'Rourke." Leaning a stiff shoulder against the wall, he scribbled his signature across Aimes's chart, then rubbed his burning eyes. How long had it been since he'd eaten? Six hours? Seven?

"You'd better hustle your bones down here," Shannon Pratt advised. "We're swamped, and we've got a live one coming in. The switchboard just took the call. Something about an abandoned baby, a newborn with possible exposure, dehydration, jaundice and cephalhematoma."

Dallas scowled to himself. What was the old saying? Something about no rest for the wicked? The adage seemed to apply. "I'll be down in a few minutes." God, what he wouldn't do for a hot shower, hotter cup of coffee, and about ten hours in the rack.

He only took the time to leave the chart in the patient's room and give the third-floor nurses' station some instructions about Bill Aimes's medication. "And make sure he takes it," Dallas warned. "It seems Mr. Aimes thinks he can self-diagnose."

"He won't fool us," Lenore Newell replied, and Dallas was satisfied. Lenore had twenty years of nursing experience under her belt, and she'd seen it all. If anyone could get Bill Aimes to swallow his medication, Dallas decided, Nurse Newell could.

Unwilling to wait for the elevator, he took the stairs to the first floor and shoved open the door. The bright lights and frenetic activity of the emergency room greeted him. Several doctors were treating patients, and there was a crowd in the waiting room.

Shannon Pratt, a slim, dark-haired woman and, in Dallas's opinion, the most efficient nurse on staff, gave the doctor a quick smile. "They're on their way. Mike just called. They'll be here in about five minutes."

Mike Rodgers was one of the regular paramedics who drove ambulance for Riverbend Hospital.

"How's the patient?"

Shannon glanced at the notes she'd attached to a clipboard that she cradled with one arm. "Looks like the information we received from the first call was right on. The paramedics confirmed what the woman who called in already told us. The baby—only a couple of days old—has some signs of exposure as well as possible jaundice and slight swelling on one side of the head—the, uh, right," she said, rechecking her notes. "No other visible problems. Vital signs are within the normal range."

"Good. Order a bilirubin and get the child under U.V. as soon as I finish examining him. Also, I want as much information from the mother as possible, especially her RH factor. If she doesn't know it, we'll take blood from her—"

Shannon touched Dallas lightly on the arm. "Hold on a minute, Doctor. The mother's not involved."

Dallas stopped. He glanced swiftly at Nurse Pratt—to see if she was putting him on. She wasn't. Her face was as stone sober as it always was in an emergency. "Not involved? Then how the hell—"

Pratt held up a hand. "The woman who found the child—"

"The woman who *found* the child?" Dallas repeated as they passed the admitting desk, where Nurse Lindquist, a drill sergeant of a woman, presided. Over the noise of rattling gurneys and wheelchairs, conversation, paging and computer terminals humming, Dallas heard the distant wail of a siren.

Pratt continued, "The mother isn't bringing him in. This is a case of abandonment, or so the woman who called—" she glanced down at her notes on her clipboard again "—Chandra Hill, claims. Apparently she's saying that she discovered the baby in her barn."

"Her *barn?*"

"Mmm. Doesn't know how he got there." Shannon rolled her large brown eyes and lifted one slim shoulder. "I guess we'll find out soon enough."

Dallas swore silently. "If she's not the mother, how can we do anything with—"

"We're already working on consent forms," Pratt cut in,

ahead of him, as she usually was in a case like this. "The police are involved, and someone's looking up a judge to sign the waiver so we can admit the kid as a Baby John Doe."

"Wonderful," Dallas growled under his breath. With his luck, the kid's mother would show up, demand custody and file a complaint against the hospital. Or worse yet, not show up at all, and the child would have to be cared for by the state. "Just damned wonderful." What a way to end a shift!

The siren's wail increased to a glass-shattering scream that drowned out all conversation. Lights flashing, the white-and-orange rig ground to a stop near the double glass doors of the emergency room. Two men Dallas recognized hopped out of the cab and raced to the back of the emergency van.

"Okay, listen up," Dallas ordered Pratt. "I'll need that bilirubin A.S.A.P., and we'll need to test the child—drugs, HIV, white count, everything," he said, thinking of all the reasons a person might abandon a child. Maybe the woman couldn't afford proper medical attention for herself and the baby; maybe the child needed expensive care. "And get ready with an IV or a bottle..." God, what a mess!

The paramedics shoved open the back doors of the ambulance. Pulling out a small stretcher and carrying it between them, Mike Rodgers and Joe Klinger ran across the short covered span near the doors. A tiny baby, insulated by a thermal blanket, was strapped to the stretcher and was screaming bloody murder.

"Okay, Doc, looks like it's show time," Shannon observed as Dallas caught a glimpse of another vehicle, a huge red van of some sort, as it sped into the lot and skidded into a parking space.

The doors to the emergency room flew open. The paramedics, carrying the small stretcher, strode quickly inside.

"Room two," Nurse Pratt ordered.

Under the glare of fluorescent lights, Mike, a burly redheaded man with serious, oversize features and thick glasses, nodded curtly and headed down the hall without breaking stride. "As I said, it looks like exposure and dehydration, heart rate and b.p. are okay, but—"

Mike rattled off the child's vital signs as Joe unstrapped the child and placed him on the examining table. Dallas was listening, but had already reached for his penlight and snapped his stethoscope around his neck. He touched the child carefully. The right side of the infant's head was a little bit swollen, but there wasn't much evidence of bleeding. A good sign. The tiny boy's skin was tinged yellow, but again, not extremely noticeable. Whoever the woman was who found the child, she knew more than a little about medicine.

Dallas glanced over at the paramedic. "This woman who called in—Ms. Hill?—I want to talk to her. Do you have her number?"

"Don't need to," Mike said. "She followed us here. Drove that damned red van like a bat outta hell...."

The red van. Of course. Good. Dallas wasn't convinced that she wasn't the mother just trying to get some free medical attention for her child. So how did she know about the child's condition? Either she'd diagnosed the baby herself or someone else had...someone who understood pediatric medicine. One way or another, Dallas thought, flashing the beam of his penlight into the baby's dark eyes, he needed to talk to Ms. Hill.

"When she shows up," he said, glancing at Nurse Pratt, "I want to see her."

RIVERBEND HOSPITAL SPRAWLED across five acres of hills. The building was either five floors, four or three, depending upon the terrain. Painted stark white, it seemed to grow from the very ground on which it was built.

It resembled a hundred other hospitals on the outside and inside, Chandra thought; it was a nondescript medical institution. She'd been here before, but now, as she got the runaround from a heavyset nurse at the emergency room desk, Chandra was rapidly losing her temper. "But I have to see the child, I'm the one who found him!" she said, with as much patience as she could muster.

The admitting nurse, whose name tag read Alma Lindquist, R.N., didn't budge. An expression of authority that brooked no argument was fixed on features too small for her fleshy face.

Chandra refused to be put off by Nurse Lindquist. She'd dealt with more than her share of authority figures in her lifetime—especially those in the medical profession. One more wouldn't stop her, though Nurse Lindquist did seem to guard the admittance gate to the emergency room of Riverbend Hospital as if it were the portal to heaven itself and Chandra was a sinner intent on sneaking past.

"If you're not the mother or the nearest living relative," Nurse Lindquist was saying in patient, long-suffering tones, "then you cannot be allowed—"

"I'm the responsible party." Chandra, barely holding on to her patience, leaned across the desk. She offered the woman a professional smile. "I found the boy. There's a chance I can help."

"Humph," the heavyset nurse snorted, obviously unconvinced that the staff needed Chandra's help, or opinion for that matter. Alma Lindquist lifted her reddish brows imperiously and turned back to the stack of admittance forms beside a humming computer terminal. "I'm sure Dr. O'Rourke will come out and let you know how the infant's doing as soon as the baby has been examined. Now, if you'll just take a chair in the waiting area..." She motioned a plump hand toward an alcove where olive green couches were grouped around Formica tables strewn with worn magazines. Lamps offered pools of light over the dog-eared copies of *Hunter's Digest, Women's Daily, Your Health,* and the like.

Chandra wasn't interested in the lounge or hospital routine or the precious domain of a woman on an authority trip. Not until she was satisfied that everything humanly possible was being done for the baby. "If you don't mind, I think I'll just see for myself," she said swiftly. Lifting her chin and creating her own aura of authority, Chandra marched through the gate separating the examining area from the waiting room as if she'd done it a million times.

"Hey! Hey—you can't go in there!" the nurse called after her, surprised that anyone would dare disregard her rules. "It's against all procedure! Hey, ma'am! Ms. Hill!" When Chandra's steps didn't falter, Nurse Lindquist shouted, "Stop that woman!"

"Hang procedure," Chandra muttered under her breath. She'd been in enough emergency rooms to know her way around. She quickly walked past prescription carts, the X-ray lab and a patient in a wheelchair, hurrying down the tiled corridors toward the distinctive sound of a baby's cry. She recognized another voice as well, the deep baritone belonging to the redheaded paramedic who had hustled the baby into the ambulance, Mike something-or-other.

She nearly ran into the paramedics as they left the examination room. "Is he all right?" she asked anxiously. "The baby?"

"He will be." Mike touched her lightly on the shoulder, as a kindly father would touch a worried child. "Believe me, he's in the best hands around these parts. Dr. O'Rourke'll take care of the boy."

The other paramedic—Joe—nodded and offered a gap-toothed smile. "Don't you worry none."

But she was worried. About a child she'd never seen before tonight, a child she felt responsible for, a child who, because she'd found him, had become, at least temporarily, a part of her life. Abandoned by his own mother, this baby needed someone championing his cause.

The baby's cries drifted through the partially opened door. Without a thought to "procedure," Chandra slipped into the room and watched as a scruffy-looking doctor bent over a table where the tiny infant lay.

The physician was a tall, lanky man in a rumpled lab coat. A stethoscope swung from his neck as he listened to the baby's heartbeat. Chandra guessed his age as being somewhere between thirty-five and forty. His black hair was cut long and looked as if it hadn't seen a comb in some time, his jaw was shaded with more than a day's growth of beard, and the whites of his eyes were close to bloodshot.

The man is dead on his feet. This was the doctor on whom she was supposed to depend? she thought angrily as her maternal instincts took charge of her emotions. He had no right to be examining the baby. Yet he touched the child gently, despite his gruff looks. Chandra took a step forward as he said to the nurse, "I want him on an IV immediately, and get that bilirubin. We'll need a pediatrician—Dr. Williams, if you can reach him." The physician's gaze centered on the squirming child. "In the meantime, have a special crib made up for him in the pediatric ward, but keep him isolated and under ultraviolet. We don't know much about him. See if he'll take some water from a bottle, but keep track of the intake. He could have anything. I want blood work and an urinalysis."

"A catheter?" Nurse Pratt asked.

"No!" Chandra said emphatically, though she understood the nurse's reasoning. But somehow it seemed cruel to subject this tiny lump of unwanted human flesh, this small person, to the rigors of twentieth-century hospital technology. *But that's why you brought him here, isn't it? So that he could get the best medical attention available?* Belatedly, she held her tongue.

But not before the doctor's head whipped around and Chandra was suddenly caught in the uncompromising glare of Dr. Dallas O'Rourke. She felt trapped, like a specimen under a microscope, and fought against the uncharacteristic need to swallow against a suddenly dry throat.

His eyes were harsh and cold, a vibrant shade of angry blue, his black eyebrows bushy and arched, his skin swarthy and tanned as it stretched tight across the harsh angles of his cheekbones and a nose that hooked slightly. Black Irish, she thought silently.

"You are...?" he demanded.

"Chandra Hill." She tilted her chin and unconsciously squared her shoulders, as she'd done a hundred times before in a hospital not unlike this one.

"The woman who found the child." Dr. O'Rourke crossed his arms over his chest, his lab coat stretching at the shoulder seams, his lips compressed into a line as thin as paper, his stethoscope momentarily forgotten. "Ms. Hill, I'm glad you're here. I want to talk to you—"

Before he could finish, the door to the examining room flew open and banged against the wall. Chandra jumped, the baby squealed and O'Rourke swore under his breath.

Nurse Lindquist, red-faced and huffing, marched stiffly into the room. Her furious gaze landed on Chandra. "I knew it!" Turning her attention to the doctor, she said, "Dr. O'Rourke, I'm sorry. This woman—" she shook an accusing finger in Chandra's face "—refused to listen to me. I told her you'd talk to her after examining the child, but she barged in with complete disregard to hospital rules."

"I just wanted to see that the baby was safe and taken

care of," Chandra interceded, facing O'Rourke squarely. "As I explained to the nurse, I've had medical training. I could help."

"Are you a doctor licensed in Colorado?"

"No, but I've worked at—"

"I knew it!" Nurse Lindquist cut in, her tiny mouth pursing even further.

"It's all right, Alma," O'Rourke replied over the baby's cries. "I'll handle Ms. Hill. Right now, we have a patient to deal with."

Nurse Lindquist's mouth dropped open, then snapped shut. Though her normal pallor had returned, two high spots of color remained on her cheeks. She shot Chandra a furious glare before striding, stiff backed, out of the room.

"You're not making any points here," the doctor stated, his hard jaw sliding to the side a little, as if he were actually amused at the display.

"That's not why I'm here." *Arrogant bastard,* Chandra thought. She'd seen the type before. Men of medicine who thought they were gods here on earth. Well, if Dr. O'Rourke thought he could dismiss her, he had another think coming. But to her surprise, he didn't ask her to leave. Instead, he turned his attention back to the baby and ran experienced hands over the infant's skin. "Okay, that should do it."

Chandra didn't wait. She picked up the tiny little boy, soothing the child as best she could, rocking him gently.

"Let's get him up to pediatrics," Dr. O'Rourke ordered.

"I'll take him." Nurse Pratt, after sending Chandra a quizzical glance, took the child from Chandra's unwilling arms and bustled out of the room.

The doctor waited until they were alone, then leaned a hip against the examining table. Closing his eyes for a second, he rubbed his temples, as if warding off a headache. Long, dark lashes swept his cheek for just an instant before his eyelids opened again. "Why don't you tell me everything you know about the baby," he suggested.

"I have," Chandra said simply. "I woke up and found him in my barn."

"Alone?"

"*I* was alone, and as far as I could tell, the baby was left."

He rubbed the back of his neck and winced, but some of the tension left his face. He almost smiled. "Come on, let's go down to the cafeteria. I'll buy you a cup of coffee. God knows I could use one."

Chandra was taken aback. Though his voice was gentle, practiced, his eyes were still harsh and assessing. "Why?"

"Why what?"

"The coffee. I don't think—"

"Humor me, Ms. Hill. I just have a few questions for you."

With a shrug, she agreed. After all, she only wanted what was best for the child. And, for the time being, this hard-edged doctor was her link to the baby. He held the door open for her, and she started instinctively toward the elevators. She glanced down a hallway, hoping to catch a glimpse of Nurse Pratt and the child.

Dr. O'Rourke, as if reading her mind, said, "The pediatric wing is on two and the nursery is on the other side, in maternity."

They reached the elevators and he pushed the call button. Crossing his arms over his chest and leaning a shoulder against the wall, he said, his voice slightly kinder, "Let's get back to the baby. You don't know whom he belongs to, right?"

"That's right."

"So he wasn't left by a relative or friend, someone who wasn't interested in keeping him?"

"No." Chandra felt a tide of color wash up her cheeks.

"Look, Dr. O'Rourke, I've told you everything I know about him. My only concern is for the child. I'd like to stay here with him as long as possible."

"Why?" The doctor's gaze had lost its hard edge, but there were a thousand questions in his eyes. He was a handsome man, she realized, surprised that she noticed. And had it not been for the hours of sleeplessness that honed his features, he might even be appealing. But not to her, she reminded herself.

The elevator bell chimed softly and the doors whispered open. "You've done your duty—"

"It's more than duty, okay?" she cut in, unable to sever the fragile connection between her and the baby. Her feelings were pointless, she knew, but she couldn't just drive away from the hospital, leaving that small, abandoned infant. Not yet. Not until she was assured the child would be cared for. Dr. O'Rourke was holding the door open, so she stepped into the elevator.

"Dr. O'Rourke. Dr. Dallas O'Rourke..."

The doctor's shoulders slumped at the sound of the page. "I guess we'll have to take a rain check on the coffee." He seemed as if he were actually disappointed, but that was ridiculous. Though, to be honest, he looked as though he could use a quart of coffee.

As for Chandra, she was relieved that she didn't have to deal with him right now. He was unsettling somehow, and she'd already suffered through a very unsettling night. Pressing the Door Open button so that an elderly man could enter, she watched O'Rourke stride down the hall. She was grateful to be away from his hard, assessing gaze, though she suspected he wasn't as harsh as he outwardly appeared. She wondered if his sharp tongue was practiced, his guarded looks calculated....

"There she is! In there! Stop! Hold the elevator!"

Chandra felt a sinking sensation as she recognized

the distinctive whine of Nurse Lindquist's voice. No doubt she'd called security and was going to have Chandra thrown off the hospital grounds. Footsteps clattered down the hall. Chandra glanced back to O'Rourke, whom she suddenly viewed as her savior, but he'd already disappeared around the corner at the far end of the corridor. As she looked in the other direction, she found the huge nurse, flanked by two deputies from the Sheriff's Department, moving with surprising speed toward her. Chandra's hand froze on the elevator's Door Open button, although her every instinct told her to flee.

One of the deputies, the shorter one with a flat face and salt-and-pepper hair, was staring straight at her. He didn't bother with a smile. "Chandra Hill?"

"Yes?"

He stiff-armed the elevator, holding the doors open, as if to ensure that she wouldn't escape. "I'm Deputy Bodine, and this is Deputy White." He motioned with his head toward the other man in uniform. "If you don't mind, we'd like to ask you a few questions about the child you found on your property."

CHAPTER TWO

"So I FOLLOWED the ambulance here," Chandra said, finishing her story as the two officers listened, alternately exchanging glances and sipping their coffee as she explained how she discovered the abandoned child.

Deputy Stan Bodine, the man who was asking the questions, slid his cafeteria chair closer to the table. "And you have no idea who the mother might be?"

"Not a clue," Chandra replied, tired of repeatedly answering the same questions. "I know it's strange, but that's what happened. Someone just left the baby in my barn." What was it about everyone in the hospital? Why were they so damned disbelieving? Aware of the curious glances cast her way by a few members of the staff who had come down to the cafeteria for their breaks, Chandra leaned across the table and met the deputy's direct gaze. "Why would I lie?"

"We didn't say—"

"I know, but I can tell you don't believe me."

Deputy White, the younger of the two, stopped writing in his notepad. With thin blond hair, narrow features and a slight build, he wasn't the least bit intimidating. In fact, he seemed almost friendly. Here, at least, was one man who seemed to trust that she was telling the truth.

Deputy Bodine was another story. As bulky as the younger man was slim, Bodine carried with him a cynical attitude honed by years with the Sheriff's Department. His expression was cautiously neutral, but suspicion radiated from him in invisible waves. As he swilled the bitter coffee and chewed on a day-old Danish he'd purchased at the counter, Chandra squirmed in her chair.

"No one said we didn't believe you," Bodine answered patiently. "But it's kind of an outrageous story, don't you think?"

"It's the truth."

"And we've seen lots of cases where someone has... changed the facts a little to protect someone."

"I'm *not* protecting anyone!" Chandra's patience hung by a fragile thread. She'd brought the baby to the hospital to get the poor child medical attention, and this cynic from the Sheriff's Department, as well as the good Dr. O'Rourke, were acting as if she were some kind of criminal. Only Deputy White seemed to trust her. "Look, if you don't believe me, you're welcome to check out all my acquaintances and relatives. I just found the baby. That's all. Someone apparently left him in the barn. I don't know why. There was no trace of the mother—or anyone else for that matter." To keep her hands busy, she rolled her cup in her fingers, and a thought struck her. "The only clue as to who the child might be could come from his swaddling. He was wrapped in a blanket—not the one I brought him here in—and an old army jacket."

Bodine perked up a bit. "Where's the jacket?"

"Back at my cabin."

"We'll pick it up in the morning. And don't disturb anything in that stall where you found the kid...or the rest of the barn for that matter." He took another bite of his Danish and washed it down with a swallow of coffee. Several crumbs fell onto the white table. He crumpled his cup. Without getting up from his chair, he tossed the wadded cup high into the air and watched as it bounced off the rim of a trash container.

The younger man clucked his tongue and tucked his

notepad into his pocket. "I don't think the Nuggets will be drafting you this season," he joked. He shoved out his chair and picked up the discarded cup to arc it perfectly into the trash can.

"Lucky shot," Bodine grumbled.

Chandra was just grateful they were leaving. As Bodine scraped his chair back, Dr. O'Rourke strode into the room. He was as rumpled as before, though obviously his shift was over. His lab coat was missing, and he was wearing worn jeans, an off-white flannel shirt and a sheepskin jacket.

"Just the man we wanted to see," Bodine said, settling back in his chair. Chandra's hopes died. She wanted this interrogation over with.

"So I heard." O'Rourke paid for a cup of coffee and joined the group. "Nurse Pratt said you needed some information on Baby Doe. I've left a copy of the admittance forms at the E.R. desk, and I'll send you a complete physical description of the child, as well as that of his condition, as soon as it's transcribed, probably by the afternoon. I can mail it or—"

"We'll pick it up," Bodine cut in, kicking back his chair a little so that he could view both Chandra and O'Rourke in one glance. "Save us all some time. Anything specific we should know right now?"

"Just that the baby is jaundiced, with a swelling on the right side of his head, probably from a difficult birth. Other than that, he looks pretty healthy. We're keeping him isolated, and we're still running tests, but he's eating and giving all the nurses a bad time."

Chandra swallowed a smile. So O'Rourke did have a sense of humor after all.

The doctor continued. "A pediatrician will examine him as soon as he gets here, and we'll give you a full report."

"Anything else?" White asked, scribbling quickly in his notepad again. He was standing now, but writing as quickly as before.

"Just one thing," O'Rourke replied, his gaze sliding to Chandra before returning to the two deputies. "The umbilical cord wasn't severed neatly or clamped properly."

Bodine dusted his hands. "Meaning?"

"Meaning that the baby probably wasn't born in a hospital. I'd guess that the child was delivered without any medical expertise at all. The mother probably just went into labor about three days ago, experienced some difficulty, and when the baby finally arrived, used a pair of scissors or a dull knife to cut the cord."

Chandra sucked in her breath and O'Rourke's gaze swung to her. She cringed at the thought of the baby being born in anything less than sterile surroundings, though, of course, she knew it happened often enough.

"What do you think?" O'Rourke asked, blue eyes drilling into hers.

"I don't know. I didn't really look at the cord, only to see that it wasn't bleeding." Why would he ask her opinion?

"You examined the infant, didn't you?"

Chandra's response died on her tongue. Dr. O'Rourke didn't know anything about her, she assumed, especially her past, and she intended to keep it that way. She'd come to this part of the country for the express purpose of burying her past, and she wasn't about to unearth it now. She fiddled with her coffee cup. "Yes, I examined him."

"And you were right on with your diagnosis."

No reason to explain. Not here. The Sheriff's Department and Dr. O'Rourke—and the rest of the world, for that matter—might find out all about her eventually, but not tonight. "I've had medical training," she replied, the wheels turning in her mind. "I work as a white-water and camping guide. We're required to know basic first aid, and I figure the more I know, the better I can handle any situation. So, yes, I've taken every medical course I could."

O'Rourke seemed satisfied; his gaze seemed less suspicious and his eyes turned a warmer shade of blue.

Bodine stood and hiked up his pants. "Well, even if you don't think the baby was delivered in a hospital, it won't hurt to check and find out if anyone's missing a boy."

"Missing from a hospital?" Chandra asked.

O'Rourke lifted a dark eyebrow. "What better place to steal a newborn?"

"Steal?" she repeated.

Squaring his hat on his head, Deputy Bodine said, "The black-market baby business is booming these days."

"You think someone *stole* this baby then left him in my barn? That's crazy—"

Bodine smiled his first genuine smile of the night. "Sounds a little farfetched, I admit, but we have to consider every angle. Could be that whoever took Baby Doe could have holed up in your barn for the night and something went wrong. Or they left him there while they went searching for food or more permanent shelter."

"Or you could've scared 'em off," Deputy White added.

Chandra shook her head. "There was no one in the barn. And I live nearly ten miles from the nearest store."

"We'll check out all the possibilities in the morning," Bodine assured her. Turning his gaze to O'Rourke, he said, "Thanks, Doctor. Ms. Hill."

The deputies left, and Chandra, not even realizing how tense she'd become, felt her shoulders slowly relax.

"So how's he doing?" she asked, surprised at her own anxiety, as if she and that tiny baby were somehow connected, though they weren't, of course. The child belonged to someone else. And probably, within the next few hours, Bodine and White would discover the true identity of

Baby Doe and to whom he belonged. Chandra only hoped that the parents had one hell of an explanation for abandoning their child.

"The boy'll be fine," O'Rourke predicted, stretching his long legs in front of him. He sipped from his cup, scowled at the bitter taste and set the cup on the table, content to let the steam rise to his face in a dissipating cloud. Chandra noticed the lines of strain around the edges of his mouth, the droop at the corners of his eyelids.

"Can I see him?" she asked.

"In the morning."

"It *is* the morning."

His gaze locked with hers and the warmth she'd noticed earlier suddenly fled. "Look, Ms. Hill, I think you and the kid both need some rest. I know *I* do." As if to drive home his point, he rubbed a kink from his shoulders. "You can see him around ten."

"But he *is* eating." She'd heard him say so before, of course, but she couldn't stem the question or the concern she felt for the child.

A whisper of a smile crossed the doctor's thin lips. "Nurse Pratt can barely keep up with him." O'Rourke took another swallow of his coffee, his unsettling eyes regarding Chandra over the rim of his cup. She felt nervous and flustered, though she forced herself to remain outwardly calm. "So who do you think left him in your barn?" he asked.

"I don't know."

"No pregnant friends who needed help?"

Her lips twisted wryly. "I already told the deputies, if I had friends who needed help, I wouldn't suggest they use one of my stalls as a birthing room. They could've come into the house or I would've driven them to the hospital. I think, somehow, we would've found 'room at the inn,' so to speak."

O'Rourke arched a thick eyebrow, and his lips twitched, as if he were suppressing a smile. "Look, there's no reason to get defensive. I'm just looking for some answers."

"I gave all of mine to the deputies," she replied, tired of the unspoken innuendoes. She leaned forward, and her hair fell in front of her shoulders. "Now *you* look, *Doctor* O'Rourke, if I knew anything about that baby—anything at all—I'd pass that information along."

He didn't speak, but his relentless stare continued to bother her. The man was so damn intimidating, used to getting his way—a handsome, arrogant son of a gun who was used to calling the shots. She could see he was tired, irritated, but a little amused at her quick temper. "You know," she said, "I expected the third degree from the police, but not from you."

He lifted a shoulder. "The more I know about the child, the better able I am to take care of him. I just don't want to make any mistakes."

She was about to retort, but the words didn't pass her lips. Chandra knew far too well about making mistakes as a physician. Her throat closed at the sudden burst of memories, and it was all she could do to keep her hands from shaking. She took a quick drink of coffee, then licked her lips. When she looked up at O'Rourke again, she found him staring at her so intently that she was certain he could see past the web of lies she'd so carefully woven around her life here in Ranger, Colorado. Did he know? Could he guess that she, too, had once been a physician?

But no one knew about her past, and that's the way she intended to keep it.

The silence stretched between them, and she shuffled her feet as if to rise. It was late, and she wanted to get some sleep before she returned later in the morning, and yet there was something mesmerizing about Dr. O'Rourke that kept her glued to her chair. He was good-looking in a sensual way that unnerved her, but she'd been around lots of good-looking men, none of whom had gotten under her skin the way O'Rourke had. Maybe it was because he was a doctor, or maybe it was because she was anxious about the baby, or maybe he was just so damned irresistible that even she, a woman who'd sworn off men, and most specifically men with medical degrees, was fascinated. She nearly choked on her coffee.

As if sensing she was about to flee, he finished his coffee and cleared his throat. "You know," he said, tenting his hands under his chin, "you'd better get used to answering questions, because the minute the press gets wind of this story, you're going to be asked to explain a helluva lot more than you have tonight."

The press. Her heart dropped like a stone and memories rushed over her—painful memories of dealing with reporters, photographers, cameramen. Oh, God, she couldn't face them again. She wasn't ready for the press. What if some hotshot reporter saw fit to dig into her background, through her personal life? Her hands grew suddenly damp. She slid her arms through the sleeves of the jacket she'd tossed over the back of her chair. "I think I can handle a few reporters," she lied, hoping she sounded far more confident than she felt.

"It'll be more than a few. Think about it. This could be the story of the year. Christmas is only a few months away, and the press just loves this kind of gut-wrenching drama."

"You could be wrong."

O'Rourke shook his head and stifled a yawn. "Nope. An abandoned baby, a complicated, unexplained birth, perhaps a missing mother, the mystery child swaddled only in an old army jacket—could it be the father's?—it all makes interesting copy." Rubbing a hand around his neck, he added, "You'll have a couple of reporters from the *Banner,* maybe someone from Denver. Not to mention the local television stations. My guess is that this story will go regional at least." He lifted his eyebrows speculatively, as if he believed he were far more informed than she. Typical. "And once the story hits the news services, I'll bet that neither one of us is gonna get a moment's rest." He crossed one battered running shoe over the other and rested his heels on the seat of the chair Deputy White had recently vacated.

"Are you trying to scare me?" Chandra asked.

"Just preparing you for the inevitable."

"I can handle it," she assured him, while wondering what it was about this man that made her bristle. One minute she wanted to argue with him, the next she wanted to trust him with her very life. Good Lord, she must be more tired than she'd guessed. She'd instinctively come to depend on him because he was a doctor—the one man who could keep her in contact with the baby. After all, he could stop her from seeing the child.

Deep down, though, she knew her anger wasn't really directed at Dr. O'Rourke specifically. In fact, her wrath wasn't really aimed at doctors in general; just at a few doctors she'd known in her past, especially a particularly egotistical plastic surgeon to whom she'd once been married: Douglas Patrick Pendleton, M.D., P.C., and all-around jerk.

Now she couldn't afford to have Dr. O'Rourke against her. Not only was he her link to the child, there was a chance he might help her with the press and the Sheriff's Department—not that she needed any help, she reminded herself. But Dr. O'Rourke did seem fair and was probably sometimes kind, even though he appeared ragged and cynical around the edges.

"I guess I am tired," she finally said, as half an apology. Dr. O'Rourke wasn't the least bit like Doug. No, this man with his rugged good looks, beat-up running shoes and worn jacket looked more like a mountain climber than an emergency-room physician. She couldn't imagine him reading medical journals or prescribing blood-pressure medicine or attending medical conferences in Chicago or New York.

And yet it did seem possible that he could care for an abandoned infant. On that score, Chandra was comfortable. O'Rourke, she sensed, was a good doctor, the kind of man who had dedicated himself to people in need rather than to the almighty dollar. Unless the unshaven jaw, worn clothes and fatigue were all part of an act.

She didn't think so. His gaze was too honest. Cutting, yes. Intense, certainly. But honest.

Scraping back her chair, she stood and thrust her hand across the table. "Thanks for all the help."

He clasped her palm with his big hand, and she forced a smile, though Dr. O'Rourke didn't return the favor. As his fingers surrounded hers, the doctor stared at her with those electric blue eyes that could look straight into her soul, and her face suddenly felt hot.

Quickly, Chandra yanked back her hand and stuffed it into the pocket of her jeans. Her voice nearly failed her. "I'll be back later," she assured him as she turned and marched out of the cafeteria, hoping he didn't guess that she'd reacted to his touch. She was tired, that was all. Tired and nervous about the infant. God, what a night!

DALLAS WATCHED CHANDRA HILL retreat. A fascinating woman, he thought grudgingly as he swirled the dregs of coffee in his cup. There was something about her that didn't quite click, an attitude that didn't fit with the rest of her.

Still, she intrigued him. The feel of her hand in his had caused his heart to race a second, and she'd reacted, too—

he'd seen the startled look in her eyes as she'd drawn back.
He laughed inwardly. If she only knew how safe she was
with him. He'd sworn off beautiful women long ago, and
despite her uncombed hair, hastily donned clothes and
face devoid of makeup, Chandra Hill was gorgeous.

And trouble. One hundred fifteen pounds of trouble
packed onto a lithe frame. She obviously bucked authority:
Nurse Lindquist would testify to that. At the thought of
Alma Lindquist's agitated expression, Dallas grinned. Yes,
he imagined Chandra with her sharp tongue and high-
handed attitude could get under anyone's skin.

Fortunately, Dallas didn't have time for a woman in
his profession. Not any woman. And especially not a fire-
cracker like Ms. Hill. He rubbed his eyes and blinked several times, trying to dispel her image.

He was off duty. One last look at the Baby John Doe
and then he'd go home and sleep for twelve hours. Maybe
longer. But first, he might stop by the sheriff's office and
listen to the recording of Chandra Hill's call to the emergency dispatcher. If he heard the tape, perhaps he'd get
a better perspective on what condition the child was in
when she found him. Oh, hell, it probably wouldn't do
any good. In fact, he decided, he was just curious about
the lady. And he hadn't been curious about a woman in a
long, long time.

Squashing his cup with one hand, he shoved himself
upright and glanced at the corridor down which Chandra
had disappeared.

Who was this tiny woman with her unlikely knowledge
of medicine? Jaundice was one thing, the layman could
spot that. And a lay person might notice the swelling on
the baby's head. But to come up with the medical term
after a few first aid courses? Unlikely.

Nope. For some reason, Chandra Hill was deliberately
holding back. His eyes narrowed at the thought.

Obviously the child wasn't hers. He'd checked out her trim figure and quick step. No, she wasn't the least bit postpartum, and she was far too young to have a daughter who'd gotten pregnant. But a sister? Or a friend?

Could the baby be stolen? Could Chandra have taken the child from its home, then realized it needed medical attention, concocted this story and brought him in? Dallas didn't think so. A dozen questions about Chandra Hill swam through his tired mind, but he couldn't come up with an answer.

Drawing in a long breath, he was surprised that the scent of her—a clean soapy scent unaffected by perfume—lingered in the stale air of the cafeteria, a fresh breeze in this desert of white walls, polished chrome, chipped Formica and the ever-present smell of antiseptic.

She was definitely a mystery, he decided as he shoved back his chair, but a mystery he was too damned tired to unravel.

CHAPTER THREE

SAM WAS WAITING for Chandra. As she opened the door, he jumped up, yipping excitedly, his tail wagging with unbridled enthusiasm. "Oh, come off it," Chandra said, smiling despite the yawn that crept up on her. "I wasn't gone that long."

But the big dog couldn't get enough attention. He bounded back and forth from his empty dish to her as she started for the stairs. "Don't get too anxious, Sam. Breakfast isn't for another three hours." In the loft, she nudged off one boot with the toe of the other. "What a night! Do you believe it? The police and even the doctor seem to think I had something to do with stealing the baby or kidnapping the kid or God only knows what! And that Dr. O'Rourke, you should meet him..." She shook her head, as if she could physically shake out her own thoughts of the doctor. Handsome, arrogant and sexy, he was a man to steer well clear of. But she couldn't. Not if she wanted to see the baby again. "Believe me, this is one mess," she told the dog, who was still pacing in the kitchen.

She thought about checking the barn one last time, but was too exhausted. Tossing off her jacket, she dropped onto the unmade bed, discarded her jeans and sought solace under the eiderdown quilt she'd inherited from her grandmother.

With a disgruntled sigh, Sam swept up the stairs and parked in his favorite spot on the floor near the end of the bed. Chandra heard his toes click on the old pine boards as he circled three times before dropping to the floor. She sighed to herself and hoped sleep would quickly overcome her weary body as it seemed to have done for the old dog.

Three days after moving into this place a couple of years before, Chandra had discovered Sam, so thin his ribs showed beneath his matted, dusty coat, his eyes without spark and a wound that stretched from one end of his belly to the other. He'd snarled at her approach, his white teeth flashing defensively as she'd tried to touch him. But she'd brought him water and food, and the listless dog had slowly begun to trust her. She'd eventually cleaned the wound, the mark of a cornered wild animal, she'd guessed, and brought Sam into the house. He'd been with her ever since, a permanent and loving fixture in her life.

But a far cry from a man or a child.

She smiled sadly and pulled the covers closer around her neck. Just because she'd found an abandoned infant was no reason to start dreaming old dreams that she'd discarded long ago. But though her body was fatigued, her mind was spinning with images of the wailing, red-faced infant, the sterile hospital room and the unsettling visage of Dr. Dallas O'Rourke. Even with her eyes closed, she could picture him—jet black hair, eyes as blue as a mountain lake and lips that could thin in anger or gentle into the hint of a smile.

Good Lord, what was wrong with her? In frustration, she pounded her pillow with her fist. In less than four hours, she had to get up and lead a white-water expedition of inexperienced rafters down the south fork of the Rattlesnake River. She didn't have time for complications, especially complications involving a man.

She glared at the clock one more second before squeezing her eyes closed and thinking how she would dearly love someday to have a baby of her very own.

DALLAS WASHED THE GRIT from his eyes and let the spray of the shower pour over him. He leaned one arm against the slippery tiles of the stall and closed his eyes as the jets of hot water soothed the ache of overly tired muscles.

The past thirty-six hours had been rough, one case after another. A twelve-year-old with a broken arm, a messy automobile accident with one fatality and two critically injured passengers flown by helicopter to Denver, a drug overdose, two severe strep cases, an elderly woman who had fallen and not only broken her hip, but fractured her pelvis, and, of course, the abandoned baby.

And it was the thoughts of the infant and the woman who'd found him that continued to rattle around in Dallas's tired mind. Probably because he was overworked. Overly tired. His emotions already strung tight because of the phone call....

He twisted off the faucets and pulled down a towel from the top of the glass shower doors, rubbing his body dry, hoping to infuse a little energy through his bloodstream.

He should eat, but he couldn't face an empty refrigerator. The joys of being a bachelor, he thought fatalistically, because he knew, from the experience of a brief, painful marriage, that he would never tie himself down to one woman again. No, medicine was his mistress, and a demanding mistress she was. She exacted far more attention than any woman would. Even the woman to whom he'd been married, Jennifer Smythe O'Rourke Duncan.

The bitch. He still couldn't think of her without the bitter taste of her betrayal rising like bile in his throat. How could he have been duped by her, when all along, she'd been more of a slave to her precious profession than he had to his?

He didn't bother shaving, that he could do in the morning, but walked through the connecting door to the bedroom and flopped, stark naked, onto the king-size bed. He dropped the towel onto the floor. He'd pick up it and his discarded clothes in the morning.

Muttering oaths he saved for the memory of his marriage, he noticed the red light flashing on his phone recorder, though he hadn't been paged. A personal call. Great. He didn't have to guess who the caller was. He rewound the tape and, settling back on the pillows, listened as his half brother's voice filled the room.

"Hey, Dal. How's it goin'? I just thought I'd touch base before I drop by tomorrow. You remember, don't ya?"

How could he forget, Dallas thought grimly. His half brother, Brian, was here in the waning weeks before college started, not because he was working, but because he'd spent the summer camping and rafting in the wilderness. Only now, with less than two weeks until he left for school, did Brian think about the more practical side of education.

"Hey, man, I really hate to bug you about this and I'll pay you back every dime, you know I will, but I just need a little something to keep me goin' until my money gets here."

Right. Brian's money was scholarship dollars and not nearly enough of them to pay for the tuition, books and a carefree lifestyle.

The machine clicked off, and Dallas scowled. He shouldn't loan Brian another nickel. Already the kid was into him for nearly ten thousand. But his mother's other children, Brian, Brian's twin sister, Brenda, and their older sister, Joanna, were the only family Dallas had ever known.

However, the loans to Brian were starting to bother Dallas, and he wondered, not for the first time, if he should be writing checks directly to University of Southern California rather than to the kid himself.

He'd find out this afternoon. After he felt refreshed and after he made rounds at the hospital, checking on his patients. The image of the newborn flitted through his mind again, and Dallas wondered if he'd run into Chandra Hill. Now there was a woman who was interesting, a woman who knew her own mind, a woman with a presence of authority that was uncommon, a woman who, even in old boots, jeans and a nightshirt, her hair wild, her face free of makeup, was the most attractive woman he'd seen in a long, long time.

He rolled under the covers, switched off the light and decided, as he drifted off, that chances were he might just see her again. And that thought wasn't all that unpleasant.

CHANDRA PULLED HER HAIR into a ponytail when she heard the hum of an engine and the crunch of tires against the gravel drive. She pulled back the curtains to discover a tan cruiser from the Sheriff's Department rolling to a stop near the barn. Sam, vigilant as ever, began to bark and growl.

"You haven't had this much excitement in a long while, have you?" Chandra asked the retriever as she yanked open the door. Two deputies, the same men she'd met in the hospital, climbed out of the car.

She met them on the porch.

"Sorry to bother you so early," Deputy White apologized, "but we're about to go off duty and would like to check over the barn and house."

"Just to see if there's anything you might have missed," Bodine added.

"I hope there is," Chandra replied, feeling more gracious this morning than she had last night. She thought again, as she had for the past four hours, of the dark-haired infant. She'd called the hospital the minute she'd awakened, but had been unable to prod much information from the nurse who had taken her call. "Doing as well as can be expected. Resting comfortably…in no apparent distress…."

When Chandra had mentioned that she'd brought the baby in, the nurse had warmed a bit. "Oh, Miss Hill, yes. Dr. O'Rourke said you'd probably call." Chandra's heart had nearly stopped. "But there's nothing new on the baby's condition."

So Chandra had been given stock answers that told her nothing. *Nothing!* Except that O'Rourke had had the decency to advise the staff that she would be inquiring. Surprised that he'd bothered at all, she again decided she'd have to make a friend of O'Rourke, even if it killed her.

She hadn't been this frustrated since she'd lived in Tennessee…. With a start, she pulled herself away from the painful thought of her past and her short-lived marriage, noticing that the deputies looked beyond fatigued. "How about a cup of coffee before you get started?" she asked, and the weary men, seeming much less belligerent in the soft morning light, smiled in response.

"I wouldn't want to trouble you," White said.

"No trouble at all. I was just about to pour myself a cup."

"In that case, you're on," Bodine cut in, obviously not wanting the younger man to talk them out of a quick break.

They followed her inside. Sam, ever watchful, growled deep in his throat as they crossed the threshold, but the men seemed unintimidated by the old retriever.

Chandra reached for two mugs from the shelf near the kitchen window and couldn't help asking, "Have you learned anything else?"

"About the baby?" Bodine asked, and taking off his hat, he shook his head. "Not yet. We thought maybe we could find something here. You got that jacket?"

"The what…? Oh! Just a minute." She poured them each a mug of coffee from the glass pot warming on the burner of the coffee maker. From the closet, she retrieved the ratty old army jacket and tattered blanket that had swaddled the newborn. Smudges of dirt, a few wisps of straw and several patches of a dark, dried substance that looked like blood discolored the dull green jacket. Faded black letters stated: U S ARMY, but no other lettering was visible.

"Anyone could pick up something like this in a local G.I. surplus store," Bodine grumbled to himself as he searched the jacket's pockets and discovered nothing more exciting than lint. He focused his attention on the blanket. It offered few clues to the identity of the newborn, fewer than the jacket. Frowning, he pulled a couple of plastic bags from his pocket and wrapped the blanket and jacket separately, then accepted a cup of coffee. Motioning toward his plastic-encased bundles, he added, "We'll see if the lab can come up with any clues from these."

"But don't hold your breath," White added. "Despite what Sheriff Newell thinks, the lab guys aren't gods. There's just not too much here to go on." He flashed a hint of a smile as Chandra handed him a steaming cup. "Thanks."

"Our best hope is for someone to step forward and claim the kid."

"Is it?" Chandra asked, surprised by her own sense of dread of some relative appearing. "But what if whoever tries to claim the child is a fraud?"

"We won't let that happen." Nonetheless, Bodine's eyebrows drew together and a deep cleft appeared on his forehead. He was worried. He studied the hot black liquid in his mug, as if he could find the answers he was searching for in the coffee. "Why don't you go over your story one more time." He held up a couple of fingers when he caught Chandra's look of distress. "Since we're here, talk us through it again and show us what you did last night."

Chandra wasn't all that eager to repeat the story, but she knew that was the only way to gain the deputies' confidence. And after all, they were all on the same side, weren't they? Didn't Chandra, the police and the hospital staff only want what was best for the tiny, motherless infant?

"Okay," she said with a forced smile. "It's just exactly what I said last night." As they sipped their coffee, Chandra pointed to the loft. "I was sleeping up there when Sam—" the big dog perked up his ears and his tail dusted the floor at the sound of his name "—started barking his fool head off. Wouldn't let up. And that's when I heard the sound."

"The baby crying," White cut in.

"Yes, but I didn't know that it was a baby at first." She continued while they finished their coffee, then led them back outside as Sam tagged along.

The sun was climbing across the morning sky, but frost still glazed the gravel of the parking lot. Sam nosed around the base of a blue spruce where, hidden in the thick needles, a squirrel scolded him. Deputy White tossed the jacket and blanket onto the front seat of the car.

"The noise was coming from the barn." Chandra followed her footsteps of the night before and shoved open the barn door. Shafts of sunlight pierced the dark interior, and the warm smell of horses and musty hay greeted her. The horses nickered softly as dust motes swirled in the air, reflecting the morning light.

"The baby was in the end stall." She pointed to the far wall while petting two velvety noses thrust over the stall doors.

As the officers began their search, Chandra winked at Cayenne, her favorite gelding. "I bet you want to go out," she said, patting his sleek neck. In response, the sorrel tossed his head and stamped. "I'll take that as a yes." Cayenne shoved his big head against her blouse and she chuckled. "Grouchy after you missed a night's sleep, aren't you?" She walked through the first stall and yanked open the back door. One by one, she opened the connecting gates of the other stalls and the horses trotted eagerly outside to kick up their heels and run, bucking and rearing, their tails unfurling like silky banners behind them.

Chandra couldn't help but smile at the small herd as she stood in the doorway. Life had become so uncomplicated since she'd moved to Ranger, and she loved her new existence. Well, life had been uncomplicated until last night. She rubbed her hand against the rough wood of the door and considered the baby, who only a few hours before had woken her and, no doubt, changed the course of her quiet life forever.

Inside the barn, Deputy Bodine examined the end stall while Deputy White poked and prodded the barrels of oats and mash, checked the bridles and tack hanging from the ceiling and then clambered up the ladder to the hayloft. A mouse scurried into a crack in the wall, and cobwebs, undisturbed for years, hung heavy with dust.

"This yours?" Bodine asked, holding up Chandra's father's .22, which she'd left in the barn upon discovering the infant.

Heat crept up her neck. "I must've dropped it here when I found the baby. I was so concerned about him, I didn't think of much else."

Bodine grunted as he checked the chamber.

"Nothing up here," Deputy White called down from the loft.

"I could've guessed," Bodine muttered under his breath as he turned his attention back to the stall, instructing Chandra to reconstruct the scene. She pointed out the position of the baby and answered all the questions he asked. Deputy White climbed down the ladder from the loft and, after observing the stall, asked a few more questions that Chandra couldn't answer.

The deputies didn't say as much, but Chandra read in their expressions that they'd come up against a dead end. Outside, they walked through the paddocks and fields, and even followed a couple of trails into the nearby woods. But they found nothing.

"Well, that's about all we can do for now," Bodine said as they walked across the yard. He brushed the dust from his hands.

"What about the baby?" Chandra asked, hoping for just a little more information on the infant. "What happens to him?"

"Don't worry about him. He's in good hands at the hospital. The way I hear it, Dr. O'Rourke is the best E.R. doctor in the county, and he'll link the kid up to a good pediatrician."

"I see."

Bodine actually offered her a smile. "I'm sure O'Rourke will let you look in on the kid, if you want. In the meantime, we'll keep looking for the baby's ma." He opened the passenger side of the cruiser while Deputy White slid behind the wheel. "If we find her, she's got a whole lotta questions to answer before she gets her kid back."

"And if you don't find her?"

"The baby becomes a ward of the state until we can locate a parent, grandparent or other relative."

Chandra's heart wrenched at the thought. "He'll be put in an institution?"

"Probably a foster home—whatever Social Services decides. But we'll cross that bridge when we come to it. Right now, we have to find the mother or next of kin. We'll keep you posted," he said, as if reading the worry in her eyes for the very first time.

Bodine slid into his seat, and Deputy White put the car into gear. Chandra waited until the car had disappeared around the bend in the drive before returning to the house with the rifle.

So what happens next? she wondered. If nothing else, the baby was certainly a part of her life.

As she walked into the house, she heard the phone ringing. She dashed to the kitchen. "Hello?"

"Miss Hill?"

She froze as she recognized Dr. O'Rourke's voice. "Hello, doctor," she said automatically, though her throat was dry. Something was wrong with the baby. Why else would he phone her?

"I thought you'd like to know that the baby's doing well," he said, and her knees nearly gave out on her. Tears of relief sprang to her eyes. O'Rourke chuckled, and the sound was throaty. "He's got the nurses working double time, but he's eating, and his vital signs are normal."

"Thank God."

"Anytime you want to check on him, just call," Dallas said.

"Thanks for calling."

There was a long pause before O'Rourke replied. "You seemed concerned last night and…since the boy has no family that we know of…"

"I appreciate the call."

As DALLAS HUNG UP the phone in his office at the hospital, he wondered what the devil had gotten into him. Calling Chandra Hill? All night long he'd remembered the worry in her eyes and, though he wasn't scheduled to work for hours, he'd gotten up and gone directly to the hospital, where he'd examined the baby again.

There was something about the boy that touched a part of him he'd thought was long buried, though he assumed his emotions were tangled up in the circumstances. The baby had been abandoned. Dallas's emotional reaction to the infant was because he knew that baby had no one to love him. No wonder he had felt the unlikely tug on his heartstrings when he'd examined the baby and the infant had blinked up at him with trusting eyes.

"This is crazy," Dallas muttered, and headed back to the parking lot. He would drive over to the club and swim out his frustrations before grabbing some breakfast.

RIVERBEND HOSPITAL APPEARED larger in daylight. The whitewashed walls sprawled upward and outward, seeming to grow along the hillside, spawning several clinics connected by wide breezeways. The Rocky Mountains towered behind one facility, and below it, within view, flowed the Rattlesnake River. The town of Ranger was three miles away.

Chandra parked her truck in the visitors lot and prepared herself for a confrontation with another nurse on an authority trip. She wouldn't have to pass anywhere near the emergency room, so in all probability, she wouldn't run into Nurse Lindquist again. Or Dr. O'Rourke. He'd appeared dead on his feet last night, surely by now he was sleeping the morning away.

Probably with his wife.

Chandra's eyebrows pulled together, and above her nose a groove deepened—the worry line, Doug used to call it. The thought that Dr. O'Rourke was married shouldn't have been unpleasant. Good Lord, he deserved a normal life with a wife and kids...yet...

"Oh, stop it!" she grumbled, walking under the flat roof of a breezeway leading to the main entrance of the hospital. The doors opened automatically and she walked through.

The reception area was carpeted in an industrial-strength weave of forest green. The walls were gray-white and adorned with framed wildlife posters hung exactly ten feet apart.

A pert nurse with a cap of dark curls, a dash of freckles strewn upon an upturned nose and a genuine smile greeted Chandra from behind the information desk. "May I help you?"

Chandra returned the woman's infectious grin. "I hope so. I'm Chandra Hill. I brought in the baby—"

The nurse, Jane Winthrop, laughed. "I *heard* about you and the baby," she said, her dark eyes flashing merrily. "I guess I should transfer to the night shift in E.R. That's where all the action is."

"Is it?" Chandra replied.

"Oh, yeah. But a lot of it's not too pretty, y'know. Car accidents—there was a bad one last night, not too long before you brought in the baby." Her smile faded and her pretty dark eyes grew serious. "Anyway, what can I do for you?"

Jane Winthrop was a refreshing change from Alma Lindquist.

"I'd like to see the baby, see how he's doing."

"No problem. He's in pediatrics, on two. Take the elevator up one floor and turn to your left. Through the double doors and you're there. The admitting nurse, Shannon Pratt, is still with him, I think. She'd just started her shift when they brought the baby in."

Chandra didn't waste any time. She followed Jane's directions and stopped by the nurse's station in the pediatric wing on the second floor. Chandra recognized Nurse Pratt, the slim brunette, but hadn't met the other woman, plump, apple cheeked, with platinum blond hair, a tanning-booth shade to her skin and pale blue eyes rimmed with eyelashes that were thick with mascara.

"You're back," Shannon said, looking up from some paperwork on the desk. "I thought you would be." She touched the eraser end of a pencil to her lips as she smiled and winked. "And I bet you're looking for one spunky little guy, right?" Before Chandra could answer, Shannon waved toward one of the long corridors. She leaned closer to the other nurse. "I'll be back in a minute. This is the woman who brought in the Baby Doe."

The blond nurse, whose nameplate read Leslie Nelson, R.N., smiled and a dimple creased one of her rosy cheeks. "He's already won over the entire staff—including Alma Lindquist!" She caught a warning glance from Shannon, but continued blithely on. "You know, there's something special about that little guy—" The phone jangled and Leslie rolled her huge, mascara-laden eyes as she picked up the receiver. "Pediatrics. Nurse Nelson."

"She's right about that," Shannon agreed as she led Chandra down the hallway. "Your little friend has wormed his way into the coldest hearts around. Even Dr. O'Rourke isn't immune to him."

"Is that right?" Chandra asked, lifting an eyebrow. She was surprised to hear Dr. O'Rourke's name, and even more surprised to glean a little bit about the man. Not that she cared. He was just a doctor, someone she'd have to deal with while visiting the baby.

"One of the nurses caught him holding the baby this morning. And he was actually smiling."

So there was a more human side to the gruff doctor. Chandra glanced down the hallway, half expecting to see him, and she was surprised at her feeling of disappointment when he didn't appear.

Shannon clucked her tongue and shook her head. "You know, I didn't think anyone could touch that man, but apparently I was wrong." She slid Chandra a glance. "Maybe there's hope for him yet. Here you go. This little guy's still isolated until we get the results of his tests. But my guess is, he'll be fine."

They stood behind a glass partition. On the other side of the clear wall, the dark-haired infant slept, his face serene as an ultraviolet light warmed him. There were other newborns as well, three sleeping infants, who, separated by the wall of glass, snoozed in the other room. Nearby, a nurse was weighing an unhappy infant who was showing off his lungs by screaming loudly.

"We're busy down here," Nurse Pratt said.

"Looks that way." Chandra focused her attention back on the isolated baby, and her heart tugged. So perfect. So beautiful. So precious. The fact that he was separated from the rest of the infants only made his plight seem more pitiful. Unwanted and unloved, living in a sterile hospital with only nurses and doctors—faces, hands and smells that changed every eight hours—to care for him.

A lump formed in her throat—a lump way out of proportion to the situation. She'd been a physician, for God's sake, a *pediatrician*. She was supposed to handle any given situation and keep her emotions in check. But this time, with this child, she was hopelessly ensnared in the trap of caring too much. Involuntarily her hand touched the cool glass. If only she could pick him up and hold him close....

Chandra felt Shannon's gaze resting on her, and she wondered just how much of her emotions played upon her face. "It looks as if he'll be okay once we get the jaundice under control," Shannon said softly.

"And his caput—"

"Nothing serious, according to Dr. O'Rourke, and he's the best E.R. physician I've ever met."

"And the pediatrician?"

"Dr. Spangler was on duty and looked him over last night. Agreed with O'Rourke right down the line. Dr. Williams will check the baby later this morning."

Chandra felt a sense of overwhelming relief. She stared at the perfect round cheeks and the dark sweep of lashes that caressed the infant's skin, watched as his tiny lips moved ever so slightly, as if he were sucking in his dream. On whose breast did he subconsciously nurse?

Chandra's heart wrenched again and she felt rooted to the spot. Though she'd seen hundreds of babies, they had all come with mothers firmly attached, and she'd never once experienced a pang of devotion so deep. The feeling seemed to spring from an inner well of love she'd never known existed.

True, she had been married, had hoped to bear her own children, and so, perhaps, all her motherly instincts had been turned inward. But now, years later, divorced and having no steady man in her life, her nurturing urges seemed stronger than ever, especially where this tiny baby was concerned.

"Uh-oh." Nurse Pratt exhaled softly. "Trouble."

"What?" Chandra turned and discovered two men striding toward her. Both were of medium height, one with curly black hair, the other straight brown. They wore slacks and sweaters, no hospital ID or lab coats.

"Make that double trouble," Shannon corrected.

"Miss Hill?" the man with the straight hair and hard eyes asked. "Bob Fillmore with the *Ranger Banner*."

Chandra's heart sank as the curly-haired man added, "Sid Levine." He held out his hand as if expecting Chandra to clasp it. "Photographer."

She felt Sid's fingers curl over her hand, but she could barely breathe. Reporters. Already. She wasn't yet ready to deal with the press. "But how did you know—"

"Have you got permission to be here?" Nurse Pratt cut in, obviously displeased.

Fillmore ignored her. "I heard you found an infant in the woods near your home. Abandoned, is that right?"

"I don't think this is the place to conduct an interview," Nurse Pratt insisted. Behind the glass, the baby started making noise, soft mewing sounds that erupted into the hard cries Chandra had heard the night before. Chandra whipped her head around and the sight of the infant, *her* baby—no, of course he wasn't hers, but he *was* in distress and she wanted desperately to run to him and pick him up.

"Is that the kid?" Fillmore asked. "Any idea who he belongs to? It is a he, right?" He looked to Chandra for verification as he withdrew a small pad and pen from the inner pocket of his jacket. He'd also unearthed a small tape recorder from his voluminous pockets and switched on the machine.

The baby cried louder, and Chandra felt her back stiffen. "Look, I'm not ready to give you an interview, okay? Yes, I found the baby—in my barn, not the woods—but since this is a case the police are investigating, I think you'd better go to the sheriff's office to get your facts straight."

"But why your property?" Fillmore insisted, his tape recorder in his outstretched hand. Memories, painful as razors, cut through Chandra's mind as she remembered the last time she'd had microphones and recorders waved in her face, how she'd been forced to reveal information to the press.

"I don't know. Now, if you'll excuse me—"

"Just a few more questions."

Obviously the man wasn't about to give up. Chandra glanced at Nurse Pratt and, without thinking about protocol, ordered, "Call security."

Fillmore was outraged. "Hey—wait—you can't start barking orders—"

"If she doesn't, I will." Dr. O'Rourke, who could have heard only the last of the exchange, strode down the hall. Dressed in jeans, a long-sleeved T-shirt and down vest, he nonetheless oozed authority as he glared at the reporter and photographer with a stare that would have turned the fainthearted to stone. He motioned to Shannon. "Do as Ms. Hill suggests. Call security." Nurse Pratt walked to the nearest telephone extension and dialed.

"Why all the secrecy?" Fillmore demanded, apparently not fainthearted and not the least bit concerned about O'Rourke's stature, anger or command of the situation. "We could help you on this, y'know. A couple of pictures of the baby and an article describing how he was found, and maybe, just maybe, the kid's folks will reconsider and come back. Who knows what happened to them? Or to him? For all anyone knows, this kid—" he hooked a thumb toward the glass "—could've been stolen or kidnapped. Right now some distraught mother might be anxious to have him back again, and you guys are impeding us."

He's right, Chandra thought, disliking the reporter intensely as she noticed a flicker of doubt cross Dr. O'Rourke's strong features.

"In due time," the doctor replied, his gaze landing on Chandra for a heart-stopping second. A glimmer of understanding passed between them, as if she and the doctor were on the same side. Quickly, O'Rourke turned back to the reporters. "My first concern is for the child's health."

"The kid got problems?" Fillmore persisted, his eyes lighting with the idea of a new twist to an already news-worthy story.

"We're running tests." O'Rourke, in a sweeping glance, took in the two men and Chandra, and once again she felt a bond with him, though she told herself she imagined it. She had nothing, save the baby, in common with the man.

O'Rourke wasn't about to be pushed around. "Now, if

you'll excuse me, I have a patient I have to see. If you want to continue with this interview, do it somewhere else." He turned just as two security guards, hands on holsters, entered the pediatric wing.

"Okay, what's going on here?" the first one, a man with a thick waist and a face scarred by acne, demanded. His partner stood two feet behind him, as if he expected the reporters to draw weapons.

"Just lookin' for a story," Fillmore said.

"Well, look somewhere else."

Levine threw up his hands, but Fillmore stood his ground and eyed the doctor. "What is it with you, O'Rourke? Why do you always see us as the bad guys?"

"Not bad guys, just guys without much dignity." Dr. O'Rourke stepped closer to Fillmore and scrutinized the reporter with his uncompromising gaze. "You tend to sensationalize things, try to stir up trouble, and that bothers me. Now if you'll excuse me, and even if you won't, I've got a patient to examine."

Summarily dismissing both men, O'Rourke stepped into the nursery to examine the baby. With a nudge from the guards, both reporter and photographer, muttering under their collective breath, headed out of the wing. "You, too," the heavier guard said, motioning toward Chandra.

"She can stay." O'Rourke, though on the other side of the window, pointed toward Chandra before focusing his attention on the crying infant. Chandra had to swallow a smile as she stared at the vest stretched taut across O'Rourke's back.

The guard shrugged and followed his partner through the double doors while Chandra stood dumbstruck. She didn't know what she expected of O'Rourke, but she suspected he wasn't a particularly tolerant man. His demeanor was on the edge of being harsh, and she was certain that

LISA JACKSON 303

just under his facade of civility, he was as explosive as a volcano.

On the other hand, he touched the infant carefully, tenderly, as he gently rolled the screaming baby from front to back, fingers expertly examining the child. It was all Chandra could do to keep from racing into the room and cradling the baby herself, holding the infant close and rocking him.

This has got to stop, Chandra, she told herself. *He's not yours—he's not!* If she had any brains at all, she'd tear herself away from the viewing window, walk out of Riverbend Hospital and never look back. Let the proper authorities take care of the child. If they could locate the parents or next of kin, so be it. If not, the Social Services would see that he was placed with a carefully-screened couple who desperately wanted a child, or in a foster home...

Quit torturing yourself!

But she stayed. Compelled by the child and fascinated by the doctor examining him, Chandra Hill watched from the other side of the glass.

Why she felt a special bond with the child and the doctor, she didn't know. And yet, as if catching a glimmer of the future in a crystal ball, she felt as if they, all three, were inextricably bound to each other.

CHAPTER FOUR

DR. O'ROURKE WAS QUICK and efficient. His examination took no longer than five minutes, after which he gave Nurse Pratt a few instructions before emerging from the glassed-in room. "I think he'll be out of isolation tomorrow," he said, joining Chandra.

"That's good."

"Know any more about him?"

She shook her head and began walking with him, wondering why she was even conversing with him. She thought she caught an envious look from Shannon as they left the nursery, but she chided herself afterward. Envious? Of what?

"The Sheriff's Department show up at your place?" he asked as they walked. His tone wasn't friendly, just curious. Chandra chalked his questions up to professional interest.

"This morning at the crack of dawn. The same two deputies." She stuffed her hands into her pockets. "They poked around the barn and the grounds. Didn't find much."

O'Rourke pushed the button for the elevator, and the doors opened immediately. "Parking lot?"

"Yes." She eyed him for a second, and as the car descended, said, "I'm surprised to see you here this early. Last night you looked like you could sleep for twenty years."

"Thirty," he corrected, then allowed her just the hint of

a grin, and she was shocked by the sensual gleam of white teeth against his dark skin. His jaw was freshly shaven, and the scent of soap and leather clung to him, overpowering the antiseptic odor that had filtered through the hospital corridors and into the elevator. "But I've learned to survive on catnaps. Five hours and it's all over for me." He studied her with that intense gaze that made her throat grow tight, but she held her ground as a bell announced they'd landed at ground level. "What about you?"

"Eight—at least. I'm running on empty now."

He cocked a dubious eyebrow as they walked past the reception area and outside, where the sunlight was bright enough to hurt the eyes. Chandra reached into her purse for her sunglasses and noticed that O'Rourke squinted. The lines near his eyes deepened, adding a rugged edge to his profile. The man was handsome, she'd give him that. Dealing with him would be easier if he were less attractive, she thought.

"That reporter will be back," he predicted. "He smells a story and isn't about to leave it alone. You might be careful what you say."

Though she knew the answer from personal experience, she wanted to hear his side of the story. "Why?"

His lips twisted into a thin line of disapproval and his eyes turned cold. "Words can be misconstrued, taken out of context, turned around."

"Sounds like the voice of experience talking."

"Just a warning. For your own good."

He acted as if he were about to turn away, and Chandra impulsively grabbed the crook of his arm, restraining him. He turned sharply and his gaze landed on her with a force that made her catch her breath. She swallowed against the dryness in her throat and forced the words past her lips. "When can I see the baby? I mean, really see him—hold him."

She didn't remove her fingers and was aware of the tensing of his muscles beneath the sleeves of his shirt and jacket. "You want to hold him?"

"Oh, yes!" she cried, her emotion controlling her tongue.

"You feel something special for the child, some sort of bond?" he guessed.

"I..." She crumbled under the intensity of his gaze. "I guess I feel responsible."

When he waited, for what she knew was further elaboration, she couldn't help but ramble on. "I mean he was found on *my* property, in my barn. I can't help but think that someone wanted me to find him."

"That you were chosen?" He sounded as if he didn't believe her, yet he didn't draw his arm away.

"Yes. No. I mean—I don't know." She'd never been so confused in her life. Always she'd been a take-charge kind of individual, afraid of nothing, ready for any challenge. But one tiny newborn and one very intimidating man seemed to have turned her mind to mush. "Look, Doctor, I just want to hold the baby, if it's okay with you."

He hesitated, and his voice was a little kinder. "I don't know if it's a good idea."

"What?" She couldn't believe he would dissuade her now, after he'd called her to tell her the child had improved and then had let her stick around. But that warming trend had suddenly been reversed.

"Until the Sheriff's Department sets this matter straight, I think it's best for you and the child if you stayed away from the hospital until everything's settled."

Her hopes, which she had naively pinned on this man, collapsed. "But I thought—"

"I know what you thought," O'Rourke said. "You thought that since I rescued you from those vultures, loosely called reporters, that I was on your side, that you could get at the kid through me. Well, unfortunately, it doesn't work that way. Either you're a relative of the child or you're not. And I don't like being used."

"You called me," she reminded him, and watched his lips tighten.

"I've had second thoughts."

"To hell with your second thoughts!" Her temper, quickly rising, captured her tongue. "I'm not going to hurt the baby. I'm just someone who cares, Doctor. Someone who would like to offer that poor, abandoned child a little bit of love."

"Or someone who enjoys all the attention she's getting?"

"If that was the case, I wouldn't have tried to throw the reporters out of the hospital, now, would I?"

That stopped him, and whatever he was about to say was kept inside. He stared at her a few minutes, his gaze fairly raking over her, as if he were examining her for flaws. She almost expected a sneer to curl his lip, but he was a little too civilized for outward disdain. "I'm just being straight with you. There's a lot I don't know about that baby who's up in pediatrics, Ms. Hill. And a lot more I don't know about you. If it were up to me, I'd let you hang around. Based on first impressions, I'm guessing that you do care something for the infant. But I don't know that, the hospital administration doesn't know that and Social Services doesn't know that."

He turned then, and left her standing in the middle of the parking lot, her mouth nearly dropping open.

HE DIDN'T UNDERSTAND why he'd come to her rescue in the hospital, only to shoot her down a peg or two.

Instinctively, Dallas knew that she was a different kind of woman than those he'd met. There was something about her that attracted him as well as caused him to be suspicious. She seemed at once strong willed and yet innocent, able to take care of herself and needing something—a man?—to lean upon occasionally.

There had been a desperation in her eyes, a pleading that he hadn't been able to refuse in the hospital, but here, out in the light of day, she'd looked far from innocent—in fact, he suspected that Ms. Hill could handle herself in just about any situation.

Dallas felt himself drawn to her, like a fly buzzing around a spider's web. He didn't know a thing about her, and he was smart enough to realize that she was only interested in him because he was her link to the baby. Yet his stupid male pride fantasized that she might be interested in him—as a man.

"Fool," he muttered to himself, kicking at a fragment of loose gravel on the asphalt. The sharp-sided rock skidded across the lot, hitting the tire of a low-slung Porche, Dr. Prescott's latest toy.

He must be getting soft, Dallas decided. Why else would he let a woman get under his skin? Especially a woman who wasn't being entirely honest with him.

He slid behind the wheel of his truck and flipped on the ignition. What was it about Chandra Hill that had him saying one thing while meaning another? He didn't want to keep her from the child, and yet he had an obligation to protect the baby's interests. Hospital policy was very strict about visitors who weren't relatives.

But the baby needed someone to care about him, and Chandra was willing. If her motives were pure. He couldn't believe that she was lying, not completely, and yet there was a wariness to her, and she sometimes picked her words carefully, especially when the questions became too personal. But that wasn't a sin. She was entitled to her private life.

Yet he felt Chandra Hill was holding back, keeping information that he needed to herself. It was a feeling that kept nagging at him whenever he was around her; not that she said anything dishonest. No, it was her omissions that bothered him.

He crammed his truck into gear and watched Chandra haul herself into the cab of a huge red Chevrolet Suburban, the truck that last night he'd thought was a van. Her jeans stretched across taut buttocks and athletic thighs. Her skin was tanned, her straight blond hair streaked by the sun. She looked healthy and vibrant and forthright, and yet she was hiding something. He could feel it.

"All in your mind, O'Rourke," he told himself as he drove out of the parking lot and toward the center of town. He had hours before his meeting with Brian, so he decided that a stop at the sheriff's office might clear up a few questions he had about Chandra Hill and her abandoned baby.

CHANDRA DROVE INTO RANGER, her thoughts racing a mile a minute. Automatically, she adjusted her foot on the throttle, managing to stay under the speed limit. She stopped for a single red light and turned right on Coyote Avenue. Without thinking, she pulled into a dusty parking lot and slid into one of a dozen available spaces, her mind focused on the infant. Baby John Doe. Already she'd started thinking of him as J.D. Kind of a bad joke, but the child deserved a name.

Lord, who did he belong to?

And that damned Dr. O'Rourke, telling her she shouldn't "hang around" the hospital. That man—kind one minute, cruel the next—set her teeth on edge! Well, the less she thought of him, the better.

Flicking off the ignition, she grabbed her jacket and climbed from the cab onto the sun-baked asphalt. A few blades of grass and dandelions sprouted through the cracks in the pockmarked tarmac, but the neglect seemed only to add to the casual allure of this tourist town. Most of the buildings, including the gas stations, coin laundry, banks and restaurants, sported a Western motif, complete with false facades, long wooden porches and, at the veterinary clinic, a hitching post.

Years before, the city fathers had decided to mine whatever gold was left in Ranger—not in the surrounding hills, but in the pockets of the visitors who drove through this quaint village in the foothills of the Rocky Mountains. Those same far-thinking civic leaders had persuaded the town to adopt a Wild West atmosphere, and the mayor had encouraged renovating existing buildings to adopt the appearance of the grange hall, livery stable and old hotel, the only remaining structures built before the turn of the century, and therefore, authentically from the eighteen hundreds.

In the past twenty years, all the businesses facing Main Street and a few more on the side streets reeked of the Old West. Wild West Expeditions had willingly embraced the idea.

Situated near the livery, on the second floor of a building constructed in 1987 and made to look a hundred years older, Wild West Expeditions, owned by once-upon-a-time hippie Rick Benson, was Chandra's place of employment.

She climbed the exterior stairs, noticing a soft wind rush through the boughs of a birch tree, spinning the leaves so that they glittered a silver-green.

The door was propped open. The sign above, painted red and yellow, swung and creaked in the breeze.

"Hey—I heard a rumor about you!" Rick greeted her with a toothy smile. He was a big man, six-two with an extra twenty pounds around his middle. His hair was extremely thin on top and had turned to gray, but he still wore his meager locks in a pony tail that snaked halfway down his back. He had a flushed face, an easy smile and no enemy in the world. Not even the mother of his children, who, in the seventies, he hadn't bothered to marry, and ten years later hadn't needed to divorce when she took the kids and packed them back to "civilization" in St. Louis.

"A rumor, eh?" Chandra hung her jacket on a peg near the door. The interior of the establishment was as rustic as the rest of the town. Rough-hewn cedar walls, camping equipment, including ancient snowshoes and leather pouches, hanging from wooden pegs, a potbellied stove and a long counter that served as the reception desk. "Only good things, I hope."

"Something about an abandoned kid. Found by your mutt down near the creek. I heard the kid would've drowned if Sam hadn't led you to him."

"Well, that's not quite the truth, but close," Chandra said, thinking how quickly a story could be exaggerated in the gossip-riddled coffee shops and streets of Ranger. She gave Rick a quick rundown of what really happened, and he listened, all the while adding receipts on a very modern-looking adding machine, swilling coffee and answering the phone.

"Why'd'ya s'pose the kid was left in your barn?" he asked once she'd finished with her tale.

She poured herself a cup of coffee. "Beats me. That seems to be the million-dollar question."

"Must be a reason."

"Maybe, maybe not."

"The army jacket a clue?"

Chandra sighed and blew across her cup. "I don't know. The deputies took it and the blanket, but it seemed to me they think nothing will come back from the lab."

Rick pushed up the sleeves of his plaid shirt, which he wore as a jacket over a river boatman's collarless shirt, usually cream colored and decorated by a string of beads that surrounded his neck. "Well, whatever happens with the kid, the press will be all over you." He scowled, his beefy face creased. "Bob Fillmore has already called."

"We've met," Chandra said dryly.

"Watch him. He's a shark," Rick warned, his light brown gaze meeting hers. He never probed into her private life. Not even when, two years before, she'd shown up on this doorstep and applied for a job as a white-water and camping guide. He hadn't lifted an eyebrow at the holes in her résumé, nor had he mentioned the fact that she was a woman, and a small one at that. He'd just taken her down to a series of rapids known as Devil's Falls in the Rattlesnake River and said, "Do your stuff." When she'd expertly guided the rubber raft through the treacherous waters, he'd hired her on the spot, only insisting she learn basic first aid and the lay of the land so that she would become one of his "expert" guides. She'd passed with flying colors. As far as she knew, Rick had no knowledge of her past life and didn't seem interested. She doubted that he knew that she'd been married or had been a pediatrician. He didn't care about the past—only the here and now.

Rick rubbed his chin. "Fillmore wants you to call him back and set up an interview."

"And you don't think I should."

Lifting a big shoulder, Rick shook his head. "Up to you. Just don't let that piece of slime inside here, okay?"

"You don't like him."

"No." He didn't say why, but Chandra remembered hearing that Fillmore had once written a piece about Wild West Tours. The crux of the article had been a cynical evaluation of Rick's alternative life-style, his "sixties values" in the late eighties.

"What've we got going today?" she asked. "There's a group coming in—when?"

"Soon, but I've changed things around a little," Rick replied, glancing at his schedule. "That group of six from the Hastings Ranch want a medium-thrill ride. I thought the south fork of the river would work for them. But I've got one lone ranger who wants to play daredevil...let's see... the name's McGee. Brian McGee. Young guy. Twenty, maybe twenty-two. He wants, and I quote, 'the ultimate thrill—the biggest rush' we can give him before he heads back to college. You think you want to deal with him?"

With pleasure, Chandra thought, recalling the so-called he-men she went to college with. The boys who didn't think she'd cut it in medical school. "Grizzly Loop?" she asked.

"If you think *he* can handle it. I know you can, but who knows what kind of a nut this bozo is. If he wants to play macho man and doesn't know beans about rafting, you could be in a pile of trouble."

"I'll check it out."

"Good. He'll be in at eleven."

"And the other group?"

"Randy and Jake'll handle them. Unless you'd rather—"

"Oh, no," Chandra replied crisply, noticing the teasing lift of Rick's brow. "Bring on Mr. Macho." Maybe she just needed to throw herself into her work to forget about the baby and, most especially, Dr. O'Rourke.

THE SHERIFF'S DEPARTMENT had ignored the Western motif of the other buildings in town. A single-story brick building, there wasn't the hint of pretension about the place. Inside, the walls were paneled in yellowed birch, and the floor was a mottled green-and-white tile that was worn near the front desk and door.

The receptionist recognized Dallas as he walked through the door. He'd helped deliver her second child two years earlier. With a grin, she slid one of the glass panels to the side. "Dr. O'Rourke!"

"Hi, Angie." He leaned one arm on the counter. "How're the boys?"

"Hell on wheels," she said with a heartfelt sigh. Behind her desk, officers in uniform or dressed in civilian clothes sat at desks and pushed paper, drank coffee, smoked and cradled phones to their ears as they filled out reports. "But you didn't come here to discuss the kids," Angie said. "What's up?"

"I'd like to talk to the dispatcher on duty early this morning, around one-thirty or two o'clock. A call came in about an abandoned baby."

"Let me check the log." Angie's fingers moved quickly over a computer keyboard, and she squinted into the blue light of a terminal. "Let's see… Here it is—1:57. Marla was on duty, but she won't be in until ten tonight."

"But the call was recorded?"

"They all are. You want to listen to the tape?"

"If it's all right."

Angie winked. "I've got connections around this place," she said. "Come on in." As Dallas walked through a door to the offices, he heard Angie ask another woman officer to cover for her, but his mind wasn't on the conversation. He was, as he had been ever since meeting her last night, contemplating Chandra Hill.

"So, you've got an abandoned kid on your hands," Angie said, snapping him out of his thoughts. She opened a door to an interrogation room. "Who would leave a baby alone like that?"

"I wish I knew."

"So do I. I'd personally wring her neck," Angie said fiercely. "Here, just pull up a chair. I'll get a copy of the tape. It'll be just a minute."

The room was windowless, with a long table, four folding chairs and little else. Just the basics. The faint scent of stale cigarette smoke hung in the air, and the two ashtrays on the table had been emptied, but not wiped clean.

He waited less than ten minutes for Angie to return, as promised, with a tape, a player and a cup of coffee, "compliments of the department."

"Thanks." He accepted the cup as she slipped the tape into the player.

"All the comforts of home," she teased, her dark eyes sparkling as she glanced at the bare walls and uncomfortable chairs. "Let me know if you need anything else."

"Will do."

She closed the door behind her as she left, and Dallas played the tape. Chandra's voice, at first frantic, calmed as she described the condition of the child. Cool and professional. And the medical terminology was used precisely—hardly typical of a first-aid class graduate. No, Chandra sounded very much like a physician.

Dallas sipped some of the coffee—stronger and more bitter than coffee served at the hospital—and rocked back in the chair. Chandra Hill. Beautiful and slightly mysterious. Sure, she came on strong and she seemed forthright, but there was more to her than what she said.

So what if she's a physician? Big deal. Maybe she just wants a little privacy. And, really, O'Rourke, it's none of your damned business. She brought you a patient, and you've got an obligation to care for him—and not for her.

Yet, as he heard her take-charge voice on the tape, he smiled. What, he wondered, would it be like to kiss a woman like that? Would she bite his lips and kick him in the groin, or would she melt against him, growing supple and compliant? The thought of pressing his mouth to hers caused an unwanted stirring between his legs.

"Damn," he muttered, angry at the turn of his thoughts. What the hell was he thinking?

Scowling darkly, he rewound the tape and listened to it again, his eyes narrowing through the steam rising from his cup. The tape gave him no more clues to the baby's parentage or to Chandra Hill. In fact, he thought sourly, he had more questions about her than ever.

"YOU'RE THE GUIDE?" Brian McGee couldn't swallow his surprised grin. He was handsome in a boyish way, with oversize features, large green eyes and a smile that was dazzlingly white. And he was shocked to his socks as he stared down at Chandra.

"I'm the guide," she quipped.

Brian glanced from Chandra to the counter, where Rick was busily working on the wording of a new brochure.

"I, uh, expected someone more—"

"Male?" she asked, tilting her chin upward and meeting his quizzical, amused gaze with her own steady eyes.

"Well, yeah, I was. I mean, not that you're not capable—"

"She's the best riverwoman I've got," Rick put in, never looking up from his work.

"But—"

"Come on, Mr. McGee. It'll be fun," Chandra assured him, though she was beginning to doubt her own words. This young buck definitely had ideas about male-female relationships on all levels. She grabbed a couple of life vests and a first-aid kit. "Believe it or not, you don't need extra testosterone to paddle a canoe."

He gulped. "Is anyone else going on this trip?"

"Nope. Just you and me."

McGee glanced back at Rick. "And this is a serious ride?"

Rick slid him a glance. "I guarantee you'll get the biggest rush of your life," he mocked, chuckling softly.

"That's what I want," McGee replied with a grin.

"Good." Chandra was already at the door. "The raft's tied to my rig. You follow me in yours, and we'll drop your car off at the south fork. Then you climb in my Suburban with me and we'll continue up the river. It'll only take about an hour to get there." She eyed him over her shoulder. "You have rafted before, haven't you?"

"Absolutely."

"Then let's get going."

While McGee paid for the excursion and signed the release forms, Chandra packed the truck. Within ten minutes, she was on the road, McGee following her in a beat-up Pontiac. They dropped his car off at Junction Park, and he climbed into the Suburban. Mentally crossing her fingers, Chandra hoped that Brian McGee wouldn't be too much trouble on the trip. She glanced at his profile as she put the truck into gear. For a second, she thought she was looking at Dallas O'Rourke. The profile, though much more boyish, was similar, the clear green eyes intense... but that was crazy. Calling herself every kind of fool, she snapped her sunglasses onto the bridge of her nose and vowed she wouldn't think of Dallas O'Rourke for the rest of the day!

She must really be losing it. To think that this...college boy resembled O'Rourke was ludicrous. And why Dr. O'Rourke wouldn't leave her mind alone was too obnoxious to contemplate.

"Somethin' wrong?" McGee asked, and she shook her head, as if to clear out a nest of cobwebs.

"Nope. You just..." She laughed. "You reminded me of someone I know."

His grin was enchanting. Boyish, but enchanting. "Someone you like?" he asked, his voice smooth as silk.

"I'm not sure," she said, and decided to end the conversation by turning on the radio. She wasn't interested in a college boy, or any man, for that matter.

McGee seemed to take the hint. He reached into his
pocket for a pack of cigarettes and, rolling down the
window, lit up. Tapping his foot to the sultry beat of an old
Roy Orbison song, he seemed lost in his own world, which
was fine with Chandra. She coveted her own thoughts, and
they had nothing to do with the boy next to her.

Instead, her mind was crowded with images of a tiny
baby and the doctor who cared for him. The baby, she understood. She'd wanted a child for a long, long time. But
why Dr. O'Rourke? He was the baby's physician. And a
man who was much too complicated for her—not that she
wanted a simple man. She didn't want a man at all, thank
you very much. And especially not a man like Dallas
O'Rourke.

She gripped the wheel more tightly and realized that
her palms were sweating as they drove upward, on a gravel
road that twisted and turned along the forested banks of
the Rattlesnake River.

LATE, AGAIN. DALLAS GLANCED at his watch and scowled.
Brian had suggested they meet here, at the Rocky Horror
Pub, at six. It was now 6:40, and Dallas had nursed one
beer in the smoky interior. The after-work crowd had gathered. Pool balls clicked in the corner, a lively game of
darts had begun, and the tables, as well as the bar itself,
were packed with the regulars who always enjoyed a
couple beers before heading home.

Five more minutes. That's all he'd give his irresponsi-
ble brother, then Brian could go borrow money at a bank,
like a normal person.

Dallas finished his beer just as the saloon-type doors
swung open and Brian, all one-hundred-eighty-five
pounds of cockiness, strode in. Dressed in dusty jeans, a
cowboy shirt and Stetson, Brian glanced around, spotted
Dallas and waved.

"Sorry I'm late," he announced, plopping down on a chair at Dallas's table. He waved to the waitress and pointed at Dallas's empty. "Two more of those…wait a minute. Is that a *light?* Forget it. I want the real thing. Whatever you got on tap."

"And you?" the waitress asked, her eyebrows lifting at Dallas. "Do you want the 'real thing,' too?"

"Nothing," Dallas replied, glancing at his brother. "Better watch out, Brian. You could end up with a Coke."

"Bring this guy the same thing I'm having," Brian insisted, and the waitress, rolling her eyes, left them.

Settling back in his chair, Brian took off his hat and hung it on a hook near the table. His thick hair was unruly, springy and slightly damp. "I've just had the experience of a lifetime, let me tell you."

The waitress deposited the two glasses on the table and, surprisingly, Brian paid for them both. Reaching for a handful of peanuts and shaking his head, Brian asked, "Ever shot the rapids at Grizzly Loop?"

"No," Dallas replied.

"Hell, man, you should. It was incredible."

"Sounds dangerous." Dallas waited as Brian tossed peanuts into his mouth. Sooner or later, he would get to the point, which was, of course, how much.

"It was. But the woman who was in charge, man, could she shoot those rapids. Scared the living hell out of me!"

"Woman?"

"Yeah." Brian hooked his thumb toward the windows. "She works over at Wild West Expeditions. Chandra something-or-other. Just a little thing, but, boy, does she know how to ride a river."

"Does she?" Dallas asked dryly. He took a swallow of the beer he didn't want. What were the chances of there being more than one woman named Chandra in a town this size?

"Believe me, I was skeptical. This little thing, couldn't be more than five-three or four, drives a huge red rig, carries a backpack that's half her size and shoots rapids like some damned Indian guide!"

"She blond?" Dallas couldn't resist asking.

"And gorgeous." Brian smiled slyly and winked at his older brother. "Built a little on the slim side for my tastes, but good-lookin'." Dallas felt his back stiffen. "With women like that," Brian continued as he lifted his glass to his lips, "maybe I'll just hang around for a while. I could go back to school after Christmas."

"Like hell!" Dallas replied in a loud whisper. A few heads turned in his direction, and he immediately put a clamp on his runaway emotions. What the hell was wrong with him? Brian was only kidding around, anyone could see that. Yet Dallas's temper had flared white-hot, probably because he was guilty of the same thoughts himself.

"Hey, man, I was only—"

"I know." Dallas waved off his explanation. "Maybe we should get down to business."

Brian's smile left his face, and for the first time that Dallas could remember, the younger man seemed genuinely sincere. "Look, I hate to ask you again, but I do need a few bucks to get through the next couple of terms."

"How much?" Dallas asked, taking a swallow from his "real thing."

Brian turned his glass uneasily. "I don't know. Four—" he glanced up to see how far he was getting "—maybe five grand could get me through to spring."

He wasn't asking a lot, Dallas knew. Though part of Brian's tuition and books were paid by his scholarship, his room and board were not. Brian's dad helped him a little, but the monthly checks didn't stretch far enough. And living expenses alone would mount up to more than he was asking for. However, Dallas couldn't get over the fact that Brian hadn't bothered to earn one red cent all summer. It wasn't loaning Brian the money that bothered Dallas so much as wondering if the kid would ever get enough gumption to actually get a job and become self-reliant.

"I looked for a roommate," Brian added, and Dallas's head snapped up.

"I thought you had two roommates."

"They dropped out."

"So you're living alone?"

"It's only temporary. I'll hook up with someone once school starts. There's always guys looking for a place to stay, and I'm not too far from campus...."

Without roommates to share the expense of a Southern California apartment, Brian would go through five thousand dollars quickly.

Dallas frowned and rubbed the back of his head. "I'll send you the money once you get back to L.A.," he said, eyeing his half brother and wondering why, with the same mother, they were so unlike each other. Dallas had never shied from work; in fact, he'd been accused of having no emotions, no room for anything in his life but his profession. He'd put himself through school with a little help from a small inheritance from his grandmother. When that had run out, he'd borrowed money from the government. School had been a grind—long hours, no money, no room for anything but classes, studying and sleeping. And it had taken him years to pay off the debt. However, he didn't wish what he'd gone through on anyone, especially his younger brother.

Brian looked straight at Dallas. "I was kinda hoping you'd, uh, give me the check now." He licked his lips nervously, and Dallas noticed a tightening around the corners of his half brother's mouth.

"Are you in some kind of trouble?"

"Nah! Nothing serious," Brian said quickly, his mouth twisting into a boyish grin again. "It's just that I've got a temporary cash-flow problem and I thought…well, I was hoping…"

Dallas reached into his jacket pocket and pulled out his check book. "How much?"

"Just a couple of hundred…"

Wondering if he was doing more damage than good, Dallas wrote a check for three hundred dollars and handed it to his brother.

With obvious relief, Brian stuffed the check into his wallet. "I don't know how to thank you."

"Finish school."

"No worry about that. Oh, by the way, I bought you something."

"You *bought* me something?"

"Yeah, well, I couldn't resist."

"But I thought you were broke."

"I am. But I've got a bank card and…I guess I was in a generous mood."

Dallas was about to protest. No wonder the kid couldn't stretch a buck, but Brian withdrew some sort of coupon from his wallet and slid it across the table. It was a pass for a white-water camping trip from Wild West Expeditions.

"You need to lighten up," Brian said. "I thought you should do something besides hang around the hospital all the time."

"This must've cost you—"

"Relax, will ya. Think of it as your money. Have Chandra take you up to Grizzly Loop—I told the old man who runs the place you're to specifically ask for her. You'll never be the same, I guarantee it." He reached into his shirt pocket, grabbed a pen and, clicking it, scratched Chandra's name on the coupon. "There ya go! The experience of a lifetime!"

"If you say so," Dallas said, his lips twisting at the thought of spending a day alone with Ms. Hill. It could be interesting.

And dangerous. He didn't know anything about her, and her story about the baby didn't ring quite true. No, he was still convinced she was hiding something—something she didn't want him to find out about her. What it had to do with the abandoned infant, he didn't understand. But he would. In time, he'd figure it out and, he thought bitterly, he probably wouldn't like what he found.

Except that she was interesting, far more interesting than any woman he'd met in a long, long while. He considered her tanned skin and gray-green eyes. A day or two alone with Chandra Hill could spell more than trouble. His emotions were already on edge whenever he thought of the woman—which was too damned often. But the idea of being close to her, seeing her without all her attention centered on that baby, was far too appealing to turn down. And, even if she were trouble, he decided he was willing to take that chance. He slipped the pass into his wallet.

CHAPTER FIVE

A COUPLE OF DAYS LATER, Dallas had his first weekend off in two months. Seated in his pickup, he stared through the glass at the rustic building where Chandra worked.

Baby Doe was doing well. Just yesterday, Dr. Williams had allowed the infant to be put in the general nursery with the others. Had the child a parent, he would be released soon. However, no one as yet had claimed the baby, despite the front-page story in this morning's *Banner*. Dallas glanced to the passenger seat, where the paper still lay open. "Mystery Baby Abandoned in Barn." Fortunately there were no photographs of the child. Chandra had only been quoted once, and it seemed that Bob Fillmore, a man Dallas didn't trust an inch, had gotten most of his information from the Sheriff's Department.

However, the first story in the *Banner* was unlikely the last. The press would keep sniffing around, Dallas thought, his gaze returning to the rough-finished building where Chandra worked. Fillmore, like the proverbial dog after the bone, wouldn't stop until he'd dug through every corner of Chandra's life. Things could get ugly.

Retrieving the coupon from his wallet, Dallas reached for the door handle and wondered, not for the first time, what the devil he was doing here. He was afraid his reasons had more to do with Chandra than with relaxing in the mountains. Yes, he was curious about her, but logic told him he was making a big mistake by taking up his brother's offer. Long ago, Dallas had decided he didn't need any complications in his life. Hadn't he had enough of complex relationships in L.A.? Weren't difficulties in his life in southern California the express reason he had retreated to this sleepy little mountain town? To his way of thinking, women always spelled trouble—with a capital *T*.

Chandra Hill would be no different—perhaps she was the most complex of all the women he'd ever met. Certainly she was fascinating. And she was crazy for that little boy. He'd checked with the nurses in pediatrics. It seemed Chandra was more often in the pediatrics wing of Riverbend Hospital than not. In two days, she'd visited the child five times—drawn inexplicably to the baby, as if she were the infant's mother or, at least, were nurturing some maternal bond.

He started up the steps leading to Wild West Expeditions. It wouldn't hurt to find out a little bit about the mysterious Ms. Hill, he decided. After all, he did have some stake in Baby Doe's future, in so far as he was the admitting physician. And the child had no one to fight his battles for him. Unless Dr. Dallas O'Rourke stepped in. His mouth twisted at the irony of it all—he'd never considered himself a hero of any kind. And here he was, deluding himself, making excuses just so he could spend a little time with Chandra Hill. Just like a schoolboy in the throes of lust. He hadn't felt this way in years.

"You're a case, O'Rourke," he muttered under his breath as he leaned on the door at the top of the stairs. It opened easily, and a brass bell jangled as he crossed the threshold.

Chandra was inside. Alone. She was seated at a makeshift desk, and glanced in his direction. Her fingers froze above the keyboard of a calculator, and surprise and anxiety registered in her even features. "Dr. O'Rourke," she said quietly. Standing, she yanked her glasses from her face and folded them into a case. As she approached the counter separating them, she asked. "Is...is anything wrong? The baby—is he—"

"He's fine," Dallas said, cutting in, and noticed relief ease the tension from her shoulders.

"Thank God. When I saw you here...well, I assumed the worst."

She blew her bangs from her eyes in a sigh of relief, and Dallas couldn't take his eyes from her face as he crossed the room and slapped his coupon onto the desk. "Actually, I'm here to cash this in."

Chandra picked up the voucher and eyed it carefully. "You want a white-water trip?"

"Overnight campout, I think it says."

"When?" She seemed ill at ease, drumming her fingers as she read the damned coupon again.

"As soon as possible. I've got three days off and thought we could get started whenever your schedule allows." He watched her and wondered if she'd try to beg out, try to palm him off on someone else—a man probably. He didn't blame her and, considering his fantasies of late, she would probably be right. Nonetheless, more than anything, Dallas wanted to spend the next couple of days alone with her.

"This coupon has my name on it," she said, glancing up at him with assessing hazel eyes. "Did you request me?"

"It was a gift. From my brother."

"Your brother?" She pulled her eyebrows together, and a deep line formed on her forehead.

"Half brother really. Brian McGee."

"McGee? Oh!" A smile of recognition lighted her eyes. "Mr. Macho."

"Was he?" Dallas wasn't certain he liked this twist in the conversation. Obviously Chandra had noticed Brian's dubious charms, and Dallas had hoped that she would be a little more selective. He saw her as a cut above the women Brian usually dated.

"He wasn't too thrilled to have a woman guide," she explained with a soft chuckle that struck a chord deep within Dallas. "But he changed his mind."

"Whatever you did, he sang your praises for two hours."

She laughed, and the sound was deep and throaty. "I scared him."

"You what?" Dallas couldn't help the grin that tugged at his lips. The thought of this little woman besting his brother was music to his ears.

"I scared the living tar right out of him." She glanced to the coupon and back to Dallas, and the laughter died in her eyes. "Am I supposed to do the same for you?"

"Do you think you can?"

"Without a doubt," she said, arching one fine eyebrow.

Was she teasing him? Women rarely had the nerve to joke with him; he'd heard his nickname, Dr. Ice, muttered angrily behind his back more than once. The name and the reputation suited him just fine. Kept things simple.

"Well, Ms. Hill, you're on."

"In that case, call me Chandra—I'll try to forget that you're a doctor." She flashed him a cool smile of even, white teeth that made him want to return her grin.

"Will that be possible?"

"Absolutely. But I think we should get some things clear before we set out—in case you want to back out." She leaned over the counter that separated them. "When we're in the boat, *Dallas,* I'm in charge. And that goes for the rest of the trip, as well. It was hard enough to convince your brother of that fact, so I hope I don't get any guff from you. Understood?"

For a little thing, he thought, she certainly could lay

down the law. He couldn't help feeling slightly amused. "What time?"

"Let's see what we've got available." She turned, picked up a clipboard with several charts attached to it and ran her fingers along the top page. Scowling, as if she was disappointed to find she wasn't booked up, she said, "Be back here at ten-thirty today. I'll have everything ready by then."

"What do I need to bring?"

"Besides your nerve?" she asked, and slid a list of supplies across the desk. One column listed the equipment and food that would be provided, the other suggested items he might bring along. "Just remember we travel light."

"Aye, aye, captain," he said mockingly, and started for the door.

"One more thing," she called. He stopped short, turning to catch a glimpse of what—worry?—on her small features. "Will you be coming alone—the coupon is only for one. Or is anyone from your family...your wife, anyone, coming along?"

At that he snorted. "My wife?" he asked, and thought of Jennifer. Though they'd been divorced for years, she was the only woman who had become missus to his mister. "Nope. Just me." With that, he strode through the door.

Chandra let out her breath. If Rick was here right now, she'd personally strangle him. What did he mean to do, hooking her up with O'Rourke? And what about the cryptic comment from O'Rourke about his wife? Was he married or not? Already, Chandra was getting mixed signals from the man, and not knowing his marital status made things difficult. Not that his marital status mattered, of course. Dallas O'Rourke was nothing more than the doctor who had admitted the baby.

Nonetheless, Rick Benson had a lot of explaining to do! Putting her name down on the form!

Within ten minutes, her boss waltzed through the door. "What's gotten into you?" she demanded.

"Hey—what's wrong?"

"Everything." She threw up her hands in disgust. "You signed me up for an overnight with Dr. O'Rourke. Remember him? The guy who's about as friendly as a starving lion and as calm as a raftload of TNT going over the falls!"

"Hey, slow down. What's all this about?" Rick asked before spying the coupon on the desk. "Oh."

"'Oh' is right."

"Don't blame me. That college kid insisted that you give his brother the ride of his life."

Chandra's eyes narrowed suspiciously.

"The kid even paid for an overnight, but if you don't want to do it, I'm sure that Randy would—"

"No!" Chandra cut in, feeling cornered. "I already said I'd meet him today. I can't back down now."

"Sure you could. Get a headache or claim you have P.M.S. or—"

"Just like a man!" she said, throwing up her hands and glaring at him. "I swear, Rick, sometimes I think you're on *their* side."

"On whose side? Men's? No way, Chan, I'm just walking a thin line between the sexes." He looked up, trying to swallow a smile. "I hired you, didn't I? You should have heard all the flack I took about that."

"I know, I know," Chandra said, though she still felt betrayed. It wasn't that she didn't want to be with Dr. O'Rourke, she told herself; the man was interesting, even if his temper was a little on the rough side. But the thought of spending a day *and* a night with him...

"Hey—isn't he the guy who took care of the baby at the hospital?" Rick asked as he walked into the back room.

He returned with a gross of pocket knives, which he put on display in the glass case near the door.

"Just the admitting doctor."

"Well, he works at the hospital, doesn't he? Maybe you could get a little more information on the kid. I know that you've been eatin' yourself up over it."

"Is it that obvious?"

"And then some." Rick opened one pocket knife to display the blades, then locked the case. He moved back to the desk, where Chandra had tried to resume tallying yesterday's receipts. "If you ask me, you're getting yourself too caught up with that little tyke."

"I don't remember asking." She took her glasses out of their case, then slid them onto her nose.

Rick pushed the sale button on the cash register and withdrew a five-dollar bill. A small smile played upon his lips. "This trip with the doc might be the best thing that happened to you in a long time."

O'ROURKE WAS PROMPT, she'd give him that. At ten-thirty, his truck rounded the corner and pulled into the lot. He guided his pickup into the empty slot next to Chandra's Suburban. "Ready?" he asked as he hopped down from his truck.

"As I'll ever be," Chandra muttered under her breath, forcing a smile. "You bet." Dr. O'Rourke—no, Dallas— was as intimidating outside the hospital as he was in. Though he was dressed down in faded jeans, beat-up running shoes, a T-shirt and worn leather jacket, he still stood erect, his shoulders wide, his head cocked at an angle of authority. *What am I doing?* Chandra wondered as she, balancing on the running board of the Suburban, tightened a strap holding the inflated raft onto the top of her rig.

"Need help?"

"Not yet." She yanked hard, tied off the strap quickly

and hopped to the ground. Dusting her hands, she said, "Just give me a hand with your gear and we'll get going. You follow me in your truck. You can park at the camp. We'll take my rig up the river."

"Sounds fair enough," he said, though he couldn't hide the skepticism in his voice.

Within minutes, they were ready—or as ready as Chandra would ever be—and the Suburban was breezing along the country road, which wound upward through the surrounding hills. Behind her, Dallas drove his truck, and she couldn't help glancing in the rearview to watch him. There was something about the man that was damned unsettling, and though she told herself differently, she knew her attraction to him—for that's what it was, whether she wanted to admit to it or not—had nothing to do with Baby J.D.

The drive took nearly two hours, and in that time the smooth asphalt of the country road deteriorated as they turned onto a gravel lane that twisted and turned up the mountains.

Tall pines and aspen grew in abundance along the roadside, their branches dancing in the wind and casting galloping shadows across the twin ruts of the sharp rock. Through the forest, flashes of silver water, the Rattlesnake River, glinted and sparkled in the trees.

Chandra pulled off at a widening in the road, just to the south of Grizzly Loop. Dust was still billowing from beneath her tires as Dallas's rig ground to a stop. Through the surrounding stands of trees, the river rushed in a deafening roar and the dank smell of water permeated the air.

Dallas cut the engine and shoved open the door of his truck. "I must be out of my mind," he said as he hopped to the ground. "Why I ever let Brian talk me into this..." He shook his head, and sunlight danced in his jet-black hair.

"So it wasn't your idea?"

"No way."

Chandra opened the back door of the Suburban and started pulling out crates of supplies. "Let me guess. You didn't really want to come today but your male pride got in your way, right? Since your brother—"

"Half brother," Dallas clarified gruffly.

"Whatever. Since he made the trip, your ego was on the line. You had to prove you were man enough to challenge the river." She smiled as she said the words, but Dallas got the distinct impression that she wasn't just teasing him. No, she was testing his mettle.

"Maybe I couldn't resist spending time with you," he said smoothly, then cringed at the sound of his own words. Good Lord, that corny line could've come straight out of an old black-and-white movie.

"I figured as much," she tossed back, but a dimple in her cheeks creased, and her hazel eyes seemed to catch the rays of the sun. Her eyes sparkled the same gray-green as the river that he glimpsed through the trees. "Well, are you going to give me a hand or what?"

"I thought you were the guide."

"On my trips, everyone pitches in." She reached into the truck again, withdrew some tent poles and tossed them to him. "I think we should set up camp at the edge of the forest."

"Whatever you say. You're the boss," he mocked, carrying tent poles, tarp and a heavy crate down a dusty path through the trees. Branches from the surrounding brush slapped at his thighs, and a bird, squawking at his intrusion, soared upward past the leafy branches to the blue sky.

For the first time, Dallas didn't doubt the wisdom of this little adventure. Though he hated to admit it, he decided that Brian might have been right about one thing—

he did need a break from his sterile routine. For the past three years, he'd had no social life, contenting himself with work and sleep. He swam daily in the pool of a local athletic club, taking out his frustrations by swimming lap after tiring lap, and he skied in the winter.... Well, he hadn't last winter or the winter before that. He'd been too busy....

"This should do."

He hadn't even been aware that Chandra had joined him or that the path had ended at a solitary stretch of sand and rock. Chandra strapped on a tool belt and took the tent stakes from his hands. "Put the rest of the equipment right there and unload the back of the Suburban. But don't bring down the first-aid kit, life preservers or anything else you think we might need on the trip—including the small cooler." When he didn't move, she smiled sweetly and added, "Please."

Dallas wasn't used to taking orders. Especially not from some tiny woman puffed up on her own authority. And yet, she'd been straight with him from the beginning, so despite his natural tendency to rebel, he dropped the things he was carrying and, turning, started back up the path.

When he returned, Chandra was bent over her work. The stakes were driven into the earth, and the ropes were strung tight. She leaned her back into her efforts as she stretched the nylon tarp over the poles.

She'd tied a handkerchief around her forehead and had begun to sweat; shiny drops beaded over her eyebrows and along the gentle ridge of her spine where her blouse separated from her shorts. He wondered about the texture of her skin, so firm and supple, then closed his mind to that particular topic. What was coming over him? Since he'd moved to Ranger, more than his share of women had shown interest in him. Patients, nurses, even fellow doc-

tors had been bold enough to try to get to know him, but
he'd held firm. No woman, no matter how beautiful, no
matter how interesting, was allowed past a certain point.
He had made the mistake of putting his faith in a gorgeous
woman once before, and he wasn't about to suffer that fate
again.

Even if, as he was beginning to suspect, Chandra Hill
was the most exciting female he'd met since stepping foot
on Colorado soil.

Ignoring the obvious curve of her behind, he dropped
the rest of their supplies. "Here, let me give you a hand
with that."

"You know how?" she asked skeptically.

"Mmm."

"Don't tell me, you're an Eagle Scout in disguise," she
joked sarcastically, but took the sting off her words by offering him that sexy smile again.

"Nope. The military."

"You were in the service?" she asked, turning all her attention his way. Her face, touched by the sunlight, seemed
younger and more innocent than he'd first thought, and
yet there was a trace of sadness in her eyes, a flickering
shadow that darkened her gaze momentarily.

"My father was," he clarified, wondering why he was
giving her any information about himself. "Career military doctor."

She rocked back on her heels and wiped her palms on
her shorts. "And you decided to follow in his footsteps?"

"Something like that," he admitted, though the subject,
as far as he was concerned, was closed. He'd come on this
trip with the firm intention of gaining some insight on Ms.
Hill, not the other way around.

They finished setting up camp, and Chandra, swinging
a rope over a tall tree branch, hoisted a nylon bag of food
twenty feet into the air. "Bears," she explained when she

caught his questioning gaze. "They're as hungry as Yogi and twice as clever. So let's not leave any 'pic-i-nic baskets' around. Even this—" she hooked a thumb toward the tree "—might not be effective."

"No one mentioned bears on this trip."

"Don't worry, I'll protect you," she said, and laughed. That husky sound continually surprised him. Checking her watch, she said, "Come on, let's go. We want to get back here before dark."

He had no choice but to follow her back up the path, and though he tried to train his eyes on the steep curving trail, his gaze wandered continually to the movement of her tanned legs and the sway of her hips beneath khaki-colored shorts.

Her clothing, an aqua T-shirt and shorts, wasn't innately sexy, but there was something about her, some emotions simmering just beneath the surface of her calm smile, that hinted at a slumbering sexuality ready to awaken. His thoughts leapt ahead to a vivid picture of her lying naked on that sandy beach, hair wild and free, water from the river still clinging to her skin. Her arms were outstretched, her legs, beneath an apex of blond curls, demurely crossed, but her dark-tipped breasts pointing upward, beckoning—

"Ready?"

His heart slammed against his chest as he started from his fantasy and found her staring up at him. They had emerged from the forest, and the sunlight seemed harsh after the filtered shadows of the woods.

"Anytime you are," Dallas replied, his voice lower than usual as he shook the inviting image of her bare body from his mind with difficulty.

"Good." Crawling into the cab of her truck, Chandra added, "Hop in." She fired the engine and threw the big rig into gear. Dallas had barely settled into his seat and closed the door when she tromped on the accelerator and they were off to God-only-knew-where.

Dr. O'Rourke wasn't exactly as Chandra had expected him to be. He was quiet—too damned quiet. She never knew what he was thinking, and now, bumping over the lane to the start of Grizzly Loop, she wished she'd never agreed to be his guide. His brooding silence made her nervous, and the directness of his gaze made it impossible for her to relax. And that didn't even begin to touch his sexuality, which, now that she was alone with him in the wilderness, seemed more potent than ever.

She switched on the radio, hoping that music would dull the edge of tension that seemed to emanate from the man beside her. A Kris Kristofferson ballad drifted from the speakers.

"Where, exactly, are we going?" the doctor finally asked.

"To a point known as Fool's Bluff."

"Appropriate," he muttered, and slipped a pair of mirrored sunglasses onto the bridge of his hawkish nose.

She let that one slide. But as the gravel of the lane gave way to rocky ruts, she hazarded a glance at this man who was to be her companion for the next thirty-six hours. He was handsome, no doubt of that, and his profile, made more mysterious by the dark glasses, was potently virile and male. His features were hard, his hair wavy and willful, for the black strands appeared to lie as they wanted, refusing to be tamed by any civilized comb or brush.

He seemed to fill up the interior of her truck, the smell of him pure male and soap scents. His long legs were cramped, even in the roomy interior.

She knew that he was watching her from the corner of his eye, and she felt self-conscious. Never before had she needed to rack her brain for conversation; her clients had always, through anxiety or their outgoing personalities, managed to keep up a steady stream of small talk.

But not Dr. O'Rourke. No way.

The noon sun was intense, and the sky offered no traces of clouds. Chandra drove along the winding road that followed the twisted course of the river. Through the passing trees, flashes of gray-green water sped by. "Okay, let's go over a few safety rules," she said as she fished a pair of sunglasses from the glove box and slid them onto her nose. "First, as I told you before—I'm in charge. I'll let you guide the raft, but if we're getting into trouble, you've got to trust me to take over."

O'Rourke snorted, but inclined his head slightly.

"Secondly, you wear your life vest and helmet at all times."

"I read all the rules," he said, rolling down his window and propping his elbow on the ledge. Cool mountain air, smelling of fresh water and dust, rushed through the rig's interior, catching in Chandra's hair and caressing the back of her neck.

She rattled off a few more pieces of information about raft safety, but Dallas was way ahead of her, so she fell silent, watching the road as the Suburban jarred and bumped up the hillside. Shafts of sunlight pierced through the pines and aspen that clustered between the road and the river. Nearby, the mountains rose like stony sentinels, sharp-peaked and silent.

The road began to lose its definition, becoming nothing more than a pair of tire tracks between which grass, weeds and wildflowers grew.

"This part of the river is known as Grizzly Loop," Chandra said, glancing over at Dallas.

"So, there are really bears up here. I thought you hauled our provisions into the trees just to scare me."

"Did I...scare you?"

His smile was arrogant and mocking. "I was terrified."

"Right," she said sarcastically. "As for grizzlies, you'll see about as many as you see rattlesnakes. The river and parts of it were named a long time ago. I suppose there were a lot of bears here once, and there could be rattlesnakes, but I've never seen either, nor has anyone I know. Disappointed?"

"Relieved."

The radio, playing a mixture of soft pop and country, finally faded in a crackle of static, and the grass strip between the tire ruts grew wider. Long, sun-dried blades brushed the underbelly of the truck. Chandra fiddled with the dial, found no discernible signal and flipped off the radio. "I guess we'll have to settle for brilliant conversation."

"Suits me." He leaned against the passenger window and studied her more closely. "What do you want to talk about?"

"Baby Doe," she said automatically. No reason to beat around the bush, and that way she could avoid discussing her life.

"What about him?"

"Has anyone tried to claim him?"

Dallas shook his head, and Chandra felt a release of anxiety, like the rush of water from a burgeoning dam. Ever since she'd found the small child, crying and red faced in her barn, a tiny idea had sprouted in her mind, an idea that had grown and formed until she could recognize it for what it was. She wanted the baby, and though she'd argued with herself a million times, she knew that she was on a path to requesting guardianship. It was time she became a parent. She needed the baby, and, oh, Lord, the baby needed the kind of loving mother she could well become.

They drove a few more miles until they reached Fool's

Bluff, which was situated some forty feet above the river. The rocky ledge provided a view of the curving Rattle-snake as it sliced through a canyon in the mountains. "That's where we'll be going," Chandra said, parking the truck and climbing out to point south, toward the wayward path of wild, white water.

"It looks pretty tame from up here," Dallas observed.

Chandra laughed. "Don't you know that looks can be deceiving?"

"I'm beginning to," he said, and he sent her an assessing glance that caused her heart to trip-hammer for a second as their gazes touched then moved away. Quickly, she turned back to the truck, and balancing on the running board, began to unleash the raft.

Dallas worked on the other side of the Suburban, and soon they were packing the raft and a few supplies along the narrow trail leading through the undergrowth and pines surrounding the river. "You're sure this is safe?" he asked, a smile nudging the corner of his mouth.

"You're insured, aren't you?"

He snorted. "To the max. I'm a doctor, remember? Insurance is a way of life."

"Then relax. You've got nothing to worry about," Chandra mocked, her eyes seeming to dance.

But Dallas wasn't convinced. With the single-minded perception he'd built a reputation upon, he realized that the next hours, while he was alone with Chandra in the forested hills, might prove to be his fateful undoing.

CHAPTER SIX

LIKE AN AWAKENING SERPENT, the river bucked and reared, rolling in a vast torrent of icy water that slashed furiously through the terrain. Chandra propelled the raft through the rapids, concentrating on the current, guiding the craft away from rocks and fallen trees.

The raft hit a snag and spun.

Adrenaline surged through Chandra's blood as the raft tilted, taking on water. *Hold on,* she told herself. Freezing spray splashed in her face, and water drenched her shirt and shorts as she tried to concentrate on the idiosyncrasies of the river. The raft pitched and rolled as the Rattlesnake twisted back upon itself. "Hang on," she yelled, putting her shoulders into the task of balancing the inflatable boat.

Blinking against the spray of water, she was aware of Dallas shifting the position of his oars, of his body moving with the flow of the current as easily as if he, too, were a river guide.

The raft hit a submerged rock and bounced upward, landing back on the water with a slap and a curl, spinning out of control for a heart-stopping second before Chandra found the channel again.

Dallas, his black hair wet and shining, his face red where the water had slapped him, paddled with the current, helping Chandra keep on course.

"You lied. You *were* a Boy Scout," she screamed over the roar of wild water.

His laugh filtered back to her. "No. But I was taught to be prepared for anything."

"By your father?"

He didn't answer, but threw his back into his oar, and the craft whipped past a slick boulder that protruded from the frigid depths.

They shot past the final series of ripples, and finally, as the Rattlesnake's strength gave out, their craft slowed in the shallows to drift lazily in the ebbing current.

Chandra let out her breath in relief. Though she was always eager to challenge the river, she was also relieved when the most difficult part of the journey was over.

"You do this every day?" Dallas asked, settling back against the stern of the raft to look at her.

"No, thank God! Sometimes I guide trail rides or supervise campouts or rock climbs. In the winter, I work on the ski patrol and give lessons."

"The outdoorswoman who does it all."

"Not everything," she countered, shoving her wet hair from her face. "I don't hunt."

"No?"

She narrowed her eyes against the lowering sun and paddled slowly, anticipating the next series of rapids. Though smaller than the last, they were still treacherous. "I'm afraid that if meat didn't come wrapped in plastic on little trays in the store, I'd become a vegetarian."

He smiled at that, and his grin, honest in the outdoors, touched her.

"Show time," she said as the river picked up speed again, and together they slid through the rapids, following the Rattlesnake's thrashing course until, half an hour later, they glided around a final bend to the beach beneath Fool's Bluff, where their camp was waiting.

"Home sweet home," Chandra quipped, and Dallas couldn't help thinking she was right. The faded tents and supplies stacked nearby, the bag of food swinging twenty feet in the air, the tall pines and rocky shore all did seem as much home to him as anyplace he'd ever lived.

Skimming her paddles through the water, Chandra guided the boat to the bank. Near the beach, she hopped into the icy water. Dallas, sucking in his breath, followed suit, and soon they'd pulled the raft onto the beach, leaving it upside down to drain.

"Now what?" Dallas asked.

"Well, you can change into some dry clothes, or you can leave those on, they'll dry soon enough. We'll get started on dinner. Then, once it's dark, we'll tell ghost stories around the campfire and scare ourselves out of our minds," she deadpanned.

Dallas laughed, and Chandra couldn't help but grin. Beneath his hard facade, Dallas O'Rourke was a man with a sense of humor, and here in the mountains, he seemed less formidable, more carefree. What else was he hiding beneath his surgical mask and professional demeanor? she wondered before closing her mind to a subject that was strictly off-limits. He was the client, and she was the guide. Nothing more. And yet, as the time she shared with him passed, she found her thoughts drifting to him as she wondered what kind of a lover he would be. What kind of husband? What kind of father?

Before twilight descended, they drove upriver in his truck to retrieve the Suburban. By the time they returned, the sun was behind the mountains and long shadows stretched across the beach. Dinner consisted of sandwiches, fruit and cookies that Rick always purchased from a bakery on the first floor of the building housing Wild West Expeditions.

"Not exactly Maxim's," he remarked, leaning his back against a large boulder and stretching his legs in front of him.

"You complaining?"

"Me? Never."

"You could have bought the deluxe trail ride and rafting trip," she said. "The one with caviar, champagne, Thoroughbreds and a yacht."

His mouth lifted at the corner and he said lazily, "My brother's too cheap."

"Are you two close?" she asked, and was rewarded with silence. Only the swish of water and drone of insects disturbed the silence. The sky, as if painted by an invisible brush, was layered in bands of pink and lavender. Above the darkening peaks, the boldest stars glimmered seductively.

Chandra, leaning against a log, drew her legs to her chin and wrapped her arms around her shins. "It's gorgeous up here, don't you think? The first time I saw this place, I *knew* this was where I had to stay."

"Where're you from?" he asked. She turned to find him watching her so closely that her breath stopped for a second. For the first time since the river run, she realized that she'd be spending the night with this man—all alone in the wilderness. Though it wasn't a new experience— she'd led more than her share of trail rides and camping excursions—she could feel in the air that this night would be different. Because of Dallas. There was something that set him apart from the other men she'd guided along the river—or was there? She edged her toe in the sand, unwilling to admit any attraction for a man she'd met so recently, a man who could, for all she knew, be married.

The scent of water filled her nostrils and the night seemed clearer than usual. The evening air was warm, its breath laden with the scents of spruce and pine.

"I take it you're not a native," he pressed, those inscrutable eyes still staring at her.

"No, I'm originally from Idaho," she admitted. "Grew up there. My dad was a real outdoorsman, and since he had no sons and I was the oldest daughter, he spent a lot of time showing me the ropes of canoeing, horseback riding, swimming, rafting and mountain climbing."

"And you made it a profession?"

Picking up a stick, she nudged over a rock, exposing a beetle that quickly scurried for cover. "With some stops along the way," she admitted. "Why are you so interested?"

He looked at her long and hard. "Because I've never met a woman who, with a few first-aid courses, could so quickly and accurately diagnose a patient as you did. You were right on target, Ms. Hill."

"Chandra. Remember?" she said, and considered telling him the truth. He deserved that much, she supposed. "And you're right," she admitted, though she couldn't confide in him, not completely. There was too much emotional scarring that she wouldn't reveal, at least not yet. So she hedged. "I've had more training than basic first aid. I was in medical school for a while, but I dropped out."

"Why?" he asked. The word seemed to hang between them in the night air. The moon had risen, and dusk, like a familiar warm cloak, closed them off from the rest of the world. The river rippled by, shimmering with the silvery light of the moon. The mountains, craggy and black, loomed toward the twilight sky.

"I didn't think it was right for me," she lied, cringing inwardly. Why not tell him the truth and get it over with? But, though she tried, the words wouldn't pass her tongue. Standing, she dusted her palms on her shorts. She felt a chill, though the air still held warmth from the afternoon, and she didn't know how much she should tell Dallas.

He was leaning forward, hands clasped, watching her every move, but when she didn't explain any further, he stood and walked toward her, his gaze still fastened on her face. He stopped just short of her, and she was all too aware that he was standing inches from her, his sleeve, still damp, brushing the crook of her arm. She tried not to notice how close he was, how intimate the night had become. Dry leaves fluttered in the wind, rustling and whispering as the breeze moved along the course of the river.

Lifting her head, she focused on the straight line of his chin, his square jaw, the way his hair ruffled in the wind. As if he understood her pain, he didn't ask another question, just took her in his arms and held her. Her throat burned with his sudden gentleness, and tears threatened her eyes. She didn't try to break away, just let his arms and the sounds of the river envelop her. How long had it been since someone had held her?

His breath whispered across her crown, and his body was warm, a soothing balm for all the old wounds. Her arms wrapped around his as if of their own accord, and he groaned. "Chandra," he whispered, and his voice had grown husky.

Good Lord, what was she doing, embracing this…this stranger, for crying out loud? And why did she feel the need to tell him her life story? This was all wrong. Even if his arms felt right, he was a client, a doctor, for God's sake, not a man she could get involved with. He could be married, for all she knew! She tried to break away, but his arms, strong as hemp, wouldn't budge. "I think…this isn't right…. I don't know anything about you." She gazed up at him steadily. "Look, Dallas, I don't fool around. Especially with married men."

"Then you're safe."

"You're not married?"

The muscles surrounding her tensed. "Not anymore."

"Oh." She didn't know what to say.

She tried to slip out of his arms, but his grip tightened. "I still don't think this is very smart."

"I know it isn't."

"I don't get involved with *any* men," she clarified, her voice unusually low, her pulse beginning to race wildly. They were talking about a very serious subject, and yet she felt that there was an undercurrent in their conversation, and she couldn't concentrate on much more than the feel of his hard body pressed so close to hers.

Embracing him was crazy! Downright insane. She didn't even know the man—not really. All she had were impressions of an honest, overworked physician, who at times could be cuttingly harsh and other times as textured and smooth as velvet.

"I know you were right on the money with the baby," he said, his breath fanning across the top of her head. "I've seen you handle Alma Lindquist and Bob Fillmore. I know for a fact that I couldn't put you off when you demanded to know about the infant's condition. And I've seen you navigate one helluva river. My guess is that you do whatever you set your mind to, Ms. Hill."

"Chandra," she reminded him again, but the words strangled in her throat as his night-darkened gaze locked with hers for a heart-stopping instant. She knew in that flash of brilliance that he was going to kiss her and that she was unable to stop him. He dropped his head then, and his mouth molded intimately over hers.

It's been so long... she thought as a river of emotions carried her away. The smell of him was everywhere— earthy, sensual, divine. And the feel of his hands, so supple against her skin, caused tiny goose bumps to rise on her flesh. He locked one of his hands around the back of her neck and gently pulled her hair as his tongue traced the rim of her mouth.

Her breath was stilled, her heart beginning to pound a cadence as wild as the river rushing through this dusky canyon.

This is a mistake! she told herself, but didn't listen. She heard only the drumming of her heart and the answering cadence of his. Warm, hard, primal, he provoked a passion so long dormant, it awoke with a fury, creating desire that knew no bounds. He shifted his weight, drawing her down, and her knees gave way as he pressed her slowly, intimately, to the beach.

Cool sand touched her back, and he half lay across her, the weight of his chest welcome, the feel of his body divine. She didn't protest when his mouth moved from her lips to the slope of her chin and lower, against her neck. She was conscious only of the feel of the coming night, the cool sand against her back, the whisper of his lips against her skin, the firm placement of his hand across her abdomen, as if through her clothes he could feel the gentle pulsing at her very core.

He moved slightly, and his hand shifted, climbing upward to feel the weight of her breast. Chandra moaned as her nipple, in anticipation, grew taut and desire caused her breast to ache.

Dear Lord, this is madness! she thought, but couldn't stop. She gripped his shoulders and sighed when she felt him push aside the soft cotton of the T-shirt until his flesh was nearly touching hers and only the simple barrier of white lace kept skin from skin.

"Chandra," he groaned, as if in agony, against her ear. "Oh, God…" He tugged off her T-shirt then, as the first pale glow from the moon filtered through the forest. He stared at her, swallowing hard as his gaze centered on the dark nipple protruding against filmy lace.

Chandra shivered, but not from the coolness of the night so much as from that critical gaze that seemed to caress the border of tan and white flesh across her breast, below which the white skin, opalescent and veined with blue lines, rounded to a pert, dark crest.

Dallas closed his eyes, as if to steady himself, but when he looked at her again, none of his passion was gone. "This is crazy," he whispered, and she couldn't reply; her mouth was dry, her words unformed. But she felt him reach forward again, slowly push down the strap of her bra, peel away the gossamer fabric and allow her breast to spill free.

"You're beautiful," he said, and then, as if he knew the words were too often spoken in haste, looked her straight in the eyes. "It's probably as much a curse as a blessing."

Beautiful? She wasn't blind and knew she was pretty, but beautiful? Never. She felt herself blush and hoped the night hid the telltale scarlet stain creeping up her neck. "You don't have to say anything," she replied in a voice that sounded as if it had been filtered by dry leaves.

His arms surrounded her, and he drew her close, his mouth finding hers in a kiss that drew the very breath from her lungs. No longer tenuous, he pressed his tongue into her mouth and explored the wet lining, one hand surrounding her back, the other softly kneading her breast.

Chandra melted inside. Heat as intense as a fire burning out of control swirled inside her, through her blood and into her brain. She wrapped a leg around him and arched upward. He slid lower, then snapped the fastening of her bra, letting both breasts swing free. He captured one nipple in his teeth and sucked as if from hunger, his tongue flicking and massaging the soft underside of her skin.

Her passion igniting, Chandra cupped his head and pulled him closer, crying out in bittersweet agony when, as he breathed, his hot breath fanned her wet nipple.

"Please," she whispered, caught in this hot whirlpool of desire and unable to swim free. "Please."

He found the fastening on her shorts, and his fingers brushed against her abdomen and lower still.

Somewhere in the trees high above, an owl hooted

softly, breaking the stillness of the night. Dallas's lips stopped their tender exploration, but the breath from his nostrils still seared her sensitive skin. He jerked his head away. "This is a mistake," he muttered, swiping a hand impatiently through his hair, as if in so doing, he could release the tension that was coiling his muscles. He rolled away from her. "Damn it all to hell, Chandra, I don't know what got into me."

Embarrassment crept up Chandra's spine at his rejection. Silently calling herself a fool, she scrambled for her clothes.

"Look, I'm sorry—"

"Don't apologize," she interrupted. "There's nothing to apologize for. Things just got out of hand, that's all." She wished she felt as calm as she sounded, but inside, her heart was pounding, and she wanted to die of mortification. She'd never played loose and fast. Never!

She'd been the butt of cruel jokes while in medical school. Doug's friends had wondered aloud and within her earshot if it were possible to light a fire in her or if she, so conscientious with her studies, were frigid. Doug had stood up for her, if feebly, and they had married, but she'd never forgotten how wretched those remarks had made her feel.

Nonetheless, she didn't see herself in the role of femme fatale, and this little escapade with Dallas was certainly out of character.

"This doesn't happen to me," he said.

"And you think it does to me?"

His lips compressed into a hard line, and Chandra nearly laughed. What did he think of her? She should be incensed, but she found his confusion amusing. She smothered a smile as she pulled her T-shirt over her head. "Well, what just happened between us is usually not part of the expedition, not even the most expensive trips," she teased, hoping to lighten the tension. Dallas wasn't in the mood for jokes. "Don't worry about it," she said, though she could think of nothing but the touch of his hands on her skin, the smell of him so close, the taste of his lips on hers. She turned back to the campsite. "Come on. We should start dinner, and if you think just because I'm a woman that I'm going to do it all myself you've got— Oh!"

He caught hold of her wrist and spun her around. She nearly tripped on a rock, and he caught her before she fell. Strong arms surrounded her, and his face, not smiling, but as intense as the night closing in on them, was pressed to hers. "I just want you to know," he said so quietly she could barely hear him above the wind soughing through the pines, "I don't play games."

She gulped. "I wouldn't think so."

"So when something like this…happens, I can't just take it lightly and shrug it off like you do."

"It's easier that way," she said, lying.

In the darkness, his eyes narrowed. "Just what kind of woman are you?"

She sucked in her breath, ragged though it was. "What kind of woman am I?" she repeated, incredulous. "I'm a woman who doesn't stand around waiting for a man to trip all over himself to open her car door, a woman who doesn't believe in love at first sight, a woman who would someday like a child but doesn't necessarily need a man, and a woman who expects any man she meets to pull his own weight," she managed to spit out, though she was all too aware of the feel of his hands against her skin and the tantalizing passion flaring in his eyes.

His grin slashed white in the darkness, and his hand was tight over her wrist. A chuckle deep and rumbling erupted from him. "Are you really so tough?"

"Tough enough," she replied, tilting her chin defiantly, though inside, she quivered. Not that she'd let him know. She didn't want Dallas to suspect any weakness. She twisted in his arms, afraid that if he saw into her eyes, he'd read her hesitation. Together, while the river flowed on in bright glimmers of silver moonlight, they stared at the water, and Chandra couldn't help feeling as if they were the only man and woman on earth.

"Come on," she finally said, afraid this intimacy would only make spending the night together more difficult. She drew her hand from his and, reluctantly, he let her go. "I'm starved."

They barbecued steaks and warmed bread, boiled potatoes and stir-fried fresh vegetables. Conversation was minimal. After dinner, they sat near the tents, the lanterns glowing in the wilderness and attracting insects. The smell and sound of the river filled the night, and Chandra felt more at peace than she had in a long, long while. There was something comforting about being with Dallas, something warm and homelike. And yet, there was another side to him, as well, the volatile, passionate side that kept her on edge. They drank coffee slowly, sitting apart, not daring to touch.

She wrapped her arms around her knees and stared at the man, whom she'd met as a doctor for J.D., but now knew as…well, not a friend…but more than an acquaintance. *And possibly a lover?* her mind teased, but she steadfastly shoved that absurd thought into a corner of her mind. Though she wanted to think of him as a man, she forced herself back to the issue at hand. She had more important things to think about.

"How long will Social Services wait until they place the baby?" she asked, sipping from her cup.

"As soon as we release him from the hospital. Probably in a day or two."

"That soon?" Chandra's heart took a nosedive. She'd have to work fast.

"He can't stay in the hospital forever." Dallas reached for the coffeepot, still warm on the camp stove, and, holding the enamel pot aloft, silently asked if she'd like more.

Shaking her head, Chandra bit her lower lip, her mind racing in circles. If no one claimed the baby, she'd try to adopt him. Why not? Tomorrow, when she returned home, she'd call her lawyer, have all the necessary applications filled out, do whatever she had to do, but, damn it, she intended to make a bid for the baby....

As if he saw the wheels turning in her mind, Dallas said, "What's on your mind, Chandra? You've been bringing up the baby all day." He stretched out on a sleeping bag and levered up on one elbow while his eyes, cast silver by the soft shafts of light from the moon, centered on her.

Could she trust him? She needed a friend, an ally, but Dr. O'Rourke was an unlikely choice. Licking her lip nervously, she decided to gamble. "I hope to adopt him," she admitted, holding his gaze.

"If no one claims him."

"If J.D.'s—" she saw the doctor's bushy eyebrows elevate a notch "—that's what I call him. You know, for John Doe." When he nodded, she continued. "If J.D.'s mother shows up, she'll have to prove to me that she's fit. What kind of woman would leave a baby in a barn?"

"A desperate one?"

"But why not stick around? Or knock on my door? I would've helped her, taken her and the child to the hospital," Chandra said, shaking her head and turning her attention back to the few swallows of coffee left in her cup. "Oh, no, there's no reason, no good reason, to leave a baby to die."

Dallas finished his coffee. "The baby didn't die," he pointed out. "Maybe the mother was in an abusive situation. Maybe she was trying to protect the child. The reason she didn't show her face is that she doesn't want her husband or boyfriend or whoever to show up, claim the baby, then perhaps hurt him or her. She could be on the run for a good reason."

"There are agencies—"

"Not enough."

Chandra glanced up at Dallas and noticed the serious lines deepening along his eyes and mouth. So there was a humanitarian side to Dr. O'Rourke. The man had many layers, Chandra decided, and she would all too willingly unravel each and every one to get a glimpse of the real man hidden beneath his cold, professional facade.

"I work in E.R. We see a lot of 'accidents' to children and women," he added, his voice deep and grim. "You don't know that the boy's mother wasn't a woman who, given her fear and limited knowledge, did the best she could."

"Leaving a baby alone and defenseless is never the best. That woman—whoever she is—had other options. She didn't have to take the coward's way out. She could have taken that baby with her wherever she was running."

"And what if she had a couple of other kids?" He sighed and threw the dregs of his coffee into the woods. "There's no reason to argue this. We don't know the woman's motives, but I think there's a chance the mother will surface, and when she does, she'll want her baby back."

Chandra knew he was right, and when her gaze met his eyes, she noticed a trace of sadness in their steely depths. Her heart grew suddenly cold.

"Just don't get too attached to…J.D…. Don't be giving him names and thinking about swaddling him in blankets and knitting little blue booties. You could get hurt."

"It's a chance I'll have to take."

Dallas drew one knee up and leaned over it. His face,

illuminated by the fire, was serious as he studied the crackling flames. "There are other ways to become a mother—easier ways. Ways that will ensure that no one takes the child away from you."

She snorted. "Most of those ways involve a man." She stared boldly across the short space separating them, and asked, "Are you applying for the job?"

He returned her gaze for a long, tense moment, and Chandra wished she could call back the words, said too quickly. He probably thought she was seriously propositioning him.

"I just thought you could use some friendly advice," he finally said.

Chandra felt a rush of warmth for the man. "Thanks."

"You're still going to go through with it, aren't you?" When she didn't reply, he continued, "You know, you might still need a man. The system still likes to place children in homes where there is a role model for each parent. And, no, since you asked a little earlier, I don't go around fathering children." An emotion akin to anger pinched the corners of his mouth. "Call me old-fashioned, but I think it's a father's duty, responsibility and privilege to help raise his child."

"Well—" she stood and dusted her hands "—now we know where we stand."

"Almost." He tossed down his cup and stood, closing the distance between them. He grabbed both her shoulders in big, hard hands. "Be careful, Chandra. If you don't watch out, you and the baby and God-only-knows who else might be hurt by this."

"It's my business," she said simply, unmoving.

"It's my business, too, like it or not. We're both involved." He dropped his hands, and Chandra took the opportunity to step back a pace, to keep some distance from him. Her crazy heart was thundering. What was wrong with her? She'd been with dozens of men on trips like this. A few had even made the mistake of making a pass at her. But until tonight, resisting a man's advances had come easy.

To make herself look busy, she rinsed her cup in the warm water simmering on the stove. "I'd better get this food back in the bag and hang it from the tree, then we can turn in." She wished she'd never gotten close to O'Rourke. He'd only reinforced her fears that adopting the baby would be difficult, even painful, and might not work. But then he didn't know her, did he? He couldn't understand that once she'd set her mind on something, it would take the very devil himself to dissuade her.

Later, tucked snugly in her sleeping bag, she thought about the night stretching ahead of her, of the starlit sky, the mist rising off the river, the man who slept only a few feet away. Kissing him had seemed natural and safe. She touched her lips and quietly called herself a fool. Dallas O'Rourke was a doctor, for crying out loud, a man married to his job, a man who might stand in her way in her efforts to adopt J.D., a man of whom she knew very little. She'd had a physical response to him, that was all. It was no big deal. She hadn't been with a man since her divorce, and in those few years, she hadn't so much as let another man kiss her, though more than a few had tried.

It wasn't that she was a prude; her response to Dallas was evidence to the contrary. She just didn't want an involvement with any man, including Dr. O'Rourke.

CHAPTER SEVEN

CHANDRA WAS UP at the crack of dawn and insisted they break camp early.

"That's it? We're finished?" Dallas asked, his chin dark with the shadow of a beard, his eyes a midnight blue as he stretched and yawned. A few clouds hovered in the sky, but the temperature was cool, the mountain air crisp with the promise of autumn.

"Not quite. We still have one run before you can return to civilization. We'll eat, take down the tents, check the supplies and make sure we haven't sprung any leaks in the raft. Then we'll shoot the lower flats."

"Lower flats? Calmer than Grizzly Loop, I hope."

"Different," she replied as she retrieved the supply sack. Fortunately, no bears had disturbed the food, though once before, on a camping trip in the mountains, she'd awakened to see her fat supply sack flapping in the breeze. It had been slashed at the bottom, the contents long gone, with only scraps of carton and paper and the wide tracks of a bear visible the next morning. That trip, they'd relied on the fish they'd caught and a few berries for the day. Fortunately, this time she wasn't embarrassed by a persistent and clever bear making a mockery of her precautions.

After a quick breakfast of muffins, fruit and coffee, they made preparations to break camp. Before she folded up her tent, Chandra changed into a swimsuit, shorts and blouse. She tied her hair away from her face, ignored any thoughts of makeup and yanked on a nylon parka.

Dallas, who hadn't bothered shaving, wore a khaki-colored pair of shorts and blue pullover. "You know, we could call it quits here," he said as he loosened a rope and his tent gave way.

"Your brother paid for a specific excursion," Chandra replied. "I wouldn't want to disappoint him."

"He'll never know."

Bending over her own flattened tent, she smiled at him over her shoulder. "Cold feet, Dr. O'Rourke?"

"I just thought I'd save you some trouble, that's all." His blue eyes gleamed with a devilish spark.

"No trouble at all."

Dallas didn't argue any further. Chandra could sure change a man's mind, he thought as he watched her move expertly through the campsite, packing gear, bending over without even realizing she was offering him a view of her rounded buttocks and tapered legs.

"Well?" she asked, turning to cast him an inquiring look. Her rope of tawny hair fell over one shoulder.

"You're the boss." He slapped his knees, and as he stood, he looked younger, more boyish, as if he were really enjoying himself.

She chuckled. "Now we're making progress." They packed the remaining gear and carried it up the shaded path to the strip of road where their trucks were parked.

Dallas pumped the throttle and flicked the ignition switch of his truck. The engine revved loudly, and despite his reservations, he felt a surge of excitement at the coming raft trip. Being alone with Chandra in the wilderness was more than a little appealing, and he remembered their embrace vividly, more vividly than he remembered caressing or kissing any other woman in a long, long while.

He forced his thoughts away from the impending rafting trip and the possibilities of kissing her again, of the silken feel of her skin against his, of the proud lift of her breasts, pale in the moonlight.

"Stop it," he muttered to himself, grinding the gears as he shifted down and wrenched on the wheel in an effort to follow her Suburban onto the flat rise of dry grass. She parked in the shade of some aspens that bordered the field. He stopped and willed his suddenly overactive sex drive into low gear.

The river curled close to the shore, cutting through the dry land in a shimmering swath that reminded him of a silvery snake.

Chandra cut the engine, hopped to the ground, locked the door, then climbed into the passenger side of Dallas's truck. She shoved her sunglasses onto the bridge of her nose and pretended she didn't notice the handsome thrust of his chin or the way his eyes crinkled near the corners as he squinted against the sun. She didn't let the masculine scent of him get to her, either.

He was just a man, she told herself firmly, forcing her gaze through the windshield to the rutted lane that wound through pools of sunlight and shadow. But he was her link to the baby—that was why she was attracted to him, she thought.

Deep in her heart, though, she knew she was kidding herself. Dallas was different, a man who touched a special chord deep within her, a chord that she didn't dare let him play.

She drummed her fingers on the armrest, and the hairs on the back of her neck lifted slightly when she felt him glance in her direction.

"Nervous?" he asked.

She shook her head. "Anxious to get back," she said

evasively. Just being around Dallas was difficult; she felt she was always walking an emotional tightrope.

"Already she wants to get rid of me," he mocked.

Chandra laughed a little. "It's the baby. I wonder how he's doing," she replied, though the infant was only part of the reason. She needed to find her equilibrium again, something that proved impossible when she was with Dallas.

"I'll bet he's screaming for breakfast, or—" he made a big show of checking his watch "—or lunch. Demanding food seems to be what he does best."

Chandra glanced at the doctor, caught the sparkle in his eyes and was forced to smile. She relaxed a little, her spirits lifting with the morning sun as it rose higher in the sky.

Once they'd parked near the river, they checked the equipment one last time, shoved the raft into the frigid water and hopped in. The current was lazy near the shore, but as the craft drifted to the middle of the river, the stream picked up speed, narrowing as the current turned upon itself and the surge of white water filled the canyon.

The raft plunged into the first set of rapids, and the river became a torrent that curled around rocks and the shore. Chandra, jaw set, narrowed her eyes on the familiar stretch of water, shifting her weight and using her paddles against the primal force of the river.

Over the deafening roar of the water, Chandra shouted orders to Dallas, who responded quickly, expertly, his shoulders bunched, his eyes glued to the frothy water and rocks stretching before them.

He moved as they approached a rock, and they skidded past the slick, dark surface. Chandra bit her lower lip. Downstream, Ridgeback Ripples foamed in furious waves, and Chandra braced herself for the pitch and roll that would occur as they rounded the dead tree that had fallen into the river.

She managed to steer clear of the fallen pine, avoiding the part of the stream that swirled near the blackened, dead branches. The water was clear, the rocks below shimmering gold and black. She shoved in her paddle, intending to move into deeper water.

"Watch out!" Dallas yelled.

Too late! The raft hit a snag in the water and responded by spinning, faster and faster, out of control. Water thrashed over the side. Chandra paddled more firmly.

The raft plunged deep, then bobbed up again, bucking wildly, out of control.

Hang in there, she told herself, refusing to lose her calm. They rammed a large rock and pitched forward. Chandra fell against the inflated side. Before she could get up on her knees again, the raft, still spinning, hit a shoal and buckled, flipping over.

"Hold on!" Chandra screamed as she was pitched overboard. Roaring ice-cold water poured over her in a deluge, forcing its way down her throat. Sputtering, she couldn't see, but reached out instinctively, grabbing hold of the capsized raft.

Dallas! Where was he? Oh, God! She surfaced, pulled by the drag of the current as it whisked the overturned raft downriver. Water rushed everywhere. "Dallas!" she yelled, coughing and looking around her as she tried vainly to tread water. Trees along the bank flashed by, and the sun, still bright, spangled the water, the light harsh against her eyes.

She didn't see him.

Come on, Dallas, come on. Show yourself. She looked upriver and down, searching for some sign of him as she was carried along with the current. "Dallas!" she screamed. Oh, Lord, was he trapped beneath the raft?

Trying to grab on to a rock with her free hand, she scraped her arm. If she could only stop and look for him! Her heart pumped. She gasped in lungfuls of air and water. Adrenaline surged through her blood, bringing with it fear for the man she'd only recently met. *Where was he?*

If she'd inadvertently hurt him…

"Dallas!" she screamed again, just as the rapids rounded a bend and dumped into a relatively calm pool. She flipped the raft over, half expecting him to be caught beneath the yellow rubber.

Nothing.

Oh, God. Please don't let him drown! She couldn't lose someone in her care again…someone who had trusted her with his life…someone she'd begun to care about. "Dallas!" she screamed, her voice growing hoarse as she shouted over the roar of the river. "Oh, God, Dallas!" Her heart dived, and she struggled until she found a toehold where she could stand and scan the river as it roared by in fierce torrents. Coughing, her teeth chattering, she prayed she'd see him, his lifejacket keeping him afloat, his helmet preventing a head injury. "Come on, Dallas…please!" The river flowed past in swift retribution. "Dallas!" she yelled again, her voice catching in fear. *Think, Chandra, think! You know what to do!* She wouldn't just stand here. She'd had survival training, and she'd find him. He had to be alive—he had to! But fear kept her rooted to the spot, drew her eyes to the dark and suddenly evil-looking river.

She forced her legs to move with the current, knowing that he would have been swept downstream—

"Hey! Chandra!"

His voice boomed, and she turned to find him waving his arms on the shore at a bend in the river. He was the most beautiful sight she'd ever seen. Wet, bedraggled but grinning, he shouted her name again. Relief brought tears to her eyes, and she nearly fell on her knees and wept openly. Instead, she sent up a silent prayer of thanks. To think that he might have drowned…oh, God.

Still dragging the raft, she sloshed through the shallow water near the shore, wading toward him, and he, grinning sheepishly, slogged upstream. They met in waist-deep water, their lips blue, water running from the helmets and down their necks. Without thinking, Chandra flung her arms around him, wanting to feel his heartbeat, the strength of his body.

His arms, as sturdy as steel, surrounded her, drawing her close, and for a second in the frigid water, they forgot all propriety. She wanted to laugh and cry, scream in frustration and kiss him, all at the same time. Relief poured through her. Her senses, already charged by the fear that had stolen into her heart, filled with him. He smelled of the river, but his touch was warm and electric. He smoothed a strand of hair from her cheek, as if he, too, were savoring this moment when they were both alive. Her heart wrenched and her throat clogged. She pounded a fist against his chest. "You scared me half to death," she said, drawing her head back to stare up at him.

"It was my fault."

"Yours?" Shaking her head, she wouldn't let him take the blame. "No way. I was in charge. I shouldn't have let her capsize."

"But I steered the raft into the snag—"

"The current did that. It was my job to avoid the situation." Suddenly weak, she sighed and, ripping off her helmet, tossed the hair from her eyes, spraying his chest with icy pellets of water. "I'm just glad you're in one piece." His arms tightened a little, and when she glanced up at him again, her breath caught in her throat. His gaze, blue and intense, drilled deeply into hers. He, too, removed his helmet and cast it beside hers on the rocks of the shore.

"I'm glad you're in one piece, too," he said, his breath warm against her chilled skin. He lowered his head and kissed her, his cold lips molding to hers, his hands drawing her so close, she could scarcely breathe.

His tongue pressed lightly against her teeth and she responded, her heart soaring that they'd both survived the accident. Her mind, usually calm and rational, was now fuzzy with emotions she didn't want to dissect. She lost herself in his touch and the smell of his clean, wet skin. Clinging to him, her breasts flattened against the hard wall of his chest, she thought of nothing save his touch and the tingling of her skin whenever their bodies pressed close against each other.

He slid his hands across her back, and through her wet shirt she felt the warmth of him. He scaled her ribs with gentle fingers and slowly eased a palm over her breast.

She gasped, and he kissed her harder, his tongue plunging deep as his fingers moved insistently beneath the top of her swim suit, to her nipple, stroking the already hard peak until her entire breast ached.

The cold seeped away. The water rushing past their knees and slapping their thighs didn't exist. Chandra was only aware of Dallas, his kiss and the expert touch of his hands on her flesh.

She shivered deep inside as desire crept through her blood. Moaning, she wound her arms around his neck, her own tongue searching and tasting, delving and flicking.

He groaned in response and slid downward, moving his hands slowly to her buttocks, kissing the column of her throat.

Chandra sucked in her breath and he pressed his warm face against her abdomen before he pulled down her vest and suit and then rimmed her nipple with his tongue.

"Oooh," she whispered over the rush of wild water. Her fingers twisted in his hair as he suckled. Between the cold air and the warmth of his body, Chandra was suspended in tingling emotions that wouldn't lie still. She knew she should stop this madness, but couldn't. His body, hard and anxious, demanded exactly what hers wanted so desperately.

When he drew his mouth from hers, he gazed up at her and shook his head. "What're we going to do about this?" he wondered aloud, obviously as perplexed with the situation as she was.

"I don't know."

He slowly covered her breasts and stood, his arms still surrounding her. "Overused phrases like 'take it slow' or 'one step at a time' seem the appropriate thing to say, but I'm not sure slow is possible with you. And I'm sure it isn't with me." He sighed loudly in frustration. "You turn me inside out, Ms. Hill," he admitted, "and I don't think this is the time in my life for that kind of imbalance."

"Imbalance?" she repeated, shivering. "I'm causing you an imbalance?" Shaking her head, she turned back to the raft. "Well, we certainly wouldn't want to mess around with your well-ordered life, Dr. O'Rourke," she said, her anger rising. "It's not like I planned this, either, you know. It just happened!"

She was suddenly angry, and wondered if her fury was aimed mostly at herself. "Let's just forget this happened and get on with the trip."

"I don't know if I can."

She'd been reaching for the rope when his voice arrested her. Turning, she found him still standing in the river, his features thoughtful, almost disbelieving, as if something were happening to him that he couldn't control.

She cleared her throat. "We only have about a mile of river left, then we can pack up. You can go your way and I can go mine. And trust me, I won't try to imbalance your life again. Just make sure your brother doesn't buy you another expedition, okay?"

She grabbed his helmet off the beach and tossed it to him, then strapped hers on. "Let's get this over with."

"You're the boss."

"Right. So get in and we'll shove off!"

They both climbed into the raft, and Chandra, determined to be professional, guided them downstream. They didn't say another word, though a few blistering phrases leapt to Chandra's mind. She'd love to tell Dr. O'Rourke what she really thought of his attitude.

She didn't like being played with, and yet, every time he kissed her, she hadn't stopped him—hadn't been able to. Her traitorous body seemed to tingle with anticipation at his touch, and that thought alone disgusted her.

He was just a man! How many times did she have to remind herself of that one simple fact? She hazarded a glance in his direction and took comfort in the fact that he seemed as irritated and out of sorts as she was. And she consoled herself that he wasn't immune to her.

The raft glided around the final bend in the river. Chandra, feeling a mixture of relief and sadness, spied her truck parked beneath the tree. Soon, this wretched, lovely trip would be over.

Dallas saw the play of emotions on Chandra's face. She barked orders at him as he helped her drag the raft out of the water and lash it across the top of her rig. Silently, still wondering what the hell he was going to do with her, he admired how quickly and efficiently she worked, her arms tanned and strong, her fingers sure as she tied square knots and half hitches, and stored the gear in the back of her Suburban.

She moved with the natural grace and assuredness of an athlete, and yet her femininity was impossible to ignore. Her legs were supple and tanned, her buttocks round and firm, and her breasts, hidden beneath several layers, were soft, fleshy mounds that fit so perfectly in his palms.

But more intriguingly feminine than her obvious physical attributes was the sparkle of green in her gray eyes, the lift of her lips when she smiled, the arrogant toss of her hair over her shoulders. Chandra Hill was used to dealing out authority, probably from her year or two in medical school. He wondered how she could have ever given up medicine. Maybe she hadn't been able to afford the schooling. She claimed that she'd found out once she'd enrolled that she wasn't cut out to be a doctor, but he doubted that story. Chandra Hill seemed to be a woman who set goals for herself and then went about attaining them, no matter what the odds.

Somehow, guiding the idle rich down a dangerous stretch of water paled when compared with the ecstasy of saving a life. There were downsides to being a doctor, and tragedies that were impossible to ignore, but he'd learned to live with those, and he couldn't imagine giving up his livelihood as a physician. He'd rather cut off his right arm.

"That's it," she said, opening the driver's side of her truck. Dallas slid into the sunbaked interior and rolled down his window. He propped his elbow on the window frame as she started the truck and headed up the mountain road in a plume of dust. Reaching into the compartment between the two bucket seats, Chandra found a pair of sunglasses—ostensibly to replace those she lost during the rafting excursion—and set the shaded lenses across her nose. "Well, what d'ya think? Ready to go out again?"

"Maybe," he said, and she cast him a quick glance.

"Even after that spill?"

"Does it happen often?"

"This is only the second time," she said, a frown puckering her brow as she braked and the Suburban hugged a sharp turn in the road and slid to a stop. "Shh—look."

She pointed to the undergrowth where a doe stared at them with huge, liquid eyes. A fawn pranced behind its mother until it saw the truck and froze, unmoving, blending into the background of dry grass, brush and trees.

"You love your job, don't you?" he asked.

Lifting a shoulder, Chandra shoved the rig into first and appeared to concentrate once again on the road that wound through the forest.

"And you're never going back to finish studying medicine," he predicted.

She flashed him a dark look. "I don't think so," she said, unhinged by his sudden display of compassion. "I—um—the trip's over. I really have to get back," she said, though a part of her wanted this trip to last forever.

"Someone waiting for you?"

She smiled slightly. "Oh, yes," she admitted, thinking of Sam. The old dog would be looking for his dinner. She'd fed him early yesterday morning, leaving enough food for two days along with several gallons of water, but by this time, he'd be starved. And lonely.

"There is?"

"Mmm. And he's very jealous."

Dallas cocked a thick eyebrow, his expression neutral, though his eyes had darkened a shade.

"His name is Sam and he lives with me," she clarified, smiling inwardly when she caught a gleam of jealousy in Dallas's eyes. Did he really think she would let him kiss her when she was seeing someone else? "He wanted to come along, but I told him that he'd just be in the way."

"Is that so? And how'd he like that?"

"Not at all. In fact he growled at me all night long."

The doctor's eyes narrowed, and all of his friendliness, so visible earlier, disappeared from his features. "You're *involved* with someone? And he lives with you?"

"Has since I moved in," she teased, waiting as Dallas

opened the door. "He's become very possessive. In fact, he's been known to bite intruders."

A slow smile spread across Dallas's chin and Chandra couldn't help but chuckle. "Tell your 'friend' that I'm not afraid of him," he said with a laugh as he slammed the door shut.

"He'll be disappointed."

"I'll bring him a steak bone. Will that solve the problem?"

"He'll be forever in your debt," she said, ramming the Suburban into reverse and roaring off, her laughter hanging on the air as Dallas fished his keys from his pockets.

What was wrong with him? He'd almost acted as if he were planning to see her again. And he wasn't. If he'd learned anything from this fiasco of a trip, it was that he had to keep his distance from Chandra Hill. The woman was just too damned attractive for her own good. Or his.

But the thought of not seeing her again bothered him, and he took heart with the realization that, as long as Baby Doe—or J.D., as she insisted upon calling him—was a patient at Riverbend Hospital, Chandra Hill would be underfoot. She could very well pretend interest in Dallas just to get close to the baby. In fact, her interest in the infant explained why a strong-willed woman like Chandra could so easily be seduced.

He believed her when she said she didn't get involved with her clients—so why him? A physical attraction she couldn't deny? He scoffed at the idea, though his passion for her was something he could barely control. But, no, he suspected that Chandra was just using him to get close to the baby. Still, he couldn't just forget her. She was an impossible woman to forget.

He opened the door of his truck and sighed. Damned if you do and damned if you don't, he decided, pushing the key into his ignition. He didn't want to see Chandra again—well, at least he told himself that he didn't—and yet, he couldn't imagine not ever looking into her eyes again or catching the glimpse of her smile.

He hadn't felt this way since Jennifer. That realization was more shocking than a plunge in the icy depths of the Rattlesnake. He'd fallen hard once before, and, after more emotional pain than he'd ever thought existed, he'd proclaimed that he'd never fall again.

Since the divorce, he'd clung to his vow as if to life itself. He'd made sure that he had no time for a woman in his life, no time for anything but his work. And he'd been happy, or so he'd told himself.

CHAPTER EIGHT

CHANDRA, ONE HAND PRESSED against the glass, stared at the baby. He was awake, his eyes bright, his face relaxed as he lay in the bassinet in the nursery with the other infants. There was a group of six small bodies wrapped in warm blankets, sleeping or blinking or yawning. Nurse Nelson was changing a squalling, tiny red baby without a trace of hair.

"Hi," she said from the other side of the glass that separated the nursery from the hallway where Chandra stood. "Would you like to hold him?" Leslie finished with the diaper, then motioned to J.D.

"Are you serious?" Chandra asked in a voice loud enough to be heard through the glass.

"Why not?" Opening the door a crack, Leslie flashed her dimples and tucked a blanket around the baby she'd been changing. "All these other guys—" she gestured to the bassinets with their squirming bundles "—get more than their share of attention. Of course, they're lucky. They have mothers." She disposed of the dirty diaper, then walked to J.D.'s bassinet and wrapped his blanket tightly around him. "Come on, you," she said as she carried him through the double doors and placed him in Chandra's waiting arms.

Chandra's heart felt as if it might break. The baby cooed and shifted, nuzzling her chest. Emotions tore at her soul. Tears gathered behind her eyes, and her throat closed as she gazed down at this precious child with the perfectly arched eyebrows, pudgy round cheeks and loud voice. Any lingering doubts she had concerning this baby were quickly washed away. She had to adopt him. She had to! She had no other choice. She thought of all her reservations, but she couldn't help herself. Who cared if the baby's natural mother showed up? This child needed her. And she needed him. Desperately. To make her life complete. Or would it be? Even with J.D., her life might still be missing something vital, the third part of a perfect family—the husband and father.

She rocked gently back and forth, ignoring her disturbing thoughts, whispering to the infant, touching his downy hair, unaware that Dallas was watching her as Leslie Nelson returned to the nursery. On rounds, Dallas had worked his way through the second floor and ended up at the nurses' station, where he'd stopped when he'd spied Chandra cradling the infant.

A smile toyed with the corner of her lips, and her eyes were downcast, focused on the bundle in her arms. Dark lashes, looking slightly damp, swept her cheek as she, dressed in denim skirt, white sweater and suede vest, held the baby. She was talking to the infant, maybe singing to him. Dallas could only hear a word or two, but the scene resurrected an old dream of his—the dream of one day being a husband and a father. Now this woman—this woman he barely knew, with her blond hair and mischievous gray-green eyes—awakened feelings in him he'd hoped he'd long since destroyed. An unfamiliar tightness bound his chest, and he couldn't for the life of him drag his eyes away from Chandra and the child.

He folded his arms across his chest and wondered if Chandra's love for this child—for she obviously already did care for the baby as if it were her own—would cause her any heartbreak.

"Hush, little baby, don't say a word,
Mama's gonna buy you a mockingbird…"

Dallas felt an unlikely tug on his heart.

"And if that mockingbird don't sing,
Mama's gonna buy you a diamond ring…"

He cleared his throat, and she jumped, her head snapping up, her eyes focusing on him. "Looks like I've got some competition," he said, sauntering slowly up to her.

She blanched, as if she felt guilty for being caught with the child. "Com—competition?"

"For your affection."

"I didn't know it was a contest," she replied, turning her gaze back to the swaddled child in her arms. "And neither does he—do you, J.D.?"

"So, you're still calling him J.D.?"

A wonderful, soft shade of pink crawled up the back of her neck and stained her cheeks. "It sounds so much more…" She blinked as if she truly were embarrassed. "So much more personal than Baby John Doe."

"You can call him whatever you like," Dallas said, wondering if she were setting herself up for an emotional fall from which she'd never recover. She was building her dreams on this child, he could see that hope shining in her eyes, and it broke his heart. The child had only been here a few days. The mother—or some other relative—could still turn up. If not, the baby would end up with Social Services, a foster home, then be adopted. "Can I buy you a cup of coffee?"

One eyebrow lifted, and he could see that she was surprised by his offer. Surprised but pleased. "Thanks, I'd like that—but I have an appointment. Maybe some other time."

"Later today?" What was wrong with him? Why couldn't he just leave her alone? She'd been on his mind, in his thoughts, ever since she'd left him at the river just yesterday. Last night had been pure hell. Her vision had followed him into bed and never left him even as he'd dozed in the final hours before dawn. He'd awoken fully aroused, hoping his dream had been real. "I know we didn't part on the best of terms."

"I thought that's the way you wanted it."

He wished it were that simple. "To be honest, when it comes to you, I don't really know what I want," he admitted, baring his soul for the first time in years.

"That's what I like," she said sarcastically, "a man who knows his own mind."

He reached for her arm, wanting to shake some sense into her. Couldn't she see that this was hard for him? But he didn't touch her as she was holding the infant—the only person, it appeared, she truly cared for. "I'm trying to be big about this," he insisted, knowing emotion registered in his eyes. "It's not easy for me. All I'm asking is for a little of your time."

She eyed him speculatively, chewing on the corner of her mouth while she chased away what appeared to be indecision. So she was as wary of him as he was of her. "Sure. Coffee would be good," she finally said, her gaze lingering for a second too long in his. Beyond that, she didn't commit, just checked her watch, frowned and reluctantly handed the baby back to Nurse Nelson. "But not today. I've really got to run," she said as she clipped down the hall to wait for the elevator. Dallas watched her disappear through the parted doors.

He knew where she lived—she'd given her address to the dispatcher when she'd called 911—someplace on Flaming Moss Road, clear out of town.

"Dr. O'Rourke. Dr. Dallas O'Rourke." The page

brought him out of his thoughts, but he decided he'd call on Chandra. To hell with the fact that he didn't need any complications. She definitely was a complication, but like it or not, she was already a part of his life. At least until the identity of the baby was discovered. After that…well, he didn't want to project that far into the future. Soon the baby would be released from the hospital and, no doubt, Ms. Hill would lose interest in him.

Dallas plucked a pen from his pocket and clicked it several times before writing instructions on a patient's chart. But as he started down the corridor toward the maternity wing, he passed the elevators and smelled the clean scent of Chandra, the whisper of her perfume still clinging to the air.

What was he doing thinking about her? he wondered angrily. He couldn't start fantasizing about her while he was working. He had a job to do, a job that required complete concentration. A job that was his whole life!

He stopped by a phone to pick up his page, and while the operator connected him to Dr. Spangler, Dallas rubbed his chin. He couldn't afford to get involved with a woman; he knew the price he'd have to pay. Closing his eyes briefly, he muttered irritably, "Come on, come on," hoping the operator would put him through to Spangler and get his mind off Chandra.

But her image wouldn't leave him alone. As he waited, his damned thoughts drifted to her again. He decided he was handling the situation all wrong. As long as she was distant, she would always be the forbidden fruit and her allure would never diminish. Before he got caught up in something he couldn't control, he needed to know more about her. He'd trusted a woman at face value once, and she'd proved far from the woman he'd thought he'd married. As for Chandra, what would it hurt to check out her story before he or the hospital was duped? She seemed sincere, and yet her tale about finding a baby and not knowing the mother was hard to believe.

He had a friend in Denver, a guy he'd gone to school with, a private detective who made a decent living out of poking into other people's lives. Guilt stiffened the back of his neck; he knew that Chandra was a private person and she'd be furious if she had any idea he was checking her out. But if he were going to see her again, it only made sense—

"Dallas?" Spangler's voice broke him out of his thoughts. "Would you mind looking in on a patient in 107? Eleanor Mills. Fractured tibia…" Dallas's mind jerked back to the present, but he knew he wasn't finished with Chandra Hill.

Roy Arnette stared at Chandra as if she were certifiably insane. "You want to adopt the kid you found in the barn?" he repeated, eyeing her over the tops of his wire-rimmed glasses. Roy had been her attorney ever since she'd landed in Ranger, and he was as straitlaced as a Victorian corset and just as inflexible. At sixty-three, he sported a thick shock of white hair, dark eyebrows and a quick smile. He was tall, six-two or three, and dressed the part of a Texan, with his gleaming lizard-skin cowboy boots and string tie. Even his office had a Southwestern motif, which fit right into the town's Western look. Cacti sat in clay pots in the corner, pictures of coyotes and adobe Indian villages graced the walls, and a Native American rug in hues of rust, blue and gray was spread over a bleached plank floor.

"That's right," Chandra said. "I want you to draw up the necessary papers and file whatever petitions are necessary. I want that child for my own."

Roy shook his head. "Whoa, darlin', aren't you gettin' the cart before the horse? You don't even know that baby won't be claimed. Hell, it's only been a few days."

"And any mother worth her salt would never have left J.D. in the first place."

"J.D.? You've already got a name for him?"

"Yes," she said firmly. She was on her feet, pacing in front of Roy's red-oak desk, a bundle of restless energy.

"As your lawyer, I'd advise you to take this slow," he drawled, licking his lips and staring up at her with worried eyes.

"I don't want to take it slow. In fact, the sooner we can get the child, the better."

"It's not that easy. You're not dealing with a private adoption, you know. The state's gonna have to get involved. Social Services. And there may be other people—the child's kin or just some couples anxious for a child of their own—who might want him."

"Who? If the boy had any family, surely they would've come forward."

"If they knew about him. And even if not..." He reached behind him to a stack of newspapers, unfolded one and searched until he'd found the section he wanted. With a rustle of paper, he snapped the page open, pressed the newsprint onto his desk and pointed a long finger at the personals column. "Take a look-see."

Chandra swept her gaze over the advertisements:

ADOPT—Loving couple awaits your newborn. Expenses paid. Contact our attorney...

ADOPTION—Dear Birthmother: Professional couple willing to give your newborn love and affection. Expenses paid. Secure future for your child with all the opportunities you'd hoped for. Contact the law firm of...

LOVING ARMS WAITING TO ADOPT...

CHICAGO COUPLE WILLING TO ADOPT YOUR NEWBORN...

WANTED TO LOVE: YOUR NEWBORN...

There were more. Lots more. The requests for babies filled two columns. Chandra felt her knees go weak. She sank into one of Roy's overstuffed leather chairs positioned near the desk and let the breath out of her lungs at the thought of the uphill battle that was before her.

"This is just one paper, from Denver. Ads like this appear in newspapers all over the country. Sterile couples want babies. I have three clients myself who are interested in private adoption. But you know this—it isn't new to you. You worked with kids, and in a hospital."

Of course she knew the facts, but she'd been hiding from them, unwilling to accept the reality that someone else might want her baby. And that was how she'd come to think of J.D.: as hers.

"There's something else you might consider," Roy said, refolding the paper and speaking to her in a kindly voice that reminded her of her own father. "When the judge grants someone custody of the child, he'll probably award that custody to a married couple."

"But—"

Roy held up a flat hand. "I know, I know, single person's rights and all that baloney. But you can argue till you're blue in the face, I'm just tellin' you the facts. A married couple—a *stable* married couple—with a house and a few dollars in the bank to provide security for the baby will have the best shot at adopting B.J."

"J.D.," she corrected automatically. "I think I'd do a damned good job as a mother."

"And a father?"

"Yes, and a father!" she argued. "Look at my job, for crying out loud!"

"Being a father takes more than a job," Roy said calmly, reminding her without words that he and his wife had raised five children. "It's a way of thinking—the male perspective. And there's the most obvious reason for placing a child with a couple."

"Which is?" she asked, knowing and dreading the answer.

"That if one of the parents dies, the kid's got a backup. He won't be orphaned again."

Chandra's shoulders slumped. She couldn't argue against that simple logic, and yet, she told herself, if she gave up now, didn't even fight for custody, she'd always look over her shoulder and wonder if she'd made a mistake. "I don't care what the odds are, Roy," she said, slowly lifting her gaze to meet the questions in his. "I want you to do everything in your power to see that I adopt J.D."

"And you—are you willin' to do the same?"

"Do you even have to ask?"

"Then, if I might make a suggestion," he said, his lips twitching a little, "you might want to find yourself a husband. It'll increase our odds of winnin'."

"Got anyone in mind?" She threw the words back at him, in no mood for jokes.

"That's your department. I'll do my bit—you do yours."

"I won't get married," she said, shoving herself upright.

"No hot prospects?"

Unbidden, a picture of Dallas O'Rourke formed in her mind, a picture she quickly shoved aside. "No," Chandra replied with a wry smile, "no prospects whatsoever."

"Then you'd better start prayin'," Roy advised, "'cause without a little help from the man upstairs, I don't think you've got a ghost of a chance."

"Try, Roy, okay? Just try."

"I'll do my best. You know," he said with an ingratiating grin, "I always aim to please."

Chandra left the attorney's office with her spirits dragging on the concrete sidewalk that flanked the building. She spent the next few hours at the office of Wild West

Expeditions planning a day trip for the following weekend. When Rick asked her about her trip with Dr. O'Rourke, she didn't go into much detail, deciding the less said on the subject of Dallas, the better.

For the next few days, Chandra went about her life. She stopped by the hospital on the way to work, then again before she went home. Even the days on which she led a trail ride or guided a rafting excursion, she found time to spend a couple of minutes staring at the baby.

Every day she expected him to be released, but the doctors at the hospital were taking no chances. J.D. had come into the hospital dehydrated and undernourished, as well as jaundiced, and the swelling in his little head was still apparent, though only slightly.

Soon, however, he'd have to leave.

DALLAS WANTED NO PART of the baby. Or so he told himself. Getting involved with the infant was as dangerous as falling for Chandra Hill. Yet, even he was intrigued by the infant with the dark eyes, lusty voice and shock of black hair.

No wonder Chandra wanted to adopt him. Had circumstances been different, Dallas would have been interested in the boy himself. But, of course, he had no room for a child in his life—a child or a woman. And this baby, whoever he was, had parents out there somewhere. Sooner or later, they'd show up, either together or alone, but someday a woman would claim to be J.D.'s mother.

"And then what are we going to do?" he asked the baby as he rubbed a large hand over his tiny ribs. The infant stared up at him with those eyes that reached right into Dallas's soul. The doctor knew what it was like to be unwanted and unloved, and he pitied this poor child.

It would be a blessing if Chandra were allowed to adopt him, Dallas thought; at least, then J.D. would know a mother's love. He wrapped the baby back in his blanket, and rather than kiss the downy head, Dallas patted the little bottom. "You're gonna be okay," Dallas assured him, though he wished he could predict the baby's future. As well as his own. He hadn't seen Chandra all day, and he'd made excuses to show up in pediatrics hoping for a glimpse of her.

Deciding he was hopeless, he headed back to the emergency room.

CHANDRA DID EVERYTHING possible to assure herself the best chances of adopting J.D. She filled out all the appropriate papers and even began interviewing baby-sitters. She wanted all her ducks in line before she talked to Social Services.

In the meantime, Roy Arnette assured her he was doing everything possible to petition the court for guardianship. Aside from having Chandra fill out forms and sign statements, he'd begun collecting personal references from her friends and acquaintances, even checked on her parents in Idaho, since she knew few people in Ranger. In fact, she was beginning to feel that the hospital staff, particularly the nurses on the pediatric floor, were fast becoming the best friends she had in town.

Even Dr. O'Rourke was more than an acquaintance. She'd seen him several times at the hospital, and for the most part he'd been friendly, though professional. Never once had the rafting trip been mentioned between them. And, if O'Rourke remembered the passion that had burned so brightly for a few magical hours, he didn't show it. Once she'd thought he'd been staring at her, but that flicker of interest she'd seen, or hoped to see, in his eyes was quickly replaced by the cool exterior that had earned him the name Dr. Ice.

"No woman has ever gotten through to him," Shannon

Pratt had divulged once when she and Chandra were sharing a cup of coffee in the cafeteria. "I remember when he came here, several of the single nurses zeroed in on him." She'd smiled at the memory. "Every one of them struck out. And these gals were big leaguers. He wasn't the least bit interested."

Chandra had stared at the bottom of her cup, wishing she could confide in Shannon, but unable to bring up the rafting trip. What had occurred between Dallas and her had been special. "Surely the man must have dated someone."

"Not that I know of. Rumor has it that he was burned badly by his ex-wife." Shannon had finished her coffee. "Believe me, if there were a way to that man's heart, no one's found it yet. And the best have tried."

Now, two days after Shannon's revelation about Dallas, Chandra stopped by the hospital again. Gathering all her courage, she dropped by Dallas's office, hoping to see him, but his receptionist told her that he wasn't available.

In the pediatrics wing, Leslie Nelson was off duty, but Shannon was stationed at the second-floor desk. She let Chandra hold J.D., and once again Chandra's heart wrapped possessively around this little boy. "It's going to be all right," she whispered into his cap of dark hair. "We're going to work this out."

Eventually, she gave the baby back to Shannon, who suggested Chandra drop by at feeding time so that she could give J.D. his bottle. Chandra asked a few questions, but was told that, as far as Shannon or any of the nursing staff of the hospital knew, no one had yet found the mother.

From the hospital, Chandra called the Sheriff's Department and was eventually connected with Deputy White, who informed her that there was nothing new on the case. No one, it seemed, was missing an infant. All the hospitals in a three-hundred-mile radius had been contacted, and no babies had been stolen from the nurseries. It was as if J.D.'s mother didn't exist.

"Nobody just leaves a baby in a barn," Chandra told herself as she walked through the breezeway connecting the parking lot to the hospital. Of their own accord, her eyes swept the staff lot, but Dr. O'Rourke's truck wasn't tucked into any of the parking spots reserved for hospital physicians, and she chided herself for looking.

"OH, FOR CRYING OUT LOUD!" Chandra felt like cursing when, two hours later, she drove down the lane to her house. A tan station wagon was parked near the back porch, and the driver, sitting and smoking, was Bob Fillmore from the *Banner*. Blast it all, she should've known he wouldn't give up. One little article wasn't enough.

Sam, teeth bared, black lips snarling fiendishly, paced by the vehicle. The hairs on the back of his neck stood on end, and every time Fillmore moved, Sam lunged at the car, barking ferociously.

Just what I need, Chandra thought, bracing herself, though the retriever's antics amused her. Sam yipped excitedly as she parked her rig near the back porch.

Knowing that she couldn't duck the reporters forever, she decided to tell everything she knew to Fillmore, hopefully ending any interest the press could have in her.

"Slow day for news?" she asked, hopping out of the truck and forcing a smile she didn't feel. "Sam, down!" She snapped her fingers and pointed to the ground at her feet. Sam reluctantly trotted over and lay by her side, his steady gaze never leaving the car.

"That animal should be locked up!" Fillmore tossed his cigarette butt onto the gravel as he crawled out of his car, but his eyes never left the retriever. "I thought he was going to tear me limb from limb."

"That's the general idea," Chandra said.

Suddenly, the reporter was all business. "Back to your question—about the news? Seems that most of the news is right in your backyard these days. I didn't get much of an interview at the hospital. And the Sheriff's Department hasn't been overly helpful. I thought you could fill in a few of the holes in my story." As if he read denial forming on her lips, he continued, "Look, you're the only one who knows exactly what happened, and I just want to get this story right. The kid's parents may be looking for him right now. He could've been stolen, right? You might be doing them and the baby a big favor…." He let his sentence trail off, implying that there might be a big reward for finding the child. As if money were the answer.

Her stomach lurched and a bad taste filled her mouth. The dislike she'd felt for Bob Fillmore grew more intense. "I just want to do right by the child," Chandra said in the same confidential tone he'd used with her, "and I don't want to interfere with the investigation by the Sheriff's Department." She said nothing about wanting to become the baby's mother. Right now, a statement to that effect would have the same result as spraying gasoline on a slow-burning fire. Fillmore's interest in the story—and in Chandra herself—would definitely heat up. Time enough for that later.

He smiled easily. "No chance of messing anything up with the police. I just have a few questions. Simple ones. Really. Questions that might help the baby find his mom."

Chandra bit back a hot reply about the woman who had forsaken her son. And as for Fillmore, she didn't trust the reporter for a minute. In Tennessee, her life had been ripped open, the focus of several "in-depth" interviews after Gordy Shore had died and his parents had filed suit against her. All of those reporters had seemed a cut above

Fillmore, and they'd made her life a living hell. There was no telling what the reporter from the *Banner* might do.

Yet she couldn't very well hide the truth, could she? She couldn't refuse to talk to the man. She'd only make him think she had something to hide. Frowning, she unlocked the back doors of the Suburban and pulled out two sacks of groceries. Sam followed obediently at her heels and only growled when Fillmore, trying to help, grabbed the handle of a gallon of milk. "I could carry those bags."

"Already got 'em." Balancing the groceries, she unlocked the back door, and Sam streaked inside. The retriever settled on the rug under the table and, with one final growl of disapproval, watched Fillmore enter the cabin.

Chandra stuffed a carton of eggs into the refrigerator. "You know, I thought people usually called ahead for an interview."

"I did. This morning. No answer. I left a message. When you didn't call back, I figured the time and place was okay with you."

"And what if I hadn't shown up?" she asked, waving him into a chair. Casting a glance at her answering machine, she noticed the red light flashing. She had no option but to get this over with.

"I would've waited. Speaking of which—" he checked his watch and scowled "—the photographer should be here by now. He knew about this shoot. Would you mind if I used your phone?" He was already picking up the receiver when Chandra nodded. The man was pushy, no doubt about it. He dialed quickly, then tapped a toe while he waited. "Yeah. It's Fillmore," he said into the mouthpiece. "I'm lookin' for Levine. Should've been here by now. I'm at the Hill place on Flaming Moss Road...yeah, eighteen, twenty miles out...well, tell him to get his butt in gear, okay? We're waiting."

Chandra, only half listening to the reporter, pulled out a couple of sodas from the refrigerator. Her throat was already parched, and at the thought of an interview, her mouth turned as dry as a desert wind. She held one can up silently and Fillmore, still growling orders into the phone, grinned and waved an affirmative. While he was finishing his call, she cracked ice into a couple of tall glasses, not really in the mood to sit down and sip Pepsi with the man from the *Banner.* Her only consolation was that she figured it wouldn't hurt to have the reporter on her side, pretend to go along with him and then, at the first available instant, make some excuse to end the interview early. He'd have a deadline, so he wouldn't be back, and that, thankfully, would be the end of the press camping out on her doorstep. She hoped. If not and he got wind of the fact that she was planning to adopt J.D., so be it. At least he wouldn't be out to smear her. She felt better about offering him the cola.

"Look," she said, once he'd hung up and settled into a chair at the table. She placed one of the dewy glasses in front of him and resisted the urge to press the other to her forehead to ward off a headache. "I just don't want this to get out of hand. No media circus on this, okay?"

"I'm just here to tell a story." After draining half his glass, Fillmore reached into his jacket pocket and pulled out his tape recorder, pen and notepad. "Okay, let's start at the beginning. How did you find the baby?"

Chandra had gone over the same tale so many times that she said the words without much emotion, explaining about discovering the child, calling 911 and driving to meet the ambulance. No, she didn't know to whom the baby belonged. No, she couldn't imagine who would leave a baby alone. Yes, the baby had needed medical attention, but he had seemed strong enough.

They were both about finished with their drinks when

Fillmore brought up the baby's future. "What if the mother shows up?"

"Then I guess the court decides if she's a fit parent," Chandra replied, studying the melting ice in her glass. She hoped her face was impassive.

"And where do you fit into it?"

Yes, where? "I don't know," she answered truthfully, just as Sam's ears pricked forward and the dog scrambled to the door with a bark. Chandra glanced out the window and her heart dropped. Dallas's truck slowed to a stop by Fillmore's car. *Great,* she thought, knowing instinctively that Fillmore wouldn't budge if he recognized the doctor who had admitted J.D. into the hospital.

"Well, well, well, the good Dr. O'Rourke," Fillmore drawled, a satisfied smile slithering across his lips. "What's he doing here?"

"I wouldn't know," Chandra said, rising to answer the door. Dallas had, indeed, arrived—all six feet of him greeted her as she swept the door open and invited him in. "Hi," she said, motioning toward Fillmore. "Join the crowd."

Dallas grew rigid and as he walked into the kitchen, the temperature seemed to drop ten degrees. Both men stared at each other for a few agonizing seconds. "Fillmore," Dallas finally said, not bothering to hide his distaste for the man. "What're you doing here?"

"Just checkin' out a story. What about you?" The reporter clicked his pen loudly, and the tape in his machine continued to whir.

"I took an excursion with Ms. Hill over the weekend. She left something in my truck."

"Excursion? You mean a rafting trip?" Fillmore glanced from Dallas to Chandra and back again.

Dallas shrugged. "My brother thought I could use a little R and R." He reached into the pocket of his jeans and pulled out her bandanna, the one she'd used to tie back her hair, clean and pressed.

"So how was the trip? Exciting?"

Dallas turned chilling eyes on the reporter. "Very. Ms. Hill is an excellent guide. In fact, have you ever been on one of those trips down the Rattlesnake at—what was it called?" He looked to Chandra for help, but she had the feeling he knew exactly what he was saying. "Grizzly Loop? I think it's just your speed, Fillmore."

Bob Fillmore smirked, as if he refused to be goaded by Dallas.

"And if Chandra can't help you, maybe the owner can. What's his name—Rick Benson—you remember, the guy you did the piece on a few years back."

The muscles in Chandra's neck tensed. This was no time to intimidate the reporter, for God's sake! What was Dallas doing?

"I'll keep it in mind," Fillmore replied as he scraped his chair back and stood. Chandra hoped fervently that he was finished. "Tell me, Doctor, since I'm writing about the abandoned child, what's his status with the hospital?"

Dallas looked in Chandra's direction. "He's about to be released."

No! So that's why Dallas was here, to break the news and prepare her. Chandra's heart leapt to her throat. "Released to whom?" she asked, trying to keep a calm appearance.

Dallas slanted a glance at the reporter, as if he realized he'd said too much.

"That's right," Fillmore added, "who'll get the kid?"

"I think that's up to Social Services."

Fillmore grinned. "This is getting better by the minute. When, exactly, will he be released?"

"Dr. Williams and Dr. Spangler will decide."

"They the kid's pediatricians?"

"That's right," Dallas said as Sam barked loudly.

A compact Ford, silver-blue in color, roared down the drive, leaving a plume of dust in its wake.

What was this? Chandra wondered. More bad news?

"About time," Fillmore muttered, scooping up his notepad and tape recorder as he scraped his chair back. "It's Sid. He'll want a few pictures of the barn, you know, where the kid was found. And he might have a few questions. Then we'll be outta your hair."

Chandra could hardly wait. They walked outside, and Sid Levine, gathering camera bag, umbrella, light meter and other equipment, unloaded his car. "Hi, fella," he said to Sam as the retriever bared his teeth and galloped toward the newcomer. Sid reached down and scratched Sam behind the ears. "Hey, slow down, I'm not gonna hurt anything."

Growling, Sam sniffed at the proffered hand then, traitor that he was, began wagging his tail so hard that it thumped against the fender of the Ford.

"We were on our way to the barn to get some pictures of the inside," Fillmore said, waving the photographer along as he crossed the yard.

"I'll be there in a minute. Just let me take a few shots out here," Levine said, apparently used to Fillmore's brusque manner.

Inside the barn, Chandra, as she had with the sheriff's deputies, pointed out the stall where she'd found the baby. One of her favorite geldings, Max, a curious buckskin, strolled inside and stood waiting for some oats to be tossed his way. The other horses poked their noses into the barn door and their shadows drifted inside, but they didn't follow the buckskin's lead. Even Cayenne, usually friendly, eyed the intruders, snorted disdainfully and refused to amble inside.

Max draped his head over the top of the stall and eyed

Fillmore, who was busy in the end box where the baby was found, then nuzzled Chandra's jacket, looking for a piece of carrot or apple. "Sorry, buddy," she whispered to the horse, who snorted and stamped a foot impatiently.

Dallas had followed her into the barn. He leaned against the ladder to the hayloft while Fillmore asked still more questions and the photographer scurried inside, sending up dust motes and disturbing the cobwebs that draped from the windows. Chandra could feel Dallas's gaze on her back as she petted Max's velvety nose and answered the questions as best she could. Fillmore tried to ignore the doctor, but Chandra couldn't. His presence seemed to charge the air in the musty old barn, and she sensed that some of the reporter's questions were worded more carefully just because Dallas was within earshot.

"This it?" Sid Levine asked, looking around the barn, searching, it appeared, for sources of light. A grimy circular window over the hayloft and a few rectangles of glass at eye level over the stalls gave little natural illumination to the interior.

"In here," Fillmore replied from the stall.

Once again, Chandra pointed out the position of the child. Then, while the reporter asked a few more questions, the photographer took aim and began clicking off shots. Dallas said nothing, just watched the men going through the motions of creating news.

It's almost over, Chandra thought, *it has to be.*

"So...you been a resident of Ranger long?" Fillmore asked.

"A few years," she replied.

"And before that?"

Chandra felt the sweat break out between her shoulder blades. She didn't want her past splayed all over the front page of the *Ranger Banner.* She'd buried her life in Tennessee and hoped that it would stay that way.

"I'm originally from Idaho, up near McCall," she said easily.

"Ahh," Levine said, nodding to himself. "So that's where you get the interest in rafting and trail riding."

"Grew up doing it," she replied. "My father was a real outdoorsman." From the corner of her eye she saw Dallas straighten a little, but Fillmore, evidently satisfied, snapped off his tape recorder and checked his watch. "Thanks for your time. I've gotta shove off if I'm gonna put this story to bed tonight."

The muscles in Chandra's back relaxed a little. If they would just leave, she could find out about J.D. It seemed forever before Fillmore's car was moving down the drive and the afternoon sun was warming her back as she and Dallas watched the reporter take his leave.

Levine was still finishing up in the barn, but Chandra couldn't wait. "What's going to happen to the baby?" she asked, laying a hand on Dallas's arm. She attempted to keep the desperation from her voice, but found it impossible. "What will Social Services do?"

"Probably place the child in a temporary home until a judge decides where he'll be placed permanently."

"Oh, God," she whispered, her throat dry. J.D needed someone who loved him, someone who would care for him. While he was in the hospital, he was being cared for, even loved a bit, by the nurses, and Chandra could see him every day. But now...

To her surprise, Dallas placed a comforting arm around her shoulders. "Don't worry. He'll be fine." Her throat clogged at his tenderness.

"How do you know that?" she demanded, her eyes beginning to burn with unshed tears. She hadn't realized until just then how much she'd thought of the baby as hers. Everyone had been warning her that he could be taken away, but she hadn't listened.

"He'll be placed with someone who'll care for him."
Dallas smiled down at her and squeezed her a little. "And
I'll make sure that whoever gets him will allow you to see
him."

She couldn't believe it. "You can do that?" she asked
skeptically.

"I can try." A sliver of uneasiness clouded his features.
"But don't get too involved. You don't know what will
happen."

"I know, I know," she said, her throat clogging as
Dallas offered her the comfort of his arms. She laid her
head against his shoulder, drinking in the smell of him,
glad for the strong arms that surrounded her. How right
it felt to be sheltered by him. For years she'd stood on her
own, relied on no one, and now all she could think about
was leaning on Dallas. "The mother might show up. Damn
that woman, anyway!"

She heard a camera click behind her and jumped.
Dallas whirled, his eyes blazing, as Sid Levine lowered
his .35 millimeter and snapped the camera back into his
case. "All finished," he said, and his eyes held a spark of
nastiness that Chandra hadn't seen before.

"I hope I don't see my picture on the front page," Dallas
said, and the treachery on the photographer's face was replaced by a glimmer of fear as he slid into his Ford and
took off.

"Bastards. Every last one of them," Dallas growled,
his eyes narrowing on the silver car as it roared down the
lane.

"Just tell me about the baby." Chandra couldn't worry
about the reporter or his sidekick. All that mattered was
J.D.—her J.D.

Dallas shoved his hands into his pockets of his jeans.
"That's why I stopped by," he said, and Chandra felt a
jab of disappointment. There was a little part of her that

wanted him to have come to visit her on his own. "I talked to Williams, and it's just a matter of days—possibly tomorrow or the day after—whenever Social Services decides to get their act together."

"Oh, God," she whispered, knowing that soon it would all be over. But she hadn't lost. Not yet.

"Maybe it won't be so bad," Dallas said. "As I said, I'll try to arrange it so you can still visit with the baby—"

"Oh, thank you," she said, and, without thinking, she flung her arms around his neck. "Thank you." She felt his arms wrap around her, hold her snug against him for a heartbeat, and for a second she felt as breathless as she had that night by the river. Her heart thundered as his hands moved slowly up her rib cage. But he stopped, pushed her slowly away from him, and when she lifted her eyes to his, she saw his features harden.

He held her at arm's length and dug his fingers into her shoulders. "Look, Chandra, you don't have to thank me, okay? You don't have to do anything to show your appreciation."

"Meaning?"

"Meaning that just because I'm helping you with the baby doesn't mean that there's anything else between us. You're not obligated to show your appreciation."

"Well, that's a relief," she shot back. Did he really think that she would stoop so low as to manipulate him and play with his emotions? "And here I thought I'd have to do something like go to bed with you just to get you on my side."

He sucked in a quick breath at her sarcasm. His eyes flashed, and he looked as if he'd been slapped.

"That is what you were insinuating, wasn't it? Well, let me tell you something, *Doctor,* I *don't* sleep with men to get what I want. Ever."

He lifted a skeptical eyebrow and she couldn't help

ramming her point home. "You know, I thought you were different, that you weren't the typical egomaniac M.D. who thinks he's God's gift to women. But it turns out that you're just like all the rest—misconstruing motives, thinking women are coming on to you. All I wanted to do was say thanks."

"Then just say it."

"I did." She shoved her hair from her eyes and planted her hands firmly on her hips. "Now, if you'll excuse me—and even if you won't—I've got work to do." In a cloud of dust and anger, she stormed to the barn, furious with herself and outraged with him.

Once inside, she climbed the loft ladder, kicked down a couple of bales of hay, then hopped to the floor. Finding her pocket knife, she slit the twine, snapped her knife closed and grabbed a pitchfork. She began tossing loose hay into the manger, throwing her back into her work, filling her nostrils with the scent of sweat, horses, dung and dried grass.

Max, snorting expectantly, wandered back to his stall, tentatively nudging his nose into the fresh hay.

A shadow from the open door fell across the floor. Chandra stiffened and turned, facing O'Rourke again. He looked as he did the first night she'd seen him, unapproachable and deadly serious. "I thought you were leaving," she said, throwing another forkful of hay into the manger.

"And I thought we should clear the air."

"About what?"

"Us."

"Us," she threw back at him. "What 'us'? I'm just *using* you, remember?" She plunged her pitchfork into the loose hay again and threw the bleached strands into the next manger. Brandy, a chestnut mare, ambled inside, her white blaze visible as she sniffed the feeding trough.

Before Chandra knew what was happening, Dallas had closed the distance between them. He grabbed her shoulders with hands made of steel. Spinning her around, he forced her to face the conflicting emotions shading his eyes. "I don't think you're purposely trying to *use* me," he said fiercely.

"What a relief," she shot back, her voice dripping sarcasm.

"But what I do think is that, whether you like it or not, you see me as a link to the baby. You're so desperate to be a part of that child's life that you'll manipulate anyone to get what you want."

"And what I see is a man who runs away from his emotions—a man afraid of being spontaneous because it might upset the careful balance in his life!" Breathing hard, she held the pitchfork with one hand. She didn't want to see the anger in his eyes or feel the warm pads of his fingers digging into her skin. Nor did she want the male smell of him to fill her senses.

She ripped herself free. "Look, don't feel *obligated* to do anything, all right? You don't owe me anything, and I can handle my life by myself. And that includes doing what I have to do to be close to the baby. You can walk away from this…just turn—" she pointed to the door "—and leave. That's all there is to it."

"I wish." He lifted his hands as if to touch her face, dropped them again, then swore under his breath. "Damn it all to hell, anyway," he muttered before grabbing her again and pulling her roughly against him. Startled, she dropped the pitchfork and it clattered to the dusty concrete floor.

This time his lips crashed down on hers with a possessive savagery that sent one pulsating shock wave after another down her body. He breathed in her breath, his lips moving insistently, his big hands splayed across the gentle slope of her back.

She tried to drag her mouth away, pushed with all her strength, but was unable to break the manacle of his embrace. Instead she was subjected to an elegant torment as his tongue sought entrance to her mouth and his hands moved insistently, rubbing her clothes against her skin.

She moaned softly, her head falling backward, her throat exposed. One of his hands curled in the thick strands of her hair, and he drew her head back farther still, until he could press hot, wet kisses against the curve of her shoulder.

"No...please...stop..." she whispered, hardly believing the words came from her lips.

His touch was electric, his tongue, teeth and lips nipping and creating pulses of desire that swirled deep inside.

"You don't want me to stop," he whispered against her ear, his breath tantalizing and wet.

"Yes...no... Oh, Dallas, please..." With all her might, she coiled her strength, then pushed away from him and found to her mortification that she was panting, her heartbeat thrumming, her pulse pounding in her temples.

Running a trembling hand through her hair, she stepped backward until she ran into a post supporting the hay loft. The splintered wood pressed hard against her back. "For someone who doesn't want to get involved, you're pretty damned persistent," she said, trying to sound haughty, and failing.

"What I want and what seems to keep happening between us aren't necessarily the same." He, too, had trouble finding his breath. He ran a shaking hand over his lips.

"Then I guess the answer is to stay away from each other."

"You think that's possible?" he asked, sliding her a look with his knowing blue eyes.

"Anything's possible if you want it bad enough."

"Is that so?"

"Absolutely."

"I hope you're right, Ms. Hill," he said as he walked to the door. He stopped and looked over his shoulder. "Because if you're not, we've got one helluva problem on our hands."

CHAPTER NINE

DALLAS DRAGGED HIMSELF out of the pool, his body heaving from the exertion, his lungs craving more air. He'd swum over a mile in less than forty-five minutes, and he was breathing hard, his heart pumping crazily.

"What're you tryin' to do, kill yourself?" the man in the next lane asked. The other swimmer ripped off his goggles and cap, letting his wet hair fall nearly to his shoulders.

"I was a little keyed up," Dallas replied. He didn't know the man's name, wasn't really interested. He saw him here at the pool a couple of times a week and usually they swam their laps at about the same pace. Not this morning. Dallas had been wound tighter than a clock spring, his muscles tense, his attitude one notch shy of downright surly.

All because of that damned woman. He didn't know whether to hate her or to love her. She'd upset his well-ordered life, and for that, he was angry with her; but she brought out a part of him he'd kept hidden, a part that felt younger and carefree. He supposed, if he didn't love her, at least he owed her one.

He climbed to his feet, grabbed his towel and rubbed the rough terry cloth over his face, neck and shoulders. Seeing her yesterday with the reporter should have been warning enough, but no, he'd hung around and let down his guard enough to allow that louse of a photographer to snap a picture of them together. Not that it really mattered, he supposed. The picture probably wouldn't be printed, and if it was, so what?

Worse yet, he'd let the man goad him into tracking her down in the barn and acting like some horny barbarian. God, what was happening to him?

In the shower room, he ignored the other men who were in various stages of dressing, shaving or blow-drying their hair. They joked and laughed over the whine of hair dryers and electric razors, but Dallas barely noticed. He'd never been part of that club of men who sought camaraderie in the locker room before facing the day.

He washed the chlorine from his skin and hair and, as they had for the past week, his thoughts swirled around Chandra. Chandra the camping guide. Chandra the seductress. Chandra the would-be mother. God, she was crazy for that kid; that much was obvious.

But Dallas wasn't too sure about how she felt about him. Unless her emotions were as jumbled as his. Dunking his head under the shower one final time, he twisted off the knob and tried not to think about last night, how he, after a short shift at the hospital, had gone home and fallen into bed, only to dream about her—her honey-gold hair, her laughing eyes, her luscious pink lips and her breasts, round and full with dark, sweet tips.

Suddenly embarrassed at the swelling that the thought of her always brought to mind, he turned on the faucet again, gave himself a douse of ice-cold water, then muttering obscenities under his breath, wrapped a towel around his hips and walked briskly to his locker. He changed into clothes quickly, shoved his fingers through his hair and, slinging his bag over his shoulder, strode outside.

The day echoed his mood. Gray clouds clustered over the mountaintops, threatening to explode in a deluge of late-summer rain. Well, great, let it pour. Maybe the drops from the dark sky would cool his blood. He hoped so. Ever since he'd met Chandra Hill, it seemed he'd been battling his body, his mind telling him not to get involved, his damned body wanting nothing more than to plunge into her with a fierce possession.

He'd *never* felt this way before. *Never.* Even with Jennifer, there had been an edge of control in their lovemaking, and not once had he discovered that his passion had ruled him. But now, with Chandra, he couldn't stop thinking about making love to her over and over again.

He unlocked his truck and slipped behind the wheel. Jamming his key into the ignition, he decided that he'd be better off not seeing the lady again.

Maybe another woman... He considered the women he knew and, without even realizing the turn of his thoughts, his mind had wandered back to Chandra Hill. Yesterday's kiss...a simmering passion...

Getting to know her more intimately would either be a blessing or a curse, and he strongly suspected the latter. He shoved a tape into the player and, muttering oaths at the other drivers, he eased his truck into the snarl of traffic and turned toward the hospital.

"I HAVE NO CHOICE but to release him," Dr. Williams said with a quiet authority that brooked no argument.

Chandra had caught up with him after his rounds, and they were now in his office at the hospital, he seated on one side of a glossy black desk, she on the other. Behind him, through the window, she noticed the dark clouds that hinted of a late-summer thunderstorm. The thunderheads reminded her of Dallas and the storm she often saw gathering in his eyes, but then, just about anything these days caused her to think about Dr. O'Rourke.

Or the baby. And that was why she was here. She hadn't slept a wink last night, worried about the child. She'd spent the night tossing and turning, her mind spinning with schemes to get custody of the boy, and oftentimes, she hated to admit, those schemes also involved Dallas.

Dr. Williams was staring at her, waiting for her to say something.

"I just think it might be best for the child if he stayed here at the hospital a few more days."

"Why? He's healthy."

"But—"

"Really, Miss Hill, the hospital has done everything it can for the child." Williams gave her a soft smile that was barely visible beneath his neatly trimmed red beard. "He'll stay the night, and tomorrow the caseworker from Social Services will come for him."

"And take him where?" Chandra asked, managing not to sound frantic.

"I don't know." Williams sat back in his chair and shook his balding head. "Her name is Marian Sedgewick, and she's coming for the baby at about eleven. I'm sure you could call her and find out more about his placement."

The phone on the corner of his desk rang shrilly, and Chandra rose. "Thanks, Doctor," she said.

"Anytime." But he was already picking up the receiver.

Chandra walked along the hall of the pediatrics wing, refusing to be discouraged. This was to be expected. The baby couldn't stay here forever. But she'd have to move quickly. Near the nurses' station, she stopped and rummaged in her purse for change, then placed a call to Roy Arnette.

"I'm sorry, but Mr. Arnette isn't in right now. Can I take a message?" Chandra left her name and number. Deflated, she walked to the nurses' station, where Shannon Pratt was busy fielding phone calls.

"Go on back," she mouthed, the phone cradled between her shoulder and ear, as she wrote hastily on a clipboard.

Chandra didn't need any more encouragement. She

hurried to the nursery and spied J.D., wrapped in a white blanket, his eyes moving slowly as he tried to focus. Her heart squeezed at the sight of his chubby face. Where would he be tomorrow? Who would change him, feed him, kiss him good-night?

An uncomfortable lump filled her throat as Shannon, all smiles, bustled by. "It's been a madhouse this morning," she apologized. "Leslie told me you were coming in to feed him." She motioned toward J.D.'s crib.

"I'd love to."

"Well, we could use the extra hands." Shannon walked into the nursery, still talking. "This is, and I quote, 'highly irregular,' but I talked long and hard and got the okay from my supervisor who, in turn, worked it out with admin. So we're all set." She handed Chandra gloves and a mask. "You can scrub up in the lavatory, and once you've donned all these glamorous accessories—come back. Believe me, your little guy will be hungry...."

Your little guy. If only. Chandra scrubbed her hands and arms and yanked on her gloves. The smell of antiseptic and newborn babies reminded her of her own practice. She'd been happy back then, treating the patients, getting to know their mothers, fitting into the cozy community of Collier, Tennessee and thinking she would put down roots and start her own family.

But Doug had had other ideas....

"Hey, you look like one of us!" Shannon said as Chandra walked out of the washroom. "And look who's waiting...."

"J.D.," Chandra said, grinning behind the paper mask. "How're ya, pumpkin?" She took the little bundle eagerly, held his tiny, wriggling body close to hers. Nurse Pratt handed her a bottle of formula, and the baby, still blinking up at Chandra, began to suckle hungrily. Tiny little noises, grunts of pleasure, accompanied the slurping sound as he tugged on the nipple.

"You've named him?"

Chandra, startled, jumped and the bottle came out of J.D.'s tiny mouth. He let up a wail that could put a patient in cardiac arrest. Quickly, she nudged the nipple back between the baby's tiny lips. "I'm sorry," she said to Shannon, "I was so into this, I forgot you were there. And, yes, I decided he needed a name."

"Well, I think it's a much better name than Baby John Doe." With a twinkle in her eye, she hurried back to the nursery and, with a black marking pen, wrote "J.D." in large letters on the tag of his bassinet.

Chandra smiled. For the first time since she'd moved to Ranger two years before, she felt a part of the community. Living as she did, miles out of town, meeting only a few townspeople at the market or at work, she hadn't cultivated many friends. Most of the people she dealt with were tourists who wanted a thrill before returning to their cities and nine-to-five jobs. A few returned from one year to the next, but her only real contacts with people in town were the men she worked with.

The nurses and staff of the hospital seemed special. She wondered if it was the hospital surroundings. For the first time since she left Collier, she wondered if leaving her profession had been the right choice.

So she was here. Again. Being set up for a fall. Dallas saw Chandra with the baby, this time taking a bottle from him and swaying gently, brushing the top of his downy head with her lips.

Was she out of her mind? Didn't she know she was playing Russian roulette with her emotions? Yet he, too, could feel the tug on his heartstrings, the unlikely and unwanted pull of tenderness for the child. Seeing them together, she cradling the little dark head so close to her breast, the baby nuzzling closer, caused a tightness in his chest and a deep sadness that he would never be a father, never a husband. He'd tried once and failed.

The familiar metallic taste of loathing filled his throat when he remembered his wife and her betrayal. Though he hadn't loved her as he should have, he'd been faithful to her and fair, and he'd cared about her. And she'd driven a knife into his heart, cutting him so deeply, the scar would never heal. He'd never feel free to love someone like Chandra, to father her children....

He coughed loudly. What the hell was he doing even thinking such ludicrous thoughts? It was one thing to fantasize about making love to her, to consider bedding her and having a quick affair that would end as surely as had his own brief marriage. But to consider a lifetime together, marriage and children? What in God's name was wrong with him?

Clearing his throat, he approached her. She turned, and the sight of her hair fanning her face nearly undid all his hard-fought resolutions to keep away from her. Her lips moved slightly, smiling at the sight of him.

"Thank God you're here," she said, and he realized that she'd somehow become dependent upon him.

This very headstrong, independent woman was beginning to trust him, and he thought guiltily of his detective friend digging into her past. He could call off the investigation, but decided it wouldn't hurt to know more about her. She seemed to have brushed their episode in the barn from her mind.

She said breathlessly, "I just talked to Dr. Williams. They're releasing J.D. tomorrow."

"So it's been decided."

"'Morning, Doctor." Shannon emerged from the nursery and turned her attention to Chandra. "Here, let me change him."

"He hasn't burped yet," Chandra protested, drawing her fine eyebrows together.

"That's all right." Nurse Pratt wriggled her nose at the tiny baby. "We'll take care of it, won't we? And I'll take your lovely accessories…" Shannon accepted the baby, bottle, gloves and mask from Chandra, and after a few quick words with Dallas about a peculiarly obstinate patient in CICU, carried J.D. back to the nursery.

Dallas took the crook of Chandra's arm in his broad hand and pulled her gently toward the nurses' station. "I wouldn't worry too much about the baby. He'll be in good hands."

"How do you know?" She stopped short, looking up at him. "*What* do you know?"

"Rumor is that the child will be placed in temporary custody of the Newells."

"The sheriff?"

"He and his wife, Lenore. She's a part-time nurse here and they've done this sort of thing before. Lenore's known for taking in stray dogs, cats and opening their home to runaways or children who are waiting to be placed in more permanent quarters."

Anxiously, Chandra bit her lower lip and Dallas experienced a sudden urge to kiss her and tug on that very lip. "Come here," he said, all thoughts of denying himself long gone. He pulled her around a corner and down a short hallway to a quieter part of the floor. At the end of the hall, in the landing of the emergency stairs, he tugged on her hand, yanking her hard against him. She gasped, and he captured her lips with his. Seeing the startled look on her face, the surprise in her wide, gray-green eyes, he expected her to frantically push away, but she didn't resist.

His mouth moved over hers, and she leaned against

him, circling his waist with her arms, her breasts crushed against the hard expanse of his chest. This time she seemed to melt against his body. He twisted his hands in her hair and played with her lower lip, touching it with his tongue before drawing it into his mouth.

Chandra's heart thumped crazily. What was he thinking, kissing her here, in broad daylight, where at any minute— Her senses reeled, her body reacted and a tingling blush suffused her skin. She closed her eyes and let herself get lost in the smell and touch and taste of him. There was the faint odor of chlorine that clung to his skin, the smell of soap. And his hair was still damp. Somewhere, faraway, a metal cart rattled.

"What the hell am I going to do with you?" he muttered into her hair, breathing deeply, his heart drumming so loudly, she could hear the wild beat.

Before she could answer, he kissed her again, long and hard, creating a whirlpool of emotions inside her. She sighed into his open mouth, and his tongue touched hers before he closed his mouth and every muscle in his body tensed. He dropped his hands to his sides then, and she nearly fell over.

"What?" she asked, before seeing that his eyes, now open, were focused on something or someone standing just beyond Chandra's shoulder.

Chandra turned and found herself gazing into the flushed face of Nurse Alma Lindquist. "Excuse me," the big nurse said, obviously embarrassed. "I, uh, well, I'm looking for you, Doctor, and Shannon said she saw you goin' down this hall." She turned her gaze to Chandra. "She didn't mention—"

"What is it?" Dallas was all business, and Chandra felt like crawling into a hole. Caught like a couple of lusty teenagers—by Alma Lindquist, of all people. Alma's eyebrows were arched over her glasses, and a tiny I-got-you grin was barely visible on her face. Chandra was absolutely mortified.

"Dr. Warren isn't in yet, and I need to get into the medications for E.R. However, if you're busy—"

"I'll be right there," Dallas said, his eyes glittering as Alma tried and failed to smother her knowing smile. She sauntered off down the hall, and Chandra's face felt red-hot.

"This was a mistake," Dallas said, jamming his hands through his hair and shaking his head. "Look, I can't get involved with anyone. It just wouldn't work."

"I don't remember asking you," Chandra replied, though his words stung.

"But you haven't exactly been backing off, have you?"

"I've done nothing to encourage you," she reminded him, wounded. "You came on the rafting trip. I didn't invite you."

"My brother—"

"Whatever. It doesn't matter. And you showed up at my house the other night—and barged into my barn. Again without an engraved invitation."

"And you camp out here at the hospital."

"Because of the baby!" she shot back, knowing in her heart what she would never admit to him. "Don't you understand?" she said instead. "J.D. means everything to me!"

"Oh, Chandra..." he said, and a dark emotion flickered in his eyes.

"And don't give me all the reasons I shouldn't try to adopt him, because I'm going to," she replied, embarrassed and angry and frustrated. She tossed her hair over her shoulders.

"You're serious about adopting him?" Dallas asked, obviously skeptical.

She wished she could call back the words, but the

damage was done. There was no reason to play coy. "I hope to. I've already told my attorney to draw up the necessary papers. I'll petition the court—"

"And what did your attorney say?"

"Well, after he tried to talk me out of it," she replied, sliding the doctor a glance, "he told me I'd better go about increasing my chances."

"How?"

"By getting married."

Dallas blanched. Rock solid, all-business Dr. Dallas O'Rourke actually lost his color. Good! Chandra had the feeling O'Rourke needed to be shaken up once in a while.

"That's right, Doctor, I guess I'm in the market for a husband." She straightened her blouse. "Seems that the courts will look more kindly on a couple rather than a single woman."

"You're joking!" He was absolutely stricken, and Chandra's heart nosedived.

"Only about being in the marriage market," she said. "But I'm not going to let any prejudice against single women stop me. If I have to fight this through the Supreme Court, I will."

"Or get married?"

"That was a joke, Doctor," she said, and then decided to drop the bomb. "I was married once. It wasn't all it was cracked up to be."

He didn't move, but his eyes didn't leave hers and she silently counted her heartbeats. "Maybe you married the wrong man," he finally said.

"I did," she admitted, quivering at the thought of discussing her short-lived marriage with him. Once the divorce had been finalized, she'd never spoken of Doug or her marriage to anyone. Not even to her family. "But even if I did marry the wrong guy, I'm not sure I would recognize the right one if he landed on my doorstep."

"Oh, Ms. Hill, I think you would."

She lifted a shoulder dismissively. "I'm not going to lose any sleep over it. See you later," she said breezily, as if his passionate kiss and harsh words hadn't bothered her in the least. With a forced smile, she turned and left him there, trying not to notice that the taste of his lips still lingered on hers.

DALLAS TRIED TO IGNORE the fact that he was jealous—of a man whose name he didn't know. Whoever Chandra's ex-husband was, he was a damned fool.

Now, as Dallas folded his arms over his chest, he tried to keep his thoughts on the business at hand, which was his patient. "The nurses say you've been giving them trouble, Mr. Hastings."

"Call me Ned. And don't give me no guff about not takin' those pills. I've lived eighty-five years without takin' pills, and I'm not about to start now."

"Even though you're in intensive care and have had one heart attack already? All the medication does is help regulate your heartbeat."

Ned scratched his head, his mottled scalp showing through thin gray hair. "I know you're just doin' your job, Doc, and I 'preciate it, but I don't need any goldurn pills to keep my ticker from conkin' out."

"I'm not so sure about that."

"And about those nurses of yours. Always fussin' over me. Pokin' and proddin' and cluckin' their tongues. You're lucky I'm still in this hospital."

Dallas swallowed a smile. The old coot was lovable in his own way. But stubborn. "I don't think you're being realistic about your health."

"Hell, I didn't get to my age by lyin' in a hospital, with tubes run through my body and pills bein' stuck in my mouth every hour of the day. I live alone, I'm proud of it, and I don't need no mamby-pamby women stewin' over me."

"I see he's his usual jovial self," Lenore Newell said. She placed the thermometer into a disposable cover, and with a smile, stuck the thermometer under Mr. Hasting's tongue. "This should keep you quiet a while," she said.

He sputtered, but didn't spit the thermometer out as Dallas had expected.

Nurse Newell took the old man's pulse and, while eyeing her watch, added, "Some people would think spending a few days being pampered by women would be heaven."

"Humph," Ned growled around the thermometer. "They're just plain stupid or they haven't been in this damned place," he mumbled.

"Shh," she ordered, winking at the doctor as she waited for the beep and digital readout of her patient's temperature.

"Keep giving him the medication," Dallas said, seeing the glint of fondness in the old man's glare. "And don't take any abuse from this guy."

Hastings's thick eyebrows shot up.

"I'll be back," Dallas promised him. As he left the room, he heard Ned Hastings still growling around the thermometer.

Lenore caught up with Dallas in the staff lounge. "Cantankerous old son of a gun," she said with a ready smile. Behind big glasses, her eyes gleamed with affection.

"He keeps life interesting," Dallas remarked.

"Don't they all?"

Dallas poured himself a cup of coffee while Lenore rummaged through a basket of tea bags. The lounge was nearly empty. Three nurses surrounded a round table by the window, and a couple of residents, who looked as if they'd each pulled thirty-six-hour shifts, were stretched

out on the couches, one in scrubs, the other wearing a
rumpled lab coat and slacks. Each supported more than a
day's growth of beard and bloodshot eyes.

"Been here long?" Dallas ventured.

One of them, the lanky one with long blond hair,
shoved a hand through his unruly locks. "Days, weeks,
years...I can't remember."

"We came on duty in 1985," his companion joked. He
was shorter and thin, with a moustache and eyes that appeared owlish behind thick glasses.

"Time for a break," Dallas suggested.

"Man, I'm gonna sleep for a week," the tall one said.

"Not me. I'm going out for a five-mile jog and set of
tennis."

"Yeah, right!" They struggled to their feet and headed
out the door.

Dallas stirred his coffee before glancing at Lenore. "I
heard you might have another mouth to feed."

She smiled. "Yep. The abandoned baby. Judge Reinecke
seems to think that the baby would be best at our house,
at least for a while. We've cared for more than our share
of orphans."

Dallas stared into his coffee, not knowing whether he
should bring up Chandra or not. Maybe she was better off
away from the baby. But he remembered her look of desperation at the thought that the child would be taken away
from her. Knowing he might be playing with emotional
fire, he nonetheless had to do anything in his power to
help her. "Look, there's a woman, the woman who brought
the baby in, Chandra Hill. I know she'd like to visit the
baby fairly often."

Lenore dunked a tea bag into a steaming cup of water.
"I've heard about her. Seems she's pretty attached to the
boy."

"Well, it wouldn't hurt for her to drop by."

"Of course not. Tell her to stop in anytime."

"Lenore! Hey, what's this I hear about you and the Baby John Doe?" one of the other nurses called over. "You got any room left over there?"

Dallas took his coffee and left as the two other nurses joined into the conversation. He'd done what he could. Now it was up to Chandra.

He spent the rest of the day in the hospital and finally, at five, stopped in at pediatrics for one last look at J.D. Holding the child, he sighed. "What're we gonna do with you?" he wondered aloud. "You're giving the woman who found you fits, y'know."

The baby yawned, as if he were bored to death.

"Okay, okay," Dallas said, smiling down at the child. "We'll see what we can do."

He left the infant with a nurse and walked outside. The storm that had threatened earlier had cleared up and the day was dry and warm, no lingering clouds in the sky. Whistling under his breath, he walked to his truck and stopped when he spied his half brother chewing on a toothpick, one lean hip resting against the fender, his knee bent and the sole of one boot pressed against the front tire. A grimy duffle bag had been dropped on the asphalt near the truck.

"I thought I might have to spend the whole weekend here waiting for you," Brian said as Dallas approached. As usual, Brian's cocky grin was in place, his eyes squinting slightly against a lowering sun. His jeans were so faded, they'd ripped through the knees, and the denim across his butt was frayed, on the point of giving way completely. His shirt was bright orange, faded neon, and said simply, SURF'S UP!! diagonally in purple letters that stretched from his right shoulder to his left hip.

"What's doing?"

Brian grinned, as if he read the caution in Dallas's eyes.

He straightened and held out his hands, surrendering to his half brother's suspicion. "Don't worry, I haven't gone through the money yet. I just came by to say I'm shipping out. On my way back to school."

About time. "That's good."

"Right, and I probably won't see you until Christmas. You'll come to Mom's?"

"I'll see. Christmas is a long way off."

"She'd be disappointed if you didn't come."

Well, maybe. From Brian's point of view, their mother loved Dallas as much as she did her other children. But Dallas remembered a time when, after the divorce from his father and her remarriage, Eugena O'Rourke McGee had been so involved with raising a daughter and the twins that she hadn't so much as smiled at him. She'd been tired most of the time from chasing the younger kids.

Dallas, a reminder of her marriage to a military doctor who had never been able to show any emotion, was, for the most part, left on his own. He'd been enrolled in boarding school while his parents were married, and his status didn't change when his mother remarried, even though none of her other children had ever stepped foot in a school away from home until college. Joanna, Brian and Brenda had been raised at home.

Yes, there was the possibility that his mother might miss Dallas at Christmas, but not for the reasons Brian expected. In her later years, she'd developed a fondness for her firstborn, probably born of guilt, but never had Eugena given him the love she'd lavished on her younger children.

Dallas was no longer bitter about that particular lack of love; he just didn't dwell on it.

"Ahh, come one, it'll be fun. And Joanna and Brenda will kill ya if ya don't show up."

That much was true. For all the love he hadn't received

from his mother, his sisters had adored him. "I'll think about it."

"See that you do. Well, I'm outta here." Bending down, Brian slung the strap of his duffle over his shoulder and offered his brother one of his killer smiles. "Thanks a lot. For everything. And, oh—did you manage to go on the raft ride?"

Dallas grinned. "An experience of a lifetime."

"What did you think of the lady?"

"She's something else."

"I'll say." Brian's grin turned into a leer. "Strong little bugger. And great legs! Boy, I bet she's a tiger…" His voice faded away when he caught the set of his brother's jaw. "So you noticed?"

"Just that I already knew her."

"A nice piece." When Dallas's lips thinned, Brian laughed. "Of work. Hey! What did you think I meant?" He glanced down at his brother's hands and grinned even more broadly. Dallas realized that he'd instinctively clenched his fists. "Hey, bro', is there something you're not tellin' me?"

Dallas forced himself to relax. This was just Brian going into his macho-man routine. "Nothing. Just that I already know her."

"And you've got the hots for her."

Dallas didn't reply, but just glared at his half brother, wondering if they had anything in common at all.

"Well, go for it, man! I don't blame you. The lady's nice…real nice."

"What do you mean, 'go for it'?"

"Ask her out, spend some time with her, get to know her. For crying out loud, here you are and—pardon me for pointing it out—in the middle of no-friggin'-where, and a woman like that falls into your lap. Take a chance, man. I know you got burned by Jennifer the Jezebel, but not all women are Wicked Witches of the West."

"I should take advice on my love life from you?" Dallas asked, slightly amused.

"Well, you'd better take it from somebody, 'cause the way I see it, your 'love life,' as you so optimistically call it, doesn't exist."

Dallas wanted to smack the smug smile off the younger man's face, but, for once in his life, Brian was right. Instead, Dallas stuck out his arm and shook his brother's hand. "Thanks for the advice."

"Don't thank me. Just do something, man."

"I could give you the same words of wisdom."

Brian's grin was positively wicked. "Not about *my* love life, you couldn't." With a cocksure grin, he strolled over to his car and yanked open the door. Throwing his bag into the back seat, he crawled into the interior, started the engine of the old Pontiac Firebird and took off in a cloud of exhaust that slowly dissipated in the clear mountain air.

Brian's advice hung like a pall over Dallas as he drove to his condominium. This morning he'd wanted to drive Chandra from his life forever. Then he'd seen her in the hospital and could hardly keep his hands off her. No, he'd better face facts, at least for the present. Brian was right; he should kick up his heels a little. He didn't have to fall in love.

That thought hit him like a bucket of ice water. In love? *I guess I'm in the market for a husband.*

Her words ricocheted through his mind. Had she been joking, or had she been hinting? "Quit this, O'Rourke, before you make yourself crazy."

But forget her he couldn't, and before he knew it, he was making plans to see her again. As soon as he walked into his home, he dropped his mail, unopened, on the table, then picked up the phone book. He punched out the

number of Wild West Expeditions. Chandra answered, and
he couldn't stop the tug of the muscles near the corners of
his mouth.

"I thought we should get together after work," he said,
feeling the part of a fool, like some creepy lounge lizard.
God, he was just no good at this.

"Why?"

"We left on the wrong note. How about I take you to
dinner?"

A pause. A thousand heartbeats seemed to pass.
"Dinner?" she finally said. "I don't know...."

"Neither do I, but I've been thinking and..." He let
out his breath slowly, then decided honesty was the best
policy. "Well, I'd like to see you again."

"Even though I'm only interested in a husband or, more
precisely, a father for my yet-unadopted child."

There it was—that biting sarcasm that he found so fascinating. No wimp, Ms. Hill. "Even though," he said, smiling despite himself. "Dress up. I've got a surprise for you.
I'll pick you up at your place at six-thirty."

"What if I already have plans?" she asked, obviously
flirting with him a little. It occurred to him that she was
as nervous about this as was he.

"Cancel them." He hung up, feeling a little like a jerk,
but looking forward to the evening ahead. This morning
he'd tried to drive her from his mind, but now, damn it all
to hell, he was going to fulfill a few of his fantasies with
the gorgeous Ms. Hill.

After all, it was just a date, not a lifetime commitment.

CHAPTER TEN

A DATE? SHE COULDN'T believe it. Yet here she was, pawing through her closet of work shirts, jeans and a few old dresses trying to come up with an outfit for Dallas's surprise.

And her heart was pounding as if she were a schoolgirl. *Take it easy, Chandra,* she told herself, knowing that Dallas's mood could change as rapidly as the weather in these mountains.

She settled for a rose-colored skirt and a scooped-neck blouse, and was just brushing her hair when Sam, ever vigilant, began to growl. "Jealous?" Chandra teased, her heart surprisingly light as she patted the dog on his head, and was rewarded with a sloppy lick of his tongue.

Dallas stood on the doorstep, balancing two grocery sacks. "Wait a minute—I thought we were going out," she said as she opened the door and he stepped inside.

"We are." He placed the brown paper bags on the kitchen counter. "Got a picnic basket?"

"You're kidding, right?" she asked, but caught the glint of devilish mischief in his eyes. *This* was the serious Dr. O'Rourke—this man who seemed hell-bent to confuse her? It seemed that he enjoyed keeping her equilibrium off-balance.

"Someone told me I wasn't spontaneous enough, that I needed to get out of my rut," he said with a shrug. "So— the basket?"

"Right. A picnic basket." Wondering what he was up to,

she rummaged in the closet under the stairs and came up with a wicker basket covered with dust. She blew across the top and dust motes swirled in a cloud. "Doesn't get much use," she explained, finding a cloth and wiping the woven wicker clean.

"I thought we'd take a ride into the hills."

"Like this?" She eyed his slacks and crisp shirt. "Are you crazy?"

"Just spontaneous."

"Yeah, right," she replied, but wiped out the interior of the basket and lined it with a blanket. Dallas reached into his grocery bag and filled the basket with smaller sacks, a bottle of wine, glasses and a corkscrew. "Did you bring the horses, too, or is that what I'm supposed to provide?"

"The horses and the destination."

"Oh, I get it—you're counting on me to provide you with a free trail ride, is that it?" she teased, feeling her spirits lifting along with the corners of her mouth.

He laughed and the sound filled the cabin, bouncing off the rafters as he snapped the lid of the basket shut. Approaching her slowly, he held her gaze with his. "Are you going to fight me all the way on this?"

"I don't have a side saddle." Oh, Lord, he was so close she could see a small scar near his hairline, obviously old and faded with the passage of time from ruffian boy to man. She had to elevate her chin a fraction to meet his gaze, and her throat caught at the depth of blue in his eyes.

"Improvise," he suggested, his breath tickling her scalp.

"I could change—"

"And leave me overdressed? No way!" His gaze lowered, past her lips and chin, along the column of her throat, to the scooped neck of her blouse and the beginning of the hollow between her breasts, just barely visible. "Besides, you look—" He broke off, his Adam's apple working in his throat. Reaching forward, he touched a strand of her hair and wound its golden length around one finger.

The moment, only seconds, seemed to stretch a lifetime, and as he laid her curl back against her cheek, his finger grazing her skin, her diaphragm pressed so hard against her lungs, she had trouble breathing.

"I think we should go," she said, stepping back from him and feeling clumsy and embarrassed and totally unbalanced. Just being close to him caused her to lose her cool façade. This one enigmatic man had managed, in the span of one week, to create havoc with her emotions. "I—I'll saddle up."

"*I'll* saddle up. You bring the basket." He swung out the door, and Sam, with one look over his shoulder, trotted after him.

"I'm going to change your name to Judas," Chandra warned, swinging the basket from the table and following man and dog to the barn. She was struck by the natural way Dallas strode across the yard, as if he belonged here. Sunlight gleamed in his dark hair and warmed her crown. His dress clothes seemed appropriate somehow, though she could just as easily envision him in faded jeans, a work shirt open and flapping in the breeze as he chopped firewood. And Sam, the turncoat, padded happily behind him, tongue lolling, tail moving slowly with his gait.

Within minutes, Dallas had saddled Max and Brandy, and they were riding along a dusty trail. Chandra had hiked her skirt around her thighs and felt absolutely ridiculous as well as positively euphoric. The sky was a clear cobalt blue, and two hawks circled lazily overhead.

The mountain air was clean, the horses' hooves thudding softly, stirring dust, causing creatures in the brush to scurry through the undergrowth. Once in a while, Sam gave chase, startling the horses as he dashed by, barking wildly at some unseen prey.

After nearly an hour of riding through the forest, the trail forked, and Chandra veered sharply to the right, back-trailing downhill.

"You sure you know where you're going?" Dallas asked.

"Positive." She nudged Brandy in the sides as the pines and blue spruce gave way to a meadow. The game little mare sprinted forward, ears pricked, nostrils flared, her hooves pounding across the field of dry grass and wild-flowers in shades of pink, blue and lavender.

Chandra's skirt billowed behind her, and her bare legs held fast to Brandy's sides. Wind streamed through Chandra's hair, and she laughed as she heard Max close to Brandy's heels, his galloping hooves loud against the dry ground.

"Come on, Brandy," Chandra said, leaning over the little mare's shoulders and watching the horse's ears flatten against her head. She picked up speed, but it was too late. Max, black legs flashing in the sun, raced past. Dallas rode low in the saddle, his shoulders hunched forward, the picnic basket propped between the saddle and his chest.

"We should've beaten them," Chandra told the mare as she pulled up. Both horses were sweating and blowing hard. Chandra, too, was having trouble breathing, but Sam wasn't even winded. He saw a squirrel, streaked off across the meadow and splashed through the creek that zigzagged through the grass. Spring water gurgled and rushed over rocks, and the big gold dog bounded through the stream before disappearing into the woods.

"Should we worry about him?" Dallas asked, swinging off Max at a bend in the creek where the water pooled and reflected the intense blue of the sky.

"He'll be back. He's used to it." Chandra hopped to the ground and felt the tickle of grass against her bare ankles. "That's how I found him, you know. He crawled into the yard, ripped from stem to stern by something—bear, raccoon, possum or something else, I suppose—and I had to sew him up. I've had him ever since."

Dallas's eyes narrowed on the forest into which the dog, joyfully yelping and giving chase, had disappeared. "Hasn't learned much."

"He'll be all right," Chandra replied.

While the horses grazed near the stream, Dallas and Chandra unfolded the blanket in the shade of a pine tree. He uncorked the wine and poured them each a glass of Chablis. "What are we drinking to?" she asked, and his blue eyes deepened to a mysterious hue.

"How about to us?"

She laughed, tucking her legs beneath her as she sat on the edge of the blanket, her skirt folded over her knees. He wasn't serious. This was all a lark, a fantasy. "Us? I thought there wasn't any us—that you couldn't get involved or muck up your life with a woman." She took a long swallow of wine and watched the play of emotions across his face.

His jaw slid to one side, and his hair was rumpled by the breeze that blew from the west. "I didn't want any complications."

"Didn't…?"

"Still don't," he admitted, lying on the blanket and leaning back on one elbow while he sipped from his glass. "But sometimes things change. And what you don't want changes with it." He plucked a dry blade of grass and chewed on it. "From the minute I saw you in the emergency room, I knew you were going to be trouble—big trouble." He squinted as a pheasant, wings beating frantically, rose from the grass as Sam leapt and barked in the frightened bird's wake. "And I thought the only reason- able thing to do, the only sane path to take, was to avoid you."

She smiled. For the first time since she'd met him, she

felt that Dallas was being honest with her. His eyebrows were pinched together, and his lips, moving on the straw, pursed hard, as if he were angry with himself.

"So…" she prodded.

"So I did. And then my brother gave me that damned coupon."

"But you still weren't convinced that I wasn't trouble," she said.

"Hell, no. Then I knew you were more trouble than I'd even imagined." He laughed again and took a long swallow of his wine. "And that's when things got really out of hand." He looked at her directly then, his gaze holding hers. "I couldn't keep my hands off you, and that's not the way it usually is with me. In fact," he admitted, glancing away, as if the admission were embarrassing, "I was starting to become obsessed."

"With…?" she asked warily.

"You." A muscle in his jaw convulsed, and Chandra realized just how difficult it was for him to bare his soul. They weren't so different, she decided; they both bore wounds that wouldn't heal. "Anyway, I wasn't sleeping at night, and I couldn't think of anything but you. Making love to you."

Chandra nearly dropped her glass. Her hands began to sweat, and she took a long swallow of wine to avoid those blue, blue eyes.

"So that's when I decided never to see you again."

She glanced up sharply. "But you're here—"

"Believe it or not, I ran into Brian and he told me I was crazy to keep avoiding you. He told me I should loosen up, enjoy life, take a chance or two…." Dallas lifted a shoulder and beneath the crisp white fabric, his muscles moved fluidly.

A tight knot formed in the pit of Chandra's stomach.

He reached over and refilled her glass before adding more wine to his own.

"So, for the first time in my life, I took Brian's advice. Believe me, it wasn't easy." He studied the label for a second before propping the bottle against the inside of the wicker basket.

Chandra felt as if time were suspended between them. Surely she could think of something clever to say, something that would lighten the mood. But all words escaped her, and she could feel his gaze moving slowly over her, caressing her, causing her skin to tingle under his silent appraisal. "So what is this?" she finally asked, her voice as soft as the wind in the pines. "A seduction?"

"If you want it to be."

"No!" she said quickly, breathlessly. She'd thought of making love to him. But it was one thing to fantasize, another to actually do it. She gulped her wine and glanced his way, hoping that she could see some indication that he was joking, but not a glimmer of humor sparked in his eyes.

"Afraid?"

"Look, Dallas. Maybe you can make all sorts of plans—you know, buy the wine, pick out the right cheese and bread, and just…just map out some way for us to get together. But it doesn't work that way with me. I can't just drink a little wine and say, 'what the hell,' and start stripping off my clothes. It's just not me…." Slowly, she climbed to her feet and dusted her hands. "This isn't going to work." She whistled to the horses, and while Brandy ignored her and continued to pluck grass, Max responded.

She reached for his reins, but Dallas caught up with her and gently grabbed her wrist. "I've been accused of being blunt," he admitted. "Too blunt."

"Well, at least you don't leave me guessing." She tried

to pull away, but his grip tightened, and slowly he tugged, forcing her to face him.

"It's just that I want you," he said. "I want you so much, I can't think of anything else. I ache for you at night, embarrass myself during the day when I start to think of you. I've tried to fight it—hell, I had myself convinced that I didn't want, didn't need, a woman. And I was right. I don't need just any woman, Chandra. I need you."

Her heart turned over, and she felt the pads of his fingers, warm and smooth against the inside of her forearm. Her heart nearly stopped as she dropped the reins and stared into eyes the color of a mountain sky.

"You want me, too." He placed the flat of his free hand over her heart, his fingertips skimming her bare skin, his palm resting over the neckline of her blouse, seeming to press against her breast.

Her heartbeat quickened, and her breath, unsteady to begin with, came in quick bursts through her lips.

"W-wanting isn't enough," she said.

"It was enough on the rafting trip." He kissed the side of her neck then, and her throat constricted. Somewhere she heard a dog barking and the jingle of a bridle, but those sounds were in the distance, and now she heard only the rapid tattoo of her heart and the rasp of air through her lungs.

Dallas pulled her blouse down over one shoulder and placed his lips against her skin. An endless ache started at the apex of her legs and moved slowly upward.

The fingers surrounding her wrist pulled gently, insistently, forcing her to follow him to the ground, and she didn't resist, fell willingly against him, their arms and legs entwining, his body wedged between hers and the bent grass.

He moved his mouth over hers, fiercely, possessively, until it seemed that the fever in his blood had ignited all her senses. She felt the pressure of his tongue, the urgency in his hands, the hot, throbbing desire that blossomed inside her.

He pulled her blouse from the waistband of her skirt and slowly ran his hands over her ribs, moving upward, brushing the lace of her bra. She moaned into his mouth as his thumb skimmed against her already taut nipple.

"Dallas," she whispered as he unbuttoned her blouse and the cool mountain air caressed her skin. He shoved the blouse aside, and then with her above him, craned his neck so that his lips touched her bra and the lace-encased nipple. She writhed, and he pulled her downward, one hand splayed against the bare skin of her back, the other tangled in her hair. He kissed and teased her through the lace, his tongue wet and wonderful in delicious ministrations that caused her to convulse.

"Please, please, please..." she moaned, and he groaned against her flesh, unhooking the bra and letting her breasts fall free, unbound, above him. He took one eagerly into his waiting mouth, suckling hungrily, his tongue and teeth pulling and tugging, creating a whirlpool of warmth deep within her body.

She found the buttons of his shirt and quickly dispensed with them, pushing the white fabric over corded shoulders that flexed, strong and sinewy against her fingers. She arched against him as the shirt was discarded, and her breasts felt the rough hairs of his chest when he lifted his head to stare up at her eyes.

"Chandra," he whispered, his voice rough and pleading, his hands smoothing her back, exploring the cleft of her spine. "You're so gorgeous," he whispered, moving his gaze from her eyes and past her parted lips to her breasts, white and firm, floating above him, enticing him to delirious heights of sexuality.

Never had he felt so free, so anxious, so aroused. His lust was like a living, breathing creature he couldn't control.

With his hand, he sculpted her, teasing the hard nipples and kneading the warm flesh of her breast. Shockwave after delicious shockwave spread through him, and she responded by throwing her head back, her luxurious mane of golden hair falling over her shoulders and back. He didn't stop. Couldn't. He fastened his mouth over her nipple again and slowly slid his hand beneath the waistband of her skirt, skimming her abdomen and reaching lower still.

Sweat broke out on her body, and though he relieved her of her skirt and panties, a dewy sheen covered her body as he continued to touch her, kiss her, caress her.

She found herself helping him with his jeans, and he kicked them off, then lay under her, wanting to delve into her and never stop. When he firmly grasped one buttock, she pressed herself hard against him.

"Make love to me, Chandra," he whispered into her hair. "For now and forever, make love to me."

She closed her eyes and swallowed as he ran one finger down the hollow of her breasts, down past her navel and farther still, until she bucked above him, and he reacted, capturing her lips in his and rolling her over in one quick motion. As he stared down into her eyes, he parted her legs with his knees and hesitated, seeing the trust in her gaze, knowing that she was envisioning a future together.

"Oh, Chandra," he whispered. "I want you…." And in that moment, he knew that life would never be the same. He'd planned all this, to the very seduction. A man of medicine, he never lost his cool, but with this woman, he could very well lose his equilibrium forever. Trying to stay rational, he reached in the grass for his jeans, dug into the pocket for a condom in his wallet. Muttering in frustration, he held up the packet for her to inspect, as if in so doing, they could stop this madness before it went any further.

But it was too late; the bridge had been crossed. A shadow of doubt crossed her eyes for just one second. "Don't stop," she said, as if certain he would deny her. Quickly, he readied himself. She trembled as he brushed the hair from her eyes, and in that moment when their gazes crossed a chasm of doubt, he entered her, in one swift thrust of warmth and need. A hard, primal sound escaped his throat, and he moved, slowly at first, feeling all of her, still aware of her fingertips featherlight against his shoulders, her mouth yielding softly to his.

He couldn't stop and wouldn't. His tempo increased, and through fleeting thoughts of satisfying her, he lost control, plunged deep and hard, whispering her name as a litany until he could hold back no longer and he erupted with a roar.

Chandra convulsed beneath him, arching her hips and receiving him with all the ferocity of his own passion. She dug her fingers deep into his shoulders and cried out, and his name echoed through the hills.

"Dallas, oh, Dallas," she said, her throat working, tears filling the corners of her eyes.

Breathing raggedly, afterglow converging upon him, he saw the silent tracks of her tears. Pain shot through him as he realized he'd pushed himself upon her, forced her through seduction and gentle ministrations to have sex with him. Self-loathing swallowed him. "Oh, God, I'm sorry," he said, his throat rough. He pushed her bangs from her forehead, and self-contempt edged his features. What the hell had he been thinking? "I didn't mean to hurt you—"

"No!" She gasped, drawing in deep breaths. "You didn't. Really. It's…it…" She dashed her tears aside with the back of her hand. "It was wonderful. It's just…well, it's been so long."

"For me, too," he admitted, relieved that she wasn't feeling any remorse. He took her into his arms and kissed her crown. "I'm afraid I lost control."

Softly she sighed, and her skin flushed a beautiful pink. "You weren't the only one."

"You're not mad at me for planning this?"

"I could've stopped it." When he was about to protest, she shook her long blond mane. "Really, I could have. If I'd wanted to. But I didn't."

"No regrets?" he asked, kissing a stray tear that slid from her eye.

"None."

Sam loped over to them. Wet from a romp in the creek, he shook himself so hard that his license and collar rattled. Chandra screeched, and Dallas, laughing, picked her up and carried her toward the pool of spring water.

"You wouldn't," she cried, eyeing the frigid water.

"Something's got to cool us off."

"Dallas, no—"

But he waded into the clear depths and sucking in his breath, plunged them both into the icy pond. Shrieking and laughing, Chandra sputtered upward for air, only to find his smiling face next to hers. "You're horrid!" she cried, but laughed when he tickled her.

"Wicked. I'm wicked. Not horrid."

"Worse than that, I think," she said breathlessly as she struggled for the shore. He caught up with her and wrapping arms around her waist, pulled her tight against him. Wet, cold lips pressed anxiously against hers.

"You can't get away from me," he stated.

"Is that a challenge?" She lifted an eyebrow and eyed the shore, judging how far she would have to run should she want to prove him wrong.

"Don't even think about it!"

That was it. With the flat of her hand, she sprayed water in his face, then, laughing, she stumbled up the creek bank, only to be caught midstride and pulled back into the water. "As I said," he repeated, "you'll never get away from me!" He gathered her against him, sliding her intimately against him, pressing kisses against her nape and neck.

"So who's running?" she asked, and kissed him back. She wondered if she loved him and decided it didn't matter. She cared about him, felt a special fondness toward him, and the passion between them was enough to satisfy her. She thought fleetingly of the future, but dismissed it. Today, for the first time in her life, she'd live for the moment.

Eventually the cold water was too much to bear and they returned to the meadow, where, after dressing, they finished the wine and ate sourdough bread, cheese, grapes and strawberries. The sun sank lower on the horizon, and shadows played across the dry grass.

Chandra lay on the blanket, picking a few wildflowers and twirling the stems between her fingers. "You said you didn't want to get involved," she ventured, glancing over her shoulder. Stretched out on the other side of the blanket, Dallas seemed content to stare at her.

"I didn't. Probably still don't. But I am."

"What happened? I mean—that made you so afraid?"

"Afraid?" He rolled onto his back and stared at the sky, still blue as the sun sank lower in the west. "I've never thought of it as being afraid. Cautious, maybe. Smart, for sure, but afraid?"

She arched an eyebrow. "That's the way I see it."

Scowling, he sighed. "I don't believe in reliving the past. No point to it."

"Except when it affects the future."

Dallas stood and dusted off his pants. He walked to the edge of the creek, where he bent down, picked up a smooth, flat stone and sent it skimming over the water to plop near the far bank as rippling circles disturbed the surface.

Chandra followed him to the shore, and, with a twinkle in her eye, picked up a flat river rock and skipped it over the water just as easily as he had. "What is it with you?" he asked, his features pulled into a look of puzzlement. "Studying to become a doctor, guiding white-water trips, backpacking and skipping stones?" He raked his gaze down her body. "For a woman with so many obvious feminine attributes, you sure like to perform like a man."

"Compete," she corrected. "I like to compete with men."

"Why?"

She shrugged. "I guess I'm the son my father never had. He taught me how to throw from my shoulder instead of my wrist, how to rock climb, and he gave me the confidence that I could do anything I wanted to, regardless of my sex."

Dallas eyed her. "You were lucky."

"I think so. My sisters were both glad that I was the chosen one and they didn't have to do any of the tomboy stuff. I think they missed out. But we weren't talking about me," she reminded him.

He feigned a smile. "You remembered."

"What happened to you?"

"It was simple, really," he said in an offhand manner that seemed meant to belie the pain. "My folks split up when I was still in boarding school. My dad was career military, very rigid, a physician, and my mother got tired of moving around. I can't say as I blame her, Harrison O'Rourke would've been hell to live with. He's...clinical, I guess you'd say. Didn't believe in showing his emotions, not to me or Mom. It's amazing she stayed with him as long as she did."

Dallas reached down and skipped another stone, and Chandra's chest grew tight. Talking about his past was difficult for him; she could see the reluctance in his eyes, the harsh lines near his mouth. "Anyway, she remarried. Happily, I think. And ended up pregnant right away. Joanna was born a year later, and only sixteen months after that the twins came along. You met Brian." Chandra nodded. "He has a twin sister named Brenda—she's, uh, much more rational than he.

"So, Mom had her hands full, and I was old enough to be on my own, anyway. I finished high school and was accepted at UCLA in premed."

To gain your father's approval, she thought, her heart twisting for a boy who felt unwanted.

"I met the girl of my dreams before I graduated," he said, his voice turning sarcastic. "Jennifer Smythe."

A painful jab cut into her heart, though why it mattered, Chandra couldn't fathom. "Why was she the girl of your dreams?"

He snorted. "She was perfect—or at least, I thought so. Beautiful, smart, clever, witty and a graduate student in law. Even though she was a few years older than I was, I thought the right thing to do was get married, so we did."

Chandra studied his profile—so severe with the onslaught of memories.

"The marriage was mistake number one. She passed the bar exam and within a few weeks, was hired at a firm where she'd worked during the summers. It was a respectable firm, and the partners were interested in young women to balance the plethora of old men. She supported me while I finished school. Mistake number two. She always felt I *owed* her something."

Dallas frowned darkly and shook his head. "This is really pretty boring stuff—"

"Not at all," Chandra interjected, surprised that he was letting her see so deeply into his private life.

He shot her a look saying more eloquently than words that he didn't believe her, but he continued, though reluctantly. "What I didn't know was that Jennifer didn't want a kid. Period. Now, she never told me this, but she was the only child of rich parents and couldn't see tying herself down to an infant. She thought that between her career and mine, we had it made." Sam galloped up, and Dallas reached down to scratch his ears. The old dog whined appreciatively, and Dallas had to smile.

"Eventually, I graduated and was hired at a hospital in Orange County. Even though we had a few bills, I thought this was the time to start a family, but Jennifer wasn't interested. I should've let it lie, I suppose, but I wanted kids. Badly." He cast Chandra a rueful grin. "In fact, I was obsessed. A bad trait of mine. I figured my folks didn't do the family bit right, so I was going to be the perfect father. As if I knew the first thing about raising kids!"

His eyes darkened, and any trace of humor disappeared from his features. He shook his head, as if in disbelief at his own naïveté.

Chandra felt a whisper of dread as he continued.

"The kicker was that Jennifer did get pregnant, right about the time we were buying our first house. She never told me, of course, and had the pregnancy terminated. I only found out because of a mutual friend who knew the doctor who performed the abortion."

Chandra swallowed hard against the outrage that burned her throat. No wonder he was so bitter. A shadow, dark and pained, crossed his eyes, and the skin around his mouth grew taut.

"That was the last straw. I stormed over to her office, and I didn't care who heard the argument. I was furious that she wouldn't at least have talked to me, have worked things out before she took such drastic measures. But Jennifer wasn't the least bit reticent, and she told me then that she would never have children. It was her body, it had nothing to do with me, and as she saw it, I shouldn't get all worked up over it. Besides, she pointed out, I was doing well at the hospital, and I put in long hours. I didn't need the responsibility of children to make demands on my time—not to mention hers. What did upset her was that I embarrassed her by coming into the law firm in a rage."

Chandra placed a hand on his arm, but he didn't seem to notice. "So that's it. I couldn't deal with her from that point on. I tried to tell myself that losing the baby was for the best, that being married to a doctor was difficult for any woman, that maybe Jennifer would change her mind and there would be other children. But I was kidding myself. I never forgot."

He shoved his hands into his pockets and rotated his neck, stretching his shoulder muscles. For a second, Chandra thought he'd finished, but his next words came out in a rush of disgust.

"You'd have to meet Jennifer to understand this, but she assumed everything was A-OK. She was delighted with our new lifestyle. We had money and social status and interesting careers. She was moving up in the law firm at an incredible pace. Her only real worry was that my position as an emergency-room physician wasn't all that glamorous. She thought I had the brains and skill to become a specialist, a notch up in her estimation. I fought her on that one. I like what I do and couldn't see giving it up."

He rolled his eyes to the sky, now streaked with gold and pink, as if he couldn't believe he'd been so foolish. His shoulders, which had been rigid, began to slump.

"Things got worse, of course. Living in L.A. was a grind. Jennifer and I barely saw each other. When I was offered a position at Riverbend, here in Ranger, I thought maybe we had a chance to start over. But I was wrong. Even though I said I'd set her up in her own practice here, Jennifer wouldn't hear of the move. It was obvious at that point that her job was more important than our marriage and she wasn't about to move to 'some podunk little town in the mountains.' She would be bored stiff in a small town in Colorado, without the nightlife and the glitz.

"Besides," he added bitterly, "she was up for a big promotion. If push came to shove, she'd rather live in L.A. without me than move to Colorado. So we separated. I moved. She stayed. We saw each other a couple of times a month and it was a sham. There was no reason to try to hold the marriage together."

He kicked at the grass. "We agreed on a quick divorce. Three weeks after the divorce was final, Jennifer married her boss, a man twice her age who had grown children and didn't want to start another family. The next time I saw her, she admitted that the baby she'd aborted wasn't even mine."

Chandra thought she might get sick. How could someone use this man—this wonderful man?

"Jennifer had been having an affair with her boss for years—which explained her meteoric rise in the firm of James, Ettinburg, Smith and McHenry," he said, his voice still edged in anger. "And I was the dupe who believed that we still had a chance." He snorted in self-disgust, and Chandra wished for the right words that would ease his pain, but there were none and she had to content herself with touching his arm.

"The irony of it all was that it didn't matter. Sure, I would've wanted my own kid, but I would've brought up Jennifer's baby as if it were my own. But it was too late."

"And that's when you gave up on love and marriage?" Chandra asked, her heart aching, her fingers still gripping his forearm.

He slanted a glance down at her. "I think a man who's so involved with his work has no right to ask a woman to be a part of his life."

"You're wrong," she whispered. "Oh, you're so wrong." Moved by his agony, she threw her arms around him and kissed his lips. "You would make a wonderful husband and a terrific father!" Then, realizing what she'd said, she dropped her arms and swallowed hard.

"Why, Ms. Hill," he drawled, his eyes sparkling, "is that a proposal?"

"I already told you, I'm not interested in getting married," she said quickly, a flood of embarrassment washing crimson up her neck. How could she have done anything so rash? This entire evening had been an exhibition in throwing away her self-control. What was happening to her?

"But *I* should be ready to walk down the aisle again?" He laughed without a trace of mirth, and she realized that the two women in his life who should have loved him, his mother and his wife, had hurt him so badly, he might never trust another woman again.

"You know, Chandra," he was saying, still discussing marriage, "there's a saying that what's good for the gander is good for the goose. Or something like that." He picked a stick from her hair, and she smoothed a wrinkle from his shirt, wondering what marriage to him would be like. Would there be long days of comfortable familiarity or passionate nights of lovemaking and unexplored emotions?

"What about you?" he asked suddenly, and her insides turned to jelly. "I bared my soul. Tell me about your ex-husband."

Chandra wanted to tell him everything, but found the words difficult. "He was a doctor," she finally said, and Dallas froze, his face instantly serious.

"Was he the reason you dropped out of medical school?"

"I, uh, really didn't drop out," she said, then at his look of amazement, shook her head. "I can't talk about it, but Doug was and is a major reason that I decided to give up my practice."

Dallas's hand covered hers. "Whatever happened," he said gently, and Chandra felt tears prick her eyes, "it was a mistake. Whatever he did, it was wrong."

"You don't know—"

"No, but my guess is that you're a helluva doctor."

She blushed, and blinked back tears. "Come on, O'Rourke," she said, eyeing the darkening sky and sensing that they'd said enough for one evening. Someday she'd tell him everything, but not tonight. She didn't want to ruin this night with more bitter memories. "We'd better go while it's still light."

They rode back to her house in relative silence. The forest seemed to close around them, and dusk sent long, purple shadows through the woods. Even Sam seemed to pick up on the mood, and he followed behind Brandy, keeping to the trail, never bounding off into the undergrowth.

By the time they returned to the house, the first stars winked in the sky. The temperature had dropped several degrees with the coming night. Together, Chandra and Dallas took care of the horses, removing the saddles, blankets and bridles, and brushing the animals down. Dallas forked hay into the manger while Chandra filled the water trough and measured out oats.

Max, grinding his ration of grain, nuzzled her chest. "Oh, you think you should get some special favors, do you?" she asked, chuckling, then found apples for each eager set of lips.

Once the horses were cared for, Dallas and Chandra walked across the yard to the house. The moon had risen and offered a silvery light to the shadowed hills.

Chandra asked Dallas in for coffee, and it felt natural to sit with him at the table, cradling cups, watching the steam rise. He was silent, brooding about something, and yet the silence was companionable. An unspoken question lingered between them—just how far would this relationship take them? Was this to be only a one-night stand? An affair? Or a lifetime together?

The coffee was nearly gone when Dallas scraped his chair back. "So where do we go from here?" he asked, his gaze roving through the small rooms and up the stairs to the loft, where her bed was visible through the slats of the railing.

"Do we have to make a plan?" She held her empty cup in a death grip and stared into the stain on the bottom of the earthenware as if she could read the future from the dregs of her coffee. But she knew that they couldn't just let things lie as they were.

Yet, they hardly knew each other. One afternoon of making love hardly seemed enough of a basis to plan a future together.

"You told me once that you were in the market for a husband."

"That was a joke—"

"Kind of a joke," he said, his gaze holding hers. "You were half-serious."

The air seemed to grow cooler yet. Chandra rubbed her

arms. The conversation was making turns she hadn't expected, turns she wasn't certain she could deal with. But she had to be honest with him. "Well...actually I'm in the market for a father for J.D. If I adopt him, and I intend to, I'll need a father figure for him, or so my attorney insists. So being a husband would probably be secondary," she admitted, hating the awful truth, but knowing it had to be said.

"That could get messy." He glanced out the window to the night beyond the glass before returning his gaze to her. "J.D.'s dad—whomever you choose—might not like me hanging around."

So he wasn't interested. Of course not. What had she expected? she silently chided herself. A proposal? "I suppose not." She tried to hide the disappointment in her voice and refused to back down. She gambled, wondering if she'd lost every last ounce of her sanity. "You told me that you wanted children. And J.D. does need a father—a father he can depend upon, a father to love him." She rotated the cup in her hands and, gathering all her courage, looked Dallas steadily in the eyes. "This could be an opportunity of a lifetime—for both of you."

"Are you propositioning me?" he asked, but there wasn't a glimmer of humor in his eyes.

Why not? she thought, her palms beginning to sweat. "I—I think that getting married for the sake of the baby wouldn't be such a bad idea," she said. "People marry for much worse reasons. And it—it wouldn't have to be forever. You said that if your wife's baby hadn't been yours, you still would have raised it as your own. Well, J.D. doesn't even have a biological father."

Dallas gazed at her face. "What that boy needs is two parents who love each other, two people who will provide a stable life for him."

"No baby is assured of that," she said boldly.

He rubbed his palms on his pants. He appeared more nervous than usual. "I'll be honest with you. I don't know if I can change, Chandra. I was sure that I'd never marry again, never have children. Hell, until today, I was convinced that I should avoid you."

"And now?" she asked breathlessly, her own hands sweaty around her empty cup.

"And now you've nearly convinced me to take the plunge. I'm on the verge of doing something we might regret for the rest of our lives." He held her gaze for what seemed a lifetime, staring at her as if measuring her. "This is absolute madness."

"I don't think so." Good God, was she actually saying this—trying to convince him to walk down the aisle with her? Why? Just for J.D., or did she feel a pang of guilt for making love with Dallas this afternoon? Or were there deeper reasons still, reasons she couldn't yet confront? She studied the handsome lines of his face and knew in an instant that she wasn't speaking from remorse. No, she liked Dr. O'Rourke and thought living with him wouldn't be unpleasant. He evoked emotions within her she didn't want to analyze, so she justified marrying him by telling herself it was all for the baby.

Dallas shoved his hands into his pockets, but he never stopped staring at her. "I don't know if it would work— hell, I'm half-certain it won't, but I'm willing to marry you—for the sake of the child, to help you win custody. Because I don't think that kid could find a better mother."

Time stood still. The clock by the front door was ticking loudly. Here was her chance. He was offering to marry her for J.D.'s sake. And hers. A thousand doubts, like dark moths, flitted through her mind. She ignored them. Touched, she swallowed back the tears that formed in the corners of her eyes. "You—you don't have to be so noble."

He snorted, and the muscles of his shoulders bunched. "Noble? I've never done a noble thing in my life."

"But…this…" She shook her head, and he touched the tip of her chin, raising her face with one long, insistent finger.

"There's a benefit for me, too, you know."

She was afraid to ask, but a warning sensation swept through her, chilling her blood.

"I'll be making love to you every night, and that's worth something. In fact, it's worth a lot." He smiled then, softening the blow.

Nonetheless, all of her romantic fantasies turned to dust. He only wanted to sleep with her. Nothing more. And yet there were times when his gentleness nearly broke her heart.

"I just want you to understand," he said softly, "that I'm not going to accept anything in name only. I won't expect you to cook or clean or pamper me, but I'll want you in my bed. And I'll want to know the truth about your past and the baby."

That seemed more than fair—if a little cold. Gathering her courage, Chandra lifted her chin and met his gaze with hers. If he had the right to bargain, so, she reasoned, did she. "Fair enough," she agreed, her voice shaking. She couldn't believe she was discussing *marriage,* for crying out loud. She'd sworn off men and marriage, and here she was bargaining.

Not exactly the silken thread from which romantic dreams were woven. "But, if you marry me, I'll expect you to be faithful."

His lips moved slightly, and he cocked a dubious eyebrow. "A tough request, Ms. Hill," he mocked, "since I've been celibate for three years. It'll be damned hard to give up all that womanizing. Nonetheless, you've got yourself a deal."

With that, he took her hand and drew her to her feet. Rounding the table, he yanked her toward him, deftly swept her into his arms and carried her up the stairs, sealing their bargain with a kiss.

CHAPTER ELEVEN

MARRIAGE. THE WORD RATTLED around in Chandra's brain until a headache threatened the back of her eyes. And to think how she'd practically gotten down on her knees and begged him to marry her! Good Lord, was she going out of her mind? The idea of marrying him for J.D.'s sake had seemed so right last night. Curled in his arms as she'd tried to sleep, she'd known she'd made the right decision. But this morning, with dawn streaking the hills and the soft call of a morning bird in the distance, she told herself she was crazy. She couldn't marry Dallas. Not even for J.D. Or could she?

She hadn't turned on any lights as she'd crept downstairs to stand at the window, steam from her coffee rolling across her face as she gazed at the sunrise, blazing magenta in the distance. Dallas was now awake and in the shower. A few minutes earlier, he'd leaned over the rail and playfully suggested that she might join him. She'd declined, telling him she had to feed the horses, but glancing up at him and catching a glimpse of his naked, well-muscled torso, corded shoulders, beard-darkened chin and blue eyes, she'd almost given in. "Your loss," he'd said with a flash of white teeth, and she'd believed him.

But she had needed time to sort through everything in her mind. Yes, she wanted the baby. Desperately. But to marry a man who wasn't in love with her? What kind of future would a loveless marriage bring? For herself? For J.D.? For Dallas?

Upstairs, the water was still running, but soon she'd have to face him again. And do what? Say last night was a big mistake? Surely he had misgivings—second thoughts?

She gulped her coffee and it burned the back of her throat. "Come on." She whistled quietly to Sam, then, snagging her denim jacket from a peg by the door, set off across the yard. Her boots crunched in the gravel and made footprints on the frost. The air was clear with the sharp bite of autumn. A few dry leaves blew from the trees and danced across the drive.

She shoved open the barn door, and Max nickered eagerly. "Hungry?" she asked, snapping on the lights as the smell of horses, dung, leather and dry hay greeted her. "Stupid question, eh? When are you *not* famished?"

Max snorted. The horses were anxious, pawing or snorting, liquid brown eyes trained on her. "Breakfast's coming," she promised as Brandy shoved her velvet-soft muzzle over the stall. Cayenne eyed Chandra as well, and the other horses nickered softly. "Yeah, you guys all know I got myself into a lot of trouble yesterday, don't you?"

She climbed the loft and kicked down a couple of bales, only to hear the barn door open. "Chandra?" Dallas asked, and the horses swung their attention toward the noise.

"Up here." She hopped down and pulled out her knife, slashing the twine as Dallas grabbed a pitchfork and began scooping hay into the manger.

"I thought maybe you'd run out on me," he said, his eyes dark in the barn. "I figured you might have come down with a case of cold feet."

No reason to lie. "Second thoughts."

Dallas threw another forkful into Max's manger, and his shoulders moved effortlessly beneath his shirt. Chandra's throat went dry at the thought of touching his arms and running her fingers along the ridge of his spine.

"You don't have to go through with it, you know."

"I just don't want to make a mistake." She found the grain barrel, scooped up oats with an old coffee can and began pouring the grain along the trough.

"It's your decision, Chandra," he said slowly.

"Doubts, Doctor?" she accused as she patted Cayenne's head. The sorrel gelding tossed his mane and dug his nose into the grain.

Dallas lifted a shoulder. "It's one thing to be spontaneous, but I'm not sure we really thought this out last night." As Chandra walked past him toward the grain barrel again, he touched her lightly on the shoulder, forcing her to meet his gaze. "Believe it or not, I think we can make this work, but it is a little premature. So let's take things a little slower—one step at a time. Then if either party changes his or her mind, no big deal. We'll call the whole thing off."

Relief surged through her, and it must have been evident in her face, because he laughed.

"You know, Ms. Hill, this was your idea. I'd be satisfied with a hot and heavy affair."

Her cheeks burned hotly. "But that wouldn't help J.D."

A hint of a darker emotion flickered in his eyes, and his mouth tightened slightly. He dropped his hand and started shoving the rest of the hay into the manger. As he hung the pitchfork on the wall, he spotted a mousetrap, tripped, without a victim. "You need a cat," he observed.

"You have one?"

He shook his head. "Animals complicate life."

"So how're you going to deal with a wife and child?"

"And a dog and a small herd of horses," he added, resetting the trap and placing a piece of grain on the trip. "That's the hundred-thousand-dollar question, isn't it? Too bad I don't have any answer. What about you, Ms. Hill, how're you going to deal with a husband and a child?"

"The child will be easy," she predicted, his good mood

infectious. She couldn't help teasing him a little. "But that husband—he's gonna be trouble. I can feel it in my bones."

His grin widened slowly. "You'd better believe it." Quick as a cat, he grabbed her and yanked her, squealing and laughing, into his arms. "Somehow, I think you'll find a way," he whispered, just before his lips crashed down on hers in a kiss that melted her knees.

When he finally lifted his head, he stared long into her eyes. "Yes," he said, as if answering some questions in his own mind, "this is going to be interesting. Very interesting." He glanced at his watch and groaned. "We'd better get moving. I've got to be at the hospital by eight. And you've got a wedding to plan."

Chandra didn't know whether to laugh or cry.

"You're getting married?" Roy Arnette's jaw dropped open. "What is this, some kind of joke?" Seated behind his desk, he'd been surprised by her visit, and was even more surprised when she'd told her intentions.

"No joke, Roy," she assured him, declining comment on the fact that Dallas, only three hours earlier, had given her an out, should she want one.

"Hell, Chandra, you *can't* just up and marry someone for that kid."

"Isn't that what you told me to do?"

"But I was *kidding!*" Sitting on his side of his desk, he yanked on his string tie. "You told me you weren't dating anyone."

"I wasn't."

"And what—the bridegroom fairy came in, waved a magic wand and, poof, instant husband and father?" Frowning, he pushed an intercom button and ordered coffee from his secretary. "Well, tell me, who's the lucky guy?"

"Dallas O'Rourke."

"*Doctor* Dallas O'Rourke? You can't be serious! After what happened to you with Doug—he was a doctor, remember? That was part of the problem—so now you're planning to marry an emergency-room physician? Come on!"

"I'm serious," she insisted. "Look, don't blame yourself. This is my decision."

"What do you know about the guy?" he asked, shaking his head. "What?"

A soft tap at the door announced the secretary's arrival. With a smile to Chandra, she placed a tray laden with coffee cups, a plastic carafe, a small basket of doughnuts and a folded newspaper on his desk. "Thanks, Betty," Roy said as the tall woman poured them each a cup of coffee.

Roy offered her a doughnut, but Chandra shook her head and the attorney, too, left the pastries untouched. He took a long sip from his cup and said, "All right, let's start over. When are you getting married?"

"We haven't discussed it yet," she admitted. "In fact, we haven't exactly ironed out many details. I'm meeting him tonight at the hospital, and he's taking me over to the Newells'."

"The sheriff? You're going to see the sheriff?"

"J.D. is being released today. The Newells have been granted temporary custody as foster parents." Chandra reached for her cup and caught a glimpse of the folded newspaper. Her heart did a somersault. "Oh, no," she said, snatching up the paper and snapping it open. On the front page in big bold letters the headline read, MYSTERY BABY FOUND IN BARN, and near the article were two pictures, one of the barn, the other of her and Dallas, his arm around her shoulder, his mouth pressed close to her ear.

She quickly read the article, which was more informative than the one single-column report that had appeared the day after the baby was found. She and Dallas were identified, in the caption under the picture, and though nothing was blatantly stated, there was an insinuation that she and he, the woman who had discovered the baby and the physician who had first examined him, were romantically involved. There was a plea, within the text, for the real parents of the child to come forward and claim him.

Her heart wrenched painfully. "No," she whispered to herself. "Not now!"

"What? Not now what?"

She handed the paper to Roy, and he scowled as he skimmed the article. "Well, this isn't too bad. Fillmore isn't known to be overly kind with his pen, so you'd better consider yourself lucky. At least it isn't a hatchet job, and since you and Dallas are planning to tie the knot, I don't see that there's any real harm done."

Perhaps not, but Chandra felt as if someone had just placed a curse on her. That was crazy, of course. She wasn't even the kind of woman who believed in curses or voodoo or omens. And yet, her skin crawled as she stared down at the photo of her and Dallas huddled together, consoling each other...and falling in love.

"BASTARD!" DALLAS SLAMMED the newspaper into the trash basket in the staff lounge, causing more than a few heads to turn and gaze speculatively in his direction. He didn't really give a damn. He didn't blame Fillmore for the article; the baby was news. Big news. But the picture of Chandra and him was hardly necessary.

He'd only been at the hospital half an hour and already he'd noticed a few sidelong glances cast his way, a couple of smirks hidden not quite quickly enough. It had started with Ed Prescott. As Dallas had locked the door of his truck in the parking lot, Prescott had wheeled his red Porche into his reserved spot.

"Well, O'Rourke, you old dog," he'd said as he climbed out of the sporty little car and caught up with Dallas's impatient strides. "You made the front page."

"What?" Dallas hadn't seen the paper yet as the weekly *Banner* was usually delivered by mail.

"Haven't you seen it?" Laughter had danced in Prescott's keen eyes. "Here, take my copy!" He'd slapped the newspaper into Dallas's hands and walked briskly toward the building. Prescott's chortling laughter had trailed back to Dallas as he'd opened the folded pages and found his life unraveled in, of all places, the *Banner*.

"Stupid idiot son-of-a-bitch," he growled now, wondering if he were leveling the oath at Prescott or himself. And just wait until Fillmore got wind of the fact that he and Chandra were getting married and hoping to adopt J.D. He'd never hear the end of it!

At the elevator, he waited impatiently, pushing the button several times and opening and closing his fists to relieve some tension. "Come on, come on," he muttered as the elevator stopped and three young nurses emerged.

They saw him, and nearly as one, tried to smother grins as they mouthed, "Good morning, Doctor."

It was all he could do to be civil. He climbed in the car and pushed the button for the fourth floor. He'd check his patients in CICU and ICU, then retreat to the emergency room, where he was scheduled for the day. If everything was under control, he'd head up to pediatrics before J.D. was to be released. Then he'd go to his office, return some calls and check his mail. His investigator friend from Denver had called and said a package should arrive—the information about Chandra. Good Lord, what had possessed him to order an investigation?

He wasn't looking forward to scanning the P.I.'s report, and yet, he may as well. After all, he planned to marry the woman; it wouldn't hurt to know what he was in for.

Crossing his arms over his chest, he watched the numbers of the floors light up. Chandra was so enraptured with little J.D., Dallas was concerned for her. Even if he and she were married, there were no guarantees that they would be chosen as the adoptive parents. What then? Dissolve the marriage? Strike two? "Hell, O'Rourke, you've really got yourself in a mess this time!"

The elevator thudded to a halt and the doors opened. Jane Winthrop, a nurse who usually worked in admitting, was waiting for the car. Pushing a medicine cart, she nearly ran into him. "Oh, Doctor," she said with a smile. "Excuse me."

Was there a special gleam in her eye? Of course not. He was just being paranoid. "No problem," he replied, skirting the cart with the tiny cups of pills arranged neatly on the shiny metal surface.

"I saw your picture in the paper today," she said, and he jerked his head up to meet her eyes, but found no malice in her gaze. "I sure hope that Chandra Hill gets to adopt that baby. He belongs with her, you know. That's why he was in that barn. It's God's will."

The doors closed, and Nurse Winthrop, her cart and her wisdom disappeared.

Rubbing the tension building in his neck, Dallas turned toward ICU and knew that it was going to be a long day. He decided to go directly to his office and only stopped by his receptionist's desk to collect his mail.

There it was, along with the letters, advertisements and magazines—a package with a Denver postmark. His heart stopped for just a second, and he felt guilty as hell, but he took the stack of mail and a fresh cup of coffee into his office. He set the coffee on the ink blotter and dropped the correspondence and bills onto the desk, then ripped his letter opener through the package from Denver.

He couldn't believe he was so anxious that his stomach had begun to knot. There was a computer report, a note from Jay and a few copies of newspaper clippings, mainly of a trial in Tennessee, a malpractice suit brought by the parents of Gordy Shore, a boy who had died while in Chandra's care.

Dallas let his coffee grow cold as he continued to read, and he learned more than he wanted to know about his future wife.

"A SHOOT DOWN the south fork, a trail ride over Phantom Ridge and a day hike along the west bank of the river," Rick said, eyeing his schedule. He tapped his finger on the last expedition. "Chandra, you can handle the day hike. Randy's got the trail ride, and Jake will take our friends from Boston down the river. All right with you?"

"Fine," she agreed as Jake and Randy began packing gear for their expeditions.

"Good, then I'll hold down the fort here."

Chandra eyed the younger men. Jake was tall and strapping with wheat-blond hair, a tan and blue eyes that cut a person right to the quick. Randy was more laid-back, with a moustache, day's growth of beard and red-brown hair a little on the shaggy side. She turned to see Rick staring at her, his expression uncharacteristically serious. These men, who often joked with her, were the only family Chandra had in Ranger.

"Saw your picture in the paper," Randy said as he tucked trail mix and a couple of candy bars into a backpack. The horses were stabled out of town, so he would meet his clients, drive to the stables and start the ride from that point.

"I hope you're not talkin' 'bout that damned *Banner*," Rick growled, frowning.

"'Fraid so. Chandra's big news around this town,"

Randy teased. "You and the doctor looked pretty chummy to me."

"We are," she said with a shrug.

"And here I thought you'd always had the hots for me, but were just too shy to make the first move."

"If only I'd known," she quipped. These men could tease her and needle her because she knew they cared. Once she'd proved herself on the river, they'd both taken on the roles of brothers.

"I just hope O'Rourke knows what a prize he's found," Jake said forcefully. Jake was always more serious than Randy.

"Dallas O'Rourke?" Rick asked. Still behind the desk, he absently counted out the cash, the "seed money" as he called it, that he kept in the safe at night before replenishing the till each morning.

"The one and only."

"How'd you land that one?" Rick asked.

"Must have been that little sashay you took down Grizzly Loop," Randy teased.

"Get a life, Randy," Chandra said, refusing to be baited.

"And keep that rag that some people consider a newspaper out of my shop," Rick ordered. "I'd just as soon wring Bob Fillmore's neck as say hi."

Chandra spent the next hour stocking the shelves with supplies, then met her group of hikers and drove them to the foothills. They spent most of the day walking the trails that crisscrossed Rattlesnake Canyon. At noon, dusty and hot, they paused to eat at the river, then headed downstream until they'd circled back to the car. Clouds were beginning to form over the hills, and the temperature descended as she dropped her tired party off at the offices of Wild West.

For the next hour, she cleaned up and helped Rick close the shop before driving through town and along the road that led to the hospital. At five-fifteen, she dashed up the stairs to the pediatrics wing and discovered Leslie Nelson at the desk. "Is he still here?" she asked without preamble, but she knew from Leslie's sorry expression that J.D. had already been released. Fear, cold as a night wind, touched her soul. What if things didn't go as planned? What if she never saw J.D. again?

Leslie sighed unhappily. "The caseworker—what's her name—Miss Sedgewick... She was here earlier with Sheriff Newell, and the baby was placed under his care. You know Lenore, don't you?" Chandra shook her head, and Leslie waved aside her doubts. "Well, she's just about the best person J.D. could be placed with. She *adores* kids, and since hers left home, she's been taking in strays, so to speak, kids with all sorts of problems—drugs, family breakups, abuse or runaways. She's one in a million."

"I guess I should be relieved," Chandra said. But she wasn't. She was used to finding J.D. here, and now things had changed. His little life was on its own path, out of her control....

"I think so, and I'm sure she'd let you visit J.D. as often as you want." Leslie leaned over the desk and motioned Chandra closer, as if to tell her a secret. "Just between you and me," she said confidentially, "it's a good thing he's been moved."

"Why?"

"The press! Ever since that story came out in the *Banner* this morning, the phone's been ringing off the hook. Newspaper reporters from as far away as Chicago and Seattle trying to get more information. We're routing all the calls to Dr. Trent's office—he's the chief administrator—and we're not to talk to anyone about the baby."

So the media circus had begun. Chandra's stomach turned over. "Is Dr. O'Rourke in?"

"He was in earlier—checked on a couple of patients, but I don't know his schedule."

"Thanks, Leslie." Chandra turned to leave as the phone at the nurses' station began ringing insistently. Walking on numb legs toward the wing that held the clinic and doctors' offices, Chandra hoped to find Dallas. She'd known the press would come sniffing around, of course, but she'd hoped the public wouldn't be interested.

Dallas wasn't in his office. The receptionist told her he'd be back within the half hour and that she could wait in the lounge. Chandra tried, but the chairs were too uncomfortable and her thoughts were whirling. What if the reporters started digging into her past? The headlines haunted her...

Local Doctor Accused Of Malpractice
By Young Patient's Parents
"My Boy Could Have Been Saved,"
Gordy Shore's Mother Testifies
Doctor Chandra Hill Pendleton Sued By Shores

THE HEADLINES HAD kept coming. Doug's practice had been mentioned, as well as hers, causing a deeper rift in their marriage. Then some of Doug's patients had requested that their files be sent to other cosmetic surgeons. "This'll all blow over," Doug had said, trying to console her, but he couldn't understand the pain and guilt she felt over losing a beautiful boy and suffering the hate of his parents.

No wonder she'd taken back her maiden name and left Tennessee with all its painful memories. Perhaps leaving Collier had looked like the coward's way out, but there had been nothing left for her in Tennessee: no medical practice, no friends, no husband and certainly no children. No, it had been better to make a clean break. And she was still a physician, though unlicensed in Colorado.

Face it, she silently advised herself as she flipped through a dog-eared women's magazine that didn't hold her interest. *You're a lousy judge of character. You married Doug and became friends with Willa and Ed Shore. They all turned on you.*

And now you're planning on marrying Dallas O'Rourke. Good Lord, Chandra, will you never learn?

Bored with waiting, she watched as the receptionist answered the phone and juggled appointments. When the woman's back was turned, Chandra slipped down the hall and pushed open a door with brass letters that spelled "Dallas O'Rourke, M.D." Fortunately the door was unlocked, and Chandra, feeling just a tingle of guilt, rationalized her behavior by telling herself that she was about to become Mrs. Dallas O'Rourke. She needed a little information on the man.

The room was cluttered. A suede-and-leather jacket had been tossed carelessly over the back of one chair, and a tie dangled from the handle of the window. His desk was piled high with papers, though there did seem to be a few distinct piles, as if there were some semblance of order to the paperwork. Medical journals and encyclopedias filled a bookcase and laminated certificates were mounted over the desk. The view from his window overlooked a parking lot, and the two chairs angled near the front of his desk appeared seldom used.

A stack of mail was opened and strewed over the papers on the desk. As she quickly skimmed the letters and bills, her own name leapt out at her: "INVESTIGATIVE REPORT ON CHANDRA HILL."

Chandra's insides froze and her heart turned to ice. Her throat worked, though she couldn't speak. Surely, she'd read the heading incorrectly! She skimmed the first page and felt sick. Dallas had been checking up on her? The tightness in her chest constricted a notch as she sifted through the pages, obviously already read by Dr. O'Rourke. "Why?" she whispered. Why would he ask her to marry him and then check up on her? Or maybe it was the other way around? She found the postmark on the envelope. No. He'd only received this damned report today.

Her hands shaking, she dropped into a chair and began reading about herself, starting with her date of birth and her parents, and later, as they came along, her sisters. Her history inched its way through the pages, a listing of her accomplishments in elementary and high school, as well as in college and medical school. Even names of her friends were listed and those of a few of the men she'd dated.

Nausea churned in her stomach. Her life reduced to eighteen pages of a computer printout, including copies of the newspaper articles about her, her credit history, her health and her marriage and divorce from Doug.

Her stay in Ranger was tagged on at the end, listing Rick as her boss. The first story in the *Banner* about J.D., which had been published just last week, was the final entry.

"Oh, God," she whispered, dropping her head into her hands. How could she ever face Dallas again? Mortified and furious, she clamped her jaw and bit down hard in order to get control of herself. She couldn't let him reduce her to the rubble she'd once been. Never again would she feel this way! She forced her pain to shift to anger. It wasn't hard. She was beyond furious. If and when she ever set eyes on Dallas again, she'd tear him limb from limb! Who did he think he was, sneaking around behind her back, digging up her life to file it neatly onto some private investigator's computer disk?

The door opened, and she twisted her head to find Dallas striding into the room. His eyes dropped to the report in her hands and he sucked in his breath. "What're you doing in my office?"

Chandra stood slowly, dropping the report and pushing herself upright. He was standing in the doorway, his shoulders nearly touching the frame, his face unreadable.

She didn't care how big or intimidating he was. Rage scorched her blood. How could he—this man she'd planned to marry—do this to her? Inching up her chin, she picked up the horrid pages and waved the report in the air. "And what are you doing checking up on me?"

"You're supposed to wait in the lounge."

"Stupid me! I thought being your fiancé gave me a few privileges."

"Not snooping in my office."

"But it's okay for you to snoop into my life, is that right?" She slapped the damned report onto his desk. "How *dare* you have me investigated like some criminal! Who do you think you are that you can open up my life and check me out? I thought—no, I hoped—you were above that sort of thing!"

A muscle in the corner of Dallas's jaw came to life, but there was no anger in his eyes. "What did you expect, Chandra?"

"Trust!" she shot back, and he winced.

"And I expected the truth, which you seemed to twist around to suit your advantage."

"I did not—"

"You came waltzing in here with a baby whom you claim you've never set eyes on before and a load of medical knowledge. And you ended up turning this hospital upside down—"

"I've done no such thing!"

Dallas snorted, his face a steely mask. "You read the headlines today in the *Banner?*"

"Yes, but—"

"You see the picture?"

"What, exactly, is your point?" she asked, leveling a glacial stare at him.

"I just wanted to know whom I was dealing with."

"Because you thought I might have stolen the baby, then, seeing he needed medical attention, brought him in here?"

"At first, yes, but—"

"Well, you're way off base, Doctor!"

"I know that now." Unbuttoning his lab coat, Dallas dragged one hand through his thick hair. "But I didn't—not in the beginning."

"And you check up on any person you've never met before?"

"Any person I think I might marry."

She stiffened. Marriage? Now? After this damned report? She didn't think so. "When you ordered that investigation, you couldn't have had the faintest idea we might discuss the remote idea of wedded bliss!" She shook her head, disbelieving that their relationship had come to this. She was trembling inside, her breathing erratic, and she went to the window to open it a crack and let in some fresh air. "You really are a bastard, O'Rourke," she said quietly.

A cold smile crept across his lips. "Coming from you, that's quite an indictment. Your résumé—" he motioned to the damning report "—is chock full of deadbeats. Especially your ex-husband."

She felt as if she'd been slapped. "A failing of mine, I guess. I just can't say no when a real jerk asks me to marry him!"

"*You* asked me, lady. Not the other way around." He flung the white jacket over an already crowded spoke of a brass hall tree before glancing at her again,

Chandra felt the color drain from her face. "You arrogant son of a—"

"Don't," he cut in. "Let's not sink to name-calling. *Bastard* and *jerk* were good enough. I got the message."

That was it. She'd had it! She grabbed her purse and started for the door. He reached for her arm, but she spun away from him.

"Chandra, wait!" Her hand was on the doorknob, and she, ignoring him, yanked hard.

With a curse, he slammed the door closed. "Don't go—"

She turned frigid eyes on him. "Don't you have some patients to see or, at the very least, some new person in your life that you can sic a private detective on?"

"There's only one new person in my life," he admitted.

"Meaning me?" she spat. "Well, scratch me off the list. I'm not into the humiliation game, okay? I don't hang out with people who dredge up my dirt." She sighed loudly, trying to rein in her galloping rage. With difficulty, she stared into his cobalt blue eyes—eyes that seemed to see into the darkest corners of her heart. "It's too bad, you know," she said shakily. "Maybe if you'd grown up with a little love, if someone had cared for you, you'd know how to care back, how to treat people, how to—" She stopped suddenly when she saw the raw pain in his eyes. She knew then that she'd hit her mark, that she'd wounded him as deeply as he'd hurt her.

Stonily, he stepped away from the door. "I don't think we have anything more to discuss," he said, his voice flat. He moved to the desk, snatched up the damaging report and held it out to her. "You can have this."

Why did she suddenly feel like a heel? She was in the right, damn it! She snatched the report from his hands, but felt the overwhelming need to apologize. She knew she had a sharp tongue, but she didn't usually try to cut someone she cared for so deeply. "Look, I'm sorry. That crack about your family—was...uncalled-for..."

"Don't worry about it." He sat down in his chair and picked up the telephone receiver, staring at her impatiently, waiting for her to leave.

Sighing, she wadded up the damned report and tossed it into a wastebasket near his desk. "Can't we start this afternoon over?" she said, her fury spent.

"Why?"

"Because there's more to us than what's contained in some investigator's printout."

He dropped the receiver. "Let's not delude ourselves, okay? What we've got is a baby—that's all. He's our one common bond. Unless you want to count sex."

Swallowing hard, she glanced through the window to the traffic moving steadily in and out of the parking lot. He was right, of course. Though she'd like to think that love was involved, it wasn't. Love, as far as Dallas O'Rourke was concerned, didn't exist. She'd have to settle for this man who didn't love her, so that she could become J.D.'s mother.

"Well, as long as we understand each other," she said, managing to keep her voice steady.

"You still want to marry me?" he asked, squinting at her, as if looking for flaws.

"I still need a father for J.D."

Dallas drummed his fingers on his desk and pulled his forehead into a frown of disgust. Chandra felt as if her life were on a balance, slowly wobbling, and she was unable to right it.

"I guess I shouldn't have checked up on you," he finally said. "But I thought, when you first brought J.D. to the emergency room, that you could have stolen him or that you were covering for the real mother—that you had a sister or cousin who was in trouble. Believe it or not, I just wanted to help, and I had to be sure that the story you were giving me wasn't a line."

"And now?"

He slid a glance to the wastebasket. "I think the report's filed in the appropriate slot. All I need to know now is that you're playing straight with me."

"I've never lied to you."

"Except about your practice."

"Well, now you know."

"Not everything, Chandra."

"I—I'll tell you about it," she said nervously, her hands beginning to sweat. "But not now. Trust me on this?"

His jaw slid to one side, and as he stood, he retrieved his leather jacket from the hall tree.

"For God's sake, Dallas, don't you trust anyone?" she asked, hating the silence that was radiating from him. She knew why he had trouble trusting people. God knew that she hadn't been completely honest with him herself, and yet she hoped that he would give her the benefit of the doubt.

He slid his arms into his leather jacket, adjusted the collar and looked at her. His features had lost some of their severity, but he didn't smile. "I'm trying," he admitted, "but it's not easy." He walked to the door and held it open for her. Then, as if to leave the argument behind them in the office, he asked, "Okay, it's confession time, how did you get past the sergeant?"

"The what?"

"Dena—the receptionist. She takes her job seriously."

"I've worked in hospitals," Chandra explained. "And your door was unlocked."

"My mistake," he said, smiling crookedly. "Well, one of my mistakes. I seem to be making more than my share lately." He reached forward and took her hand in his.

"Come on," he said with a slow smile. "I think there's someone waiting to see you."

"J.D.?" Her heart soared.

"Mmm." He tugged on her hand and led her out of the office before locking the door. "High crime element in the neighborhood," he explained with a glimmer in his eyes. "You never know who you'll catch prowling around."

"Very funny."

"I thought so." He guided her through the corridors to an exterior exit. "Oh, by the way, I thought we'd get dinner first, then visit your friend. But we have one stop first."

"A stop?"

"City Hall. I think we'd better stop by and apply for a marriage license. Unless you're chickening out."

"Me? Chicken out?" she asked, her heart racing. This was it. Her out. If she only dared take it. She licked her lips nervously as she stared into his incredible blue eyes. "No way."

CHAPTER TWELVE

LENORE NEWELL COULDN'T HAVE been more delighted with company, or so it seemed to Chandra. She insisted Chandra drink a glass of iced tea while she held the baby. Lenore prattled on and on about the children she'd cared for over the years. The living room of the Newell home, a quaint two-storied farmhouse flanked by a wide front porch, was filled with pictures of children, dozens of them, some who had only stayed a few weeks, others who had lived with the Newells for years.

Over the fireplace, a family portrait, showing Lenore and Frank some twenty years younger and surrounded by four beaming-faced boys, gave testament to the Newells' strong family ties and the house itself seemed cozy and warm.

The furniture in the living room was upholstered in well-worn floral prints that matched a circular rug. Crocheted cloths covered the end tables, and a cuckoo clock near the chimney chirped the hours.

"He's just as sweet as he can be," Lenore said, touching J.D.'s cheek with her finger. The baby, sleeping in Chandra's arms, yawned, then snuggled closer. "I just can't imagine anyone in her right mind giving him up." She glanced over at Dallas, who was standing near an upright piano littered with more photographs of children and teenagers. "Frank says no one's come in to claim him yet. Can you believe that?"

"Hard to," Dallas drawled.

Lenore sighed. "Well, the child's better off with a family who loves him!" She sat in a chair next to the rocker in which Chandra was holding the baby. "Are you thinking of trying to adopt him?"

The question didn't surprise Chandra. Surely Lenore had guessed how close she felt to the baby. "I hope to."

"Good! This child needs a mother." She turned her gaze back to Dallas, and added with a crafty wink, "He could use a father, as well, you know."

"We're already a couple of steps ahead of you, Lenore," Dallas confided, slouching against the upright.

"Are you?" She arched her eyebrows in anticipation of a little small-town gossip. Dallas didn't give her any more details, but Chandra, sending him a murderous look, decided Lenore had the right to know everything.

"Dallas and I plan to be married."

Lenore's mouth rounded, and she couldn't hide the surprise and ultimate delight in her eyes. "Married!" She turned to Dallas for confirmation, but received only a noncommittal shrug. "Don't tell me Dr. Ice is melting."

"Very funny, Lenore," Dallas observed with a dry smile as the screen door squeaked on rusted hinges and Frank Newell, tall and whip-lean, strode into the foyer.

"In here—we've got company," his wife sang out. "There's beer and iced tea in the fridge."

Frank paused under the arch that separated the living room from the foyer. "Well, Doctor," he said with a widespread grin at the sight of Dallas. He motioned to the glass of iced tea in Dallas's hand. "Can't I buy you anything stronger?"

"This'll do."

"You'll never guess what!" Lenore said, bustling to her feet and heading past her husband toward the kitchen. Her footsteps retreated, but her voice still carried. "Dallas and

Chandra are going to get married and adopt the baby! How is that for perfect?"

"Is that so?" Frank asked, frowning and looking suddenly tired.

"That's the plan."

"For you and about six hundred other couples."

"What?" Lenore asked. Carrying a tray laden with two bottles of beer, a pitcher of tea, pretzels and cookies, she bustled back to the living room.

Chandra felt icicles form in her heart. "Others?"

"The phones down at the station have been ringing off the hook. Seems the story in the *Banner* got picked up by the news services and now we've got TV and newspaper reporters calling in every damn minute, along with attorneys and people wanting to adopt as faraway as San Francisco. From what I hear, the same thing's going on at Riverbend."

The bottom dropped out of Chandra's world. She felt Dallas's gaze on her as she involuntarily held J.D. more tightly. She couldn't give him up. Wouldn't. Desperation wrenched her heart, and it was all she could do to sit and rock instead of scooping the baby into her arms and fleeing. A lump filled her throat, and she sent up a silent prayer that she be given the privilege of raising this precious child.

Frank twisted open a bottle of beer. "I'm surprised the press hasn't camped out in the front yard, but I suppose it's only a matter of time." He took a long swallow and sighed, his kind eyes resting on Chandra. "You won't be out of this, you know. Bob Fillmore and the *Banner* were just the tip of the iceberg. For the next few weeks, Miss Hill, I'm afraid you'll be hounded."

"There are laws about trespassing," she said.

"And we'll uphold them. But your phone will be ringing non-stop. They've already named this guy, you know."

He nodded toward the baby. "Some reporter in Denver got wind of the fact that several couples are trying to bid for him. Our Baby John Doe is now the Million Dollar Baby."

Chandra's heart turned to stone, and Lenore protested, "He can't be raffled off like some prize quilt at a county fair!"

"I know. It's just a gimmick. But I don't think this is going to blow over." Frank offered Dallas a beer, but the doctor declined. "And I suppose you'll get your share of the press as well, O'Rourke. Yep—" he shook his head slowly before draining half his bottle "—we're all in for a lot of fun."

FRANK NEWELL WAS RIGHT. By the time Chandra arrived home that night, her answering-machine light was blinking, and the tape was filled with the names and telephone numbers of local reporters as well as a call from a couple in Salt Lake City. Chandra suspected this couple was only the first. Soon there would be a lot of couples desperately calling in hopes of adopting J.D.

"Fat chance," she muttered. The only people she telephoned were her parents. They deserved to hear what was going on in her life from her own lips.

Her mother answered and shouted for Chandra's father to pick up the bedroom extension. "I can understand you wanting the baby," her mother rambled on. "God knows you've wanted a child forever, but what about this doctor fellow? How can you be sure that marrying him won't be a mistake? Oh, well, I don't want to discourage you, honey, it's just that I don't want to see you hurt again."

"I won't be, Mom," Chandra said, winding the telephone cord around her wrist and leaning against the kitchen counter.

"Of course she won't, Jill," Chandra's father cut in.

"Chandra knows what she's doing. I'm behind you one hundred percent, girl."

"Well...well...well, so am I," her mother stuttered. "I just think you can take this slow, you know, make sure. You've got the rest of your life—"

"Not if she wants to adopt that baby—"

"Do whatever you think is best," Jill said, sounding irritated with her husband. "And know you've got our blessing. If you tell us when the wedding's scheduled, we'll be there!"

"With bells on," Chandra's father added.

"That I don't know," Chandra replied. They talked a little longer, about everything and nothing, her father asking about her job, her mother sneaking in questions about Dallas. Finally, with both parents in agreement at last that their daughter was old enough to make her own decisions, they hung up and Chandra turned on the answering machine. Whistling to Sam, she walked outside to the small garden, where a few tomatoes still ripened on the vine and the golden tassels on the corn stirred in the breeze. On the other side of the garden was the orchard where pears and apples littered the ground, beyond which were the forested hills. This small ranch would be a perfect place to raise a child, she thought, her heart tearing at the prospect of losing J.D.

And what about Dallas? What would be the point of marrying him when they had no child to hold them together? *You could have other children, Dallas's children.* If he were willing. And there weren't any guarantees that they would be able to conceive. All the advertisements seeking adoptable children were proof enough of the infertility rate. The thought of carrying Dallas's child nearly brought tears to her eyes. For years, she'd given up on the dream of having her own children, and now, with Dallas, it was possible, and what a wonderful baby they could make together. Her throat was suddenly clogged with unshed tears. Dallas's baby! Oh, God, how perfect! Absently, she rubbed her abdomen. A brother or sister for J.D....

She pulled a weed from the garden and tossed it over the fence. Would she be willing to marry Dallas without the prospect of a child? Without J.D.? She cared for him, perhaps even loved him, but was it enough? She felt confused and frustrated and wanted to do something, *anything* to ensure that the baby would be hers. Sitting around and waiting was killing her. *Calm down,* she told herself. She felt the breath of night as the sun sank below the horizon. Would Dallas ever want her to be a part of his life without the baby?

"Oh, God, what a mess," she said with a sigh as she climbed onto the split-rail fence separating garden from orchard. She sat quietly, watching the sky darken in shades of rose and purple. An owl, hunting early this evening, landed in the gnarled branches of the apple tree.

Then the tranquillity was shattered by the intrusion of headlights flashing brightly on the side of the barn.

Another reporter?

She squared her shoulders and squinted against the coming darkness before she recognized Dallas's rig. Relief swelled through her. Maybe he had good news. Or bad. Her pulse thundered, and she waited until he climbed from the cab of his truck before balancing on the lower rails, waving her hands and calling to him. Sam was already bounding through the pumpkin vines and through the yard, yipping excitedly. Even the old dog had allowed Dallas into his heart.

Dallas paused to scratch Sam's ears, then glanced up, catching Chandra's gaze. His face was grim, his expression sober, and Chandra's heart dropped to her knees. Something was wrong. Horribly wrong! J.D.! She vaulted over the fence and told her racing pulse to slow. Maybe

J.D. was fine, but she couldn't quiet the screams of desperation that tore through her heart.

"What is it?" she asked, forcing her voice to stay calm. She couldn't lose control. "Something's wrong. Is it J.D.?"

"The baby's fine," he assured her, but drew her into the warm circle of his arms and held her close to calm her. His breath fanned her hair and she felt the tension in his muscles.

"But there's trouble," she guessed as they stood in the rows of corn, the thick leaves rustling in the breeze.

"There could be." He took her hand and pulled her gently in the direction of the orchard, where they sat on the fence rails and stared across the valley. "My beeper went off as I was heading back here. Dr. Trent, chief of administration, wanted me to stop back by the hospital."

"And?"

"He showed me the first of what appears to be an onslaught of gifts, cards and letters for Baby Doe. One corner of his office was filled, and that's just the start. The hospital fax machine has been working overtime with pleas from barren couples from Colorado, Utah, Arizona and California who want to adopt the baby. Lawyers are calling or showing up in person, and the switchboard has been jammed, which is causing all sorts of problems for the hospital."

Her stomach somersaulted.

"Trent's not too happy about this, to say the least, and he called me in because of the article about you and me. Seems it's already gotten around the hospital that you and I are an item. And I didn't deny it. I told Trent we were getting married and hope to adopt the baby."

Chandra's heart was beating like a drum. "What did he say?"

"'Good luck,' and I quote," Dallas replied, holding one of her hands in both of his. "Trent showed me some of the requests for adoption. You wouldn't believe it. Frank was right. Some people are so desperate that they're offering gifts to the hospital, and we're not just talking peanuts. One physician and his wife from South Dakota are willing to buy some very expensive equipment for the pediatric wing."

"But that's bribery—"

"Another couple—both lawyers—offered free legal services to the hospital."

"I can't believe it."

He slung an arm over her shoulder, and his expression had become sober, his eyes dark with emotion. "I think it's time we thought about this long and hard. There's a good chance that the baby will be adopted by someone we don't know, someone who lives thousands of miles away from here."

So this was it—he was breaking up with her. And they'd lost the baby. Chandra wanted to crumble into a million pieces, but she wouldn't give up without a fight.

"I don't believe all this," she argued heatedly. "I can't believe that the state or the hospital would...would stoop to blackmail!"

"It's not the hospital's decision, anyway. And a good thing. Trent always has his eyes on possible endowments. But his hands are tied. He and the hospital lawyers are just trying to figure out what to do with all the gifts that are coming in—the pediatric wing is already filled with stuffed animals."

"So we still have a chance," Chandra said, unable to calm the fear that rushed through her blood.

"If you're still willing to toss our hat into the ring."

"Absolutely!"

His lips twitched and a glint of admiration twinkled in his eyes. "I had a feeling you wouldn't back down."

"No way. We haven't lost yet."

"Well, then, I don't think we should wait. Forget the marriage license and waiting period. I think we should fly to Las Vegas tonight. The sooner we're married, the sooner we'll be able to fight this as a couple."

"You're serious?" she whispered, touched. She wanted to throw her arms around him and kiss him over and over again.

Dallas reached into his pocket and withdrew two airline tickets. His eyes never left her face. "Well, Ms. Hill, this is it. Do or die. Are we going through with this?"

Her throat closed for a second. Marriage. Just like that. A quick elopement to the tower of glitz in Nevada. So much for moonlight and roses, candlelight and wine. Romance didn't have any part of this transaction…well, at least not much. But she couldn't deny the feelings of love that were sprouting in her breast, nor could she voice them. She managed a smile. "Where would we live? What would we do—"

"We can live here—or you can move into my condo."

"No, here," she said, her mind spinning with plans for the future. "The cabin's big enough, and I need to be near the horses, and J.D. would love to live out here in the country—" She gathered in her breath and stopped. "But what do you want?"

He hesitated for a minute and drew his gaze away. "I just want to make you happy," he said, and Chandra could hardly believe her ears. This man who had told her all they had in common was the baby and sex?

"You don't have to pretend to fall in love with me," she said, and watched his eyes cloud. She rushed on. "We both know that this is only for the baby."

"And what happens if we lose him?" Dallas asked.

She sighed and her heart seemed to break into a thousand pieces. "That can't happen."

"What if it does?"

Then I'll set you free. Oh, Lord, would she be able to? Or was she falling hopelessly in love with a man who couldn't learn to give love in return? "You won't have to be obligated to me, Dallas. I'll sign whatever prenuptial agreement your lawyers come up with."

"I think it's a little late for prenuptials—that is, if you still want to get married. Well?" He stared at her so intensely that her breath was lost somewhere in her throat. "What do you say?"

"I'd say we'd better get a move on if we're going to catch our flight." She hopped lithely off the fence, determined to ignore the omnipresent doubts.

Together, they walked through the garden and into the house, where she threw her one good dress and a few essentials into a small bag. Then, making sure that her horses and Sam were fed, she climbed into Dallas's truck, and they headed to Denver where they planned to take a ten o'clock flight to Las Vegas. The way Dallas explained it, they'd be married sometime after midnight, stop long enough to drink a bottle of champagne over an extremely late dinner, then catch an early-morning flight back to Denver.

They'd lose a night's sleep, but not much more as they would go to their respective jobs as Dr. and Mrs. Dallas O'Rourke tomorrow morning. Just like that. Quick and simple. She wondered what she'd tell her parents, who expected to be invited to the wedding, and her sisters, who had both shied away from marriage. Then, of course, how was she going to handle her new role as Dallas's wife? Life was suddenly becoming complicated.

As Dallas drove through the night-shrouded mountains toward Denver, she glanced at him. His profile was strong and handsome, and his eyebrows were pulled low over his eyes as he squinted against the glare of oncoming headlights.

As far as husbands went, she knew, Dallas would be better than most. Good-looking, rugged, definitely male, passionate and, for all intents and purposes, honest. And as far as their lovemaking was concerned, even now she felt goose bumps. Maybe in time he would learn to love her. They could learn together.

But she didn't kid herself. He wouldn't be easy to live with, and he did brood. His temper was as volatile as hers and as many times as she longed to make love to him, she'd just as soon strangle him.

Well, if nothing else, she decided, seeing the lights of Denver glow ethereally against the night black sky, marriage to him would never be dull.

As FAR AS ROMANCE WENT, the ceremony left a lot to be desired. The minister was red eyed and drowsy, and his breath was laced liberally with liquor. He wore a clerical collar, black jacket and slippers.

His little wife, a mere slip of a woman, smiled through her yawns, and his sister, whose floral dress stretched at the seams, played piano.

Chandra, dressed in a simple pink dress, held Dallas's hand as the minister went through the ritual. Dallas seemed amused by the scene. Wearing black slacks and a white shirt, he was dressed more like a patron of the neon-lit casinos than a bridegroom.

No rings were exchanged, but upon the orders of the minister, Dallas swept Chandra into his arms and kissed her long and hard in the little chapel on the outskirts of Las Vegas.

"It doesn't seem real," Chandra observed as they walked back to the rented car, dodging traffic, that rushed by in the early-morning hours.

"We've got a signed certificate. It's legal."

"But—"

He snorted as he opened the door of the white sedan for her. "The last time I got married, we had a bona fide church, preacher, six attendants, a three-tiered cake and all the trimmings. It didn't make for any guarantees."

Sighing, she scooted into the interior of the Plymouth. Her first wedding had been complete with a long, white, beaded gown, bridesmaids in lavender silk and ushers in matching tuxedos. A huge reception with flowing champagne, an incredible ice sculpture and hors d'oeuvres hadn't created a perfect marriage. Far from it. Dallas was right. And yet, as she caught a glimpse of her ringless left hand, she wondered if she'd made the biggest mistake of her life.

"My folks will kill me," she said, thinking of the calls she would have to make, the questions that would be hurled at her, the explanations she'd have to repeat over and over again.

"Mine will be relieved." He started the engine and edged the Plymouth into traffic, toward the hotel where they'd registered earlier.

"Will they?"

His grin turned cynical. "Oh, sure. My mother won't have to feel guilty about not paying me enough attention, and my father will probably think now he'll finally get that grandson he thinks he's owed. I'm the last of his line of O'Rourkes."

"He'll get that grandson," she said firmly, eyeing the glitter that was Las Vegas. People spilled out of casinos, music and conversation filled the air, and the night was as bright as day, lit by a trillion watts of neon.

Dallas stopped for a red light, and in the glow, his face turned hard, his lips compressed. "Sorry to shatter your dreams, Chandra, but J.D. won't count. At least not with my father."

"He damned well better," she said, her fists clenching in determination.

"You don't know Harrison O'Rourke. He's from the old school, and J.D. won't be blood kin."

"And therefore worthless?"

"As far as the family tree goes," Dallas said, frowning as the light changed and he stepped on the accelerator. "Nope, Harrison will expect an O'Rourke son—not a daughter, mind you." He slid her a glance and grinned cynically. "So don't go disappointing him."

"Wouldn't dream of it," she said, her temper flaring at Harrison O'Rourke's antiquated ideas. "I'll tell you one thing, if and when I ever get the honor of meeting your ogre of a father, he'd better treat all our children equally— and that includes J.D. and our daughters!"

Dallas shook his head as he turned toward the hotel. "So now we've got daughters?"

"We might!"

"Even if we don't adopt J.D.?" he asked, turning his gaze her way for just a second.

"I—I can't think about not having J.D. Not yet," she said softly. She clutched the handle of her purse in a death grip and tried to think about anything other than the awful fact that little J.D.'s future was out of her hands.

Dallas drove to the rental-car parking lot of the hotel. Twenty stories high, the concrete-and-steel building glowed like the proverbial Christmas tree. A marquee announced a famous comic as the weekend's entertainment, and liveried bellboys and ushers welcomed them.

The lobby was awash with light, and a fountain spraying pink water two stories high was situated in the central foyer. Veined marble and forest green carpet covered the floor.

Chandra could hardly believe that she was actually here, married and about to spend the wee morning hours of her honeymoon in the bridal suite.

With the help of the bell captain, they were whisked to the nineteenth floor and left in a three-room suite complete with complimentary champagne, heart-shaped tub and a round bed covered with silk sheets.

"Don't you think this is overdoing it a little?" she asked, eyeing the bed, beyond which the view of the city, lights winking endlessly, stretched into the desert.

"I thought it was the least I could do. This won't be much of a honeymoon."

She swallowed a smile and arched a coy brow. "You think not?" She glanced meaningfully at the bed. "Somehow, I think you'll find a way to make up for lost opportunities."

"You might be right," he agreed, striding so close to her they were almost touching. Only a breath of air separated their bodies, and Chandra's pulse quickened. Slowly he surrounded her with his arms and lowered his mouth to hers. "Maybe we should open the champagne and toast the bride and groom…."

Her breath was already lost in her lungs. "Later," she whispered.

"You're sure?"

Oh, God, was that her heart thumping so loudly when he hadn't yet touched her? "Yes, Doctor," she whispered breathlessly, "I'm positive."

With a wicked grin, Dallas lifted her off her feet and carried her quickly to the bed. "You know, Mrs. O'Rourke, I like the way you think." He dropped her on the silken coverlet, and his lips found hers, molding intimately over her mouth as his body formed to hers. She welcomed his weight and the gentle probing of his tongue.

His fingers worked on the small buttons of her dress, and the pink fabric parted. Dallas groaned as he shoved the dress off her shoulders and stripped it from her body. He moved his hands easily over the silk of her slip and touched the lace that covered her breasts. "You're so beautiful," he murmured against her hair.

She opened his shirt and touched the fine mat of hair on his chest. He caught his breath, and she watched in wonder as his abdomen sucked in and became rigid. "So are you," she whispered, fascinated by this man.

His lips found hers again, and he made short work of their clothes, kicking them into a pile and never once releasing her. Chandra's skin seared where his fingers touched her body, and her breasts ached for more of his sweet, sweet touch. She arched against him, feeling the magic of his hands, lost in the wonder of his mouth.

He kissed her face, her neck, her hair. She writhed against him, trying to get closer, and when his tongue rimmed the delicate circle of bones at the base of her throat, she cried out. He moved lower still, kissing her breasts and suckling on her nipples while he explored her back and hips with sure hands.

"Dallas," she whispered, her voice rough and low, "Dallas." She traced a path along the curve of his spine, and he held back no longer. Suddenly he was atop her, his knee between hers, his chest heaving.

Their lips locked, and he entered her for the first time as her husband. "I can't wait," he whispered, and began his magical rhythm. Chandra clung to him, moving with him, feeling the sweat collect on her skin. She thought he whispered words of love, but in her fevered state she might have heard her own voice as they exploded together and she cried out.

"Dallas!"

"Oh, love, oh, love," he sighed, collapsing against her, spent.

They held each other for endless minutes as the fog of afterglow surrounded them. Chandra closed her eyes, for she knew she might cry, not from sadness, but from deeper emotions that tore at her heart.

When her heartbeat was finally normal, she opened her eyes and found him staring at her. "You okay?" he asked, and she smiled, shyly and self-consciously, as if she'd been a virgin.

"I'm fine. You?"

He swept back the hair from her face and kissed her forehead. "Well, I'm a helluva lot better than fine. In fact, I think I'm great."

She giggled, and to her mortification he picked her up and carried her, stark naked, into the bathroom. "What're you doing?" she asked as he dropped her into the tub and twisted on the faucets.

"If this is going to be a honeymoon, we've got to make the most of it," he replied, his eyes glinting devilishly as warm water rushed into the tub.

"By bathing?"

"Or whatever." He lit two candles, brought in the champagne and turned out the lights. She couldn't take her eyes off his lean muscles, how they moved so easily under his skin. She was intrigued by all of him—the way his dark hair matted across his chest, the corded strength of his shoulders, the white slash of a smile that flashed crookedly in the light of flickering candles.

He stepped into the tub and gathered her into his arms, and their slick bodies melded together. "This is crazy," she said with a laugh as he positioned her legs around him.

"This is wonderful," he corrected. The water rose to their chests, and he turned off the faucets. In the shadowy light, he gazed at her with eyes that seemed to shine with love.

"Now, Mrs. O'Rourke," he said, tracing a drip from her neck to the hollow of her breast, "let's find a way to stretch out these few hours as long as we can."

HOURS LATER, AFTER SIPPING champagne in the tub and making love on the round bed until they were both exhausted, they awoke and headed downstairs. Dawn was just sending shafts of light across the desert floor and through the streets of the now-quiet city. The neon lights, so brilliant the night before, were dimmed as Dallas drove toward the airport.

He parked the rental car in the lot near the terminal before they headed inside, ready to return to Ranger and fight for custody of J.D. Chandra was prepared for an uphill battle, but anything as precious as that baby was worth whatever it took. By sheer determination alone, she should be allowed to adopt the child she had saved.

As she walked down the concourse with Dallas at her side, her new role as his wife started to sink in. She felt suddenly secure and worked at convincing herself that she and Dallas would be given custody. No parents would love a child more.

From the corner of her eye, she saw Dallas slow near an airport shop, and she wondered if he was going to buy some souvenir of the trip.

"Goddamned son of a bitch!" he growled, stopping short and fishing in his pocket for change. He dropped several coins onto the counter.

Before the startled cashier could ring up the sale, Dallas grabbed a newspaper and snapped it open. There on page one, in grainy black and white, was a picture of J.D.

Baby Abandoned In Colorado Barn, the headline screamed, and in smaller letters, Mother Still Missing As Hundreds Hope To Adopt The Million Dollar Baby.

Chandra's throat went dry. She curled her fingers over Dallas's arms, seeking strength. "How—how did they get that picture?" she whispered, her eyes skimming the newsprint and her legs threatening to give way when the article revealed that the child was living with Sheriff Newell. "How did they get this information?"

"Ranger's a small town," Dallas replied, tight-lipped, a deep flush staining the back of his neck. Never had she seen him more furious. "Gossip runs rampant."

For the first time, Chandra had to face the fact that the odds against them were insurmountable. They were just a couple—a recently married couple—who would stand in line with hundreds of other couples—every one of them as anxious to adopt the baby as she and Dallas were.

"Come on," Dallas said, his voice sounding strangely faraway. "We've got a flight to catch."

Her throat caught, and tears threatened her eyes. *You're just tired,* she told herself, all of her earlier euphoria long gone.

"We haven't lost yet," Dallas reminded her, and he grabbed hold of her elbow and propelled her toward the boarding gate.

"You're right," she said, then shivered. Inside, she knew she was in for the fight of her life.

CHAPTER THIRTEEN

So HERE THEY WERE at home—a married couple. They'd driven directly to the cabin and now, after showering and changing, they were preparing to go into town.

Chandra poured herself a cup of coffee and smiled as she poured another for Dallas. It would be easy, she thought, to get into a routine with him, to wake up every morning in his arms and to read the paper, drink coffee and work around the house and outbuildings.

He planned on moving first his clothes and then his furniture as soon as possible. They'd even talked of expanding the cabin, and Dallas wanted to talk to an architect about the remodeling. Things were moving swiftly, but for the first time in years, Chandra felt comfortable depending upon someone besides herself.

She heard him on the stairs, and glanced up to see his handsome face pulled into a frown as he buttoned his shirt.

"I could help you with that," she offered, and he flashed her a slice of a grin.

"You're on."

When he reached the kitchen, she kissed his chest and slipped each button through its hole.

"If you keep this up, I'll never get to work," he said, his eyes lighting with a passionate flame.

"Uh-uh." She finished the shirt and handed him his coffee cup. "Come on outside, I think we should talk."

"About...?"

She braced herself. "Me and what happened in Tennessee."

"You don't have to—"

"Of course I do," she said as he placed a hand on her shoulder. "We've got to start this marriage with a clean slate—no lies, no misunderstandings, no surprises."

Together they walked outside and Chandra felt the morning sun against her back as they leaned over the rail of the fence and watched the horses picking at the dew-laden grass. Sam trotted behind them only to be distracted by a squirrel.

"What happened?" Dallas finally asked, and Chandra decided to unburden herself.

"Medicine was my life," she admitted, thinking of all those grueling years in med school when she had not only worked for hours on end, but had to endure being the butt of too many jokes. Feeling Dallas's eyes upon her, she forced the words about her past from her throat. "I went to school in Philadelphia, then took a position with a hospital in Collier, Tennessee.

"You know about the patient I lost, a seven-year-old boy. His name was Gordy. It…it was messy." Her throat clogged momentarily, but she willed herself to go on, to get over the pain. "You saw the newspaper articles, but they didn't explain exactly what happened. I was sued for malpractice by the parents, though they brought him in much too late. They thought he had the flu, and he just got worse and worse. By the time we rushed him to the hospital…well, he died of pneumonia within the hour. The parents blamed me." She swallowed hard, looking not at Dallas but concentrating on a swallow as it flew about the barn roof. "There was an investigation, and I was cleared, but…well, I had other personal problems."

"Your marriage."

"Yes," she said with a sigh. "Everything seemed to unravel. So," she finished, trying to force a lightness into her voice, "I ended up here, with a job as a white-water and mountain guide."

"Don't you miss it?" He touched her lightly on the arm, and her heart warmed at the familiarity they'd slipped into.

"What—medicine?"

"The healing."

"Sometimes, but not often. I'm still a doctor," she said. "It wouldn't take much to get licensed here, but I guess I wasn't ready to start practicing again." She felt inexplicably close to tears, and he threw his coffee cup on the ground and took her into his arms.

"Losing a patient is hard, but it happens," he whispered.

"Children shouldn't die."

Gently, he rotated her, forced her to look at him, and Chandra didn't pull away from him as he kissed her lips. "No," he agreed, "no child should ever die, but, unfortunately, it happens. We try our best, and sometimes it isn't good enough." He looked down into her eyes, his own shining in the morning sunlight.

"I couldn't help feeling guilty, that if I would have gotten to him sooner, I could've saved his life."

"How could you have known?"

She shook her head and sighed, resting her cheek against Dallas's chest, feeling his warmth seep into her and hoping some of the old feelings of remorse would disappear. "I was married to Doug at the time, and he couldn't understand why I took it so hard. I wanted out of medicine, at least for a while, and he...he objected. We were making good money. He was a plastic surgeon in Memphis, and he didn't want our lifestyle to change. He told me that if I quit practicing that I would only be proving that I wasn't cut out to be a doctor, that all of his friends in medical school, the ones who had predicted I couldn't make it, would be proved right."

"Wonderful guy," Dallas remarked, his voice steely.

"We had our share of problems."

Dallas kissed her crown. "He was wrong, you know. Wrong about you. My guess is that you were and still are a damned good doctor."

"Have you ever lost a patient?"

"Too many."

"A child?"

"There've been a few. And I know what you went through. Each time, you can't help feeling that somehow you should have performed a miracle and saved his life."

Her throat knotted, and she couldn't swallow. Tears, unwanted, burned behind her eyes. "Yes," she whispered as he pulled her closer, holding her, murmuring into her hair, kissing her cheek. She wouldn't cry! She wouldn't! She'd spent too many years burying the pain and her past. "All those years of school, all those hours of studying, all those nights of no sleep, and I couldn't save one little boy!" Slowly, she disentangled herself and swallowed the lump that seemed determined to lodge in her throat.

"It's over," Dallas promised. "You've got a new start. We've got a new start. So it's time we took the first step and tried to adopt that baby together."

Chandra smiled through her tears and took Dallas's hand.

CAMERAS FLASHED, MICROPHONES were thrust in their faces and reporters, en masse, had collected around the Newells' house.

"Is it true you're married?" a woman with flaming red hair asked as Chandra tried to duck past the crowd.

"Yes."

"And you met Dr. O'Rourke when you brought the baby in—is that right?" another female voice called.

"No comment," Dallas growled.

"Oh, come on, Doctor, give us a break. Tell us a little about the baby. Where do you think he came from? Have you checked with any of the local clinics and found out if a woman in the third trimester never delivered?"

"No," Dallas said.

"You have no idea where the mother is?"

"None." He helped Chandra up the stairs of the New-ells' front porch as reporters fired questions nonstop. To keep the crowd at bay, a deputy was posted near the front door, but he let Chandra and Dallas pass, presumably on orders from the sheriff or his wife.

"Isn't it a madhouse out there?" Lenore asked, her eyes shadowed with worry, her face grim.

"I guess it's to be expected," Chandra replied, anxious to see the baby.

"I suppose." But Lenore's face seemed more lined this morning, her lips pinched into a worried pucker. "I've taken in a lot of children in my day, but I've never seen the likes of this," she admitted, parting the lace curtains and sighing at the group of reporters camped in her yard. "And I've quit answering the phone. Seems everyone in the state is interested in adopting little J.D."

Chandra's heart sank like a stone. Even though she held J.D. and gave him a bottle, she felt as if she were losing him, that the cord that had bound them so closely was being unraveled by unseen hands. As she held the bottle, she stared into his perfect little face. She didn't kid her-self. Sooner or later, if the media attention surrounding J.D. kept up at a fever pitch, other would-be mothers would be trying to see him and hold him. They would argue that Chandra, just because the child was discovered in her barn, had no more right to be with him than they did. It wouldn't be long before the courts or the Social Services stepped in, and in the interest of fairness, she might not be allowed to see him.

"Has it been this way for long?" Dallas asked Lenore.

"Since before dawn. And the phone has been ringing since about six last night. Someone must've let it slip that the baby's here because before that there was nothing. I was living a normal life. I don't like this, I tell you."

"Neither do I," Dallas replied, and Chandra bit her lip to keep tears from spilling on the baby who would never be hers.

As CHANDRA SETTLED into a comfortable life with Dallas, the interest in the baby didn't decrease. While she was busy making closet space for Dallas's things, helping him fill out change-of-address forms and planning the addition to the house, her name and picture appeared in newspapers as far away as Phoenix and Sante Fe. At first she was considered a small-time heroine, the woman who had discovered the baby and rushed him to the hospital. Over the next week, her life was opened up and dissected, and all the old headlines appeared.

The story of little Gordy Shore and his death was revived, and her marriage to Doug Pendleton, subsequent divorce and change of name and lifestyle in Colorado were hashed and rehashed in the newspapers and on the local news. She'd given two interviews, but quit when the questions became, as they always did, much too personal.

It was known that she was trying to adopt the baby, along with hundreds of other applicants, and it had even been speculated that her marriage to Dallas, at first a seeming fairy-tale romance of two people who meet via an abandoned infant then fall in love, was a fraud, a ploy for custody.

"I don't know what I expected," she admitted to Dallas, upon reading a rather scorching article in the *Denver Free Spirit*. "But it wasn't this."

Dallas, who had been polishing the toes of his shoes,

rested one foot on the seat of a chair and leaned across the table to stare more closely at her. "Giving up so soon, Mrs. O'Rourke? And here I thought you liked a battle."

"Not when the stakes are so high," she admitted, her stomach in knots. She hazarded a quick glance at him. "And I'm not giving up. Not yet."

"Not as long as there's an ounce of breath in your body, I'd wager," he said, winking at her.

She rolled her eyes, but giggled. The past few days had been as wonderful as they had been gut wrenching. Though she was worried about adopting J.D., her life with Dallas was complicated, but interesting, and their love-making was passionate. She couldn't resist him when he kissed her, and she felt a desperation in their lovemaking, as if they each knew that soon it would be over. If they weren't awarded custody of J.D., they would have no reason to stay together. That thought, too, was depressing. Because each day she was with him, she loved him a little more.

Sam whined to go out, and she slung the strap of her canvas purse over her shoulder. "I guess I'd better get to work," she said. "And I'll talk to my attorney today, see what he's come up with."

"I'll walk you," Dallas offered, holding open the door for her as Sam streaked across the yard. The morning was cool, the sky, usually clear, dark with clouds. Even through her jacket, Chandra shivered.

She reached for the handle of the door of her Suburban, but Dallas caught her hand.

"What's up, Doctor?" she asked, turning to face him and seeing his gaze was as sober as the threatening sky.

"I think I've gone about this marriage thing ass-backward," Dallas admitted.

"We both have."

"Right. But I decided that we need to set things right.

So, I hope this is a start." He reached into his pocket and withdrew a small silver ring, obviously old, with a single diamond surrounded by smaller sapphires.

"Where did you get this?" she whispered as he slipped it over her finger, and the ring, a size or two too big, lolled below her knuckle.

"It was my grandmother's. Harrison's mother. I don't remember much about her—except that she was kind and loving, and the one person in the world who would always stand up for me." He cleared his throat suddenly, and Chandra's heart twisted with pain for the man who had once been such a lonely boy. "She died when I was about eight and she left me this—" he motioned to the ring "—and a little money for college and medical school."

Chandra, her throat thick, her eyes heavy with tears of happiness, touched the ring with the fingers of her other hand.

"You can have it sized," he said. "Or if you'd prefer something new—"

"Oh, no! It's…it's perfect! Thank you!" Moved, she threw her arms around his neck and kissed his throat, drawing in deep breaths filled with his special scent. "We're going to make this work, Doctor," she whispered into his ear. "I just know it!"

Opening the door of the Suburban, she saw the ring wink in the little morning light that permeated the clouds. She wondered vaguely if Jennifer had worn this very ring, and a little jab of jealousy cut through her. But she ignored the pain; Jennifer was history. Chandra, now, was Mrs. Dallas O'Rourke.

She pushed all negative thoughts aside as she drove into town and stopped at Roy Arnette's office. The lawyer was waiting for her, his glasses perched on the end of his nose, his mouth tiny and pinched. "Have you talked to the Newells today?" he asked as she sat down.

"It's only nine in the morning."

Roy sighed. "Then you don't know."

"Know what?" she asked, but she read the trouble in his eyes, and her throat seemed to close in on itself.

"There's a woman. Her name is Gayla Vanwyk. She claims to be the baby's mother."

"But she couldn't be—" Chandra whispered, her world spinning wildly, her heart freezing.

"Maybe not. But the police are interested in her."

"But where did she come from? How did she get here? She could be some kook, for crying out loud, someone who read about J.D. in one of these—" She thumped her hand on a newspaper lying open on Roy's desk. "She could just be after publicity or want a child or God only knows what else!"

"Look, Chandra, I'm only telling you what I know, which is that the police are interested in her enough to have some blood work done on her."

"Oh, God—"

"If she's the natural mother..."

Tears jammed her throat, and Chandra blinked hard. "If she is, why did she leave him?" she demanded, outraged.

"If she's the natural mother, this complicates things," Roy said. "She'll have rights."

"She gave those up when she left him!"

"Maybe not, Chandra," he said as gently as possible, and Chandra felt as if her entire world were crumbling.

Dallas! She needed to talk to Dallas. He'd know what to do. "I won't lose him, Roy, I won't!" she cried, though a horrible blackness was seeping into her soul. Again she saw how small her chances of becoming J.D.'s mother actually were. Sobs choked her throat, but she didn't let them erupt. "I want to see her," she said with dead calm.

"You can't. The police are still talking to her."

"I'll wait," she insisted, somehow managing to keep the horrid fear of losing the baby at bay. "But at the first opportunity, I want to talk to that woman!"

"SHE'S DEFINITELY POSTPARTUM," Dallas said quietly. The bottom dropped out of Chandra's world as she sat slumped into a chair in his office, her heart heavy. "Now we're waiting for the lab to check blood types." He looked tired, his blue eyes dark with worry, his hair uncombed. He rubbed his neck, as if to straighten the kinks, and Chandra was reminded of the first time she'd seen him in the emergency room so few weeks before. He'd been weary then, too, but she'd known that this man was different, special. And now he was as sick with worry as she was. Maybe even more so.

"So she's had a baby," Chandra whispered with a stiff lift of her shoulder as she feigned nonchalance. "That doesn't mean she had *this* baby."

"Very recently."

"Does she look like J.D.?"

He shook his head. "Who can tell? She has black hair, dark eyes. And it doesn't matter, anyway. The boy could look like his father—or someone else in the family."

Chandra's hands were shaking. She clasped them together and saw the ring, Dallas's grandmother's ring, her wedding ring, a symbol of a marriage that, perhaps, was never meant to be. Taking in a shuddering breath, she stared past Dallas to the window where the first drops of rain were slanting over the glass. Thunderheads brewed angrily over the mountains, and the sky was dark as pitch. "I can't believe it. Not after all this... She can't just appear and claim the child...."

Dallas rounded his desk and took her hands in his; the stones of the ring pressed into his palm. "Don't tell me you're a quitter after all, Mrs. O'Rourke."

"It seems the odds are against us, aren't they?" Chandra had only to crane her neck to see the newspapers littering Dallas's desk. "That name—the Million Dollar Baby—it's stuck. Did you know that? Some couples are actually in a bidding war to gain custody. What chance do we have?"

Dallas's eyes flickered with sadness. He pressed a kiss against her temple. "We haven't lost yet."

"But it doesn't look good."

"We won't know if she's even possibly the mother until the blood work is analyzed. Even then, we can't be sure. She has no birth certificate—claimed she had him out in the woods near your place. She can't or won't name the father."

Chandra's shoulders slumped. Even if this woman did prove to be a fraud, she was just the first. Woman after woman could claim to be mother of the baby, and sooner or later the real one might show up. If, God willing, she and Dallas were allowed to adopt J.D....

Her heart ripped, and she bit her lip to fight back tears. Dallas was right about one thing, they hadn't lost yet, even though the odds of adopting the child seemed to be getting slimmer by the minute.

Dallas drew her to her feet and wrapped his arms around her, as if he really cared. Her heart nearly crumbled, and she wanted to lean against him, to sob like a baby, to cling to him for his strength, but she wouldn't break down. Instead, she contented herself with resting her head against his chest and listened to the calming rhythm of his heartbeat. God, how she loved him. If he only knew.... But she couldn't tell him. Not yet. She'd seem like some simpering female, depressed and clinging to a man who had no real ties to her.

GAYLA VANWYK WASN'T TOO HAPPY about being in the hospital, that much was certain from the crease in her brow and the pout of her full lips. Dallas guessed her age at twenty-three, give or take a couple of years. She was a beautiful girl, really, with curling black hair that framed a heart-shaped face filled with near-perfect features. Her exotic eyes were deep brown, rimmed with curling ebony lashes and poised above high cheekbones.

She sat in Dr. Trent's office, smoking a cigarette and staring with obvious distrust at the people in the room. Dallas stood near the window and looked down at the parking lot where, wedged between the cars of doctors, nurses, staff and patients, were double-parked vans and cars. Reporters milled about the parking lot and lobby.

"Shouldn't I have my attorney here or somethin'?" Gayla asked, eyeing the men and women who had dealt with the infant.

Dr. Trent, as always soft-spoken, smiled kindly. "This isn't an inquisition, Miss Vanwyk. These are some of the doctors who examined the child when he came into the hospital, and they'd like to explain his conditions to you." He tried to calm her down, to explain that they were only interested in the health of the baby, but she wasn't buying it.

"Look, I've done all I have to," she said, crushing her cigarette in a glass ashtray Trent had scrounged out of his desk. "I know my rights. I want my baby back."

"As soon as the test results are in, we'll forward them to the police and Social Services," Trent said.

"Good. And how long will that take?" She stood up, ending the interview, and deposited her pack of cigarettes into a well-worn purse.

"A day at most, but Social Services—"

"Screw Social Services, I just want my kid."

"You left him," Dallas said, unable to let the conversation end so abruptly.

"Yeah, I had to. No choice."

"Why not?"

"That's personal," she said, narrowing her eyes on him. "And I don't have to talk to you. You're the doctor who wants to adopt him, aren't you? You're married to the woman who found him."

"I just want to get to the truth."

"Well, you got it." She turned on her heel and left the scent of heavy perfume and smoke wafting after her.

"If that's the mother, I don't envy the kid," Dr. Spangler said, fiddling with the buttons on his watch. "Maternal, she's not."

Dallas shoved his hands into the back pockets of his pants. "I don't buy it," he said, his eyes narrowing a little as he considered the woman's story. Even if she was the baby's mother, she seemed more defensive than concerned about the child.

In his own office, he punched out the number of his friend in Denver, the private investigator. Why not check out Miss Vanwyk? If she proved, indeed, to be J.D.'s mother, and the state saw fit to grant her custody, there wasn't much Dallas could do about it. If, however, she wasn't the baby's mother, or he could prove her unfit, then at least the baby would be placed in a home with loving parents—not necessarily with Chandra and him, but with people who loved him.

And what will you and Chandra do? Call the whole thing off? Divorce? Or start over? Living together not for the sake of a child, but because you love each other.

Love? Did he love her already?

Impossible. Love was out of his realm. Or was it? After all, he had given her the ring, a ring he'd never even shown to Jennifer.

At the realization that he'd fallen all too willing a victim to love again, Dallas flung one leg over the corner of his desk and wondered how he could convince Chandra that, with or without the baby, they belonged together

"Killingsworth Agency," a female voice cooed over the phone, and Dallas snapped his wandering thoughts back to attention. First, he had to find out about the woman claiming to be the baby's mother; next, he'd deal with his marriage.

THREE DAYS LATER, Chandra was a nervous wreck. Certainly blood tests couldn't take so long...unless they were testing DNA.

She'd begged Dallas for information, but he claimed he, as a prospective adoptive parent, was being kept as much in the dark as she. It was all she could do not to find Miss Vanwyk and demand answers.

"In due time," Dallas told her. "You can't risk talking to her now. It might jeopardize our chances of adopting the baby."

And so she kept away. But the press didn't let up, and Chandra felt as if her life were being examined through a microscope. As was Gayla Vanwyk's. Chandra's life seemed to be a story right out of the most sensational of the tabloids, and she had trouble sleeping at night. Were it not for Dallas's strong arms on which she had come to depend, she doubted she would be getting any rest at all.

As for work, things were slowing down as summer receded into fall. And though Chandra needed to fill her idle days, Rick wouldn't hear any arguments from her. "Listen, you look like you haven't had a decent night's sleep in two weeks, and we're not busy, anyway. Until all this hubbub about that kid dies down, you take some time off. Consider it paid vacation or a honeymoon or whatever, but you take all the time you need to put your life in order. Listen to someone who knows what he's talking about—this is free advice, Chan. If I would've spent more time working things out with Cindy, she'd probably still be here with the kids and I would still be playing Santa Claus instead of getting Christmas cards from St. Louis."

Never, in the years she'd worked with him, had Chandra heard him complain about the split from the woman who'd borne his children. Though he hadn't married anyone else, hardly even dated, Rick just didn't talk about his past.

Chandra grabbed a rag from behind the register and slapped at a cobweb hanging from the wagon-wheel chandelier. "But I can't just sit around the house and stare at Sam all day," she protested, frowning as she spotted another dangling string of dust.

"Why not? It'd do you some good. You haven't taken any time off since you started working here."

Randy breezed through the door and heard the tail end of their argument. "Hey, you may as well take advantage of Rick's good humor," he said, his eyes twinkling. "I am. I'm gonna find me a woman and a kid and get married and take a few months' paid vacation—"

"Get outta here," Rick said, chuckling to himself. "No, not you, Randy. But you, Chan, do yourself a favor. Get to know that husband of yours."

That husband of mine, she thought ruefully. For how long? Snagging her long denim coat from the peg near the door, she hurried outside and shivered in the cold mountain wind. The first snow of the season had dusted the highest peaks, but here, in the lower valley, raindrops danced in the parking lot, creating shallow puddles that she had to dodge as she made her way to her Suburban. The thought of living without little J.D. was crippling, the thought of living without Dallas devastating. In a few short weeks, they'd become so close, and their marriage, though it hadn't been based on love, had provided, in many ways, the happiest moments of her life—though her parents had been shocked when she'd called them with the news.

"You shouldn't have been so hasty!" her mother had warned. "What do you know about this man?"

Chandra's father had come to her rescue. "Oh, hush, Jill. She's old enough to know what she's doing!"

"And that's what you said when she married Doug!"

Now, remembering the telephone conversation, Chandra smiled at her parents' happy bickering. They'd be lost without each other. They depended upon each other, and, yes, they argued with each other, but she never doubted that their love ran as deep as any ocean and their devotion to each other, as well as to their three daughters, was stronger than any force on earth.

She'd hoped for that same kind of love and devotion in her own marriage to Doug, and it hadn't occurred. But this time...if only Dallas could love her....

She wasn't ready to go home, knowing that there would be more messages from reporters on her answering machine. She drove instead to the hospital, hoping that she could share a cup of coffee with Dallas or just talk to him.

In the parking lot, Chandra encountered reporters, hand-held cameras, microphones and tape recorders. A police cruiser was idling near the entrance, and Chandra recognized the flat, frowning face of Deputy Stan Bodine behind the wheel. Chandra waved at him as she drove to a rear parking lot.

She left her Suburban far from the main doors and dashed through the physician's lot to a side entrance. Inside the hospital, she shook the rain from her hair and rubbed her hands from the cold, then hurried to Dallas's office.

He wasn't in. Dena checked his schedule and relayed that Dallas wasn't due back in the hospital until two, at which time he was to report for his shift in ER.

Chandra visited the nurses in the pediatrics wing, then took the elevator to ER. Dallas hadn't signed in yet. There were a few patients in the waiting room as Chandra started for the door. She was near Alma Lindquist's desk when she heard the voice of a distraught mother.

"But he hasn't taken any liquids. I can't get him to drink, and his temp's been at a hundred and four for a couple of days. The pediatrician says it's just the flu, but I'm worried."

"Who's your pediatrician?" Nurse Lindquist inquired.

"Dr. Sands, and I trust him, but Carl is so sick…"

Chandra couldn't help but overhear the conversation, and she looked at the small boy cradled in his mother's arms. His face was pale, and he could barely keep his eyes open. "Has he had any blood work done?" she asked.

"No, I don't think so," the mother replied, her own face pasty with worry.

"You haven't had a white count?"

"Not that I know of." The mother looked perplexed. "Dr. Sands says there's a virus going around…."

Alma rose from her chair. "Mrs. O'Rourke, this isn't…"

But Chandra didn't hear her. As she looked at the little boy, images of another sick child came to mind. She saw Gordy Shore's listless eyes and pale face, his lethargy palpable.

"Admit this child immediately. Get a white count, and if that's elevated, have his lungs X-rayed." Chandra turned to the mother. "Have there been any other symptoms— vomiting? Diarrhea? Swelling?"

"No, he just barely moves, and he's usually so active," the mother replied, obviously close to tears.

"Don't worry. We'll take care of him."

"Thank God."

"Has Dr. Sands listened to his lungs—"

"Last week," the mother replied.

"Admit this child," Chandra ordered again, but Nurse Lindquist's lips pressed into a stubborn line. Obviously, she wasn't taking any instructions from a woman who held no authority at Riverbend, but Chandra, spying Dallas walking from the stairs, flew past her. "That patient," she said, motioning to the little boy, "is supposed to have the flu, but he hasn't had a white count and…" She rattled off the conversation to Dallas and, thankfully, he listened to her.

"There are other patients," Nurse Lindquist objected as Dallas approached, but he surveyed the waiting room where a few people sat patiently, flipping through ragged magazines.

"Anything life threatening?" he asked.

"No."

"Admit this child—now," he ordered as an ambulance roared to the doors. "And call Dr. Hodges if we need more help." He then led the mother and child back to the examining room.

Pandemonium broke loose as another ambulance, siren screaming, pulled up to the door. Paramedics began wheeling stretchers into the emergency room.

Chandra heard the page calling for every available staff member, and she saw the influx of personnel and equipment. Suddenly, nurses, doctors and volunteers were everywhere as the first of the patients were wheeled into examining rooms.

"Bad accident…truck jackknifed on the freeway…" she heard a paramedic explain to a nurse. "This one needs help, he's lost a lot of blood and his blood pressure has dropped—"

"Put him in room three. Dr. Prescott's on his way."

Chandra didn't even think about the ramifications of what she was doing, but followed Dallas into the examining room, where he was leaning over the boy, a stethoscope to his chest.

"I don't hear anything, but we'll have to see—"

Shannon Pratt stuck her head into the examining room. "Dr. O'Rourke, we need you! Big accident. Multiple victims. We're calling all the staff back to the hospital."

"I can handle this," Chandra said, motioning to the boy, her heart in her throat. "You had blood taken?"

"It's in the lab now."

"I'll take him to X-ray." Chandra met the questions in Dallas's gaze and didn't flinch. A special glimmer passed between them. "They need you out there," she said. Shouts, moans and the sound of rattling equipment and frantic footsteps filtered through the door.

"You're sure about this?" Dallas asked.

"Positive. Come on," she said to the boy as she lifted him into a wheelchair, "let's get some pictures taken...."

The rest of the afternoon passed in a blur. Chandra helped out where she could, but was sent home when the administration caught wind that a doctor not certified in the state was giving advice, if only to other physicians. Though she didn't actually treat anyone, the administration was taking no chances. They didn't even allow her to do volunteer work, for fear that her connection to Dr. O'Rourke, Baby John Doe and Gordy Shore—plus the fact that she was unlicensed—could be grounds for one helluva lawsuit should anything go wrong.

But Chandra was grateful to have been able to help, and she wondered, not for the first time, about becoming licensed in Colorado.

The cabin seemed suddenly lonely and empty. Dallas had told her not to wait up for him, and she felt a despondency she'd never experienced in all the time that she'd lived here.

Several calls had come in while she was out. One had

been from a reporter from Los Angeles, another from a married couple from Bend, Oregon, and a third from a lawyer in Des Moines whose clients "would pay big money" for an infant. As if she could or would help them.

Chandra took down the numbers and relayed them to Marian Sedgewick, the social worker, who, to Chandra's dismay, hedged concerning the adoption. She had mentioned that even if Gayla Vanwyk were a fraud, many couples were trying desperately to adopt the child. Though Chandra's petition was given special consideration because of all Chandra's help with the child and obvious love for the baby, there were also good reasons for placing him with someone else.

"Oh, Lord, what a mess." It seemed that the odds of adopting J.D. were impossible. Chandra wanted to cry, but didn't. Even if they couldn't adopt the baby, she and Dallas still had each other. Or did they? Without J.D. would Dallas be willing to try and make this marriage work? She could trick him, of course, by becoming pregnant with his child. He wouldn't divorce her then, not with his feelings on children and family. But could she do it?

No.

She wouldn't base this marriage on lies or trickery, even if it cost her the husband she loved as much as life itself.

Feeling as if the weight of the world rested on her slim shoulders, Chandra walked to the barn and saddled Brandy. The rain had let up a little, and the game little mare was frisky, anxious to stretch her legs as Chandra rode her over the sodden fields surrounding the house. Thoughts of J.D. and Dallas filled her mind, but she refused to be depressed. And just like the afternoon sun that had begun to peer through the dark clouds, her mood lightened.

The smell of rain-washed ground filled her nostrils, and

the cool wind raced through her hair. She thought of life without Dallas or J.D. and decided, while her knees were clamped firmly around her mount's withers, that she'd have to tell Dallas that she loved him. She'd always been truthful with him before, and now, even if it meant his rejection, she had to confront him with the simple fact that she'd fallen in love with him. If he laughed in her face, so be it. If he divorced her on the spot, she'd survive. But life would never be the same, and these past few precious days would surely shine as the brightest in her life.

She rode Brandy back to the barn, groomed all the horses, fed and watered the stock, and when she was finished, snapped out the lights. "You could use a bath yourself," she told Sam. "Maybe tomorrow, since I'm a woman of leisure for the next week or so." That thought, too, was depressing. What if she had no husband, no baby, no job? A lump filled her throat, and she scratched Sam's ears. "Well, buddy, we've still got each other, right?"

The big dog loped to the back door.

Chandra couldn't shake her dark mood. She showered, changed and started cooking a huge pot of stew. As the stew simmered, she baked cornbread and found a frozen container of last year's applesauce. Now, no matter what time Dallas arrived home, she'd have a hot meal ready and waiting. *As if that were enough to tie him to you!* What a fool she'd been! And what a mess she'd gotten herself into!

Once the bread was out of the oven, she turned the stew down and grabbed a paperback thriller she'd been trying to read ever since J.D. and Dallas had slammed into her life. But the story didn't interest her and before long she tossed the damned book aside, sitting near the fire and wishing she could predict the future.

She must've dozed, because before she knew it, Sam was barking his fool head off.

Dallas!

Her heart leapt and she wondered if she had the nerve to tell him that she loved him.

As he opened the door, she flung herself into his arms and held him close. Tears filled her eyes at the thought that she could not only lose J.D., but this man, as well.

"What's this?" he asked with a familiar chuckle that touched her heart.

"I'm just glad to see you," she said, embarrassed and sniffing.

His arms held her tight, and he buried his face in her hair. "And I'm glad to see you." He kissed her cheek and held her at arm's length, surveying her. His face drew into a pensive frown at the sight of her tears.

"The accident victims?"

"Most will pull through," he said, sounding as weary as he looked, "but we lost a couple."

"I'm sorry."

"So am I," he said, holding her and sighing in relief or contentment, she didn't know which. She caught a glimpse of naked fear in his eyes, and she wondered what had happened.

"How about a glass of wine?"

"You got one?"

"In a minute." She pulled out a bottle of chardonnay from the refrigerator, found the corkscrew and poured them each a glass. "What will we toast to?" she asked.

"How about to you?" he suggested, releasing the top button of his shirt. "You're a local hero—make that heroine."

"I am? And all this time I thought that the Bob Fillmores of the world would like to tar and feather me in the press."

"Oh, but that's changed. You vindicated yourself," he said with a twinkle in his tired eyes. "Remember the boy you wanted me to treat this afternoon? The boy with the flu. Well, you were right. He has pneumonia. And I think we treated him in time. We pumped him full of antibiotics, and he's starting to respond. Thanks to you. If he'd had to sit around the waiting room…" He shrugged. "Well, it could've been bad."

Chandra felt tears well in her eyes. Vindicated? She hardly thought so. She'd lost Gordy Shore, but this time another life had been spared.

Dallas took a swallow of his wine, then twisted one finger in a lock of her hair, staring at the golden strands as if he were fascinated with her. "You know, even old hard-nosed Trent conceded that Riverbend could use another doctor. If you're interested."

"Another Dr. O'Rourke?" she replied, shaking her head, but smiling nonetheless. "Could the world stand it?"

"Could you?" His voice was low and serious.

"I—I don't know." She blinked hard. Practice medicine again? It had been so long. And, in truth, she'd missed it. But she wasn't sure she was ready. "How would you feel about having a doctor for a wife?"

Dallas grinned crookedly, as if he knew something she didn't. He tossed back his wine and set down the glass. "Personally, I'd go for it. I wouldn't mind seeing you every day. In fact, you would certainly perk up the place, but I'm not the only one we have to consider. I don't know how our son would feel about his mother—"

Her wineglass crashed to the floor, shattering and splashing chardonnay all over the floor. Sam jumped to his feet, growling fiercely.

"Our…son?" she repeated hoarsely. Her throat closed, and for a few seconds she could hear nothing save the rush of blood through her head. "The baby—is he…?"

Dallas's face split into a wide grin. He took her hand and led her to the stairs where she sank onto the bottom step. "Gayla Vanwyk was lying. She's not J.D.'s mother.

She was hired by a couple who wanted a child so badly that they would do anything, including pay her ten thousand dollars to pose as the mother. It might've worked, too. Her blood type was compatible with the child's and since we didn't know the father, it would be hard to disprove her story."

Nothing was making much sense. "Then how—"

"The DNA testing. She balked at that, and Sheriff Newell was already checking her out. I'd already called my friend in Denver—you remember, the private investigator?"

"How could I ever forget?" Chandra said dryly.

"Well, he worked the pieces of the puzzle out and called Sheriff Newell, who confronted Gayla with the truth. She broke down and confessed. She had a baby a few weeks ago, which she sold to another couple, the Hendersons. This was just a way to make a little more cash. Charges are already being considered against the couple that put her up to it."

"But I talked to Marian Sedgewick. There are other people who want the baby—"

"I know. Influential people with money. But when push came to shove, Social Services was worried about a scandal if it turns out that any of the couples who have applied for custody of the Million Dollar Baby have done anything the least bit shady."

"So...?" she prodded, hardly daring to hope, though her silly spirits were rapidly climbing.

"So, until the mother is located, the baby will be put in a permanent foster-care situation, and hopefully those parents will be able to adopt him."

"Meaning us?" she asked. Her breath caught deep in her lungs.

"Meaning us."

Tears ran down her face. "Thank God."

"This means we have to stay married, you know." His steady blue gaze assessed her as he leaned over the stairs, his face so close, she could see the lines of worry near his eyes.

"I wouldn't have it any other way."

"No?"

"Oh, God, Dallas, don't you know how much I love you?" she asked, the words tumbling out in a rasp. "Even if we had lost J.D., I would have wanted to stay married to you. I—I…" Words failed her as she realized he might not feel the same.

But Dallas's blue eyes reflected the depth of his emotions, of his love. He gathered her into his arms. "And here I'd been thinking that you'd leave me if it weren't for the baby," he said, his voice cracking with raw emotion.

"Oh, Dallas. Never!" she cried, taking his face in her hands and kissing him long on the lips. "I just spent the last few hours scheming how to keep you married to me if we lost the baby. No matter what happens, Doctor, you're stuck with me."

"Promise?" he asked, hardly daring to believe her as he folded her into his arms.

"Forever!"

"I'm going to hold you to it, Ms. Hill."

"Mrs. O'Rourke," she corrected with a hearty laugh that seemed to spring from her very soul. She wound her arms around his neck and brushed her lips over his. With or without the baby, she knew she would love this man forever, but the fact that they were to become J.D.'s parents only made their future brighter and happier.

"Come on, *Mrs. O'Rourke,*" he said, lifting her off her feet and carrying her up the stairs. "Let's celebrate."

EPILOGUE

DEEP IN SLEEP, Chandra heard the cry, a pitiful wail that permeated her subconscious. Sam barked, and she was instantly awake.

Dallas mumbled and turned over. "Some father you turned out to be," she muttered, grinning at him just the same. They'd been married over two months and she still felt like a newlywed as each day brought more happiness.

The baby cried again and Chandra smiled. "Coming," she whispered, sliding her feet into slippers and crawling out from the warmth of the bed. She threw on her robe, padded to the bassinet and picked up the squalling infant. "Shh…" she murmured, kissing the down that was his hair. She carried him downstairs and heated a bottle, all the while rocking slowly back and forth, humming and feeling happier than she ever had in her life.

Outside, snow powdered the ground and moonglow cast the icicles and snow with a silvery sheen. As she sat in the rocker near the dying embers in the fireplace, she placed a bottle in her baby's mouth. J.D. suckled hungrily, and Sam circled three times before dropping onto the rug near the hearth.

"Merry Christmas." She heard the words and looked up to see Dallas, his hair rumpled, his eyes still heavy with sleep, looking not too different from the first time she'd seen him in the hospital emergency room.

"Merry Christmas to you, too. Even though it's only Christmas Eve."

"I know, I know." He shuffled down the stairs, clad only in jeans, and plugged in the lights of the Christmas tree. The red, green, blue and yellow bulbs reflected on the windowpanes. "Are you ready for the tribe?" he asked, tossing a mossy length of oak onto the grate before taking J.D. from her arms and feeding his son.

"Your family? Why not?"

"They're loud, opinionated and—"

"I've already met Brian."

"Well, Mom and the girls aren't as bad as he is."

Chandra laughed. "You'll have to put up with mine, too."

"Can you imagine everyone in here?" He looked around the small cabin. The addition wasn't yet finished, and with all the relatives, the room would be cramped. Fortunately, Dallas's family was staying at his condo, as the lease hadn't yet expired, and Chandra's family was going to sleep at the local hotel.

"It'll be perfect."

Dallas, still holding J.D., sat next to the hearth, and Chandra cuddled up next to him. Sam wagged his tail and placed his head in her lap.

"I have an early Christmas present for you," Chandra confided, deciding now was the time to share her secret.

"Can't it wait?"

"Nope. I think you'll want it now."

One dark eyebrow lifted in interest.

"Well, actually, you're not going to receive it until next summer, but it's been ordered."

His face pulled into a frown and she giggled. He must've suspected, for his lips slid into a wide smile. "Don't tell me—"

"That's right, Doctor. We've got a brother or sister for J.D. on the way."

Dallas swallowed hard, and he forgot about the bottle, causing J.D. to cry out.

"Here, let me handle this one," Chandra said, reaching for the baby. "You know, I was worried that someone would come and take this little guy away from us." The baby cuddled close to her breast and yawned.

"Never," Dallas promised. "I don't care how many children we have, J.D. is our first, and I'd walk through hell to keep him with us."

"Would you?" Tears glistened in her eyes.

"You and J.D. and now the new baby are the most important things in my life," he said, his voice husky. He cradled his wife and child close to him. "Nothing will ever change that. And nothing, *nothing,* will ever come between us. I love you, Chandra, and I always will."

The sound of his conviction caused the tears to stream from her eyes. "Come on," he said. "Let's change this guy and put him back to bed."

While the lights of the Christmas tree twinkled and the fire blazed in the grate, Chandra carried J.D. up the stairs. Dallas, holding her, kissed the top of her head. "I've never been this happy in my life," he admitted, and his happiness was the best Christmas present she'd ever received.

* * * * *

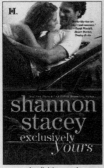 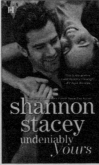 

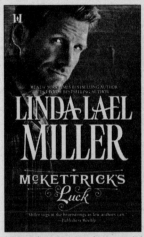

REQUEST YOUR FREE BOOKS!

2 FREE NOVELS
FROM THE ROMANCE COLLECTION
PLUS 2 FREE GIFTS!

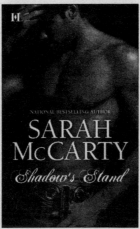

LISA JACKSON

77578 STRANGERS	___ $7.99 U.S.	___ $9.99 CAN.
77489 STORMY NIGHTS	___ $7.99 U.S.	___ $9.99 CAN.

(limited quantities available)

TOTAL AMOUNT	$	_____
POSTAGE & HANDLING	$	_____
($1.00 FOR 1 BOOK, 50¢ for each additional)		
APPLICABLE TAXES*	$	_____
TOTAL PAYABLE	$	_____

(check or money order—please do not send cash)

To order, complete this form and send it, along with a check or money order for the total above, payable to HQN Books, to: **In the U.S.:** 3010 Walden Avenue, P.O. Box 9077, Buffalo, NY 14269-9077; **In Canada:** P.O. Box 636, Fort Erie, Ontario, L2A 5X3.

Name: _____
Address: _____ City: _____
State/Prov.: _____ Zip/Postal Code: _____
Account Number (if applicable): _____

075 CSAS

*New York residents remit applicable sales taxes.
*Canadian residents remit applicable GST and provincial taxes.

HQN™ | ◆ **HARLEQUIN**®
™ www.Harlequin.com

PHLJ0112BL